"I have to tell you something," I said. "You won't believe it, but you should."

"What is it?" She sounded a little like she didn't want to know.

I took the letter from Toby and handed it to her. She looked at it a long while, and I could hear her breathe. And then she said, "Let's go downstairs and read it together, okay?"

Say you wanted a definition of the word *sad*. Say you didn't have a dictionary and needed to know. All you'd have to do to understand is to look at my mom's eyes. Look at them and you'd feel *sad* all over, infecting your blood.

"I'm so happy," I told her. And this was lie number one. A little lie, but also, in a way, the biggest. It started things.

If I wrote down all the lies that I have told since that day, I think I could fill a whole notebook and I still would not have wrote them all.

ALSO BY ELIZABETH JOY ARNOLD
Published by Bantam Books

Pieces of My Sister's Life

Promise
the Moon

Elizabeth Joy Arnold

BANTAM BOOKS

PROMISE THE MOON
A Bantam Book / June 2008

Published by Bantam Dell
A Division of Random House, Inc.
New York, New York

Bantam Books and the rooster colophon are registered trademarks
of Random House, Inc.

ISBN 978-0-385-34066-3

Printed in the United States of America
Published simultaneously in Canada

www.bantamdell.com

OPM   10 9 8 7 6 5 4 3 2 1

To our troops, past, present, and future—and to the equally heroic families who love them.

Promise the Moon

I
Natalie

I'd been kicking Josh's headstone.

In retrospect, I should've gotten the flat kind of stone instead of the sticking-up kind, because before too long the thing would probably be on the ground anyway. I'd been to the cemetery four times in the week since they'd laid the stone, three of those times without the kids, which meant I'd come for the express purpose of kicking. Which felt good while I was doing it, but once it was over all I'd gotten was a sore foot and, on the fifth day, a funny look from an old man one row down, who'd been clipping the grass around a stone with a pair of orange-handled children's scissors.

It was retribution for Toby who hadn't said a word in two months, for Anna who pretended she wasn't hurting, but still came downstairs every night to stare at the photo of herself on Josh's shoulders. And most of all for me, for leaving me with two broken kids, no money, no home, and no job. And no explanation for why he'd left.

It was Josh I really wanted to kick, of course. But mostly, mostly I just wanted to hold him.

2

Anna

My dad was a hero soldier. I looked up *hero* in my dictionary, and this is what it said:

1) A person who is admired for great courage, noble character, and good deeds.
2) A sandwich, usually made with crusty bread, a.k.a. submarine, hoagie.
3) An illustrious warrior.

My dad was the number one and number three kinds of hero both. A double hero.

He died in the war. Mom didn't tell say exactly how he died, but this is what I worked out. What happened was he went on a mission without telling us and was gone all night, after which he got shot, after which Marines men brought him home to our garage, to rest in his new Pathfinder because Mom told them it was one of his most favorite places to be. After which Toby found him. In my opinion it was not the sort of thing he should've seen.

I've thought a lot about what's the right thing people could have said to us, and have come up mostly with wrong things. These are some that came out of Ms. Thomas,

Amanda Greer, and Tim Emerson, in order. Number one: "Oh, sweet baby, are you going to be okay?" Number two: "I *totally* know how it feels because my cat died last spring." And worst of all, number three: "What did he look like without a head?"

The right thing is probably what Madison, who is my best friend, did. She didn't say anything for my whole first morning back to school, just followed me around wherever I went, sat next to me, and gave everybody else dirty looks.

The day Dad came back from heaven was, I have to say, an especially bad day. Not just because it was Friday, math test day, and I do not understand long division, but also because of art. We were doing this thing where you color patterns on paper, smear over them with black Cray-Pas, and then draw, and *voilà*, magic colors. What I drew was me, Toby, and Mom in front of our house, which looked boring so I added rain, after which Mrs. Goldberg hugged me from behind and said, "Your daddy will always be part of your family too." Which, for whatever reason, is also not a right thing to say. It makes you feel alone.

So I was not in a good mood when we found my dad's present. I had what Dad used to call "the weight" when what I used to think he meant was "the wait." Because that's what he did when he had it, hung around in bed until he felt better. But now I understand what he meant. For him the weight came after he got back from Iraq, and for me it started after he died, a punch in the stomach that makes the hurt spread heavy up your chest and down to your legs, so all you want to do is fall over and sleep.

I sat next to Toby on the bus ride home. It used to be I wouldn't be caught dead, but now he needs me so I don't care what people think. Also, the truth is that by the end of the day I need him too, because he's the only person who understands, and also he is part of home.

He rode with his forehead against the window, and I shoved up close to him. There was a white spot on his sweater and I wiped at it. "That milk?"

He didn't look at me. I licked my hand and wiped at it again. "Okay, it's pretty much gone," I said.

Sometimes I wanted to shake him and yell so loud it broke through to the inside parts of him. I knew his not talking was a sickness, like when you need to throw up. You can yell at someone all you like, but if they have to throw up they will not be able to stop themselves.

I rested my chin on Toby's head and tried to memorize everything I saw out the bus window, because in a few days this wouldn't be our home anymore. What I saw was: houses, all with roofs made out of flower pot material and little lawns; dirt that was the same color as the roofs; an empty bottle; a girl playing hopscotch. I wrote these things down in my notebook so I would remember. I had a list of everyone in my class along with who I liked and didn't like, and the color of all the carpets and curtains in our house, and my favorite places to walk. You wouldn't think you could forget these things, but you do.

I also started a list about my dad, but it didn't really work because people aren't like words in the dictionary, you can't explain them. I wrote things and then scribbled them out and tried again. *He was nice. He was funny. He used to crawl around with me and Toby on his back. He liked coffee. He had yellow hair.* But it all just sounded like I was explaining somebody who could've been anyone.

Where we were living was called Camp Pendleton, and why we had to move was because it was a place for only families of Marines to live. My dad's rank was posted outside our door, Staff Sergeant, which was no longer applicable.

Where we were moving to was my grandparents' house in a place called French Creek. Me and Toby would have to share a room, which was okay except that Toby had nightmares that woke me up. Which was also okay, though, because I'd go lie in his bed and we'd just rock until we both fell asleep. Except sometimes when he wet the bed, which was gross and not okay.

Our house was the color of chocolate milk, with yellow and pink flowers outside the door that Mom was supposed to water but usually forgot. She was waiting for me and Toby by the front door when the bus pulled up, wearing the kind of funny smile she gets sometimes, like she just tasted bad food and doesn't want to hurt the cook's feelings. She bent to hug me, right out there in the street, which normally would've been embarrassing but since Dad died I didn't care. "There's cookies in the kitchen," she said. "Anna, don't look at the pile of fabric on the bar. It's not supposed to be a scary costume but at the moment it's kind of freaky, like a black potato with eyes."

Halloween was coming, and my costume was a penguin. *Skeptical* is a dictionary word that means having doubt, and this is how I felt about my costume. Having doubt.

We went inside for our milk and cookies, and I pulled out the Cray-Pas picture I drew in art. "Want to see what I did?"

But Mom didn't look. "How d'you guys feel about ravioli for dinner?" she said, pulling out the milk. These days she only made the dinners she thought we liked, including hot dogs, bologna sandwiches, grilled cheese, and sometimes ravioli. Which was okay in the beginning, but after a while I started feeling like if I ate another ravioli I might die.

I traced my finger around the Cray-Pas Anna, and then I squashed my picture and stuffed it back in my knapsack. "Look at this," I said, and I ran to the middle of the family room, did a cartwheel, and ended with my arms in the air. "Give me a rating."

Mom smiled and said, "That was a perfect ten!" But she wasn't even looking. She was reaching for my milk, and she chugged it down in three gulps. Which hurt my feelings so I grabbed a cookie and left.

"Anna?" Mom called, but she didn't come to get me.

I went to my bedroom to read, lying on my sleeping bag because we had sold my bed. It was a good day in my reading life. I had discovered a book every person should read, with the title of *A Wrinkle in Time,* and it was everything a book should be. Scary but not too scary. About things you know you will never see but that are real enough you believe someone else might have seen them. It was the kind of book you stay up to read until your eyes feel like they are filled with glue, and it was because of that book that I was able, that day, to believe in magic.

I was there on my sleeping bag when Toby came into my room. It took all my strength to come back into the world, and I almost yelled at him for ruining the dream of it, until I saw that he was crying.

There was a Secret Special place in our house, in the up-stairs bathroom, under the cupboard where Mom kept the towels and toilet paper. The cupboard had these golf ball feet that made a space only my and Toby's hands could reach inside. It was a space that only us, and my dad, knew.

It was Dad who found the space and decided what it was for. He showed us the first day after one of his bad weeks. First days, this is how it was. His eyes would still look flat like they'd been painted on, and bruised like he'd been rubbing his fists into them hard. He still wouldn't be able to hug us or even look at us, no room to let us in. But on the day he showed us the space he'd been able to sit on Toby's bed, with me on one side and Toby on the other, and he could talk. "I have something for you," he said.

He reached into his pajama pocket and he pulled out a little heart. It was the exact size of my palm, and made out of soft fabric the color of a banana, a little mouse pillow. "Smell," he said, and he held it first to Toby's nose and then to mine. It smelled like winter and like fog, like washed clothes before they've gone into the dryer. "That's called lavender," he said.

I smiled, to be polite. It seemed like about as good a present as getting socks, and definitely not a kind of thing me and Toby could share. But that is because I didn't know.

"Thanks," I said, because I couldn't think what else to say. But then he took us up to the bathroom.

I loved our bathroom. Everything in it was white except the walls and ceiling which were blue. This is what I wrote in my list of things: *Upstairs bathroom—crack in sink shape of Big Dipper, have to wriggle toilet flusher, faucet handle shaped like jewelry.* This is what I could have written too, that when you laid in the tub you felt like you were floating on a cloud.

When we got up to the bathroom, Dad bent down and he pointed. "This," he said, "will be our Secret Special place. We'll be the only ones who know. And on days when I can't be with you, I'll do this." He held up the heart for us to see, and then he tucked it under the cabinet. We watched it disappear.

"Now take it out," he said.

Me and Toby reached under the cabinet and we both brought it out, me holding the pointy end and Toby holding the bumps. Dad held out his hand and we gave it back. Wondering.

"On days when I can't be with you," he said, "I'll leave this here while you're asleep. And in the morning, when you're missing me, you can look under the cabinet and find it. This'll be my secret message to let you know that I'm thinking about you." He gave a smile that was not a real smile, and then he said, "What it means is that I'm okay, and that I love you."

I understood. I understood exactly, and I think Toby did too. On days when he couldn't talk, the heart would be his words.

So that is what we did before my daddy died, the times when he couldn't unlock his bedroom door. Toby would wake up and he'd come to get me, and we'd both go together to feel under the cupboard. We'd take the heart out and we'd hold it, smell it. And then when we felt better we'd put the heart back in the Secret Special place, to show Dad that we loved him too. Also that we were okay, even when we weren't.

This is what I did on the day Mom told me. I couldn't breathe and so I ran up to the bathroom. And I knew what dying meant, and I knew it would not make sense to look, but I couldn't stop myself. I swept my hand around first carefully but then faster, faster, back and forth, grabbing for nothing until my knees got sore and my shoulder got sore and I got a deep indented line in my arm from the edge of the cupboard.

The heart wasn't there. Of course it wasn't, he was dead. What was there were dust and a black ball of lint. There were four little brown pellets. There was a dead ladybug. I put them all into a sandwich bag. I hid them under my mattress and slept on them every night, I don't know why. I guess because they might have been some kind of message, like a rebus:

+ + = Something

But the heart, the only message that meant anything, was gone. Until. Magic.

Toby stood in my room, watching me. He was crying, a shaking, underwater gulping kind of crying like he couldn't get enough air. He walked over and he put something on my bed, and there it was.

"Where'd you get it from?" I whispered.

He didn't answer because he couldn't talk, because seeing my dad dead and maybe bloody had swallowed up his voice. He just turned away and walked out of my room and so I followed him. He walked into the bathroom and then he looked at me, and there was a rushing through my stomach, a dark wind.

"There?" I asked, and then I sat down right on the bathroom floor and Toby sat down next to me, his knee touching my knee. We sat there not looking at each other, both of us holding the heart the same how we did on the bad days. And when we were done, I wrote a note, and we slipped the heart and the note back under the cupboard. *Who are you?* my note said. *Is this real?* Because I didn't believe it, not really, but part of me did.

Later that night we looked under the cupboard again,

and even though all of me hoped, really I was sure it would still be there. That even though I'd looked way back on the day Dad died, I'd somehow missed the heart there in the shadows. But when we looked again that night the heart, and my note, were gone.

The next morning my dad left the heart again, and again the next night it was gone. It went like that for four days, back and gone and then back, and we'd sit there on the floor, both of us holding it, smelling it. Our daddy. Our dead daddy. Who loved us enough to find a way back home.

And then on the fifth day, along with the heart, was a letter. The letter came in an envelope, with a little heart printed where the return address should be. "To Anna and Toby and Natalie," the envelope said. A letter from heaven.

I read the letter out loud to Toby, both of us sitting on the bathroom floor. I started fast, but then I got slower and I don't know how I was feeling. It is not a feeling that can be put into words. Just, wrong.

When I was halfway done, I could hear Mom coming up the stairs. I stopped reading and she just stood there in the hallway, but I didn't look up. "Hi," I said, and my voice sounded weird and Toby was gripping my knee, and Mom stood there and she stood there, and then she said, "What's that?"

I put the letter down, and Toby grabbed it. I put the envelope in his lap and I went over to Mom, and when she hugged me I stood there and I let her. And it all was exploding inside me, a wetness and a rotting-ness, but I never let Mom see me cry. Nobody knew how much I cried, not Mom or Toby, not people in school, not even Madison.

"I have to tell you something," I said. "You won't believe it, but you should."

"What is it?" She sounded a little like she didn't want to know.

I took the letter from Toby and handed it to her. She looked at it a long while, and I could hear her breathe. And then she said, "Let's go downstairs and read it together, okay?"

Say you wanted a definition of the word *sad*. Say you didn't have a dictionary and needed to know. All you'd have to do to understand is to look at my mom's eyes. Look at them and you'd feel *sad* all over, infecting your blood.

"I'm so happy," I told her. And this was lie number one. A little lie, but also, in a way, the biggest. It started things.

If I wrote down all the lies that I have told since that day, I think I could fill a whole notebook and I still would not have wrote them all.

3

Natalie

I give up!" I told Diane, flinging the upholstery needle and Anna's Halloween costume across the kitchen bar. "Why couldn't the kids choose to be something that comes pre-packaged for twenty bucks? I've stabbed myself like fifty times, and I think I'm getting lightheaded from the blood loss."

"Madison's idea," Diane said. "Sorry. She fell in love with penguins after that *Happy Feet* movie."

"Yeah, it was actually just a rhetorical question." I angled the phone against my shoulder as I pulled a roll of slice-and-bake cookies from the fridge. "I know it was Madison's idea. I just wanted to make you feel so bad you'd take over for me."

"Don't blame me! I was trying to convince Madison she wanted to wear a sheet with eyeholes."

I smiled and said, "Forget that, I don't even know if I could find a sheet in this mess. I'm usually so organized when I pack, but this week I'm using the arbitrary scoop and dump method."

"Man, I can't believe you're leaving in two days. Madison was almost in tears last night."

"I know. Anna won't tell me how hard the move is for her, but I know it's got to be."

"She's stoic," Diane said.

"What do you mean, stoic?"

"Oh, you know. I ask how she's doing, and she always says she's fine, never complains."

"Yeah, she always seems to roll with the punches." That was how she'd dealt with the depressive episodes Josh had suffered since returning from Iraq. On bad days he wouldn't leave the bedroom, would lock the door and not let us in. For me, talking to him through the door while knowing that I'd get no answer was too painful, like being hung up on, that feeling of hopelessness and not mattering. But every day after school Anna had sat by his door, sometimes for an hour or more, talking about her day, somehow managing to make herself sound upbeat.

"The therapist says she's repressing her feelings, and the goal of therapy is to lure them back out, or whatever." I set the oven to preheat. God bless Pillsbury. Within seconds you can fill your home with the scent of melting chocolate chips. Pretend you're the kind of mother your own mother was, even though you know deep down you're something else entirely. "Not that it worked," I said. "You should've seen our family sessions; all the kids did was shrug."

"They just need time to figure out themselves what they're feeling, before they can talk about it."

"But isn't that the therapist's job, to help them figure it out?" I scrubbed a hand through my hair. "I don't know, maybe I should've gotten a better therapist. I let the military recommend someone because they were willing to pay, which is so idiotic when you're dealing with your children's mental health. Like trusting your eyes to a doctor offering half-off Lasik surgery."

"They didn't give you enough in your benefits comp that you could afford somebody decent?"

"All I've gotten so far is Josh's death gratuity, and transition assistance from the VA. The casualty assistance officer I talked to told me we were eligible for all our benefits, so I have no idea what's holding them up."

When Josh had returned from Iraq last fall, the DoD had provided him counseling on coping with post-traumatic stress, and had offered separate marriage counseling and guidance for me on how to understand and help him. But when the PTSD had led to suicide, they'd acted like the connection was some algebraic equation that with study could produce definitive answers. *We are currently reviewing medical evidence pertaining to Sergeant Graham's mental condition at the time of his death,* they'd said, *to determine whether his willful misconduct was service related.* Willful misconduct, like suicide was akin to armed robbery.

"Bureaucracy. I can't even imagine what you're going through, Natalie. I mean, I *can* imagine; I think everyone here imagines it at some point, and I've actually had nightmares." She paused. Diane was in her early forties, a tad plump, and each time her husband, Jack, was deployed she let herself go, gained weight, let her graying roots take over until a month before he was due home, when she stopped eating and dyed her hair back to coppery blond. He'd been away for eight months now, and the last time I'd seen her Diane had looked at least ten years older than she actually was. "But I know it's not even close to the same thing. Listen, can I loan you some money?"

"What? No, gosh, no. We'll be fine." *Fine* wasn't the right word, of course, but I went with it. "That's incredibly nice of you, but I'm going to figure this out. Last month that grief counselor the Marines assigned me? She told me to write down a list of worries, so I sat on my bed with a pad of paper and I finally just wrote *Suck it up and deal with it* across the top. Which is exactly what I'm going to do."

"You're amazing, Natalie. If I was you, I'd've been flat on my back for the past two months, but here you are sewing Halloween costumes and packing up to start a whole new life for yourself."

"You mean attempting to sew Halloween costumes." I grabbed a stack of flattened boxes from the family room, then started for the stairs with the boxes. "There's actually a kind of freedom when you hit rock bottom and things are so screwed up they can't possibly get any worse. I guess the kids are what's keeping me sane."

"Well, I'd need alcohol to keep me sane."

"Yeah, that helps too."

I looked around me at the empty walls, nails that were put up by a previous family and would probably be used by the next. Nails that had held a wedding photo, pictures of the children at various ages. The family portrait we'd had taken for last year's Christmas postcards, in which we looked not like ourselves but like an airbrushed representation of a happy family, something that could have come printed with the frame's dimensions and price. Now packed away, and I didn't know if I'd ever take them out again. It was too painful to remember how we'd taken it all for granted, these seamless toile images of our life. How I'd believed with all my heart it was the truth.

"You're going to do so great," Diane said. "And I'm here for you if you need anything. Just call."

With no warning, I felt my face flush with tears. Diane and I were friends, but only through our daughters' friendship and I doubted I'd ever speak to her again after we'd left. I was suddenly reminded of Josh's funeral, the offers of dinner or babysitting, that had seemed more obligatory than heartfelt. I'd thought people on the base should know how to respond to death. Some of the wives hung montages of dead Marines on their walls and kept a running tally of soldiers lost. I'd expected them to swarm around me and the kids, the way I'd seen them do with other widows like it could cushion them from the pain. I'd been bracing for that swarming, both dreading it and needing it.

But it had never happened. When people had found out about Josh there'd been a strange sort of pause, like they weren't sure how to react. Most had stopped inviting us to backyard barbeques, and although they might wave if they saw me at the PX, they rarely stopped to talk. Even though I'd never quite been comfortable with the enforced closeness of a military base, when Josh had died I'd needed that, the sense of community and of family. But for some reason it was like I'd stopped existing.

I squeezed my eyes shut, thinking, *Get ahold of yourself!* and then I said the same meaningless, placating words I'd said to everyone at the funeral. "Thanks," the words went, "but we'll be fine." I don't know that anyone believed them.

I tossed one of the empty boxes into Anna's room, one into Toby's, then brought the rest to my bedroom. Moving came with the territory, something I'd signed on to like a prenup. I packed every couple of years as the fates and mystifying Marine schedules dictated, and I never really let myself put down roots, because roots made being torn away that much more painful. Some of our boxes had moved with us for years without even having been opened and so could be transferred directly from crawl space to van to crawl space again, and I had all the right plate-savers and squares of bubble wrap.

But this move was different because it was an ending. It felt almost like a betrayal, knowing Josh would never see the house we'd end up in, that I was leaving him so completely. I remembered the efficiency with which we used to pack, making a game of it, tossing things to one another and then into a box. Playing Statues where I'd work the portable radio, periodically turning it off so that they had to freeze, the kids inevitably collapsing into giggles. "You guys stink at this!" Josh would say.

The photos were the only part of our past I was keeping; everything else that made up the life we'd collected, including all our furniture, had been donated or sold. Now I was driving a '92 Buick with scabs of rust on the bumpers because both our cars were gone, the Pathfinder that Josh had died in, of course, but also the green VW I'd loved. I'd even sold the children's babyhood, their crib and clothes and Baby Bjorn all saved in the hopes of having another, but now gone to our neighbor Stephanie, pregnant with her first and just setting out on the life I'd ended. There would be no more babies for me.

I threw the last boxes on the floor, then bit the inside of my cheek, surveying the damage. There were several packing tasks I'd saved for last because I hadn't wanted to face them. But you can't ignore inevitability.

There was Josh's closet, unopened since the night I'd had to choose the clothes he'd turn to dust in. And in front of it was the large box I'd found last month in the duffle he traveled with, in which he'd kept every card the kids had ever made for him *(You are the Best Dad in the World!!!)*, the letter in which I'd first told him that I loved him, even a ticket stub from *The Shawshank Redemption,* the first movie we'd seen together.

On top of the box was the fat manila envelope the coroner had given me. I'd thrown the envelope away unopened and then, in the middle of the night, I'd retrieved it from the trash and tossed it under my bed. I felt it under me whenever I tried to sleep, couldn't stand to look at it but couldn't get rid of it either. After selling the bed, I'd thrown the envelope into one of our packing boxes, but then realized I couldn't just tote it from house to house without knowing what was inside. That would give it too much weight.

I sat on my sleeping bag and cradled the envelope in my lap. It was lumpy, heavy, Josh had been wearing his Lakers jacket that night and so had a lot of pocket room. I felt the top of the envelope: keys, something rectangular, something cylindrical, and his wallet. Harmless-feeling, the shape of things that might be in anyone's pocket. I had to make myself believe they represented nothing, except that he'd once been alive and now was not, and these things had been there for the transition. I bent up the hinges of the metal clasp, then closed my eyes and dumped it all out on the floor.

I sat with my palms flat on the carpet. Then opened my eyes and made myself look: his keys and wallet, his PDA, and a half-eaten roll of Wild Cherry Life Savers covered in pocket lint. For some reason it was the Life

Savers that got me most, their brightly colored paper a sign he'd been alive and human, had wanted pleasure, had expected he'd finish the roll. I thumbed out the top Life Saver and put it in my mouth, lint and all, closed my eyes and ran my tongue across it as if the Life Saver was something else, his skin, his mouth kissing me back.

I picked up his wallet, a Christmas present from my dad. Cheap black leather with visible white stitching, not Josh's style but kept and used because it was a gift. Inside the accordion insert were the kids' last school pictures, a photo of Josh's best friend, Nick, in uniform, and a photo of our family taken when Toby was just a baby. In the picture, I was laughing.

I looked at that picture a long while, then snapped the wallet shut and threw it into the envelope, photos and credit cards and potential cash and all, but then pulled it out again to retrieve the photos. We all seemed so happy, and that happiness was something I never wanted to forget.

Pulling out the plastic insert revealed another photo that had been tucked behind it. It was of a young Arab woman, wrapped in a dark *hijab*, the head scarf making it hard to tell her exact age; she might have been anywhere between twelve and twenty. She had a large port-wine birthmark in the shape of a hand, fingers clutching at her cheek. A wavy wisp of dark hair had escaped from her hijab, and her eyes seemed haunted but wistful, the eyes of war. The photo must have been taken in Iraq; the background colors were the dusty beige of Middle Eastern dirt and clay brick walls.

Who was she? Somebody Josh had befriended? He'd told me about many of the Iraqis he'd met, how amazed he was to see humanity managing to survive amid the inhumanity. There were heartbreaking stories of women he'd pulled from under rubble, the pain of having to tell them that the rest of their family was gone. And he'd told me about the children, their utter joy at the existence of toys and treats. I'd imagined him there, surrounded by children, the complete glee he would have felt at their excitement. "Can you believe how psyched a little boy can get over a Hershey bar or a yo-yo?" he'd written me. "Tell that to our kids, okay? Teach them about gratitude."

I slipped the photo into my pocket along with the others, and reached for the PDA Josh had been given last fall, when he was recovering from his brain injury, as part of his VA-sponsored rehabilitation. He'd been injured a year ago, had been trying to help rescue soldiers from sniper fire when an IED had gone off nearby. He'd suffered for weeks with extreme short-term memory loss, and that seemed to have been part of what had triggered the severe depression he'd struggled with ever since, the frustration of having to write everything down if he wanted to be able to remember it later.

But even when he'd mostly recovered, suffering only occasional glitches of forgetfulness, he'd still carried the PDA everywhere, writing in it constantly. I wondered if at some point he'd stopped planning, if after August 26, the day of his death, the calendar would be blank. What had he written down on that day? I couldn't look at it, couldn't look at any of it, but how could I not look?

I cradled the PDA in my hands, staring down at the scratched screen, and then I slipped it into a packing box. Someday I'd have to read it, I knew that. But not now. Not today. I covered my face and squeezed at my cheeks. *Okay. Okay.*

Standing, I felt a wash of dizziness and leaned against

the wall. The kids would be home soon, and I had one more thing to do. I slowly bent to my sleeping bag to fish out Josh's cloth heart, brought it to the bathroom where I tucked it under the cabinet, and then I leaned against the cabinet and closed my eyes.

4
Natalie

It had started two days ago when I'd come upstairs and found Toby sitting on the bathroom floor with his arm under the cabinet. Pulling out nothing but his hand and maybe a smoky skin of under-cupboard dust, smiling at it like a crazy person, like he'd reached under the cupboard and his father had reached back. And I'd immediately known what he'd been looking for.

I'd first found the heart a year ago, on one of Josh's bad days. Just a fluke, because I'm definitely not the kind of person who cleans in places you'd have to stand on your head to see. In fact, I am the opposite of that kind of person, but we'd had ants, trails of them parading brazenly up walls and into open cookie bags, defiantly wriggling their little ant behinds like they held complete ownership. I'd hidden one of the traps under the linen cabinet, and it was when I reached under the cabinet to check for dead bodies that I'd found the squishy furry thing, and screamed.

When I realized what it was, I'd imagined it as a gift the previous owner of the house had sent to his wife while deployed overseas. I imagined her carrying it with her everywhere in her pocket, upset when she realized it must've fallen out somewhere and disappeared. Feeling sentimental, I'd tucked it back under the cabinet for her, but then that same week I'd found Anna kneeling on the floor, kissing the heart and slipping it back. And I'd begun to understand what it meant.

I'd thought it was heartbreaking. But I'd never told Josh or the kids that I knew, and in the end I'd started checking for it myself on his bad days, fishing it out with the neck of a Windex bottle and smoothing it against my cheek. It was a comfort, which I guess is how I'd explain putting the heart back there now. An attempt to give comfort.

Downstairs I sliced some cookies onto a pan and slid them into the oven, then sat with my elbows on the bar, head in my hands. I'd only use the heart until we left Pendleton. I wanted so desperately to tap into Anna's and Toby's feelings, to make sure they were okay. Most of all, to make sure they knew that Josh's suicide hadn't been their fault—that he'd loved them as much as they'd loved him, that they'd always be loved like that, no matter what. Besides, how much could you screw your kids up with a few days worth of unspoken lies? It couldn't be any worse than trying to comfort them with these refined sugar and grease discs. Probably better, in the long run.

I reached for the small spiral notebook I kept in my purse. I'd initially thought of titling my new children's book *Do I Still Have a Daddy?* Then I had realized how bleak that sounded, that a book with that title would never sell. So I'd decided I'd need to make the book more universal, something that would also apply to dead grandparents, maybe even dead pets, which is how I'd come up with the idea for Carrie the Caterpillar. *Carrie the Caterpillar felt an aching in her bones. It seemed to her like something amazing was about to happen.*

But I knew why I hadn't been able to get past the first two sentences. I didn't want universality. There was no comparing Josh's death to anything else. I wanted the book to apply to my kids, and to myself, as if by writing it I could come up with answers.

I picked up a pen and stared at those two lines on the pad, until the timer went off on the cookies. I rose to transfer them to a cooling rack. Back at the bar, I looked down at what I'd written, and felt a sudden, searing pain.

I thought of Toby sitting on the bathroom floor, and the note Anna had left the first day I'd given them the heart—*Who are you? Is this real?*—both of them so desperate for Josh that they'd let themselves believe. The nights I'd sat on Anna's bed, trying to draw her out so we could talk about missing Josh, about how he'd died and the pain I knew must be under her too-quick smiles and forced happiness about school, about moving, about everything. The first time I'd tried to talk to her, she'd screamed and thrashed and refused to let me hold her, but after that she just wouldn't talk to me at all, would turn against the wall and pretend to sleep, and I didn't know if it was because she didn't understand what she was feeling or was ashamed of it, or if she just didn't want to worry me.

And even worse was Toby, with his nightmares, screaming, writhing and sweating, so similar to the nightmares Josh had after returning from his last tour in Iraq. He hadn't said a single word since the morning I'd found him in the garage with Josh, which meant he was probably playing what had happened unremittingly, a movie trailer on an infinite loop inside his head.

All the hours I'd spent with his therapist, his teacher, and the school administrators; all the hours I'd spent trying to engage him in conversation, trick him into talking, pleading with him. It was like dealing with a baby, his wordless gestures and lack of gestures, and I felt that same sense of frustration and guilt at that frustration. *Tell me what you want!*

Mornings I'd go to his bedroom and he'd be shrouded in his quilt, the only thing visible a wisped tuft of hair. I'd make a game of it, blow at that tuft. "Windy in here!" I'd say. I'd cradle his mummified self and ask if he wanted cinnamon toast. Milk with his coffee, ice with his whisky, spit with his lima beans. In response he'd just unwrap from his blanket and traipse to the bathroom to pee, and I wanted to yell at Josh, *Just look what you've done!* But instead, now I picked up my pen again. And started to write—not the universal children's book, but something just for us.

Okay. Here's the thing; it wasn't me writing, and how pathetic a justification is that? But it wasn't me. It was Josh taking over, an *Invasion of the Body Snatchers* kind of thing, writing in handwriting bizarrely similar to his neat script and bringing the letter up to the bathroom. These were the things he'd tell the children if he could, and I could feel him there as I wrote. The same delusional part of me that still, on afternoons I was too busy to touch base with reality, glanced at the clock to see how long it would be before he came home.

It was Josh's certainty I felt as he wrote through me, that he'd be able to make a difference where I'd completely failed, and I know if I'd seen this from the outside I would've wanted to shake myself, slap my cheeks, confiscate all my pens. But when I finished I felt good. More than good. Because for the first time ever Josh was apologizing to us, saying everything would be okay. And that he loved us. He missed us. He'd see us again someday.

"Dear Anna and Toby," I wrote, but when the letter was done I added, "and Natalie." Just because.

Last month I'd been bringing laundry up to the bedrooms, when I'd heard Anna talking to Toby. "Pretend this is Daddy," she said, and I'd stood in the hallway with the laundry basket and watched.

She held up Toby's stuffed bear and then slipped her hand inside a clown puppet and said, "And pretend this is a terrorist."

I'd been frozen, wanting to stop this game, but needing to know where she planned on taking it. "I'm here to help you!" the bear said. "That's how come I went away from home, not 'cause I'm mean but because I'm nice."

"I don't care!" the clown said, his voice a near squeak. "I *hate* nice people which is how come I'm going to shoot you!"

"But if you shoot me then my family's going to be really, really sad," the bear said, and the clown puppet hit him on the head. "I want them to be sad!" And the bear had fallen to the floor.

"That's how it happened," Anna said, "how the terrorist got him, but the important thing you have to remember is God got the terrorist back, and now he's probably either really sick or already dead. And every person who dies fighting bad people goes automatically into heaven."

This made me feel both sick and panicked. How did she believe that within eight hours Josh had made it to Iraq, gotten shot, and been taken all the way back home? I should've talked to her about it right then, but I couldn't because it would mean explaining the suicide, which she wasn't ready for. *I* wasn't ready for it. How did you tell children about their father putting a gun to his head? The words the grief counselor had suggested I use had seemed ridiculous to me; I'd found myself wanting to roll my eyes. So I'd said nothing, as if I actually believed the perfect words would come, words that would make it seem okay.

I knew someday they'd realize Josh hadn't been teleported to and from Iraq, but at least for now they weren't asking. And I'd convinced myself this was healthier, that the children should have someone to blame, to hate, besides their dad.

Now, as I set glasses out on the kitchen table and poured in milk, I pictured Josh and me swaying to a James Taylor song, each with a child in our arms. Josh was crooning, badly; Anna had her arms wrapped completely around his waist; and Toby was giggling as he stepped on my toes.

And there it was in that one memory, the entirety of what we'd lost, what Josh had shattered by pulling a trigger. I let myself feel it all, the family I'd thought I owned, as intrinsic to me as my own soul.

And then I clamped my teeth down on my tongue, hard, and walked outside so that I'd be waiting by the door, smiling, when the kids came home.

5

Natalie

Josh first came to one of my storytelling sessions the month after we got married, and that evening changed my life. It was at a library in Atlanta, and the book was *The Tale of the Flopsy Bunnies,* and I acted it out, the same way my mother had for me. I did all the voices—the bunnies, Mrs. Tittlemouse, Mr. and Mrs. McGregor; I used my hands, my body, actually getting on the floor to impersonate the animals, glorying in the children's laughter. And at the end of the night, Josh told me he wanted my child.

"It was like magic," he said. "It made me remember why I'm in love with you."

I raised my eyebrows at him, feeling almost giddy. "You fell in love with me because I was clucking like a squirrel? Sounds like a weird fetish."

"I'm serious," he said, and then he smiled. "I suddenly find myself wanting you to bear my children."

And so that night, what had been just a fun volunteer gig in college suddenly felt like it could be a career choice. And most important, when Josh suggested he could prove his only fetish was for me, for the first time I didn't use my diaphragm.

So this was my profession now, sitting in front of

expectant packs of toddlers spinning once-upon-a-times; sometimes my own books (the illustrious titles *Mark and the Mysterious Meatball* and *Peggy Panda Can Use the Potty!*), sometimes the books I'd loved as a kid, and sometimes pure improvisation. A storyteller is, in a sense, a bad liar. You want the kids to believe in talking chickens and running gingerbread men, so you overact, not just with your voice but also your face and your hands. And the kids believe. You can see it in their eyes. That's the best thing about the job, watching them. After a minute they stop fussing and their faces go completely still, and you know you've disappeared, smiley face and frizzy hair and all. Nothing exists except the pictures you've painted in their heads.

So I was used to fabricating stories, and that evening when I sat reading Josh's letter on the living room floor with the kids, I tried to convince myself it really wasn't all that different. Just a fairy tale with an unexpected happier-unhappy ending.

Dear Anna and Toby and Natalie,

How great it's been, exchanging the heart. I hope you understand how it means I haven't left you, not really. Because I can see you all, you know. I look down every day. Which is really why I'm writing, to say I'm still around when you need me. You can talk to me and I'll hear you every time.

When I wake up every morning I think about you, Anna, how great you're doing in school, how you've been completing your homework every night, and doing it in such pretty handwriting. It makes me and your mom so proud. I also think about you, Toby, how you've gotten so good on your bike that soon you won't even need training wheels. I'm proud of everything about both of you. You're growing up to be good people, which is the most important thing of all.

What I really want to say is that your mom's there for you, to listen to whatever you want to say. Anna, I know you must be angry and confused about why I left. I understand that completely, and I want you to talk to your mom about it, because I know that will help you feel better. And Toby especially, if I had one wish, this is what it would be: to hear your voice again. You're such an immensely strong kid, and I know you'll be able to give me this one thing.

I'm so sorry I'm not there on earth. I wish I could have just one more day with you all, so I could show you how very much I love you.

Love,
Dad

When I finished reading, we sat there without speaking while I studied Toby's face to see his reaction, but he just watched me with his head tilted, as if he were listening to a high-pitched sound.

I had a sudden memory of him at two or three, running hand in hand with Josh at the beach, a green hawk-shaped kite dancing far above their heads. "I'm flying! I'm flying!" he calls.

"Oh my gosh, he's flying!" I say. "Honey, you better grab him quick!" And Toby laughs, and Josh laughs and scoops him up onto his shoulders. Toby drops the string and the kite swoops free over the ocean, Toby's face first stunned, then dismayed, but then gleeful as the kite soars and dips toward the horizon. Laughing, laughing; when was the last time any of us laughed?

I tried to find something else to focus on in this room which now, without furniture, was completely devoid of focal points: white walls, chipped molding, a closet door that had to be opened carefully because it swung open onto the TV wires, and had more than once sent the set teetering on its edge. I finally settled my eyes on the pile of magazines that had been collecting, unread, since Josh's death. *Fact or Fad?* the top one said. *The Truth About Your Favorite Nutritional Supplement.*

"It's funny how he said he liked my handwriting," Anna said finally.

I looked at her carefully. Did she believe? It was impossible to tell. She was ten, which I knew was maybe too old for this, but she was so imaginative, had believed in Santa until just last year, and she'd tucked a note under the cabinet asking if Josh was really there.

I hoped she believed. Or even if she didn't literally believe, that it at least would prompt her to open up to me.

Toby reached toward the letter, his pupils wide, wet and black as oil, questioning like he was trying to work out a puzzle. I handed it to him and he held it on his lap and traced his finger slowly across a line.

"I know he'd rather be here with us," I said now, my voice hoarse. I swallowed, hard. "But it seems like living there's not so bad, like he's doing okay." I glanced at the kids. "Like *being* there's not so bad," I said.

Toby gave the letter to Anna, and she stared at it a long while and then set it on the floor. He rocked forward and looked down at his knees, then stood and walked out of the room.

I started to go after him, but then Anna said quietly, "That's what Dad used to say when he was in Iraq. He'd say how when we had problems we could talk to him in our heads."

"Do you want to hold on to the letter? You could read it if you ever felt sad."

Anna was quiet a minute, looking down at her knees, then said, "I guess."

And then Toby came back into the room and slowly sank back to the floor. We didn't speak, watching him while he watched us, and then he turned to Anna and pointed at the letter. Anna handed it to him, and he handed it to me.

"You want me to read it again?"

He looked up at me and gave a solemn nod. So I read the letter over, slowly. When I was done I sat back to watch him and he pointed again.

I knew what must be going on. Each time I read the letter he was hearing his father's voice, the same way I had while writing it. So I started again, and this time around it was an incantation. I'd almost memorized the words and so they lost their meaning, like the words to *Goodnight Moon* had after umpteen trillion bedtime recitations, a comfort to lose ourselves in so we could sleep.

"Love, Dad," I finished, then gave the letter back to Anna. "Anna's going to keep it," I said. "And anytime you want to hear it again, just let me know."

Toby hugged his arms around his waist. The expression on his face, the mix of dreaminess and concentration, it was Josh's look. Toby was Josh in miniature, not just in his looks but in his manner: his intensity when he tore the crusts off his sandwich, the tentative smile he wore in front of strangers. How could you be a good mother when all you felt, looking at your son, was pain?

He opened his mouth, and then sighed. And then he

opened his mouth again and spoke in a whisper, scratchy, like something in need of lubrication. "What's *immensely?*"

My eyes widened. It had been two months since I'd heard his voice, an eternity. Anna and I looked at each other and slowly, Anna smiled.

"It means hugely," I said softly. "He means you're very, very strong."

Toby nodded, as if confirming this was true, then got up and walked out of the room.

"He talked," Anna said.

All of me wanted to jump up, grab him, and bring him back into the room, but this felt so precarious, as if any overreaction might push his voice back into whatever pit had consumed it. "I know," I whispered.

"Will he keep talking?"

I smiled widely at her, then hugged her tight, my eyes stinging. Had it worked? Screw the self-recriminating parts of me, they didn't know what they were talking about. The letter had worked! I didn't know if Toby's two words were the last he'd ever speak again, but still, after two months, they felt like a miracle.

"Can we go talk to him?" Anna said.

I felt a pinch in my stomach. She was gripping the edges of the letter, wrinkling it in her fists, pressing her fists together. "Well no, sweetie. I wish you could, but that's not how it works. You belong here on earth and your dad belongs there."

She gave me a disgusted look. "*No*, I'm talking about *Toby*. We can ask him stuff and see if he says anything."

The pinch in my stomach loosened. "Oh, yes! Yes, definitely let's go talk to him. But let's be soft with him, okay? If he doesn't feel like talking we'll just sit with him, maybe read the letter again." The letter, like fairy dust, like clicking the heels of ruby slippers. Read it again and maybe magic would happen.

So we went into Toby's room. He was sitting on the floor and scribbling with blue crayon on a sheet of construction paper. I remembered Josh and Toby sitting side by side on this same floor, working on Toby's coloring book. "What color should I make her hair?" Josh would ask. "How 'bout her teeth? Her nose?" Josh coloring purple hair and green teeth, shaking his head solemnly and saying, "Poor thing's never gonna find a date..." The magnificent gusto of Toby's belly laugh.

I sat next to him. "Hey, Toby," I said. "What're you drawing?"

He kept on drawing without turning to face me, an intense look on his face. Line after line of blue scribbles. And suddenly I knew exactly what he was doing. The scribbles were how adults conveyed their love, and Toby was trying to communicate in the only way he knew how.

"You're writing back to Daddy," I said.

He continued without looking up until he reached the bottom of the paper. And then he wrote the word *TOBY* in big block letters and handed the paper to me, along with a drawing of a smiling stick figure. "Who's this?" I whispered.

He looked up at me.

"Is this Daddy?" I said, and he smiled.

It was a real smile, a genuine smile, and watching his face, something wonky happened to my emotions. I didn't feel scared or guilty, at least not explicitly. Instead my mind twisted the fear and guilt inside out and made them into a kind of excitement. We were playing "imagination," jumping off a cliff and really believing we were flying. And maybe gravity was inevitable sooner or later, but that was only something to worry about when we hit the ground.

Oh, I should've said he couldn't send letters to heaven, I knew that. I'd screwed up once and this would only compound the screwing up-ness. He must expect a letter back from Josh, bathroom cabinet as Interplanetary Postal Service, and I should've said it wasn't possible. But Toby was smiling and his eyes were pleading, please-let-me eyes, and how could I refuse them? "Okay," I said. "You can both write to him. I'm sure it'll make him happy." And who knew? Maybe it was true. Wouldn't he want to hear the things the kids would tell him? Wouldn't I?

I looked over at Anna. She was sitting with her hands pressed between her knees, sandy blond hair mussed in her face. "I don't think I want to," she said.

I tried to read her expression. "Why not?"

"Because." She turned to Toby. "Because," she said again, and then she stood and walked out of the room.

I knew I should go to her. I should admit what I'd done; it was the only sane, responsible thing to do. But then Toby spoke again: "Tell him."

"Toby," I said softly, reaching to pull him into my lap. But he pushed me away, digging his fist into the carpet, and spoke in a whisper. "Get a paper."

"Okay," I said hoarsely, "okay, you want me to write?" I quickly rose for another sheet of construction paper, and a crayon, full of both apprehension and expectation, watching him sit there with his fist still dug into the floor.

"Dear Daddy," he said, even before I'd sat down again. "Me and Anna and Mommy got your letter, and I wanted to tell you that we are moving. Mom, are we going to be there tomorrow?"

Could it really be this easy? Did I have Toby back again? There was a hyper-alertness in his face that worried me. But still, he was talking. "The day after tomorrow," I said softly.

"Okay, write that, and write the new address, and say that he should find a new place to put a letter. Maybe under a cabinet."

What would happen when we moved? Why hadn't I thought about that? "I don't know, Toby."

"Write it!"

I watched the sudden distress shadowing his face, heard the frenzy in his voice. "Okay," I said slowly, "what else?"

Toby was quiet a moment, considering. "I want to know these things: Number one, do you have TV in heaven? Number two, if you don't have TV, then what do you do all day? Number three, are there any kids there, and if there are do you like them? And also do you play with them the same way how you used to play with us?"

"Why don't you tell him about yourself?" I said. "How you're doing? What you did today?"

Toby set his shoulders. "Today I went to school."

I waited, but that seemed to be all he wanted to say about it. "Right," I said. "Today you went to school."

"Keep writing," Toby said, "okay? Write this. Write, what do you eat in heaven? And do you have friends there? And if you do, are they dead too? Write, is it scary being dead? Do you see angels, and how do they look like? And did you meet God yet?"

He paused and then he rocked forward to look at the floor. I waited, poised for a revelation, the thing he'd been keeping from me. "Also," he said, "also ask, when are you coming home?"

I felt my heart freeze inside my chest, petrified rock. I opened my mouth but there was nothing behind it, an affliction that had plagued me over the past few weeks, when the energy it took to speak lagged well behind my thoughts. "Toby..." I said finally.

Toby pounded his fist on the floor. "I know! I know what you said, but you don't know everything. You never went there."

He was crying suddenly, something he'd done only twice that I knew of in the past two months, first when my dad made some dumb-ass comment at the funeral about him having to be the man of the house, and then when he'd woken up screaming from another nightmare he couldn't tell me about. Both times the crying had ended after barely a minute, as abruptly as it had started, no winding down, no hiccups or snuffled breaths, just a sudden stillness like somebody had flicked a switch.

I stared at the wall, focusing on the blankness of it, blank except for a smudge at waist height, the size of Josh's thumb. Was it Josh's thumb? I squeezed my eyes shut and reached to hold Toby, tucked him against my neck.

How did parents resist the urge to swallow their children? Swaddle them back inside their bellies where the outside world was only muffled sound and an occasional shift in position. Expel them when they were adolescents and really needed to learn the truth about the suckiness of life. It was too much weight for a little kid to carry. It was too much weight for anyone. I rocked him in my arms like he was a toddler, two, one; I rocked both of us as if that could center us but there'd been pieces torn off me, arms, legs, internal organs, and how could I help Toby when all that was left of me was skin?

How would Josh have reacted if he could see what I'd done? I hadn't thought this through, just let the idea carry me, and now I didn't know how to take it back.

"Let's do Duck-Duck-Goose," Toby says. We're in the park, the four of us on a cool August day, the grass like blunt-tipped pins against our bare legs.

"Not sure there's enough of us," I say, ruffling his hair, recently cut, at Toby's request, in an exact reproduction of Josh's crew cut.

Josh is staring into the middle distance, and I prod him with my toe. "What do you think? You up for it?" He's been having headaches off and on for the past few months, a result of the injury he'd sustained in Iraq. That morning he'd spent an hour flat on his back with an ice pack on his forehead, while Toby hovered with his doctor's bag, taking his temperature with a plastic thermometer and plastering Band-Aids on his temples, his ears, his toes.

"Up for it?" Josh repeats.

"You know, Duck-Duck-Goose, the game."

"Oh, right, sure." He smiles, but it's not a real smile, more a stretching of lips. "Sure, okay."

"Your head's hurting."

"No, no, I'm fine!" He jumps up, tags me. "You're it!" he says, and starts running.

The three of us watch after him and Anna calls, "Dad? Daddy!" We look at one another, and then I tap her shoulder and smile. "You're it," I say, then grab Toby's hand while Anna calls, "No fair, no fair!" as we all run.

Now, lying in bed, remembering Josh ducking behind a tree, I think this: That it's easier to fake happiness than

contentment. After he'd returned from his last tour I'd
seen bright bursts of laughter, jokes, wrestling and tickling matches with the kids. But not the quiet times we'd
had, watching *Casablanca* or *Chinatown* on TV, a sleeping
child in each of our laps, Josh stroking a finger against my
palm while I rested my head on his shoulder.

My brain's been shaken but not stirred, he'd said again and
again, but of course he'd been both shaken and stirred by
his physical and emotional injuries from the war. And I'd
felt sure the real Josh must be in there, lost or hiding and
waiting for me to find him.

But maybe not. Maybe that whole time I'd been blind.
I guess that's the reason I'd wanted to write the letter, because I needed to talk to Josh just one more time, for five
minutes, with fewer words than were in one of my toddler
books. I needed to know if anything was my fault, and I
needed to know why.

Why? Why that night, after what seemed like an okay
day? Yes, he'd had bouts of depression, and there'd been
struggles from his head injury that had frustrated him and
sometimes triggered those days he spent locked behind
our bedroom door. But his memory seemed almost back
to normal, and he'd never just snapped from a good day
into a bad one; there'd always been some warning, a steady
decline.

I'd replayed everything I'd said to him and everything
he'd said to me, trying to see what I'd missed and where it
might have turned, and I'd come up with nothing that
meant anything.

It was a Sunday and we'd played tag in the park and
fed the ducks Wonder Bread, and we'd talked over dinner
and I'd gone to sleep early and I woke up and he was
dead—no note, no warning, no explanation. So I kept

having the feeling something had happened that I didn't know about, and I needed to know if there was anything I could have done to save him.

It was midnight when I retrieved Toby's letter and picture from under the cabinet. I tore it into pieces, let the pieces flutter like confetti into the toilet, flushed and watched Toby's blue scribbles swirl their way into oblivion. And I imagined Josh intercepting them before they reached the sewer lines. Piecing them together. Holding them in his lap while he cried.

6
Anna

• Daddy told us that dandelion seeds were actually fairies. In the park all of us would close our eyes, make a wish on dandelions, and blow. The wishes didn't usually come true, but sometimes they did.

• Also in the park, he sometimes would open maple seeds, to stick on all our noses.

• One time when I skinned my knee he held me on his lap and didn't let go. I fell asleep and when I woke up it was dark and everybody else had gone to bed. But Daddy still was awake, and holding me there.

Every time, my least favorite thing to pack is my animals. Imagine this, a hundred bodies squashed in a box, two hundred eyes staring up at you. I don't care that they're not real eyes, because whoever you are, when you put a lid on the box you will imagine them crying, and worry about them breathing. I wouldn't poke holes in the box, because I didn't want Mom thinking I was mental, but I will tell the truth. That I wanted to.

I set all the animals in carefully on top of a green

towel, and then I lay back on my sleeping bag with Leopolda sitting on my chest.

Leopolda is a hippo, my favorite animal even though the black of her felt eyeballs have fell off, because she was from Daddy and she's been there for everything ever since I was one day old. And also because she has a hiding place. Underneath of her zipper dress.

She has hid lots of important stuff like:

• The valentine I got from Timmy Markson,
• A butterfly I killed by accident but that was too beautiful to bury,
• The best-friend ring I got from Janice that I never showed my real best friend, Madison.

And other things, but now, she was holding a secret. A big secret, one only me and Toby knew.

Toby found it on the day Dad died, and I took it from him. And part of me wishes I threw it away, because what if Mom found it? She can't find it, not ever, because she would hate me and I know what could happen if she found out the truth.

Here is how hiding it in Leopolda felt like to me. Imagine when you have a skinned knee. And somebody's cleaning it up for you and they tell you not to look because they know it'll make you cry. But the more they tell you, the more your eyes have different ideas because it's right there and it hurts real bad and it's the only thing you can think about. Until you get the Band-Aid on, and suddenly you don't have to look anymore. Leopolda is like the Band-Aid.

"Today's Halloween, which is so stupid," I said.

Leopolda looked back at me with her white eyes. I knew if she was real, she would agree.

Last year I thought it was such a big deal. I was dressed up like Alice in Wonderland from a book I read, and I remember counting down days just like you do for Christmas. Madison still felt the same about it, I could tell. I think everybody did, except for me. But all I could think about was how Dad used to be the one who took us, not last time because he was in Iraq, but the time before and the time before.

Mom knocked on my door. "Hey, kiddo. It's that time."

"I know."

She watched my face, then sat on my sleeping bag. "So today's your last day."

"I know," I said again.

"Hard saying good-bye to a place, hunh? And all your friends. I start feeling homesick even before we leave."

I shrugged. "It's not so great here," I said, which I thought was what she wanted me to say, but she just looked at me funny. "I mean, it's okay, but I'm not so homesick."

"Well, that's good." She brushed a hand over the top of my head, then kissed me, then said, "Cereal or waffles."

"Whatever," I said, but then I said, "Waffles," just so she'd feel okay enough about me to leave.

"Waffles it is." She stood up and then she said, "Oh, and Happy Halloween!" and I smiled and looked excited. She was the only reason I even agreed to dress up as a penguin.

I was pulling a shirt over my head when Toby came into my room, already dressed in his little camouflage uniform.

"You wearing that to school?" I said. He only had

afternoon kindergarten, and probably the costume would be messed up by tonight, but he'd wanted to wear the cammies every day since Mom first got them, and now he finally had the chance.

He nodded, and then he handed me a piece of paper. Stationery, and holding it I felt my insides curling up. "You got this under the bathroom cabinet?"

He smiled. "Uh-huh, could you read it?"

My head was saying *No*, but my mouth said, "Yeah," because what else could it do? I looked down at the letter. "Okay," I said. "Okay." And then I read.

Dear Anna and Toby and Natalie,

It was so nice to hear from you, and you had some very good questions that I'll try to answer. You asked me what we eat up in heaven, and the truth is we don't actually need to eat, because we don't have regular bodies that need to be nourished. But good food is one of life's great pleasures. (Imagine what it might be like to never again taste a grilled cheese sandwich!) So God has given us the opportunity to eat in heaven. The best thing is that we can eat whatever we want here, without worrying about cavities. Of course it isn't real food, but if we are in the mood for eating, suddenly the sensation of food comes to us, exactly what we're hungry for. For example, this morning I had eggs and sausage, and the night before I had chocolate cake. It was very delicious.

Toby, it's so great that you're dressing as a Marine for Halloween. You really look like a little soldier, and it makes me so happy to know you're proud of me and who I was. I wish I could go out with you all tonight, but I want to make sure you know it's okay to have fun, to forget about hard stuff for a little while.

Please write back soon. I truly enjoyed your letter.

Love,
Dad

When I was done reading, I put the letter down. And then I squashed it and put it under my sleeping bag. Say there really was a heaven, how would Dad feel about Mom writing his letters, and making up his words? This said he wished he could go trick-or-treating tonight, and the truth was he should've been here, and I hated him for being somewhere else. If it was up to me, I'd never, ever do Halloween again. But. Mom needed us happy.

"Dad wants us to have a great time," I said, "okay? So even if you're not really having fun, let's pretend like you are, okay?"

Toby didn't answer, didn't ask why I'd squashed the letter. The whole time since I started reading it he just stood there, looking at himself in the mirror. Suddenly I noticed he was wearing the medal, the one Dad got when he came back from Iraq. "Did Mom say you could wear that?"

Toby nodded slowly, which probably meant she had not. And then he said, "Dad saw me in my cammies."

"Yeah." I hoped he couldn't see us. Embarrassing was how I felt about my penguin costume.

"Do I really look like a soldier?"

"You totally do," I said, and that was the truth, he looked like a man. Which sounds stupid to say since he's only five, but if he was taller I bet he could've done something like get on a plane to Iraq, and nobody would know to stop him.

"I need a gun."

"It's okay," I said, "you look good anyway." But it was true, the gun was the one thing missing. It used to be he had a toy rifle and an automatic that had lights and made sounds. But they both disappeared.

"You can't fight without a gun," he said.

I smiled. "Who're you gonna fight?"

He didn't answer. He just looked at himself. And then he gave a deep sigh, and left the room.

Well. I knew exactly who he wanted to fight. Because I'd wanted to fight them too for a very long time.

Probably when Toby grows up, he will be a real soldier. And I know there are a lot of soldiers, so another one might not seem important, but here is the thing. I also know Toby would be the one who cared most, more than all of the other soldiers put together. I'm pretty sure he'd be the one who could make a difference.

7
Natalie

After Anna left for school I sat with Toby on the floor of his bedroom, my notebook in my lap. Toby was hunched over a tablet of paper as he had been all morning, dressed in his little uniform, wearing the medal he must've stolen from my bedroom—trying to be his father, or make his father proud, or both at once.

I'd hoped that now he'd started talking again things might return to normal, that he'd go back to following me around the house, with the string of monotonous chatter that used to drive me crazy. But he hadn't said a word to me since last night, and I was terrified that he'd sunk back into his silence. I should've kept him awake, prodded him throughout the night with questions he'd have to answer, like revving a motor to keep it running.

I remembered the resoluteness in his face when he'd showed me what he wanted to be for Halloween, an idea it seemed he'd planned well before I'd asked him. Maybe it was ridiculous to even be taking them trick-or-treating the day before we moved, but I'd wanted to show them we could still have fun, make life as close as possible to normal. Suddenly it all seemed ludicrous.

I watched my son write to his father, and then I looked

down at my notebook and thought how utterly unqualified I was to guide parents in helping their children through grief.

I'd started writing my books when Toby was born, and the writing made me happy, dipping into the silliness of childhood. But I hadn't written anything since Josh's death and I needed to write, for the money if nothing else.

Last week I'd made up a budget, using the spreadsheet Josh had saved under the title *MoneyInMoneyOut*. We'd always been frugal and had managed to save a little; but now the *MoneyOut* number was staggeringly higher than the *MoneyIn*. I'd calculated that in order to break even, I'd need to find a job making at least fifteen dollars an hour. I wasn't delusional enough to believe I'd be handed that kind of job when I had no real work experience, and so I'd briefly contemplated welfare, bankruptcy, and a life of crime, and then had closed down the spreadsheet without saving it.

I put down my pen, then crawled over to Toby. "Hey, sweetie, you want to help me finish packing your closet?"

He glanced at me, then back at his paper. The letter I'd written late last night was gone; I'd checked soon after Anna left for school, and neither of the children had said anything about it. I didn't know what it meant that they'd kept it from me.

"You know, Daddy has a hard time reading this. Can you tell me what you want to say so I can write it down for him?"

Toby didn't answer, just brought the scribbles closer to his eyes like he was proofreading them. And I didn't need him to tell me what he wanted to say; it was written there in fifty pages of desperate, hand-cramping scribbles that, from the perspective of a five-year-old, must've taken as much dedication and determination as the writing of an epic novel. I sat there watching him, a tight band of sorrow constricting my lungs, then bent to comb my fingers through his cowlick.

"Gorgeous," I told him. "You're a man ready to face the world."

Toby watched me, unblinking. It was hard to tell if he even understood my words. He leaned against me and handed me the pages, and looking down at them I felt a flash of anger. How could Josh have done this to his son? I would die for our children; I'd cut off both arms and both legs to save them. And yes, Josh had felt immense pain, but you endured pain when you had children; you thought of them first and second and third. This was one of the natural laws of the universe, like gravity; penguins stood huddled in the cold with their eggs tucked between their legs, certain species of male spiders let themselves be eaten after procreation.

Josh had been so strong, and he'd adored the kids, I believed that absolutely, so what could have been so bad it negated his love for them? To kill himself, knowing what it would do to his children, was absolute amphibian selfishness, and part of me hated him for it.

I tried to focus on the weight and warmth of Toby's body against mine. He lifted the top sheet and underneath was a drawing of what I assumed was our family, four stick figures, two big, two small. "I'll write on here what this is," I said, "to make sure he understands it. Is this our family?"

Toby smiled and nodded, then flipped the page to reveal an orange circle, with eyes, a nose and mouth. "A jack-o'-lantern," I said, "right?" I wrote OUR FAMILY on the first, and JACK-O'-LANTERN on the second. In the next picture were two figures with boxy legs and no hair.

"Who's this?" I said.

He put the picture on the floor and laid another drawing next to it. Again two figures, now facing each other, their arms outstretched. "Are they hugging?" I said.

He shook his head.

"Fighting?"

Toby raised his chin and set another drawing on the floor. On it was a figure, its face scribbled over with cherry red, inside a blue rectangle with wheels. "This is really scary-looking," I said. And then, I realized. "Oh, Toby, is this the war?"

He watched me, not speaking. "Tell me what's going on here." I pointed to the rectangle. "Is this a tank?"

Toby's eyes filled. He stared at me a minute before he swiped the page away. And suddenly, I understood. It was Josh's Pathfinder.

Could it be that the story Anna had told him about his father's death had gotten mixed in with whatever he'd actually seen that night, and become what he now believed had happened? I didn't know if this was good or bad. Was this what Toby saw when he woke up screaming, someone fighting with his dad?

My biggest fear was that he'd seen everything, not just the aftermath. What had brought him outside in the first place? Something must have happened that I didn't know, because Toby had never gone outside on his own before. Had Josh gone into his room to say good-bye? Maybe he'd come into all our rooms that night to watch us sleep, and Toby was the only one who'd woken.

"Oh, sweetie," I said, gathering Toby up, inhaling the baby smell he still somehow managed to exude, breast milk and talcum powder, despite the fact he hadn't been near either in years. "It's okay," I whispered. "It'll be okay."

The phone rang and Toby stiffened, then wriggled to get away. I glanced toward the hallway but let the machine pick up, watching Toby stack all his pages into a thick pile. He handed them to me.

"Okay," I said softly. *Okay*, I guess, implied that I'd give the letter to his father, meaning there'd have to be another letter I wrote back. I didn't want there to be another letter. But if I didn't write back, would it feel to him like Josh dying all over again?

"You know you're going to be late for your last day," I said. "Let's get you some lunch." I took his hand and led him to the kitchen, where I pulled out bologna and peanut butter and held them up. "Which?"

"Bologna," he said softly.

"Good choice." I smiled. "Pig guts and eighty-four percent fat."

I made his sandwich and sat with him as he ate, chewing on the crusts he'd discarded. My belly fat and at least one buttock must've been completely constructed from the food my kids left behind.

He was only half done when a honk came from outside and I jumped up. "Let's go! Let's go!" I grabbed Toby's Bob the Builder knapsack and ran with him out the door, waved at the bus driver and slipped the knapsack over his shoulders, then watched him run down our front path.

There is nothing, I think, more heartbreaking than watching your kid strain to get up the tall steps of a bus wearing a knapsack almost as big as his whole body, settle in a seat and then watch you out the window as he's driven away.

Back inside I hit *play* on the answering machine. And hearing Rachel's voice, I felt squashed inside, like my heart was being flattened by the heel of a hand.

Josh and I had known Nick and Rachel Corrigan before they were even married, in Jacksonville, and when we'd all come to Pendleton we'd immediately rekindled our friendship. Nick and Josh had served together through their last tour in Iraq, and during it Rachel and I had shared dinners and coffee breaks, called each other daily on the phone. But I hadn't seen either of them since Josh had died. Rachel had left casseroles on my doorstep for a week, salty, fatty, cheesy dishes in disposable containers, but she hadn't rung the bell, had acted inexplicably distant the few times I'd called on the phone. I wanted so desperately to talk to someone who'd known Josh well, who'd cared about him. Nick had been Josh's best friend. Had he and Rachel seen some sign that I'd missed?

I played the message Rachel had left. "Hey, Natalie, it's me…I'm just calling because I guess I've seen the U-Haul out front of your house, and I was hoping to catch you before you and the kids left. I know we haven't talked for a while and I've been the world's crappiest friend, but I wanted to say I really hope you're doing okay. I think about you all the time."

I stopped the message. Then erased it. Then disconnected the machine and threw it into a packing box.

Inside Josh's closet were the cammies he'd folded on the top shelf, the shoes and belts, clothes I'd planned to donate to the Salvation Army, but then what would I have left of him? I'd saved his uniform, and two of his T-shirts were already packed with my clothes, a gray US Marines shirt which he'd worn when he went jogging, and the Volcanoes National Park shirt he'd bought on our honeymoon. The week after Josh died, I'd found the shirts in the laundry. I'd pulled them out and buried my face inside them, inhaling the scent I knew so well, just sat with them for I don't know how long, breathing what was left of him. Sometimes now I wore them to bed. I still hadn't washed them, but already they were starting to smell more like me than like him.

Pulling the clothes off their hangers, I could see on the back wall an array of colorful slips of paper, Post-it notes. I pushed the clothes to one side and peeled them carefully off the wall, one by one. *What day of the week is it?* and *Feel your chin. Have you shaved today?* and *PDA in nightstand.* I stacked the notes together, and sat with them on the floor.

At one point last year, the first month after Josh had returned from Iraq, we'd had the notes throughout the house. On the refrigerator: *Milk put away?* The bathroom mirror: *Toilet seat down?* The longest list had been the one at the front door which he'd check, go to pick up his keys, check again, pick up his wallet, and then again, take his bagged lunch from the fridge.

Things had been so hard for him, those first few weeks. He must've worried that he'd never be the same person again, but after the first month the notes had gradually come down, his memory progressively better, so it was kind of funny that he'd forgotten these. There'd been lingering holes, but not bad enough that he would've needed to remind himself to shave.

I set the notes on the floor, stood slowly, and resumed

packing. I tried not to look at the shirts I knew so well, just stuffed them into a bag without folding. And then pulling his cammies from the top shelf, I found another note pinned to the top jacket: *Hug Natalie and the kids,* it said. I looked at the note a long while, and then I unpinned it and tucked it carefully into my pocket.

The last hanger held Josh's dress suit, the suit he'd worn at our wedding. I buried my face in the jacket and rocked back and forth on my toes.

On the night of our wedding, needing to get away from the sappy dance music, we'd walked into the restaurant's back garden. "We did it," he'd whispered and we'd stood there looking at each other, smiling stupidly. And then I'd unbuttoned his jacket and leaned against him as he wrapped it around my back. In the distance I'd heard the voices of my family and our friends, clinking silverware and laughter, and I'd felt surrounded. "You're so beautiful," he'd said, and I said, "You're so full of it," feeling embarrassed and adored and yes, maybe a little beautiful. I'd put my arms around his waist and we'd rocked from foot to foot, enfolded in the jacket and the warmth of our bodies, and I'd thought, *This is the way we'll always be.*

I slipped the jacket on. "Josh," I whispered. "Hi." The sleeves were long, loose past my hands, and I raised my arms to smooth the draping fabric over my eyes, my cheeks. "Can you believe this?" I whispered. "A year ago I thought the most important thing was the grade I'd get on my Milton essay." I paused, then laughed softly. "Okay, okay, don't make fun of me, I totally didn't give a damn about Milton. But what I mean is the world suddenly feels so different, so much bigger. Just think, Josh, this is the way we'll always be."

I should give this suit away. It was only worn that one night, and somebody who couldn't afford a new suit would think it was a miracle. But I couldn't stand the thought of another man, a man I didn't know, slipping his arms into the sleeves. Being happy inside it.

So I went down to the kitchen and rooted through a box of utensils for a knife. Back in the bedroom I knelt by Josh's closet and used the knife to pry the carpet up from the tack strip, pulled it back and laid the suit over the plywood floor. I pressed my hand flat on the suit, then lay on the floor to rest my cheek against it.

I stayed there a long while, my eyes closed, then rose and carefully laid the carpet back down. Maybe the suit would be found someday; someone would notice the swelling of the carpet and lift it to see. But even years after we left, I'd be able to imagine it. Still here, waiting, in the last place he'd ever lived.

I heard the front door open, then close. Anna's voice, "Mom?" The sound of their feet on the stairs. I sat back, stared at the knife, and then slipped it into a box as Anna appeared in the doorway. "We're home," she said. There was fear in her voice, and it was only when I heard it that I realized I was crying. After weeks of holding myself steady for the sake of the kids, had I tamped my feelings down so much that now I couldn't recognize tears? I blinked quickly and forced myself to smile; the storyteller, star of Chicken Little and Dora the Explorer, whose expressions range all the way from grinning to laughing, who can make you giggle at the scary parts.

Anna kept her eyes on me, looking at the same time so young and so very old, both pale and pink-cheeked like she'd been boiled in hot water, but with bruises under her eyes the color of weak coffee. I wrapped one arm around Toby and raised the other toward Anna. She hesitated and then came to sit in my lap, and we held one another, almost tentatively, like if we held too tight, we all might explode.

8
Anna

The night before Dad left for Iraq, I wanted to sleep in his and Mom's bed, but I was too embarrassed to ask. So instead what I did was I brought my pillow and slept outside their door, close enough that I could hear Dad breathe. I heard them talking until real late, soft talking which was helping me go to sleep, until I heard Mom crying and I sat up and put my ear to the door. And this is what she whispered, how if anything bad happened to Dad, it would kill her.

That is number one.

And here is number two, what I heard her say to Grandpa at the funeral. That she couldn't feel anything anymore, and she didn't think she could do this without him.

Which Grandpa said that yes she could, that what happens is you just make yourself live for a day, and then the next day comes and you live for that day too. What he didn't say is that there might come a morning where you wake up and you look around, and you realize you are done.

I saw Mom. With a knife. Holding a knife and crying,

and I don't know if she was planning to really do anything with it. But, I could tell she thought about it.

So that night, I sat up and went to the box in the corner where my desk used to be, and I pulled out a pen and paper.

What I wanted was to really be able to write to Dad. To tell him I'm so sorry. I'm so sorry! I didn't want this and if I had one wish, the only thing I'd wish in the entire world is to take it back. That's what I needed to say, but here is something I knew. It was my job to keep Mom happy and alive, and I was pretty sure how Mom would feel if she knew what I did to him. *Dear Daddy,* I wrote.

When I was done I read the letter over and I thought it was pretty good. So I folded it, and put it under the cabinet.

I hated the letters. I hated them so much I wanted to stick fingers in my ears when Mom read them. There was only one other time Mom lied to me before, which was when she said how in the part of Iraq where Dad was going, there wouldn't be any bombs. But then, last year, he got hurt from a bomb. So.

How it felt then was how I feel now about the letters, how it probably feels whenever a person finds out that her mom lied to her. It's like somebody has done to you the same thing that you can do to a sock, stuck their hand inside your body and turned you inside out. But the thing is, I know why she did it. For the same reason I wouldn't tell Mom or Toby that I didn't believe in the letters and the same reason I would never tell what I hid inside of Leopolda. Because sometimes, it's the lies that keep you alive.

9
Natalie

The smart thing would've been for me to let Diane take the children trick-or-treating, so that I could man my door. But I wanted to walk through the neighborhood one last time, absorb the sight of it. So I left a box on the doorstep, piled with candy—carefully chosen varieties that were nobody's favorites, like Whoppers and Raisinets, to help guard against the type of kid (usually older, always a boy) who'd see the unguarded box as a personal coup.

My children's Halloween experience had always been a 180 flip from my own. My parents didn't live in a real neighborhood; there were no sidewalks, and Mom had to drive me a mile before we got to a respectable density of houses. They would buy two bags of candy, for variety and just-in-case, and we'd end up eating most of it ourselves.

But on a military base, Halloween is an event. It makes you fully understand the bizarreness of it all, witches and Spider-Men and cross-dressing teenagers milling in groups through the streets with orange bags, knocking on strangers' doors to ask them for free candy. It makes you think, *Who the hell came up with this idea?*

"Well, I think the costumes are adorable," Diane said, as we traipsed behind the kids. "Madison was mortified when she saw herself in it, but I convinced her that uniqueness was more cool than skinniness."

The costumes made the girls look like they had no legs, an oblong blob of fabric from shoulder to mid-calf. After slipping it on, Anna had stood a full two minutes in front of the mirror unspeaking, then turned away, resigned.

"This is probably the last year we'll be able to dress them as something cute," I said. "So we just took advantage."

"I know. Kind of cruel of us."

Toby was galloping beside the girls, looking exactly the way a child should look on Halloween. But Anna was almost silent as we wandered from house to house; her "trick or treat" sounded oddly flat. Even Madison was quiet, and after we'd walked several blocks I saw her take Anna's flippered hand while they continued down the street, waddling in their ridiculous costumes.

As we approached Nick and Rachel's house, I found myself hanging back. I wanted more than anything to talk to them, to know they didn't blame me for Josh's death, the way I sometimes blamed myself. And there were so many questions I wanted to ask Nick. He'd probably spent even more time with Josh than I had over the past year, so had Josh confided whatever he was going through? I wanted answers, wanted to hear the truth about how hard it had been, what might've killed him and why that day. There had to be a reason, something I hadn't known.

But Rachel didn't want to see me, that was obvious. She lived two blocks away, but she'd called and left a message this morning rather than coming to say good-bye in person. So yeah, maybe I was acting like a kid. But they were the ones who started it.

The door opened and Rachel answered looking expectant, her dark hair up in a ponytail. Immediately her face lit up, and she bent to hug first Anna and then Toby, then looked over Toby's shoulder. And saw me. She raised her hand, and I swiped a quick wave that probably looked more like I was batting at a fly.

She beckoned and I bit down on my cheek, feeling like I was two years old. But really, this was ridiculous. I squared my shoulders and walked toward the door.

"Natalie!" Rachel pulled me into a hug that smelled of floral air freshener. She was dressed in the same style she'd worn since I first met her, a filmy, loose-fitting skirt and blouse. Even her voice was filmy soft, a voice she'd admitted to me had been practiced in front of a tape recorder, in an attempt to take the South Philly out of it. "I was hoping you all would come by."

"Hey," I said, feeling suddenly shy. I glanced at the kids, then said, "You guys go on, okay? I'm just going to talk to Rachel a minute."

Diane smiled. "It's fine, I'll take them. We'll wait at the end of the street for you."

"Thanks," I said, then turned to Rachel. "Could I come in?"

"Of course! Sure!" Her voice was all exclamation points.

Nick and Rachel's house was an end unit with an identical floor plan to mine, but Rachel had actually made the place look like a home. It had always been disconcerting, walking through their door and seeing our living room festooned with tapestries and crushed silk curtains, Persian throw rugs covering our beige carpets, potted ficus and ferns in each corner. All the rooms in her house looked like they should be roped off and contain descriptive plaques. But when was the last time I'd been here? I used to come almost every morning with Toby in tow, but it had been weeks since I'd been invited.

The house smelled like coffee and cinnamon; a breeze from the ceiling fan fingered the curtains, and table lamps traced dusty peach triangles onto the walls. My throat tightened with homesickness, not for Rachel exactly, but for a way of living. I wanted to sink into one of their fluffy couches with a mug of creamy coffee the way I used to, stay forever.

"Coffee, tea, beer, or Valium," she'd say, and I'd cover Toby's ears and say, "Pot!"

And Rachel would laugh. "Keep your hands over his ears. I have to tell you what I dreamed last night."

"Sex?"

"Yeah, and not with Nick. It was scandalous."

"Awesome. Maybe we better go for the beer instead…"

Should I assume I could sit without being invited? A few weeks ago I would've felt free to look through her cupboards if I was hungry, start myself a pot of tea without asking. But she still hadn't moved away from the door. "Is Nick around?" I said. "I want to say good-bye to him too."

Rachel touched the edge of the door, then looked at her finger like she was testing for wet paint. "I guess, okay, sure."

"But you'd rather I didn't?"

"No. No! I'm sorry, it's just Nick gets upset easily."

I felt a hot vein of anger. They used to be my best

friends and now Nick couldn't handle saying good-bye to me? "Because of Josh?"

She hesitated, then said, "Because of Josh. Sorry, I'm being a total jerk; I'll call him. I'm sure he'll want to say good-bye. Nick!"

I found myself glancing toward the side table, where they'd kept a photo of the four of us, me and Josh, Rachel and Nick, taken on their wedding day back when we'd all lived in Quantico. Seeing the empty table now was like being punched in the gut. "You took down our photo," I said, before I could stop myself.

"It's in our bedroom," Nick said. He was standing at the top of the stairs, the gentleness of his almond-shaped eyes a strange disparity to his brown high-and-tight haircut and square chin. His eyes showed every emotion screened by his stoic face, and that was probably what had drawn him and Josh to each other, their similar mix of softness under hardness. He smiled. "I thought I heard your voice; it's so great you stopped by. Hold on a sec."

He disappeared around the corner of the hallway and I waited with Rachel, feeling a prickling discomfort like my skin was on too tight. "So how've you guys been?" I said finally. "I haven't seen you in ages."

"Same old," Rachel said. "Except they put Nick in recruiting, which he never wanted to do, but I think he's probably pretty good at it. Means a lot of travel, though, and not to anywhere interesting either."

"Better than restocking, though." Josh had been a Communication Center Operator for years, but since returning from Iraq he'd been assigned as a supply clerk, a huge demotion that they'd inexplicably never revoked, even after his memory had improved.

"Yeah, I guess it is. So how's Toby? He still having a

tough time of it? I meant to call sooner, but you know how time goes…" She gestured spirals in the air with both hands, like she was trying to demonstrate how time went.

"He's doing better now, I think. Still not great, it'll take a while, but I guess I'm starting to believe we'll all get there eventually."

"See." Nick strode down the stairs and handed me the framed photograph. "We keep it by the bed."

The four of us were arm in arm and laughing. I touched Josh's face and then my own, this picture of a time we'd felt so grown up but had really still been so very young. "Josh really valued your friendship," I said.

"So did I. He was honestly one of the best friends I ever had."

I studied Nick's face. He looked older than he had when I'd last seen him a few weeks ago, and he seemed to have lost weight. "Josh kept a photo of you in his wallet," I said. "I found it when I was going through his things." I shuffled in my pocketbook, and pulled out the photo.

"I look constipated," he said, smiling.

"Marines always look constipated in photos," I said, "or pissed off; it's like that look's a prerequisite for earning your stripes." I slipped it back into my wallet, then saw the photo I'd found of the girl with the birthmark. I held it toward Nick. "Hey, you don't recognize this girl, do you? Her picture was in Josh's wallet too. She's Arab, almost definitely somebody Josh met while he was in Iraq with you."

Nick looked a long time at the photo, then said, "No idea. She's probably just one of the kids he gave gifts to. He was real well known for being generous, at least around our camp, so she was probably just a fan."

"Maybe." I studied the girl's face, the sadness in her

eyes, her clawlike birthmark, then tucked the photo back into my purse.

"So where you all moving to exactly?" Nick said.

"Up to French Creek, to stay with my parents for a while."

"Cool," he said. "I mean, I'm glad you'll be near your family. I've been worried about you." I suddenly saw the anguish on Nick's face; the skin under his eyes pouchy, like his eyeballs were too heavy. All this time I hadn't seen this look from anyone other than the children. No one else had loved Josh enough, and so I hadn't been able to lean on anyone else's pain.

"Thanks," I said, wanting to talk about Josh, to cry with both of them and maybe feel a little less alone. I hated them and I needed them and I hated that I'd ever needed them. And I wanted them back.

I remembered sitting on the couch with Nick and Josh, Josh rubbing my feet as I half listened, half day-dreamed, hearing only snatches. I'd fall asleep and wake hours later to find Nick still there, their conversations softer and more intense, discussing everything from racism to pantheism to the time of day they preferred to make love. And Josh had written to me about the nights they'd spent together in Iraq, half drunk, sharing the darkest, most intimate corners of their minds, their disillusionment with the world, the need for meaning, and the meaning of meaning.

"Nick," I said. "Nick, can I ask you something?"

The doorbell rang, and I watched Rachel greet the trick-or-treaters, her smile now stiff. A fairy, a princess, a baby devil in a stroller; they were like a different species, their faces shining with the perfect joy of childhood, and I suddenly found myself wishing I could *be* them, just for a few minutes, have that sense of everything still waiting to happen.

After they'd taken their candy and Rachel closed the door, I gazed blankly at the doorknob, then squared my shoulders. "Look," I said, then turned back. "Nick...why? Why did Josh do what he did? You know what he went through in Iraq better than anybody; he was fine, he was just fine that day and then suddenly he was dead and it still doesn't feel real. Help me understand it?"

Nick hesitated, and then stepped toward me. For a second I thought he was going to reach for me and I braced myself for it, unsure if I'd push him away or let him hold me. But he just stood there with his eyebrows arched, like he was talking to a child. "I don't know any more than you, Natalie. It was a complete shock to me too."

"But he must've talked to you about how he was feeling." I was crying suddenly, with no warning whatsoever, and they both were watching me wide-eyed, like I'd just had some kind of epileptic fit. "He talked to you more than anyone!"

"Sweetheart," Rachel said, and strode to the living room for a tissue. She brought it back and waved it at me until I took it, then put her arm around my shoulders and squeezed.

"The war was hard on him," Nick said hoarsely, and then he shoved his hands into his pockets. "It was hard on everybody, but he had an especially bad time of it. You know Josh, he always believed in goodness, like everybody would be selfless and noble if they got the chance. But I think it kind of destroyed his view of the world. The things you see out there, you start questioning what it even means to be a human being. So maybe he just didn't want to live in this kind of world anymore."

"But it had to be more than that! Okay, he had bouts of depression, but he was coping with it. We played in the park with the kids that morning, and he was laughing. He was happy!"

Nick seemed to sway a little on his feet, and Rachel put a hand on his arm, then another on mine. "We hate this too," she said. "I know we haven't been there for you, which I realize is about the most selfish thing we could've done. But it's not because we don't care."

Through the window beside the door, I saw another group of kids approaching. I reached for the wall, leaned heavily against it.

"Come for breakfast tomorrow," Rachel said. "You and the kids, we'll see you off on a happier note, okay?"

I looked through the window, my eyes blurred, then rubbed my sleeve quickly over my face. "I wish I could." My voice sounded clogged so I swallowed. Swallowed again. "I'd like to but we have to leave early tomorrow. Long drive." I nodded at the street behind her. "I better go. The kids are going to yell at me for holding them up."

"Right." Rachel stretched an awkward smile, then said, "Well, we're real glad you stopped by, really we are."

"Thanks," I said. All rote words. The conversation ending used with people you never actually intended to see again.

Nick pressed me in a quick hug. I kept my arms flat at my sides. "I'll talk to you soon," he said softly.

I pulled away from him, looked from him to Rachel and back, then walked out the door without saying good-bye.

10
Natalie

I called my parents from the kitchen, then sat on the floor like the kitchen barstools I'd sold to the new owners already belonged to somebody else. My dad had never gotten the hang of answering the phone at home, his greeting still carried over from the days he'd run a consignment shop, the shop's name replaced with his own. "Will Hanson, can I help you?" As a teenager I'd found this excruciatingly embarrassing, but now it seemed heartbreaking and precious.

"It's Natalie," I said. "I just wanted to tell you we're getting a late start, but we're leaving now."

My dad grunted. This was another one of his phone quirks, that he tended to forget the person he was talking to couldn't read his expression, and expected the right reaction to indecipherable articulations.

"I'm sorry, Dad. But I still have the key so I'll try not to wake you up when we get there."

"*Don't* try. Your mother's been waiting for this, and you'll hurt her feelings."

I didn't contradict this, even though I sincerely doubted my mom even understood we were coming. The last time we'd seen her, she'd thought Anna was me. "We'll call you from the road to let you know where we are."

He grunted again, then said, "We take a nap at two o'clock."

"I know. I'll call later than that. So we better get going."

After hanging up I walked into the living room, and found Toby standing by the stairs, clutching his Pooh Bear which was now earless and eyeless and had clumped, mangy fur that made him seem afflicted with some kind of skin disease. "Where's your sister?" I said.

"She's sitting."

I smiled at him. Hearing him talk now felt even more exhilarating to me than all those years ago when he'd said his first *Ma-ma*s and *ba-ba*s. Just as much of a miracle. "Sitting?" I said. "In her room?"

He raised his chin. "She wants to be alone."

"Right," I said softly. "I guess she's saying good-bye."

Last night, I'd left one last letter in the bathroom, a good-bye letter from Josh, our good-bye to this house and this life. Good-bye because I knew this couldn't continue after we left. The letters had been a small shove on Toby's path toward healing, and now I'd have to hope the momentum would carry him. It was time to move on.

But when I'd slid a comb under the cabinet to retrieve Toby's stack of drawings, I'd discovered another slip of paper, folded, only half hidden.

Dear Daddy,
    How are you? I am fine. It's a funny coincidence, because guess what we had for dinner last night? It was exactly what you wrote in your letter. Grilled

cheese! I can't imagine never having it again, because it is truly the best sandwich in the world.

Today was my last day of school. I got an A on my spelling test but a B on the math quiz and that is mostly because I hate math.

Now here is what I really want to write about which is the most important thing I ever told you. I don't know why you had to leave us, but I know you wouldn't of left if Mom wasn't here to take care of me and especially Toby. You knew we'd be safe as long as Mom was here. So I don't blame you and I'm NOT mad, and if you decide you don't want to write again that would be okay because I think now you see how we and Mom are doing good.

Tomorrow we're leaving for our new home which is so, so exciting. I wonder what it will be like? I wonder who my new friends will be? Mom said we will be able to hang a tire swing, which will be fun! I can not wait. There is a garden where we are going to grow vegetables which will also be fun. I am especially looking forward to carrots.

Love,
Anna

I refolded the letter slowly, and held it against my cheek. I'd hoped she'd write in this letter the things she couldn't say out loud, but maybe this meant she really was okay. Except the thing was, she couldn't be *this* okay. She should be mad at Josh; she should be furious, so why would she try and placate him? Was it because she wanted to keep him from feeling bad about leaving her? To have Anna worrying about Josh's feelings was the most awful result of these letters I could imagine.

But at least she was saying something. Whether or not she truly believed Josh could read this, at least it was a crack in the door she'd slammed behind herself. Maybe she did believe the letters were real, and maybe she'd been able to convince herself Josh had died in the war, like she'd told Toby. Maybe these were both just coping mechanisms she could use until she no longer needed them, but then what? Would they just dissolve away? Flake off like a scab leaving new healthy skin (or a scar, or torn and gruesome flesh) behind?

I leaned to kiss the top of Toby's head, then took his hand and walked upstairs. I knocked gently on Anna's closed door. "Hey, there," I called.

No answer. I cracked the door open.

She was sitting in the middle of the room, facing away from me, knees hugged against her chest. "Hey," I said again, softer. "I just put the last box in the U-Haul."

She scrambled to her feet, a startled sort of move like I'd caught her doing something she shouldn't. When she turned to me her cheeks were flushed. "Okay," she said.

Toby walked in slowly and stood by Anna, then reached for her hand.

I smiled sadly at her. "We got to skedaddle." *Skedaddle*, a word infinitely lighter than what we were actually doing.

She gazed at me, her eyes unreadable, then said, "We could visit here sometime." She raised her eyebrows, waiting for confirmation, and I said, "Maybe," because it would be cruel to tell her we'd never be back.

"But probably it won't feel like home anymore," she said, and then she walked to the window. She pressed her hand against the pane, and then she turned away and strode past me down the hall.

I remembered when I'd first shown this room to Anna, how excited she'd been. It was the first room since Toby was born that she didn't have to share, because Josh thought she was too old to be sharing with a boy. And now she was two years older and would have to share again. She hadn't complained once.

I suddenly wished I'd done something special with this room, painted it purple and given her a princess canopy, a fluffy rug to cover up the worn wall-to-wall. But of course I'd thought she'd have many rooms of her own. It was another thing I'd taken for granted.

We left through the side door, even though the path from the garage to the street would've been closer. I hadn't used the garage with Toby since the day after Josh's death, when he'd kicked at me, screaming as I'd tried to usher him out. So we left through the side door and angled our way across the grass to our car.

I set a cooler in the backseat, checked for the tenth time the lock between the U-Haul and our car, made sure the kids were buckled in, and then we were gone.

This was the first time, driving away from a place we were leaving, that I didn't swivel around to watch it disappear from view.

On our way from town we stopped at the cemetery. We were probably the only ones who'd been here since the funeral, and even with all the friends we'd had at the base I didn't know if anybody would visit when we were gone.

Josh's father, also a Marine, had died in the Gulf War, and he'd been virtually estranged from his mother, Hannah, ever since he'd left home at eighteen. More than once Josh had said his life had started only when he met me. Part of me liked that, wanted to believe it was literally true, but still I needed somebody else to mourn him. The day after Josh died I'd called multiple times trying to reach Hannah, and finally had to leave a message on her answering machine with the details of the funeral arrangements. How inappropriate was that, to tell a woman through voice mail that her son had committed suicide? But at that point I didn't care; she deserved to know, but she didn't deserve tact. And apparently she didn't care either, because she'd never showed.

I handed both kids flowers from an overpriced bouquet and we walked to Josh's grave, and stood there without speaking. I laid my flowers on the grass, then touched Toby's shoulder and watched him set his crosswise to make an X. Anna looked down at her flowers, gripping them tightly, then kissed them and laid them one by one on top of the stone.

"You see us now?" Toby said softly, and I said, "What?" before I realized he was talking to his dad.

"Yeah," Anna said. "He's seeing us and he says we're doing an awesome job moving on our own."

I smiled at her, and tried to believe that she was right. Even if inside I was falling apart, wasn't I surviving? That's what life would be for us, survival, cross one bridge and then onto the next, and each would take us farther. And maybe someday, we'd actually be able to escape.

11
Anna

The last time we moved was from North Carolina. What I remember is how that time it really *was* fun. I did not even know where California was. Actually I wasn't completely sure they even looked and talked the same as us, so it all seemed like a treasure hunt, where you might find something you never knew existed.

In the morning before we left, there was a new letter from Dad under the cabinet. Here is what it said.

Dear Anna and Toby,

Today's your big move to a new home, and I'm sure that's a little scary. Moving from earth to heaven was one of the hardest things I've ever done. Especially since I miss you all like <u>crazy,</u> but you know what? One of these days you'll walk up your new driveway and find yourself thinking how good it is to be home. Which is when you realize that somehow the new house has started to become the place you belong.

It'll happen to you, I promise. Your mom loves you so much, and so do Grammy and Grandpa. In my mind, home is where you love and are loved.

Which means, with all the people who love you, the two of you are always home.

Love,
Dad

I didn't know if we'd still be getting letters in the new house. Part of me hoped no, but I have to say that another part of me would have hurt feelings, like Dad stopped caring how we were doing. Which I knew it wasn't him who wrote it, I mean *duh,* so this was a sign that I was probably going mental. But also, also I needed him to know what he did to us.

While we drove, I tried to list the good parts about moving. There could be new interesting things outside your bedroom window. There was a chance you could have a neighbor who was a girl. You could become some-one else and nobody would know it was an act.

But still, this time I couldn't make moving feel fun. It made me feel like everything I'd collected in my life was being all at once taken away.

These are the things I liked about home:

1) From my bedroom window, I could see
Mrs. Tucker in her kitchen. She was deaf and
when she talked with her hands, it was beautiful.
2) There was a stain on my ceiling that looked
like a bunny head.
3) Dad lived there.

But none of these things, including Dad, belonged to me. They're not things like coins that you can put away in a safe place, to look at later. Most of the things I'd col-lected would now belong to someone else.

These were my questions, and they made my heart hurt: What person will live in my bedroom when I'm gone? Will she notice Mrs. Tucker and the bunny stain, and if she does, will she see them as something good or something bad? What person will sit at my desk in school? Will the other kids think she's an improvement?

The people who moved into our house would not know my dad ever existed. Everything in the house that felt like him would to them feel like something completely else. Which means all the pieces of the world you thought you owned, the things you thought had a certain shape, only had that shape in your head. They disappeared without you.

12
Natalie

The yellowish streetlights and stores in French Creek seemed unchanged since the fifties: a pizza shop and a pharmacy with faded plastic Christmas décor already in its windows; a bar with dark windows and flickering neon ads. When it rained we'd smell sour milk from open dumpsters, and the pansies growing wild in window boxes. On clear days we'd be able to see the snowy peak of Mount Shasta in the distance, like an icing-laced, breast-shaped dessert.

Returning felt the same as it always did, the wash of nostalgia mixed with a strange jolt of adolescent fear. Streets became familiar and then more than familiar, the turns and ups and downs of them pure rote, like the words to a nursery rhyme. Returning home always felt the same, but I knew that now I was husbandless being home would feel like a regression, lying on the twin bed in my girl-hood room, dreaming of the future instead of the present.

My parents' house was pseudo-Victorian, scalloped shingles painted yellow, once bright but now dulled and badly chipped. The yard was surrounded by acres of woods that belonged either to the state or to the neighbors; I wasn't sure if my parents even knew which.

As we pulled into the gravel drive my dad appeared at the door. It was after midnight, I'd been driving twelve hours, and I wanted to get us all from car to bed without a discussion. Both kids were asleep. I'd carry Toby, but I knew I'd have to wake Anna, hopefully only enough to get her up and into the house where they'd forgo baths and brushed teeth and even undressing, just slip back into sleep.

But when I set my hand softly on Anna's shoulder, she screamed. I jumped back and her eyes shifted wildly back and forth. Toby started to cry.

"It's okay," I said, feeling frantic. "It's okay, we're at Grammy and Grandpa's."

My dad had come down the stairs and was now squinting in Toby's window. There was a yellow stain on Toby's shirt from where he'd been carsick, and I hoped my dad couldn't see it. Even now I wanted to be able to prove to him I was competent at motherhood, but obviously tonight I was failing miserably.

"He's crying," my dad said.

No kidding. "He's just tired," I said. "It's been a long drive, and he doesn't know where he is."

"He doesn't know where he is?"

I curled my toes inside my shoes to keep myself from snapping. Toby unbuckled himself and then crawled over the seat and across Anna's lap, his arms out to me. I lifted him and held him against my chest. "What I mean is he's in a strange place. I'm just going to get them upstairs and into bed."

"But we have *dinner* waiting."

I started to tell him we'd already eaten, but then I stopped. He looked so old in the dim yellowish light, still handsome but in a worn, bleached way: his ribbed under-

shirt and bifocals, his thick hair, which he'd kept too long
ever since his retirement, wisping out horizontally, so that
the top of his head looked almost flat. He'd made us dinner. He'd probably waited to eat with us. "Okay," I said.
"Thanks."

Anna seemed to have recovered. She walked silently
into the house, holding my elbow as I carried Toby up the
porch stairs.

Though Dad had apparently made a recent attempt to
clean, had stacked newspapers and made visible vacuum
cleaner tracks on the rug, there was evidence of neglect,
rings on the coffee table from sweating drinks, and dust
on every surface. The house smelled like Brussels sprouts
and something vaguely antiseptic, the smell of an old person's home.

My mom was sitting in the living room, in a pink
dressing gown I remembered from my childhood, flipping
through ads that had come with the newspaper, either because she liked the colorful pictures or because it com-
forted her to mime the motions she'd made back when she
could still read. She looked up when she heard us enter,
and her mouth opened into an O.

"Hi, Mom," I said.

Her expression didn't change. Anna and Toby filed
forward, unprompted, and silently gave her a hug, an act
that first astonished me and then made me want to curl up
on the floor and sob. When Mom first started getting sick,
it used to kill me inside that the kids would probably
never remember what she'd been like. But now, I was almost glad for it. It was one fewer person they'd have to
mourn.

My mom patted Anna, and then Toby, on the cheek.
"So pretty!" she said to each, as if they were crystal vases.

She was the one who'd taught me how to tell stories; I remembered her putting on voices, pulling out costumes from my dress-up box to act out scenes. Wearing fairy wings and a flowered sun hat, lying on the floor: *I drank your medicine, Peter! It was poisoned, and now I'm going to be dead…!*

When she'd first been diagnosed with Alzheimer's she'd started to write down memories from her childhood up through the present, maybe to prove to the world that she'd had a past, had once been someone, or maybe trying to affix it all in her mind. Mom's memories had taken her two years to write, and as she went on the words and concepts grew simpler, an essay written by a fourth grader, by a second grader, dictated by a toddler. The last sentence of her history: *Natalie mared to Josh and people came. It was happy.* After that, she'd given up.

I bent to hug her. She was wearing the perfume she'd worn throughout my childhood, White Shoulders, and I inhaled deeply as I kissed her cheek. "It's Natalie," I whispered. "Remember me, Mom?" She smiled and touched my arm. "So pretty," she said.

My dad paraded us all to the kitchen where the table was laid with the good china. A pot was bubbling on the stove, had probably been bubbling for hours. Chili. My dad could cook two things, chili and eggs on toast, probably had been cooking them every day ever since Mom started forgetting to turn off the stove.

I knew the kids wouldn't eat either one. The only dinners they'd eaten without fussing were hot dogs, grilled cheese, and ravioli. After Josh died I'd stopped trying to make anything else, and I knew this wasn't the time to start again.

"I'm sorry, Dad. They're probably not hungry. I

should probably just get them up to bed, and then I can come back down."

But my dad didn't seem to hear, just brought the pot to the table and started ladling the chili onto everyone's plate. "This chair's for Toby," he said, gesturing his elbow at a chair holding a phone book. The phone book was worn, dated 1983. I lifted Toby and set him on it.

"You get the drinks," my dad said. "Mom and me, we'll just have water. I bought everything else in there for you."

I opened the refrigerator to a dazzling array of juices and soft drinks. It was too overwhelming, so I just pulled out the milk and poured three glasses.

At the table, both Anna and Toby were staring at their plates. I made a face at them that I hoped could be read as *Don't worry about it, just take one bite and say it's delicious but you're full.* But as soon as I sat, Anna picked up her spoon and took a bite, and then another, then started shoveling the chili down, like a child from a third-world country who'd been presented with a chocolate sundae. Toby watched her a moment, and then also started eating. My dad nodded approvingly and I just stared.

Were my children really this polite that they'd wolf down overcooked chili just to make their grandfather happy? I didn't know if I should be worried about this, or proud.

That night I lay in bed, Anna tucked against my right arm and Toby against my left. My dad had wanted to put them both in the guest bedroom, but there was no way I'd make them spend this first night in a strange bed alone.

This was the bed from my childhood, my old room still exactly the same as when I'd left high school, friends I hadn't seen in years still tucked into the frame of my vanity mirror, the canvases of smiling suns I'd painted still covering the walls in garish orange and red. I'd lain here in this bed, dreaming of the future, *wanting* the future, and thinking I could invent it.

Anna turned against me and I buried my nose against her head, inhaled the scalpy, apple-shampoo scent of her hair. What would I have thought as a teenager if I could see myself now? I would've seen myself as an adult lying in my childhood bedroom, and I would've seen my perfect children and the things I hadn't been able to save them from, and I would've seen exactly what it meant. That I had failed.

Here I was, no money, in this aging town, living with my aging parents. I should've found a way for us to move to Minneapolis or Manhattan, somewhere vibrant and kaleidoscopic where you didn't realize you were the only thing not moving. Why was this the first time I was realizing how truly lonely this life would be?

I slipped from bed and walked outside to the U-Haul, pulled out a box labeled NATALIE, and carried it upstairs to the guest room. Then I went into my bedroom to pull out the bottom drawer of my childhood dresser, and brought it to the guest room as well. The drawer used to hold my underwear, but now was filled with chipped Christmas ornaments I remembered from childhood. I pulled them out slowly, studying each one, and then lifted the drawer's secret bottom. All my secrets had been kept in here, my diary and bad test scores, the lipstick I wasn't supposed to wear until I turned fourteen. I began transferring the contents of the packing box into the drawer.

Here were all the letters Josh had written me while he was overseas, along with old photographs, pictures that

seemed too precious and private to put in albums, shots
taken of him sleeping, our honeymoon, of me in lingerie I
hadn't worn since my body had become unfit for lingerie-
wearing. Here was a Post-it note I'd found in my jacket
pocket the week after Josh died: *Stop whatever you're doing
right now and give yourself a hug from me.* I'd been almost certain it hadn't been there when I'd worn the jacket last, so
did he write it knowing what he'd do? Was he really so
tactless that he thought it would be a comfort? What I
really wanted to believe was that he'd written it last
spring, imagining me finding it and smiling, writing something back.

Now I pressed the note between my palms, held them
up to my face. My love note back to him would be to keep
the Post-it for the rest of my life, never mind that it killed
me every time I saw it.

I'd met Josh my senior year in college. My mother had
just been diagnosed the week before, the reason for her
forgetfulness, pots left on the stove, wrong turns taken on
familiar roads suddenly devastatingly clear.

I hadn't told anyone; I was still absorbing it myself,
and even though there were times I could forget, the de-
spair came in sudden waves when I was alone. All at once
the wave would rise and drown me, tears filling not just
my eyes but my entire face.

I'd gone out for a walk off-campus, avoiding my required reading, when I suddenly found myself down on
the front stoop of a Jamba Juice, making sounds I never
would've wanted another person to hear. There was a
group of men approaching, all in uniform, and mortified
at myself, I covered my face like it would keep them from
noticing me. The men passed by, their voices dwindling,
and I peeked through my fingers to make sure they

weren't looking back. And saw a pair of legs. I widened my eyes and looked up at the length of him, the torso, the chest, the broad shoulders and the neck, at the top of which was Josh.

He reached into his pocket, pulled out a square of white cloth, and handed it to me. And where normally I would've found the idea of a handkerchief repulsive, taking Josh's handkerchief seemed, in a way, almost sexy. Because Josh was beautiful. Not classically beautiful maybe—his skin was a little too pale, his blond crew cut too short, his gaze so intense it made me uncomfortable at first to meet his eyes. But he had a magnetism, part sexual and part soothing, an attraction that pulled me in the way a familiar scent might, reminding me of something I'd once adored, something I knew had once brought me bliss, but that I couldn't quite place. And, of course, there was his uniform.

I wiped my eyes, then looked at the wet cloth. "Sorry," I said. "I mean, thanks. I'll wash this and send it to you. Or buy you a new one."

He laughed at this, and sat next to me on the stoop. "Don't worry about it." He took the handkerchief back and tucked it into his pocket, again somehow not gross but sexy. "I owe you at least ten handkerchiefs for getting me away from those guys," he said, nodding in the direction the men had gone. "They'll be talking about how many pounds they can bench-press and how many girls they've screwed. I'd rather spend time with somebody who obviously cares about something." He studied my face, then nodded slowly. "Man trouble," he said.

I smiled. "Good guess, but no."

And then I told him. He was the first and only non-family member I ever told about my mother, this stranger with his disarming smile, the shadowing in his eyes that didn't match that smile and also somehow didn't match the uniform. The eyes showed he really did understand, and when I collapsed into a second round of crying, he didn't seem uncomfortable and he didn't try to placate me; he held me and rubbed at my back, his uniform serving as a second handkerchief until, embarrassed, I pulled away.

"Don't be sorry," he said. "Tell you what. I'm going to buy you a smoothie, and we're going to talk about either politics or sports or movie stars." And so this was our first date: Mamba Mango thickshakes.

I didn't think till later what this must say about Josh, that he'd approach a woman who was in a state most men wouldn't come within a football field of, whose swollen face must have looked like a bruised tomato. He understood tears. And he'd seen me at my very worst, but he stayed. And stayed.

Now I reached back into the box and pulled out some of Josh's more recent letters and e-mails, sent that summer from Iraq. *We just drive around here and wait to get shot at,* one note said. *I feel like one of those plastic animals in an arcade game, people aiming at me for prizes while I slide back and forth on the same track.* I ran my fingers over the words, imagining them in Josh's voice. I was looking for reassurances, for Josh's strength under worse fears than mine, but reading the letters now I could see a sort of quiet desperation behind the words, too many exclamation points. How had I missed it? "*Don't forget me,*" he'd written, more than once, as if he'd actually thought that might be possible.

I pulled out all the photos, then reached back into the box for Josh's cloth heart. That night, as I'd helped Toby in the bathroom, I'd seen his eyes darting around the room.

"There's no place!" he'd said.

I'd exhaled and leaned back against the doorframe. "Oh, baby…"

His fist rammed against my leg. "I want to go back!" He hit me again, then with the other arm, fists raining little pellets against my stomach. "Now!"

I'd grabbed his wrists, and then wrapped him in my arms, burying my face in his hair. "It'll be okay," I'd said. "We'll be okay." Convincing nobody.

But I couldn't continue writing letters, I knew that much. We needed to talk about all of this face-to-face, the sadness Anna must be keeping from me, the fear she was only starting to express. I'd been hiding behind the letters. All of us had been hiding, but the thing had served its purpose. Toby was talking again and they knew their dad was watching down to make sure they were okay, and they realized dying was really not a thing to be scared about.

Those were the kinds of lessons that would stick. It was the same way I hoped how they now thought their father had died would become a sort of inherent belief. That even when they understood the truth, they'd also understand it really was the war that had killed him.

Now I held the heart to my nose, trying to absorb whatever might be left of its lavender scent, and then I slipped it into the back of the drawer and slid the false bottom over the top.

We woke the next morning to the sight of my dad standing in the doorway. If he'd knocked, I'd slept through it.

"It's seven," he said.

I blinked, tried to see through the haze of my near-sightedness and lack of sleep. "We didn't get to sleep until one-thirty," I said.

He didn't respond. Total hours of sleep was not a consideration. Good people woke by six A.M. Sleeping past seven was just slovenly.

Downstairs, a parade of cereal boxes was lined up on the kitchen table, sweet cereals I never let the kids eat at home. I felt a wash of sadness. There must be ten boxes here. My dad nodded at the kids. "Help yourself."

"You want this one?" my mother said, pointing at a box. "This one? Or this one?"

Anna reached for a box of Lucky Charms, and Toby pointed at the Fruity Pebbles, probably drawn by the foot-powered car. I poured his cereal, and then poured Honey-Combs for myself, what the hell, and we all sat and ate.

As we chewed, I watched the kids. What were they thinking? Toby had his ear to the bowl to see if the cereal crackled, and Anna was studying the back of a box the way she always did at home, sometimes reading the same text four or five mornings in a row, even when the box spouted nutritional facts or exercise recommendations. Had they even spoken since we'd gotten here? I tried to think back, and couldn't remember them saying anything. They looked okay, though. Maybe just tired.

I tried to imagine what it was like when we weren't here. My dad was never much of a talker; it was my mom who'd always taken up space. Now that she couldn't, was it always like this? Synchronous crunching, hand to plate to mouth to plate, two people living separate lives in the same place, my mother sublimated and my dad, in his own way, just as lost inside his head.

I suddenly hated myself for not having visited more often, for being so caught up in my own life I hadn't found room for theirs. I'd gloried in my independence from them, a sign of being truly adult, but how selfish of me not to have found room for this man who'd bought ten cereals for my kids. And this woman I should've let talk and talk, and listened to while she still had things to say.

"These are awesome," I said stupidly, nodding at my bowl.

"Glad you like 'em. I made them just this morning." He smiled and winked at Anna, and she giggled.

I smiled at him, then awkwardly stood and reached to hug him. My father was not a hugger but he didn't pull away, just stood there patting me softly on the back.

"I'm so glad we're going to be closer to you," I said. And meant it both ways.

13
Anna

Grammy and Grandpa's house had spiderwebs in the corners. And it took ten minutes for hot water to heat up. And also there were no lights outside so when you went out at night the trees looked like giant people, and you felt like they could maybe beat you up. But other than that, it was okay. All our things got taken out and put in their new place. My clothes, in the new closet next to Toby's, didn't look like mine anymore. My animals piled on my and Toby's bunk bed stared out at their new world.

The day before our first day at our new school, I brought my collection to Mom. I have been collecting since forever; we call it my shell collection, but it includes ingredients of everything from outdoors: shells I have found and shells I have bought, but also driftwood and sea glass, pinecones and a real nest. Also my favorite, stones I have found that look like nothing when they're dry, but you lick them and *presto* they become themselves, striped or spotted, pretty enough for jewelry. "Can I glue these to my wall?" I asked. My thinking was that every day I would wake up and see them and remember where I got them from, my life when it was normal.

Mom asked Grandpa and he said it was okay, that it

was our house now too, which made her look sad. I don't know why.

She got out her hot glue gun and I studied my new room and decided on the wall opposite my bed, the first place my eyes landed every morning and the last place they saw every night.

"You want to make a design?" she said. "Or just random."

"Let's do a big heart," I said. I thought I'd have enough to make it take up the whole wall, with enough left over to be the beginnings of a whole new collection.

First, Mom did not like this idea. Imagine a flat line. That was the shape of her mouth. But then, she smiled slowly. "A new heart for our new home, right? I love that! It'd make Dad so happy."

And I wanted to tell her that's not what I was thinking. I hated that the idea of hearts was now infected with a new meaning. A heart should always be its own thing. But then Toby smiled, which made me feel a little bit okay. Last night I saw him looking through the bathroom and our bedroom for the place where a letter could be hid. So maybe the new heart would make him forget about the old one.

We all of us had different jobs. Toby did the choosing out from my collection basket, Mom did the glue, and I was the one who decided where the pieces should go. I didn't plan it out beforehand, so when it was done it was lopsided, but in a good way. And then there were leftovers, and Mom came up with the idea to make the heart into a face. Sand dollar eyes, mica for the nose, little sprigs of hair from my broken-apart bird's nest, and then Toby got to make the mouth from everything that was left.

When we were done we stood there looking at what we'd made, all smiling. "What's her name?" Mom said.

I tried to decide what would fit her. "Josephina," I said finally. "This is Josephina Graham."

"Good choice," Mom said. "She looks just like a Josephina." Josephina was lopsidedly wonderful. You looked at her and automatically, you loved her.

Then Mom said, "I want to show you something I picked up for us last week, before we left. Hold on." She left the room and then came back and handed something to Toby and then to me. A bundle of dead weeds. "Smell it," she said. It smelled like nothing, but I smiled and said, "*Mmmm,* pretty."

Mom sniffed her bundle and then shrugged, a little embarrassed. "Okay, it doesn't have a smell. But here." She flicked a lighter and held it up to the weeds.

They didn't burn, just started to smoke, and from the smoke the smell came to me. "It smells like Thanksgiving," I said.

She smiled. "It's called sage, and I read somewhere that you're supposed to wave sage smoke when you move to a new home to bless it, to bring peace and happiness to your life inside it."

I thought about this, and what I saw was that they were two things we didn't have but needed more than anything. "Do you think it works?" I said.

Mom tilted her head. "I don't know; I just liked the idea of it, blessing the house. We'll go to every corner and wave the smoke up and down, and ask for something we want to have while we live here."

"Peace and happiness," I said. "That's what we should ask."

"Good enough." Mom lit her weeds, and then Toby's,

and then she waved the smoke at me and smiled. "We bless this house with peace and happiness."

Toby looked down at his weeds and said, "And ice cream."

Me and Mom smiled at each other. "Peace and happiness and ice cream," she said.

After the first two rooms it stopped making us laugh. I think Mom felt it too, like it was becoming a little bit real. We did our room and then hers, and then went to Grandpa's bedroom where he was helping Grammy wash sleep sand out of her eyes. Mom gave him another branch of sage, and we all four of us went around to every single room. "We bless this house with peace and happiness and ice cream," we said in every corner, and it felt like somebody might be listening.

And after we'd done everywhere, we went outside and Mom and Grandpa watched us, both laughing, me and Toby spinning in circles. Sending our spirals of smoke up into heaven.

14
Natalie

How many of my old teachers would still be teaching at Anna and Toby's new school? As I walked downtown with the kids, I found myself half hoping to see them and half scared to. The change in their age would be a sign of my age, and if they recognized me and asked how I'd been, what could I tell them? Other former students must've come back to say they'd just finished their law degree, bought a penthouse, were waiting for clinical test results from a breakthrough treatment for childhood leukemia. But here I was, moneyless, jobless, living with my parents. They'd be so proud to have been part of my education.

Anna dropped my hand as we approached, on guard against potential fifth-grade eyes. We stood by the playground watching the groups of children, maybe first or second graders, playing circle games and jump rope games and red-rubber-ball games. It was refreshing to see that they hadn't changed in all these years, that with all the exposure to alien shooting and Super Mario, they still knew what real play was about.

Anna and Toby stood watching, and then Anna said, "They look nice."

Her voice was strained, though, so I reached for her shoulder and squeezed. "They *do* look nice. And you guys never have any problems making friends. You'll love it here."

"Maybe," Anna said.

"I wanna do the swings," Toby said, pulling at my hand, and I smiled at him, feeling a tug of joy. How long since he'd wanted to play?

"On Monday you'll be able to, but let's let the other kids play with them now. C'mon, why don't we get some ice cream. There's the greatest ice cream shop downtown; they have this deal, where if you eat their whole Super Smacker Sundae, you get it for free. It's about the size of a boat, and I tried it twice, and both times I completely regretted it. But your dad tried once and he managed it. Then regretted it too, but I'm ready to try again."

"Dad went there?" Anna said.

"Uh-huh. It was years and years ago, when you were just a baby. Actually, I just realized you were there too! I think you might've tried some vanilla, or maybe you were too young."

"I don't remember it." She looked down at her sneakers, then said, "I bet I could do the super sundae. Remember last Thanksgiving? When Dad kept putting food on my plate? That was *so* funny, wasn't it?"

Anna would finish her plate and Josh would see it was empty and give her more potatoes, turkey, broccoli. "I'm not hungry!" Anna would say, and Josh would shake his head. "Look how hard your mom worked. We need to put more meat on your bones." He'd squeezed Anna's arm. "No meat!" he said, and winked at me. And Anna had finished plate after plate with no further complaint, maybe not wanting to insult me, or wanting to please Josh. The whole thing was rather weird and, now I really thought about it, somewhat troubling.

"I remember you being very sorry after," I said.

Anna smiled. "I thought I was going to puke."

"So maybe just a regular sundae," I said.

We walked through downtown, the tightness in my chest of déjà vu: the pizza shop where I'd stopped almost every day after middle school, the movie theater where I'd sat with a row of girls, all of us screaming or laughing or falling in love with Harrison Ford. Only the trees at the side of the road showed how much time had passed; planted when I was a child, their trunks the thickness of my arm, they now towered overhead with their roots kicking up the sidewalk.

I'd have to find a job in one of these shops, maybe the bakery since I'd probably at one point scarfed down every type of baked item known to mankind. Or maybe at the bank; I'd work my way up through the ranks and make enough to buy our own place nearby. It was ridiculous of me to have relied for this long on storytelling and the tiny advances from my books.

Before leaving Pendleton I'd written down a list of goals, things to get accomplished over the next year. Simple goals. Completely doable.

1. Get a REAL job.
2. Find a home.
3. Get the next book accepted for publication.
4. Make the kids laugh at least once a day.

And then, I'd written:

5. Go on a date.

Then crossed it out, and written:

5. Be happy.

Now I grabbed Toby's hand. "I think Toby wants to fly," I told Anna, and she smiled at me and grabbed his other hand, and we swung him off the ground. Toby laughed and Anna laughed. I laughed. Voilà, goals 4 and 5.

"Here we are," I said, crouching so Toby could scramble off my shoulders. The shop hadn't changed at all since I was a kid, a seventies version of the fifties with a black-and-white tiled floor, steel bar stools, and pink vinyl booths; even the woman behind the counter seemed the same, with her bleached hair sprayed to rest a good two inches over her head. I'd just pulled open the door when a voice behind me said, "Natalie?"

I froze, my stomach feeling like it had been compressed to the size of a gumball. "Seth?"

He looked exactly the same as the last time I'd seen him, senior year in college. We'd dated for four years in high school and then slept together, sporadically, in college, the only man I'd dated before Josh. Where most men my age had started to go soft around the chin, under the eyes, and at the belly, Seth looked like he'd been frozen at eighteen—neatly clipped brown hair, striped rugby shirt and all—and just now thawed.

I laughed to cover up my shock, a strange, high-pitched sound. "I didn't realize you still lived here," I said. Which was a lie. Dad had told me bits and snatches of things about him over the years, his real estate job, his marriage, his McMansion on the fringes of town. And Seth had sent me an announcement of his wedding—an announcement, not an invitation—which I'd assumed was an attempt to prove to me that he'd moved on.

"It's great to see you! Wow, what's it been? Ten years?"

"More than that." I looked down the street, and wondered how rude it would be to say I had to run, when I'd so obviously been about to enter an ice cream shop. "These are my kids," I said. "Anna and Toby. Seth's an old friend of mine, from when we were in high school." Seth extended his hand to Anna, then Toby. "Pleased to meet you," he said. "Wait, let me guess your ages, I'm good at this." He rolled his eyes to the sky. "Toby, you're twelve, and Anna, you have to be at least eighteen."

Anna watched him, unblinking, like she was trying to decide whether to smile, and Toby hid behind my leg. "Five and ten," I said, and Seth smacked his forehead with the heel of his hand.

"So how's Stacey?" I said, then inwardly winced. *How are you? What've you been up to?* were what a normal person would've said.

He snapped a quick smile. "Actually, Stacey and I separated a couple months ago."

"Oh...I'm sorry."

He shrugged. "It's for the best. I'm happier now than I've been in the past five years. I did hear about your husband, though. I can't even imagine how hard that has to be."

I willed him not to talk about the suicide in front of the kids. "Who told you?" I said.

"Actually"—he looked over my shoulder—"I heard it from your dad. I was going to send you a sympathy card, but I was in the middle of the mess with Stacey, and I didn't know if you'd want me to. I should've told you how sorry I was, though."

"No, it's okay. I didn't even have the energy to open most of the cards I got."

He reached out and gave my arm a squeeze that was probably meant to feel reassuring, but actually pulled strings that reached down to my fingers and up my arm, tugging through my chest, a drawstring pulling closed. Mortifyingly, I squeaked.

I tried to cover the squeak with a cough, then said, "Anyway, we were just about to get some ice cream. Anna thinks she can conquer the Super Smacker Sundae."

"Uh-oh, dangerous. Mind if I join you? It'll be my treat. I have a house showing at four, but I'm free till then."

I studied a smudge on the window, the size of a child's hand. Why did I feel so awkward? Maybe because I knew anyone watching us through this smudged window would think we were a family, and either feel charmed or jealous depending on their own life situation. Because even the perception would feel like a betrayal.

"Sure, of course," I said, and he opened the door, bent in a semibow, and gestured inside.

We ordered at the counter, cones for me and Toby and sundaes for Anna and Seth, and sat at a booth. As he paid, I checked my outfit, to make sure I wasn't wearing anything that made me look twenty pounds heavier than I actually was, like someone who spent a lot of time in ice cream shops. Okay, a peasant blouse and jeans. Not exactly sexy, but then again I wasn't trying to attract him, just establish that I hadn't deteriorated with age.

Seth slid into the booth across from me. "So you here to see your parents?"

I hesitated. "Actually. Actually, we're living with them. Just for a little while, till I get a job and can afford to move out." I smiled brightly, to emphasize this was just a temporary situation.

"Well, great, we can get together, maybe. You could come for dinner. I'm learning how to cook, and so far I can make three different variations on chicken that all taste pretty much the same. But I swear they're completely edible."

Toby set his cone on the table and started kicking his feet against the bench. I dipped a napkin in my cup of water, used it to wipe ice cream off his fingers. "Sure, I could go for chicken," I said.

Seth fished in his pocket for a pen and wrote on a napkin. "My number. Call anytime; all's I need is a day advance notice so I can run out to the store. But I should warn you, my place fits the exact definition of a bachelor pad."

"Leopard print bedspread and mirrored ceiling?" I said.

He laughed. "More like no bedspread and a chipped ceiling. But it's cheap, an annex over the deli. And I guess it does what it's supposed to do, least till I can find a place I want to buy." He sounded so matter-of-fact about all this, like he was discussing the loss of his wallet. "Almost everything was Stacey's, as she liked to remind me. I even got my job nepotistically; her dad's part owner of Century 21. It's a miracle he hasn't fired me."

I imagined them living for years as the kind of couple you see in restaurants bitching quietly at each other, touching at the edges of something flaming without ever quite reaching the heart of it, then finally just turning away, singed but not disfigured. "I wondered how you got into real estate. I pictured you as the kind of person who'd maybe join the Peace Corps, something less capitalistic. It didn't seem like it'd be your kind of thing."

"Yeah, it kind of wasn't. Still isn't, but it pays the rent." He held up the napkin. "Hey, Anna, Toby, look. You ever do origami?" He started folding the napkin. "Works better with thicker paper, but I can make a pretty good napkin swan."

Both kids got up on their knees to watch him fold. "You have talents I never knew about," I said.

I glanced at the white band around his ring finger, a fading scar. I didn't want to go to Seth's house. I didn't want to talk about his failed marriage or Josh's death, didn't want him to try to equate the two. And I didn't know what he expected.

Anna took the napkin from Seth, and it immediately fell apart. "Hey, you wrecked it!" Seth said.

Anna looked at the napkin a moment, then handed it back. "Oops."

"How about I buy some real origami paper before you come over, and show you my limited repertoire of animals? And Toby, I'll let you feed my cat, Binky."

He was inviting the kids too?

"You have a cat?" Anna said.

Seth started talking about his cat, the tricks he'd taught her to do. And watching him, I wasn't sure if I felt disappointed or relieved.

I cooked dinner, strip steak and scalloped potatoes, part of me still feeling the need to prove to Dad that I was a competent adult, maybe to counteract his obvious disapproval of Toby's typical hyperactive state. Five minutes at the table and he'd be out of his seat, practicing his long jump or fifty-meter sprint, making various household objects into cars. For me it was like a minimiracle; I wanted to get down on the floor with him, run and jump and laugh and laugh. But Dad, who'd never seen him any other way, would tilt his head, wearing an expression just two degrees shy of a frown. "Well, *you* didn't used to be like that," he'd said this morning. "You'd at least ask to be excused."

I brought the dishes to the table and filled Toby's plate, then my mother's. I didn't feel like talking, it seemed too exhausting, but sitting here in silence, interrupted by Mom's often inappropriate, sometimes incomprehensible interjections, was even more exhausting. I watched Anna drag her knife through her gravy, prodding her periodically to take another bite, then finally said, "We ran into Seth downtown today. He invited me for dinner."

"Oh?" Dad raised his eyebrows. "He's lonely, I think. His wife put him through the wringer pretty badly, I've heard. He's a good man." Dad nodded slowly, agreeing with himself. "He made her a good husband. I just don't understand some people."

To show him the dinner invite didn't mean what he apparently hoped it did, I said, "He invited the kids too. You knew about the divorce?"

"Oh, sure."

Mom stared at her steak like she wasn't sure what to do with it, then finally speared it and began nibbling at the edges. I watched her, a tightness in my throat, then pried the fork from her fist and began cutting her meat while she gaped at me, seemingly amazed. I brushed a strand of hair out of her eyes and handed back her fork.

"She was a real princess, I heard; probably felt like she'd married down. Marlie Sykes told me it was her father bought her engagement ring, instead of Seth, to make sure she got the right number of carats, and he bought them a house because Seth couldn't afford the kind of place she wanted to live in. Marlie said she was always talking about her debut. I'm not even quite sure what that is, exactly."

"Debutante," I said, feeling obscurely pleased. Toby clambered onto my lap and I buried my nose in his hair. "How is Marlie?" I remembered her from the weekly bridge games my parents used to host—red hair (real or fake I couldn't tell), pointy chin, a tendency to fold nearly in half when she laughed. Dad had mentioned her several times in our last few conversations.

"Oh, she's just fine," he said, a strange, overemphasized lilt to his tone, his body shifting almost imperceptibly away from Mom.

I wrapped my arms tighter around Toby. *Oh,* I thought, a sudden sorrow spreading like oil through my gut. "That's good," I said, "I'm glad." And watching Dad chew his meat, the thinness of his shoulders under his pale blue shirt, the frostlike sprays of whiskers missed by his razor, I tried to mean it.

Later that evening I sat in the living room, Dad in the armchair flipping channels, the kids on the floor staring almost catatonically at the TV, and me on the couch with Mom. I leaned forward and combed my fingers through the gauzy wisps of her thinning hair, and she closed her eyes, letting me. My frizzy hair was always so prone to tangles; how many times had she done this same thing for me? The comfort of her competent fingers, her voice soft as she talked about her day, her committee meetings and enough fleeting interests to fill an encyclopedia.

I watched Dad as I worked my fingers through the

tangles at her scalp, tugging carefully, thinking about how people moved on. Maybe necessary but also impossible; terrifying to see how easily it could happen. I brushed my lips and then my cheek against Mom's hair, then put my arms around her from behind and rested my head on her shoulder. She was so thin, her breasts deflated sacks; it was like hugging a rolled towel. "I love you," I whispered, one of the few sentiments she still understood.

She made a soft coughing sound, and then giggled girlishly. So maybe I was wrong. Maybe she didn't even understand love anymore.

15
Anna

Mr. Benning was my new teacher. I never had a man teacher before, so first I couldn't imagine it, but then I decided it would be interesting.

Toby was in morning-session kindergarten, so even though on first days you were always alone, I wouldn't be alone-alone. Already I knew I'd be in trouble at this school because all my clothes were too small. Mom couldn't afford to buy new clothes this year and so my jeans hardly reached my ankles, and at San Onofre it was okay because they knew me back in the time where my clothes fit. But here it would be different. If you ever want to find the biggest loser in a school, all you need to do is look for short jeans and there she is. You don't think about the reasons for them being short, you just assume that it is a choice.

In the morning Mom waited with us by the end of the road, and I pulled out my spiral notebook to write down what I saw:

- Red house with a partly broken roof.
- Yellow house with a pumpkin on the porch.
- Beer can.

The notebook had two hundred pages. Before I got to school I'd have to tear off the front cover because it had a picture of Snoopy, and the Snoopy would only cement the loserness into place.

"I'm visiting a nursery school today," Mom said. She was holding Toby's hand and swinging his arm. "Just to tell them what I do. It's called Crayons and Clay, Books, Bugs and Bouncing Balls. Isn't that a great name?"

I looked sideways at her. "All except for the bugs."

"Yeah, I guess I agree. It's a darned long name too; you'd think they could've forgot the bugs and you wouldn't miss it."

Toby put his thumb in his mouth and started sucking. Mom pulled it back out again. "I have a secret surprise for you guys when you get back home, something I found in Grandpa's attic that used to be mine when I was your age, Anna."

I tried to sound interested. "What is it?"

"I can't tell you!" Mom smiled. "Don't you know the definition of the word surprise?"

So we played twenty questions, and by the time the bus came I knew it was a basketball hoop you attach to the house, even though I pretended I didn't know. Because the disappointment of having a surprise that somebody guesses is a thing that makes your heart hurt.

The bus door folded open and me and Toby got inside. I took the seat right behind the driver, and Toby sat next to me. I focused on the back of the driver's head, black hair pulled back in a little black bun, and three speckles of dandruff. For some reason the dandruff made me want to crawl into her lap. Maybe because they showed that she was real.

Mom told Grandpa on the day of Dad's funeral that the whole week was "a blur." And that's what the whole beginning of my first day was like, with a few clear pictures in between. The clear pictures are:

1. Walking with a lady from the principal's office to my classroom,
2. Meeting Mr. Benning and seeing that he had a thick white mustache,
3. Staring at his mustache while he told the class who I was,
4. Noticing there were only two tables with girls at them and that neither one had empty seats,
5. Watching Mr. Benning point to an empty seat at a boys' table,
6. Sitting in the seat and looking down at my notebook, realizing I'd forgot to tear the Snoopy off, and
7. Wanting to cry.

Mr. Benning put two textbooks and a black-and-white-spotted journal on the table in front of me, and then he went to the board and started talking about poetry, and then he wrote down this poem:

Right at my feet—
And when did you get here,
snail?

I didn't understand it. It sounded too dumb to be a poem, and it wasn't just that it didn't rhyme, it was that it didn't even try. I wondered if I was too smart, or maybe too stupid, for this school. To make myself stop thinking, I opened my notebook and tried to start a list of all the things I liked so far about moving to French Creek. *Sometimes it might snow,* I wrote. But after that, my mind was empty. I had nothing.

So I tore the page out, and then I tore out the strip still attached to the rings. Dad used to play games with me, using codes, where we'd send secret notes to each other that only we could read. There were secret messages written in lemon juice that turned black when you held them over a stove. You could write the alphabet on two lines, forward and backward, and then switch letters from the top line with the line underneath. There was a code where you turned letters into numbers, A was 1 and Z was 26, and then a really complicated code that you did with a dial. But this one with the strip of paper, this was my most favorite.

I wrapped the strip in a coil around a pencil, then used my pen to write across it in four rows, one letter on each coil. This was a message Mom wouldn't be able to read, and I liked that. It felt like something just for Dad, something he really would be able to see.

I am not OK, I wrote. *I want to be there with you.*

When I uncoiled the strip and stared at the separated letters, I felt just a little bit better.

Bidwell Elementary was the fourth school I have been to. First was Mokapu in Hawaii, which I only went to for three months in kindergarten. Then came DeLalio in North Carolina, and two years later was San Onofre. This school, though, was different. Because it wasn't part of a base, it meant the kids all knew one another forever and also weren't used to new girls. Some of them tried to be nice to me; for example, a girl with earrings shaped like frogs asked if I wanted to sit next to her at lunch. But I said no, because it felt like it would be too much work.

But then something happened that I had not expected.

It was the end of the day when the boy next to me, Cameron Carson, passed me a note. He passed it in a boy's way, by crumpling it in a ball and throwing it at me. First I thought he was just being a jerk, so I was going to throw it back at his head, but then I saw there was writing on the paper, so I uncrumpled it.

How did your dad dye?

I crumpled the note and threw it back. It hit him on his nose.

He widened his eyes, but then he wrote something else on the page and threw it to me.

My mom dyed of leukemia last year

Well. This made me like him much more. Partly because we had something in common, but also because he couldn't spell the word *die* but knew how to spell leukemia.

16
Natalie

I'd borrowed a ladder and an electric drill from my dad. Climbing a ladder while holding a drill made me feel exceptionally handy. I could do anything: patch roofs, rewire electric, install plumbing fixtures. Who needed a man? Not me. I was Bob Vila, sans facial hair. Maybe I should buy a tool belt.

When I was done, I folded my arms over my chest, admiring my handiwork. Okay, it was only a basketball net, but still. It was straight; it didn't wobble; it had required a power tool.

"Dad!" I called, then knocked on the living-room window. Dad pulled back the curtain and peered out at me, glasses reflecting the sunlight. I pointed up at the net and he pulled away from the window and came outside.

"That look straight to you?" I said.

He cocked his head to one side and then the other. "Not bad for a chick."

I fake-punched him, then bent for the ball and threw it to him. "Here, catch! How 'bout a one-on-one?"

He fumbled with the ball, then grinned and sliced away from me, dribbling, then aimed for the hoop.

"Nothing but net!" I said.

Dad was one of the reasons I'd wanted to hang this hoop. It had been one of the few ways we'd connected, the two of us out here shooting baskets late at night. I remembered being exhausted after long days at school but dragging myself out here with half-closed eyes to be with him, feel his hand on mine as he taught me how to shoot.

"You still got it," I said now, as he threw me the ball. I dribbled fast, right then left for effect, and then threw. The ball hit the backboard and the hoop tumbled to the ground, taking with it a nice-sized chunk of the soffit. "Oh shit," I said. So much for self-sufficiency.

Dad bent to the net and then looked up at the house, shielding his eyes. "Okay, nothing that can't be fixed. Let me take care of it, and maybe you could watch your mom. And finish unpacking? Those boxes in the living room should maybe go up to the attic now."

"Right, okay, I'll do that." I'd been avoiding unpacking anything but necessities. But really, it wasn't like we'd be able to leave anytime soon. No point in avoiding the fact that this, for now, was home.

Mom was asleep in the living room, sitting up with her mouth open. I watched her a minute, then wiped my sleeve against the trail of drool on her chin, kissed her forehead and bent for a box. I began sorting, dividing things that could go in our bedroom from things that could stay unpacked in the attic, trying not to associate each item with the place it had in our old home, our old life. The box of fish hooks Josh had bought on a whim, which he'd used once and then felt too guilty to use again; the heating pad he'd bought me when I was pregnant, to soothe my swollen feet. Even the innocuous things, a screwdriver, a nail clipper, reminded me of Josh, and as I worked I found myself getting closer and closer to the edge, the hard knot of tears I'd hoarded in the bottom of my stomach slowly curdling. Until I got to the bottom of the box, and found Josh's PDA.

I held it flat in my palm a minute, then sank onto the floor. I turned it on, listening to the sound of Dad drilling outside, and tapped on the *Daily Log* menu item.

I chose a day at random.

And stared.

There, on every page, were dozens of entries: *New bank (Am. Nat.) on Main; T: Good b-ball hit; Vegetable chili; N: Call from dad re: Easter (here??)* All minutiae, meals he'd eaten, TV shows he'd watched, scattered around a handful of legitimate plans you might expect to be in a PDA, and what did it mean? Why would he have to tell himself that he *Hid A b-day prsnt in bott dress drwr?*

"Good as new," Dad said as he opened the front door. I stuffed the PDA down the front of my shirt. "I'll get toggle bolts from the basement for the hoop. Should have it up before the kids get home."

"Great, thanks!" I said, my voice pitched too high, avoiding his eyes.

He narrowed his gaze, looking into my face. "Everything okay?"

"Sure, I'm fine." I stood quickly. "Just unpacking's hard."

He frowned, watching me, and then he approached and patted firmly at my back, like he was trying to burp me. "I'll go down for the bolts," he said, and turned away.

I rocked back on my heels and pulled the PDA from my shirt, switched it off, and stuffed it into my back pocket.

Tonight. I'd read it tonight.

It was almost dark out before we got the chance to enact my two-on-one fantasy game, windy and so cold we could see our breath. But Anna had been so excited when she saw the hoop, actually jumping up and down and then throwing herself into my arms, that I was determined to give her the time of her life.

Dad had gone out before dinner, saying only that he had a "commitment," cleanly shaved, his hair slicked back, flushed cheeks making him look astonishingly young and handsome. A date with Marlie? At some point I should try to convince him I was okay with him finding someone new, but right now I didn't really want to know. I'd only told him to have fun. It was the most I could bring myself to do.

Mom sat on a lawn chair, watching us play, laughing when we laughed and clapping her hands when we cheered. At one point she even rose with her arms outstretched, but when I threw her the ball, crooning "Catch! Catch!" as if she were a toddler, she let the ball hit her chest and frowned, looking slightly offended.

"It's okay," I said, and took her arm. Lowered her back to the chair.

We played until Toby, who bent his knees to throw and sent the ball flying backward as often as forward, ended up cracking the window on the front door. His face froze into a comically traumatized gawk, and I laughed (while silently contemplating replacement costs) to show him it was okay. "Must've been a heck of a strong throw!" I said, which prompted him to try to throw the basketball at another window. And so. Game over. I brought Mom and the kids inside for cocoa.

"We should make this a tradition," I said as we huddled together on the sofa. I pictured us sitting there with our cocoa in December, a lit Christmas tree on one side and a lit fire on the other. "Every night we'll have cocoa, and we should each talk about the worst part and the best part of our day." I must've read about this somewhere, the idea wasn't unique, but the more I thought about it the more inspired I felt. It seemed a much healthier means of finding out what was going on in their lives and their heads, a heartwarming ritual I could picture being carried on for future generations of Grahams. "Your great-granny Natalie started this tradition!" I could hear them say.

"I'll start, okay? My least favorite thing was meeting with the head of the Baptist nursery school, who thinks fairy tales are the instrument of the devil. And my most favorite thing was seeing a little girl in the Bugs and Balls nursery school who was wearing a fairy costume and a Big Bird mask." I turned my head to smile first at Toby, and then at Anna, expecting questions, but none came. Toby swung his legs, kicking his heels back against the couch, and Anna picked at a cuticle. "So that was mine," I said. "Your turn, Anna."

She glanced at me. "My most favorite thing was basketball."

"All right, that's good. But here's a new rule. You have to talk about things we don't all know about, so we can learn something about your day. How about the good and bad things that happened at school?"

Mom rose and walked to the bookcase, picked up a ceramic chicken she'd bought at some point after she'd lost her good judgment. She brought the chicken to the armchair and sat cradling it in her lap.

Anna looked down at her knees. "Okay. My most

favorite thing was I met a person in my class, a girl, who's my new best friend, and she's really pretty and also she seems like she's smart and nice."

"Excellent!" I said. "What's her name?"

Anna scraped her nail against a loose thread in her jeans. "Anaconda," she said.

I raised my eyebrows. "Anaconda? Like the snake?"

"Oh!" She gave a quick laugh, shook her head. "I mean Anna*belle*. Because our names both start with 'Anna' we were trying to think of other Anna things, and we started calling each other Anaconda as a joke."

I smiled. "That's great! We can invite her over sometime, if you want. Maybe for dinner or a sleepover."

Anna paused, then said, "Okay."

I brushed a strand of hair from her eyes. "So now your worst thing. Can you think of something?"

She shook her head, then shrugged. "I guess my worst thing was Mr. Benning came back from lunch with tomato sauce in his mustache, and it was there all afternoon."

"Ick, gross," I said, wrinkling my nose.

She smiled. "I know."

I tried to believe in the smile. She hadn't told me anything about school when she'd first gotten home, which wasn't worrying on its own, but wasn't exactly reassuring either.

"Okay, Toby," I said. "Your turn."

Toby continued to kick one of his heels against the sofa. When he realized I was waiting for him, he said, "My best thing was we made butterflies out of construction paper, and my butterfly was red. And my worst thing was when it got stepped on."

I frowned. "What got stepped on?"

"My *butterfly*. Mrs. Lane said it was an accident."

I decided it would be best not to ask whether it actually *had* been an accident. "Well, great!" I said, not sure what exactly I was referring to as great. "Sounds like you both had an interesting first day."

"Did Dad write a letter?" Toby said.

"No." I reached for his shin to stop the kicking. "Not today, sweetie. Maybe tomorrow."

"Where's he going to put it?"

"Toby—"

"Get a paper. I'll write a letter so I can say where."

I could see the anguish in his eyes and felt an echoing punch. "It's bedtime," I said. "Let's take your bath, and then we'll see."

I let go of his shin and he kicked the couch one last time, then leapt up and walked to the bathroom.

Every night when Josh came home, Toby would jump at the sound of the opening garage door and run from wherever he'd been playing. I'd see his little pumping legs, his wide-open excitement as Josh lifted him up into his arms. "It's little man Graham!" Josh would say, and then he'd carry him to the living room while Toby told him all about his day.

Maybe it was okay to give him a few more weeks of that. It had been taken away so abruptly, and maybe the letters would ease the transition. Or maybe they would make the inevitable loss just that much harder; I didn't know. I didn't know anything anymore.

I glanced at Mom, who seemed to have fallen asleep, the ceramic chicken on the floor. I pulled a blanket over her, then followed Toby upstairs to run his bathwater, and then I went back out to the living room. Anna was still on the couch, staring at the dead fireplace. I sat next to her. "So," I said.

No answer.

"You have homework tonight?"

She shook her head. "I already did it."

"Good for you. Anna Graham, smartest ten-year-old on the planet."

She turned back to the fireplace.

"Look, Anna," I said. "You know you can tell me anything about anything, right?"

No answer.

"I just feel like there's maybe something going on with you. You're being so quiet lately."

She shrugged. "I don't know. There's nothing. First days just make you tired."

"Right," I said softly. "I know they do. And hopefully this'll be your last first day for a long time."

"Yeah." Anna sat a minute longer, not looking at me, then got up and went into her bedroom. I slowly walked upstairs to help Toby with his bath.

Later, after I'd gotten him into bed, he looked up at me, his eyes bright. "Mom, can we write now? Write, Mrs. Lane has white hair and little glasses."

I pulled a notebook and pencil from the nightstand and sat on the folding chair across from his bed so I could see Anna lying on the top bunk staring at the ceiling, palms pressed flat against the mattress.

"Also we have Show and Tell like at home. And today Jason brought a rattle, and we all shook it."

Did he mean a snake rattle or a rattle-rattle? Neither seemed like a normal Show and Tell item, both disturbing, in different ways.

"And write that tomorrow, or maybe some other time, I'm going to bring in the letters Dad wrote me. Can I, Mom?"

I imagined Toby telling the class he'd been getting letters from his dead father, and the teacher immediately calling a shrink and Child Protective Services. "No, sweetheart," I said. "The letters are something private Dad wrote just for us. He wouldn't want anybody else to see them."

"I *have* to, Mom!" Suddenly there were tears glazing his eyes. I touched his arm, but he shoved me away. "Everybody has good things to bring, and we don't have anything!"

And suddenly, seeing his desperation, I thought I understood. He'd started school in the middle of the year, with a class of kids who were already friends. What better way to become instantly popular than to Show and Tell your letters from heaven? "Sweetie," I said softly. "Why don't you bring…How 'bout Dad's Commendation Medal?" But then I suddenly imagined kids awkwardly trying to pin it onto their jackets, dropping it into the gutter. Maybe I could clip it to his coat the way kids' mittens got clipped. "You can tell them how Dad was a hero, how he helped people in the war. They've probably never seen a medal before."

He thought about this, then said, "Okay, that's true. Now write, do you wear clothes in heaven? And if you do, what kind of clothes? And where do you buy them? Love, Toby."

I bit my tongue and wrote something down, random nonsensical words. Anna hadn't moved, still lying there facing the ceiling.

"And P.S., please put your letter in the bathroom medicine cabinet," Toby said. "Okay? Bye."

I watched him, tried to smile, but it seemed to require muscles I wasn't strong enough to lift. I drew a jagged line across the page, stared down at it a moment, then quickly rose to kiss his forehead and then Anna's. "I think we're all a little homesick today," I said, studying her face, waiting for her response. Her response was to pull up her covers and close her eyes.

I stood there a long while watching, then turned out the light and walked to the living room, folding Toby's letter into a tiny square in my palm. I sat on the couch and buried my face in my hands, filled again with the realization that I wasn't old enough for this, not wise enough or strong enough. I knew that had been one of my reasons for writing the letters, because while I wrote part of me had felt Josh there with me, sharing that burden. Which was crazy, I knew that. I wasn't just lying to the kids; I'd been lying to myself.

I was almost sure Anna knew the letters were from me. Maybe it had been a mistake not to talk to her first, but why hadn't she confronted me? Was she trying to convince me she was okay? Or maybe she was getting the same peace from reading the letters that I'd gotten from writing them, even though we both knew it was a game. This sense that in a way, through each other, we actually were communicating with Josh.

But the letters were helping Toby. They'd worked where nothing else had. I'd let him settle into the habit of talking, then we'd talk about his dad, and then we'd work through whatever had made him stop talking in the first place. And then, the letters could stop.

I could feel Josh's PDA digging into my hip, so I pulled it out of my pocket, then went to the kitchen, grabbed two bottles of beer from the fridge, and brought them upstairs to my bedroom.

My shoulders were tense as I switched on the PDA. I

rolled them back to loosen them and told myself I wouldn't look at the last day unless I absolutely felt ready for it. Which wouldn't be today—of course not—so I had nothing to be scared of, right? Just notes he'd written that I could hook onto bigger memories; and memories, even though painful, were a necessary part of healing. Maybe it was strange that the notes were so copious, but that's all it was. Strange.

I flipped back to the *Daily Log*. June 18: *Mini-Wheats; Picnic—smoked turkey; In playground (headachey); aspirin 2 PM.* I ran a finger over the entry, my hand shaking. Remembering.

We're in the playground after our smoked-turkey sandwiches, Anna and Toby on swings; Toby's getting the hang of pumping, and Josh and I watch him and grin at each other, like he's just taken his first step or popped his first tooth. And then Josh gets on a swing, sways gently and then starts to pump, higher and higher. The chains are making alarming sounds, the swing-set frame is bending under his weight, and I tell him he better quit it or the whole thing's going to fall.

But he swings higher, higher, and I stop Toby's swing and pull him off and call to Anna to get down, just in case. The three of us watch Josh, laughing as he swings almost horizontal off the ground and he's laughing too, his eyes bright and face flushed pink.

He finally stops pumping and lets the swing carry him up and down while the three of us clap. "That was cool," Anna says. And even though a two-hundred-pound man on a swing might not fit anyone's definition of cool, for me it is kind of cool. It's the type of thing we used to do, skinny-dipping on public beaches at night, strolling down boardwalks with me perched on his shoulders. We'd both known how to have fun.

He lowers himself to the ground. "I'd completely forgot how that feels," he says, as we all head toward the slide, but when we get there Josh sinks onto a bench, a hand on his forehead. "Hell, why do I feel so dizzy?"

I smile. "Because you're an idiot." And he raises his eyebrows, confused, dismayed.

"Look!" Toby calls, then inches down the slide with his arms in the air, like he's on a roller-coaster hill.

I sit on the bench next to Josh. "It's okay, the idiocy's one of the things I like about you."

Josh closes his eyes. "But I feel so goddamned dizzy!" he says.

Now I ran my tongue against the ridge on the inside of my cheek carved from weeks of biting. And I made myself read on.

June 19: *Cheerios; Hillary Clinton, running pres? Chick salad.* I twisted the top off my beer and swigged at it until my eyes watered, then read the next page.

June 20: *Put gas in Pathfinder; Ham and cheese; Visa PAID!*

June 21: *A+T Dentist; Bees dying—cell phones?* My heart thumped slow and fierce against my ribs, each beat distinct and insistent. *N: Haircut—tell her nice; Saddam executed 2006 (hung).* I knew, I knew why. *Troop surge; Tomato soup; A: knows Times Tables.* He'd lied to me.

"Minor short-term memory loss," he'd told me when he called from the hospital in Iraq, and the little signs of it, misplaced shoes or words, stories or events forgotten, had always seemed insignificant. Toward the end he'd convinced me he was almost completely recovered, that he'd been tested and found within normal range. He'd still confuse words once in awhile, lima bean for lemon or dishwasher for washing machine, and I'd laugh and correct him and he'd laugh and say, "What did I say?" He'd forget we'd eaten dinner and ask what we were having, and he'd think it was a Sunday and I'd have to remind him to get up for work. But I'd believed him when he'd said these were just glitches and just as likely a result of insomnia or post-traumatic stress. It had made sense to me, especially after he'd died and I'd gone through the same thing—getting lost on my way for groceries, or looking down at the core in my hand and realizing that I'd already eaten the apple.

Sex in AM then Cereal; BTK Killer found 2005; A: Scratch on leg—fell bike. There was only one reason for him to have written such intricate details of what had happened or would happen on each day. It was because he hadn't been able to remember without them.

If the injury had been this bad, so all-encompassing that it had required this kind of concentrated effort, how could it not have become the most imperative, crucial focus of our lives? I'd known Josh since we were both on the cusp of adulthood; I'd known him forever and in all that time he'd never lied to me, or kept secrets. Josh was one of the few men I'd ever met who understood his own feelings. He'd told me the sizes and shapes of his fears and his embarrassments and angers; we were one person with two skins, so how could he not have told me this?

I heard a strange noise, and only dimly realized it was coming from my mouth, a rhythmic huffing sound, a struggle for breath. The huge calendar over the desk that he'd used to cross out days; his new habit of writing things on his palm; his insistence on buying a GPS we couldn't afford even though he never drove more than ten miles from home: There were reasons behind those things besides new eccentricities.

Accident, he'd called it, the accident of dodging sniper fire to drag men out of a blasted Humvee, of curling himself around an injured man as a medevac helicopter arrived, because he could see the snipers setting off an IED to destroy it. He'd received a medal for this, a medal in exchange for his brain.

The day after his injury I'd been informed what had happened, told he was in recovery. "No sign of internal bleeding," they'd said, "just an inch-long cut on his cheek that didn't need stitches. We'll be letting him return to the field soon as he feels up to it."

When Josh had been able to tell me what had happened, two full weeks later, he'd made light of the whole situation. "I look like Frankenstein with this scar," he said. "You're probably not gonna love me anymore. Either I have to buy a mask or you'll have to learn how to avert your eyes."

"No problem," I'd said, laughing, elated at hearing his voice. "Good thing I already found a replacement. His name's Wilson Beefcake; I met him at a strip club and I think you'll like him." After hanging up, I'd said a quick prayer of thanks and then gone on with my life.

He'd lied to me then to keep me from worrying, so I should've realized he might underplay the extent of his injury when he got home. Only later did he tell me he had minor short-term memory loss; he said that his brain was shaken up but getting better every day. How long had he thought he could keep me from seeing that it hadn't gotten better? And what kind of person was I that he couldn't trust me, lean on me? That he thought he had to go through this alone?

What if having to bear it alone was why?

I stared down at the PDA, then hoisted myself onto my feet. My stomach was smoldering, overfull, threatening to explode, and I ran to the toilet and retched, gagging again and then again. Losing myself in the ache of it so there could be nothing else.

17
Natalie

I hardly slept at all that night, going back and forth between stewing, pacing, and stewing again. I'd wanted to spend the next morning cleaning the house, focus all my attention on mundanities like decalcifying the dish drain tray so I wouldn't have to think, much less engage in civilized conversation.

But soon after the kids left for school, Marlie appeared. Which meant now that we'd been here for two weeks, Dad wanted to get back to his normal life, like when guests stay too long and you stop dressing before breakfast.

Marlie's hair was no longer red. The color and permed wave of it rather reminded me of oatmeal, but she was prettier than I remembered, in an Irish, dimpled sort of way. "I remember you when you were just a smidgen!" she said, gesturing to her waist. "But you've grown up real nice, just like your mom." With this she approached Mom, who was polishing the silver, her new favorite activity, and kissed the top of her head. "Oh, Meg, you're so much better at that than I used to be," she said. "I could never get all the crannies."

I saw the fondness in Marlie's face as she spoke to

Mom, watched my dad smiling at both of them, and I couldn't process it. Not now. "It's really nice seeing you, Marlie," I said. "I'll let you all talk. I still have some unpacking to do."

"Anything we can do to help?" Marlie said.

"Thanks," I said, "but I'm pretty much done. Just some last few things."

Upstairs I pulled out the napkin Seth had given me and dialed his number. He picked up on the first ring. "Hi, Nat," he said.

He's programmed me into his phone, I thought. "Hey," I said, then turned myself into the happy kind of person he'd want to have over for dinner. "Damn, I've never gotten used to caller ID. It's creepy, feels like the person's been reading your mind."

"Okay, I'll remember that. Next time you call I'll pretend I don't know who you are."

"And also you saying 'Hi, Nat' right away feels like we've already skipped a couple of lines of conversation. Makes me forget what I was about to say." I paused, for effect. "Okay, I remembered again. I wanted to invite myself over for dinner."

"Invitation accepted," Seth said.

I smiled. "Thanks. It's just, I could really, really use some cheering up, and you're the only one I know around here."

"Everything okay?"

"Yeah, fine," I said, an autonomic response, then, "No, actually. But I'm really not ready to talk about it. I just need a friend. I was going to come without the kids, okay?"

"Okay, sure. You want to come tonight? I can make chicken, chicken, or chicken."

"Hmmm, tough choice," I said. "I'll leave it up to you. Thanks, Seth."

I hung up and looked down at Seth's napkin, folded it in half, in quarters, unfolded it. Crumpled it and threw it across the room. I didn't know why I'd called him. I didn't want to talk about Josh, about what I'd found. What I wanted was to talk about anything but him, and I guess I'd thought being with someone completely unconnected to my present life would be a good distraction. Which... was stupid. Now I was stuck going out to dinner on a night I'd inevitably want to spend hunched in a dark corner.

I reached for the PDA and turned it on. What I'd do, I'd start at the beginning. I'd read it all, every entry, and I'd work out what they meant. I'd replay the days through Josh's eyes and live them through my eyes, and I'd figure out who he had become that I hadn't seen, and why and how I hadn't seen it, and I'd make myself believe that even through the distance he must have kept around his hollowed-out self, he'd never stopped loving us.

I clicked on a folder titled *Start Here.* The new screen had two bullets, one labeled *I Feel Okay,* the other, *I Feel Bad.* I chose the *I Feel Okay* button:

- Check "Calendar" Menu to find out day + appointments
- Meds (morning) pill case in Night Table
- Shave & Shower
- 9:00 Work: Check "Today At Work" menu
- 12:00—Call Natalie
- 2:00—Meds (afternoon) pill case in desk
- 3:30—Dr. Moore—clinic
- 5:30 Home
- 8:00 Meds (evening) pill case in Night Table

He'd had to remind himself to shave and shower. To take his medications. To call me.

I clicked on the *I Feel Bad* folder.

- Meds (morning) pill case in Night Table
- Call in sick (760–555–3146)
- Cancel Dr. Moore (760–555–7428)
- 12:00—Heart from under hall bathroom cabinet to underwear drawer
- 2:00—Meds (afternoon)
- 8:00—Meds (evening)
- 10:00—Heart in underwear drawer to under hall bathroom cabinet

This must have been a listing for the days he'd felt too depressed to leave his room. On those days, had putting the heart under the cabinet been just a following of orders rather than a desire to communicate with the children? All the times we'd taken comfort from it, all the times I'd thought it was heroic for him to have wanted to show he loved the children even on the days he was too weak to see them—had he even remembered the reason behind it?

"Natalie?" Marlie called up the stairs. "I made some muffins, can I bring you some?"

I ran my hands through my hair, scrubbing at my scalp. How much of the last months of Josh's life had been real? It was like a story from one of those TV newsmagazines—"The Man with Six Wives"—and you think, How could they not have known?

"Thanks," I said, "but I'm not real hungry. Maybe later?"

"Well, I'll try and save some for you but the way your dad eats, I can't promise they'll still be here."

"S'okay, he needs the calories more than me," I said.

The truth was that those women did know. They knew but they chose not to see. Because of course I'd recognized things were worse than he'd let on. Subconsciously I must've known; the Post-it notes I'd found in his closet, the times he'd scribble furiously on the PDA while we talked or watched the news, the absentmindedness. I must've realized what was happening, somewhere under the skin of thoughts and constant busyness I'd used to mask the realization.

He couldn't have kept these secrets without building a wall around him, and how could I have been so blind to it? I should call Dr. Moore; she'd be able to explain to me how bad he'd been, how much he might've been hiding. She was the woman he'd gone to for his Marine-sanctioned cognitive rehabilitation therapy, and he'd seen her for a month after returning last fall. Once he'd gone back to work (was this the reason he never got his Communication Center job back?) he'd been told the therapy was no longer necessary. Or was that just what he'd told me?

I sat on my bed and dialed the number listed on his PDA. When Dr. Moore picked up on the second ring, the first thing I said was, "How come nobody told me?"

"Excuse me?" she said. "Who is this?"

"I'm Natalie Graham, Josh Graham's wife."

"Natalie," she said, then, "Oh, of course. I met you last fall when Josh first started with us, yes? I heard what happened, about his death, and I'm so sorry."

"You're sorry? What good does that do?" And then I closed my eyes. "I'm sorry, I'm sorry—it's just, how come nobody told me how bad things were? You must've known he wasn't getting better."

"He was doing well, Natalie, much better than I expected actually."

"Much better? Much *better*? He killed himself!"

"Natalie." She paused, then said, "We've seen hundreds of traumatic brain injury cases since the war started, and they're probably harder on the sufferers than any other impairment. The TBI itself can directly cause depression—you combine how hard it is struggling with what you've lost along with post-traumatic stress, and depression's almost inevitable to some extent. We did check him for suicidal tendencies, though. Hold on, let me get his chart so I make sure I'm giving you the right information."

There was a click and I closed my eyes, waiting. Depression was inevitable. Why hadn't they told me depression was inevitable?

A minute later, she returned. "Well, there's not much here. Apparently we didn't save copies, which we should've done. I do know your husband had hippocampal damage that affected his short-term memory, and that only partially recovered. But he'd almost completely regained his impulse control and his self-regulation mechanisms, and he had excellent social skills. So he would've been able to do whatever he set his mind to."

Impulse control? Self-regulation? "He told me that he'd almost completely recovered. How come nobody at the clinic tried to get in touch with me?"

"He told you he'd recovered?" I heard a shuffling of papers, then a drawn-out silence before she said, "He shouldn't have said that. It's interesting...I remember he didn't want you to be part of his therapy. Usually the wife's much more involved."

"Then why did you let him decide not to involve me? Jesus Christ, he was sick! He wasn't thinking straight!"

She cleared her throat, then said, "I guess I thought there might be problems between you. I'm sorry, Natalie, but maybe he just didn't want you to know. He was very resistant to being declared incapable of serving; it's pretty common in Marines, even when their injuries are worse than Josh's. They don't want anyone to know how bad things are, and because TBIs are pretty much invisible, there've been lots of cases where they return to combat without anybody realizing how much they're struggling."

He'd stayed in Iraq for several weeks after his injury, but he'd come home months before I'd expected; he'd told me it wouldn't be until the spring at least, but he'd come back in the beginning of November. I'd been so happy to have him back for the holidays that I hadn't even questioned it, but had they realized then that he wasn't fit to serve? I remembered his return, seeing a blankness in his eyes as he'd turned to us, and then his smile, switched on rather than felt. Why hadn't I realized what that blankness meant?

"In the beginning there were real signs of improvement, so he might've thought there wasn't any reason to tell you. But after the first few months we knew we'd need to focus more on teaching coping mechanisms."

"After the first few months? Was he seeing you all last year?"

"I was seeing him ever since he came back. You didn't know that?"

"I didn't know any of this. He didn't tell me anything." I shook my head. "Can I see his medical records?"

"Oh, I'm sorry, I thought I told you we don't have copies. They've been sent to the authorities, the Department of Defense."

"Wait, what do you mean? Why?"

"We sent the first batch last January and then again in the spring, and then after his death. They haven't contacted you?"

Because they wanted to see if he was eligible for medical discharge? But why after his death? Were they investigating my benefits claim? We still hadn't gotten the bulk of our survivor benefits from the VA, I assumed because they'd been investigating his suicide. But if they'd gotten Dr. Moore's records, they must've realized it was the injury that had made him suicidal. Why would they still be sitting on the claim?

"Could you tell me something? Just tell me your opinion, okay?" I reached for a pillow, hugged it tight against me. "Why do you think he killed himself, Dr. Moore? Don't you get it? It's because I didn't know, I couldn't help."

"No," she said firmly. "No, Natalie. I honestly think it must've helped him to feel like there was some normalcy at home. There wasn't anything you could've done."

I pulled the phone from my ear and stared at the receiver, then hung up on her, hitting the receiver against the cradle hard, then lifting it and banging it down again. I didn't know who I blamed. I blamed everybody.

I want to talk to you about something, I should've said before Josh died. *Because I know the problems with your memory don't seem to be getting better, that they're actually worse than you let me know. And I love you for trying to protect me from it, but you don't have to anymore. I don't want you to, because we're going to work through this together.*

I should've been there that night, should've stayed up until he fell asleep. Should've made love to him and then stayed awake with him under me, so that he couldn't move. *Maybe you think you've lost yourself,* I should've said, *but all the things I love about you haven't changed. We'll work on this together, exercise your brain cells so much we'll force them into shape. And even if it doesn't get better, we can deal with it as long as we have each other. We can be happy again.*

Months before that, in the first conversation we'd had when he called from the hospital, I should've pressed him for more. *I don't care how bad things are for you,* I should've said. *Tell me the truth, I'm strong enough.* But instead, I'd freaked out. I told him I wanted him home. "It can't be safe being out there," I'd said. "If there's something wrong with your memory, how can it be safe? I've lost too many people already, so I can't lose you."

Too many people meaning only my mother, who I hadn't actually lost. It was only her brain that I was losing, replaced by plaques and tangles, and was that why he'd felt he had to keep this from me? He knew what it had done to me, seeing her turn into a stranger; had he suffered through this alone because he'd wanted to save me from having to go through it again? Had he really thought I was that weak?

There was a knock on the door, and Marlie poked her head in. "I had to save these from Will's clutches," she said, setting a cutting board holding three muffins, a slab of butter, and a cup of tea on the bed. "For you and the kids. I know you're not hungry now, but you will be at some point, right?"

I tried to smile at her. "Okay, thanks," I said, in a tone I was pretty sure did not sound thankful.

"Do you think ... would it be okay if I stayed for lunch? Will invited me, but I know your son'll be home for lunch, so I just wanted to check whether you minded."

Was she asking whether I was okay with Toby learn-

ing about his grandpa's adultery? Was she asking if *I* was?
"Of course," I said. "I mean, of course you can stay."

"I'll make cheddar and fresh tomato on English muffin, and a nice salad. Will Toby eat salad?"

Toby wouldn't touch the salad, and I'd give the
English muffin/tomato combo about a fifty-fifty chance,
but I said, "Sure, sounds great."

When she'd gone I turned the PDA off. I couldn't do
this now. Josh's life, our lives, the little pieces he'd thought
were important set so meticulously onto the screen. *T now
5 yrs old; Mickey Mouse pancakes w/ A.* The pieces of his
brain he wanted to keep. I wanted to see what he'd entered
on the last day, and I didn't want to let myself look. I
wanted and didn't want to see if he'd written anything after that day, how soon he'd known there would be no after.

It was last spring, and I was sitting with Josh and the
kids, playing Chutes and Ladders. Toby lands on a ladder
that shoots him up to the second row, and he jumps to his
feet with excitement, gallops in a circle around us while
we all cheer, and then he topples into Josh's lap.

Josh looks startled but lets him sit there, keeping his
hands flat on the floor. And ridiculously, childishly, I feel a
pang of jealousy that Toby's chosen his lap instead of
mine, especially since Josh doesn't seem to realize how
sweet it is to have him there. "Whose turn is it?" he says,
then reaches for the spinner and hands it to Toby. "If nobody knows, I vote we let Toby go."

Disgusting now to think about my jealousy, but I'd noticed ever since Josh had returned in November how the
children went to him first for bedtime kisses and comforting, and it had bothered me more than I'd wanted to admit. I'd thought that it must be because he'd been absent
more often than not, with the months he'd served and his

days buried under depression. But maybe it was because they'd realized what I hadn't seen, that they had to reinforce their existence to him and his love for them, drill it deep enough that it would stay.

What else had I attributed simply to post-traumatic stress and the dizziness from the medications he'd taken? A problem with short-term memory was one thing, but he'd lost more than that, and deep down I must've known it. *Sex in AM then Cereal,* he'd written.

I'd felt the new distance when we made love; the intensity seemed to have muted, and I'd lost that sense of everything else falling away, the bed beneath us, the skin between us. He'd stopped looking into my eyes when he entered me.

I'd thought it must be the war, all the horrors he'd seen distancing him because I hadn't seen them and could never really understand. And I'd thought as those images faded it would have to get better. But it hadn't gotten better, and now I realized it must have been that he'd been trying to make love to me when half of him wasn't really there.

I lay back on the bed, spilling the tea in the process. I lay there as the hot tea seeped into the butt of my jeans; I crossed my arms over my eyes and tried to wipe my mind clean. There are times when that is really all you can do. The heaviness pushes you down through the floor, through the earth, so deep that you can't even find the energy to cry.

18

Anna

The playground at Bidwell was different. Where most playgrounds had climbing things and plastic curly slides in colors you could see a mile away, this playground was just old, everything made out of rusty metal. The boys all either played some kind of chasing game or swung across the hanging bars, and the girls all played jump rope. Which first I thought was dumb, because at San Onofre we'd gotten past jump rope in the second grade, but when I sat there watching them do Miss Lucy, this is what I realized. That jump rope is, in some ways, better than most games because nobody wants you to fail.

Me and Cam sat on a green bench, which was cold enough to feel it through my jeans. When we'd first gone outside he'd just looked at me, and even without speaking I knew he wanted me to follow. So we walked across the playground together and he sat and then I sat. Strange things happen when you are new. I wondered if people were looking at us.

We didn't say anything for a while, but then he said, "That sucks about your dad."

"Yeah," I said. "About your mom too." In class I'd written back to him, *My dad died in the war. He was a hero.* And he wrote, *It is a really sad thing to dye when you are trying to do something good.* Which I thought was true, and a very smart thing to say.

We didn't talk for a long time, but we weren't quiet in a bad way. It was the way me and Toby were quiet, a way that said we knew how each other was feeling, and it was okay. I listened to the jump-ropers and played the Miss Lucy chant along in my head, and thought how funny it was that they'd have the same chant here. It made me think how all over America there were girls who had completely different ways of living, but all of us shared this one thing. Listening, it made me feel both happy and also lonesome for Camp Pendleton.

"How'd you find out about it?" he said.

First I didn't understand what he meant. But then I did. It gave me a belly cramp. I hunched forward over my knees, then swiped my foot over a hill of dirt. A jumble of ants scattered everywhere, then suddenly seemed to make a decision and followed one another into the grass.

I had thought that now Toby was talking, things might get back to normal. Or not normal, but to the point where what happened wouldn't be everywhere, like now when even little things could hurt, like seeing the color of someone's hair, or where we had to be careful what we said to each other and make sure it wouldn't make anybody remember. This, I thought, was one of the reasons why Dad's letters had been a particularly bad idea. It was like how Mom had kept Dad's voice on our answering machine up until we left, and listened to it over and over again, even though it must've been a little creepy to people who called. But for some reason she didn't see this. It was like she thought if you rubbed and rubbed at the sadness you could make it flatten, when actually the truth was it just dug the hurt in deeper.

"I heard my mom crying," I said. "So I went looking for her, and she was outside with my brother. My brother saw my dad dead."

"Whoa," Cam said.

I hunched my shoulders. "I asked what was wrong and she told me to go inside. She didn't tell me what happened until later, so I never saw him dead." Sometimes I thought it would've been better if I saw him. I felt like I should've said good-bye, and maybe if he wasn't actually dead, just hurt, I would've been able to tell. But. That is not a thing to think about.

"I never saw my mom either," Cam said. "My dad was in the hospital overnight with her, and I was waiting before I went to bed for them to call. But when the phone rang it was my aunt. She told me what flight she was taking for the funeral and asked if my dad could pick her up."

"What did you say?" I whispered.

He shrugged and looked down at his feet. "Nothing." He shuffled his sneakers on the ground. "I just threw up."

I never had a friend who was a boy before. And if I hadn't talked to Cam I never would've thought he was the kind of boy I'd want to be friends with. He was very skinny and his hair was too long over his eyes, and he was wearing an orange shirt that was kind of dirty and had a lion's head on it. I do think you usually can judge a book by its cover, but here is an example that shows you can't always. "I won't tell anybody," I said.

He nodded. "Thanks."

We looked at each other, and I thought, *Other than Toby, this is the first time I ever looked at a boy so up close.* Up close, he looked almost like a girl.

Cam leaned back on the bench, still watching me. "Want to come over this weekend?" he said. "I live near downtown, so you could bring your bike."

"Okay," I said, and then we just sat there, not talking, watching the other kids.

I wondered what parts of his mom were left in him. Sometimes I stared hard at myself in the mirror, looking for Dad. And sometimes, there he was. In my eyes. We watched each other.

19
Natalie

Y ou lied to me," I said, as Seth showed me around.
"This place is great." I'd expected yellowed paint and
the type of wood-veneer furniture sold at K-Mart, but his
annex was nothing short of elegant: high ceilings, tall,
mullioned windows, and a marble-tiled fireplace. I found
myself wondering how much money he made.

"You should come here during the day, though," he
said. "Around eight A.M. the deli starts playing Eastern
European Muzak, polka-type stuff. And when it's hot
there's this pickle smell."

"All I smell is whatever's in the oven. It's making me
hungry."

"Ah, my Chicken Surprise. Here...sit and have some
cheese. And you want red or white?"

"Red, thanks." I settled at the bar overlooking the
kitchen and studied the tray he'd set on the counter: Brie,
Gouda, tapenade, and an assortment of crackers. "You
really went all out."

"Nah, this is nothing. You should see what I do when
I'm really trying to impress a lady. I've been known to
light a hundred candles and fill a room with roses."

"Wow, who taught you that? I don't remember you lighting any candles for me."

He smiled. "Oh, I've learned a few tricks since then."

"You been dating since you got separated?"

Seth went still a moment, then said, "That was all for Stacey, actually. She liked that kind of thing."

"Ah." I stacked a slice of Gouda on another, unstacked them. "Well, I highly recommend it next time you find somebody you want to seduce."

"Right." He looked slightly annoyed as he topped my glass of wine.

I rose and walked to his bookshelf, bending to pet the gray tabby perched on the bottom shelf. "Binky," Seth said.

"I wasn't sure she was real. Has she moved since I got here?"

"No, and she probably won't. She's ancient and she couldn't be bothered."

I studied his shelf. "Aristotle? *The Canterbury Tales?*"

"Yeah, I made a pact with myself when I left Stacey, to improve my mind. So far I've gotten through three pages of *The Scarlet Letter.*"

I smiled. "Actually, that's three pages more than I've read."

And then I saw them, right above eye level, two thin books with very familiar spines. "This is a good one," I said, pulling out *Peggy Panda Can Use the Potty!* "I've probably read it about a hundred times by now, usually out loud."

He looked over his shoulder, and his cheeks flushed immediately pink. "Yeah, well, I've been following your career." He gave an almost apologetic smile. "I have that one memorized, actually. It's really reinforced to me the joys of peeing in the right place."

I laughed and slid the book back. "It's a little weird seeing it sitting next to Chaucer."

"It's alphabetical, so that was pure coincidence. But in my opinion, you're ten times better than Chaucer."

"Or at least easier to understand." I leaned back against the bookshelf and the cat gave a hoarse yowl and slithered under the sofa. "I tried starting another book recently, but my head wasn't in the right place." I considered, then unconsidered, telling him what it was supposed to have been about. I really didn't want the inevitable pitying smile. "I'm saving up so I can afford rent on a place that's not my parents' home, so I'll have to try again because I could really use the advance."

"You want help finding a house? I have connections." He waggled his eyebrows like he was suggesting he knew a guy who could bump off a home owner.

"Thanks, but you obviously don't know my net lack-of-worth. I'm still waiting for benefits from the VA, and I have to find a job, and then maybe we'll see about a house. Century 21, they're not interested in hiring somebody with zero experience in real estate, are they?"

"Probably not, unless you want to take over for the guy who empties the trash in one of those lovely brown uniforms."

"Don't make fun; I might get that desperate."

Seth cut open a piece of chicken, inspected the insides, then said, "You know, one of the mortgage companies we work with just had a receptionist go out on maternity leave. If you want, I'll find out if they need a replacement. Might just be answering phones and such."

"That'd be great, Seth, thanks. I guess answering a

phone is the one job skill I already have. Didn't even think about including that on my résumé."

He smiled. "So you mind if we serve ourselves straight out of the pans 'stead of using serving bowls? It saves on dishes."

"I've never used a serving bowl in my life," I said. "But hey, I'll do dishes."

"No, you won't." He pulled out two plates and handed one to me. "It's one of the few things in my life that give me a sense of having accomplished something. I'm just that pathetic. And I'm not letting you take it away from me."

I studied his face, basically unchanged except for the new vertical line over the bridge of his nose, and wondered what he saw in mine. What life had done to us. "Anybody who can make dinners that smell this good is definitely not pathetic," I said, filling my plate with what looked to be chicken and rice smothered in cream of celery soup. I glanced around the kitchen and, sure enough, saw the Campbell's can. "This looks awesome," I said.

"Thanks. I wouldn't call it awesome but it hopefully won't make you gag. Funny, when I first saw the recipe it was right after me and Stacey split. And I thought, if cooking's this easy, maybe everything about living alone will be." He scooped a mound of chicken onto his plate, then paused with his spoon midair. "It's amazing the things you never think about because you didn't *have* to ever think about them before, like did you know you have to order a turkey in advance if you want it fresh? When I stopped off to get dinner ingredients tonight I was going to pick up a turkey for next week, and all they had were these massive blocks of turkey-shaped ice. So I asked the butcher and he looked at me like I was on drugs."

I smiled. "So you're doing Thanksgiving here?"

He paused, then put the serving spoon down and gave a little laugh. "Yeah, I guess you'd say I'm *having* Thanksgiving here, me and a twenty-pound block of ice."

"Oh…" I said, then, "Seth, why don't you have Thanksgiving with us?"

"What? No, I mean thanks, but I don't want to be the token lonely person you invite to Thanksgiving because you're so darned thankful not to be him."

I'd rather be you than me, I thought, then said, "That's so not what it would be."

"Look, I already told my parents I couldn't go to Miami. There I'd be, with thirty old people patting my back and saying how glad they were to have me, but what a shame about my wife. I don't want to start pitying myself."

"Look at me," I said. "Look at my mom. You'd be the least pitiable person there."

Seth glanced down at his plate. "Well, thanks, I'll think about it." He brought his plate to the table.

After sitting, he raised his wineglass. "To your generosity, and our reunion," he said. We clinked glasses. "You know you introduced me to alcohol?"

I smiled. "I was such a bad influence. I kept borrowing stuff from Dad's liquor cabinet, stuff he never drank."

"And we'd replace it little by little with water. By the end I doubt there was any liquor left. I blame my drunken college years on you." He tipped his glass, looked into it, then said, "So I wanted to say how sorry I am about what's happening to your mom, and about everything you're going through. It's too much for one person."

Yes, I thought. *It is exactly too much for one person.* "I'm fine," I said. Before it was out this seemed like the right thing to say, but once I heard myself say it, it sounded completely absurd. "I was just thinking," I said, "I was trying to decide which was worse, the way Josh died or the way my mom's just slowly disappearing." And then I shook my head. "Sorry, this is a morbidly depressing conversation. I mean what good does it do to obsess about it?"

He reached to touch my hand, but in a move that I hoped seemed more subtle than it actually felt, I avoided it by stuffing a slice of garlic bread into my mouth.

Seth seemed more amused than embarrassed or hurt. "Whoops," he said, then leaned back in his chair.

I swirled my fork through my rice to avoid looking at his face. "I guess I decided Josh's death was worse. With my mom there was time to get used to the idea, except I wish I could've talked with her more the past few years. But I was so busy with the kids, and phone conversations started getting hard and then just scary, and I don't know. I guess until recently I didn't really comprehend how bad it was going to get."

"That's the thing, isn't it. If you could get just a little warning of how life would turn out, there's always ways you could do better. But what's done is done, and it doesn't help to blame yourself."

My skin suddenly felt fragile and dry, ready to break open. Somehow, since arriving at Seth's apartment, I'd managed not to think about Josh, what he'd hidden from me, not to feel it. But now suddenly it struck at me like a tire iron in the center of my chest, the same way grief hit hardest when I woke after dreams of nongrief. I leaned forward against the table, which sent wine sloshing over the sides of our glasses. I looked down at the spilled wine. "At least we still have Mom, and sometimes she has good days. But I keep thinking what I'd give for just one more hour with Josh."

Seth mopped a splash of wine off the table with his thumb, and then wiped the thumb briskly on his palm. "I'm sorry I never met him."

I watched his face a minute, then said, "You would've liked him, I think. But I don't know, I don't know; I feel like I'm going crazy."

"I'd be going crazy too."

"No, listen, it's more than that. It's bad enough not understanding why he killed himself, why he did it on that day, or if there even was a particular reason. But what I'm learning, what I found out after he died is there was stuff he wasn't telling me. I could've saved him if I knew."

Seth watched me, unblinking, then said, "What do you mean?"

"Imagine how people feel when they find their child facedown in their backyard swimming pool, and they realize if they just hadn't turned their backs they could've kept them alive. That's how I feel."

"Natalie," Seth said. "You can't save a person from depression."

I touched my cheek, the spot where Josh's scar had been, then felt my eyes start to sting. I shook my head quickly. "Josh got hurt in the war. An IED. He told me some of what it did to him, that he had a harder time remembering things, but somehow he convinced me it was getting better over the months. And I saw it, saw little things, but I was distracted with the kids, with life, and I just let myself believe him when he told me it was no big deal."

I mashed my fork against my rice, then dropped it. "But it turned out he couldn't remember anything that happened unless he wrote it down. He had this PDA where he'd been writing down almost every single thing he did every day, and I had no idea."

Seth blinked quickly, then let out a breath through his teeth. "I don't even know what to say. He lived with that without telling you?"

"Because he thought I was too weak." I took a gulp of wine, then pressed the back of my hand to my mouth. "He used to play these thought games with me; he was into philosophy and he was always coming up with questions to find out how I looked at the world. So I remember him asking me last summer if I'd rather be in a coma and dreaming that I was living out a whole perfect lifetime, or if I'd rather live a real, imperfect life."

I was lying in bed with him, on top of him actually, my head against his collarbone and his hand under my pajama bottoms. His voice had seemed to resonate louder through his chest and I'd heard his heart, the constant, steady strength of it. "We both decided if we never learned the difference," I said now, "if we really thought all our dreams were coming true, we wouldn't mind if it was all in our heads." I stretched a flat smile. "So that's what I was doing, Seth; he was letting me live out my fake fantasy of our fakely perfect world, and I didn't let myself look beyond that."

Seth reached for my hand, and this time I let him take it. His hand was smooth and warm and I felt nothing from it, no sexual spark, no comfort, just a kind of quiet deadness like I was being held by an oven mitt. "Don't go there, Nat. How can you blame yourself for stuff he never told you?"

"But he should've realized he *could* tell me," I said. "What kind of person does that make me, that he thought I couldn't help him?" I should've told him that I'd rather live a real life, as long as we were together in it. I should've told him that there were lessons to be learned from hard times, that struggles made you stronger and closer. But he thought I'd rather live inside a lie.

"I have the PDA he kept, and I started looking at it today. I wanted to go through all of it, but it was killing me."

"Then why go through it? What good does it do?"

"Because I have to find out why, don't you get it? There's got to be clues in there, stuff he didn't tell me." I stared down at my plate, suddenly nauseous, then pushed it away. "And I want to see if he wrote anything on the last day, but how the hell can I look? What if he…I don't know, told himself to load his gun, or to say good-bye to us?"

Seth watched me without speaking, everything he wanted to say explicit on his face.

"I *have* to look, I can't just have this question over my head the whole time. Like, what if he left a suicide note? I always wondered why he didn't leave a note explaining, so what if he wrote something in his PDA?"

Seth folded his hands between his knees, looked down at them. "Do you want me to look for you? I could tell you if there's anything there you should know."

I glanced at him. How much easier it would be to give the task to him, to have someone else to lean on. But if Josh really had written a suicide note, how would he have felt about the idea of Seth reading it first? "That's nice of you. But I'm gonna try and do this on my own. I haven't even told my dad about any of this, about how bad Josh's injury was, partly because it's so similar to Mom, and partly because I think Josh didn't want anybody else knowing. I mean, obviously he didn't."

"Josh must've realized you'd see what was going on when you read the PDA."

I shook my head. "I just hate this; I don't know how to deal with it all. And I hate him for making me deal with it, and then I hate myself for hating him." I looked up at Seth, feeling the raw ache of tears in my throat. "The grief counselor we were seeing said how after a suicide everybody looks for somebody to blame, and they usually end up blaming themselves. I just want to stop blaming myself."

Seth rose from his chair to kneel by my side, and pulled me toward him. And I didn't want to cry, not in front of Seth, but he was surrounding me, strong and steady, this man I'd known from *before,* before everything in my world exploded. I clutched at his shirt, and buried my head against his chest. He was soft and solid, in the way men are, and for a moment I let myself absorb it. But then I pulled away and quickly reached for my glass, took a gulp of wine, coughed a little and wiped exaggeratedly at my eyes. "I think I better get home. I've eaten so much I'm getting light-headed."

I stood and grabbed my jacket and purse, and left Seth there, on his knees, looking up at me.

20

Anna

Grandpa was kneeling on my bunk bed, hanging a reading light. Why is because he saw me using a flashlight under the covers, and batteries cost more than electricity so he went to Home Depot. I sat watching him, thinking about Mr. Burns. Mom used to go out with him. They probably had kissed. Probably when he saw her, he thought about how they used to kiss. And now they were in his apartment alone.

Grandpa turned on the light, and he held it up on the wall. "How's this spot work for you?"

I leaned back on the pillow and opened the book I was reading to test it. The book was *Stuart Little*, which Cam had gave me, but I was already bored with it. It wasn't really teaching me anything about mice, and was really more of a book for boys. "It's good," I said.

He made a mark on the wall, and I watched him attach the lamp. When he was done, he lay down next to me and said, "I don't think I've ever seen so many stuffed animals in one place."

"I like animals."

"Obviously." He smiled and picked up my stuffed

koala, Mrs. Primavera, and rubbed the top of her head. "I'm amazed you have room to sleep."

I watched him rub Mrs. Primavera, and then I leaned against his arm. He smelled like the outside, like when you break open a tree branch. And lying there I suddenly wanted more than anything to be able to tell him things. Like, for example:

Number 1. What I hid inside Leopolda
Number 2. The letters Mom pretended were from Dad
Number 3. How sometimes being asleep was the only okay part of the day

Except for about the letters, there were no grown-ups who knew any of these. And I needed a grown-up to know, because a person can only hold a certain amount of stuff alone. Which was, maybe, my reason for Number 3.

I picked up Leopolda, secret Number 1. "This is my favorite animal," I said.

"Hmmm." He smiled. "Well, he definitely looks well loved."

"She's a *she*. See the dress? It zippers up, so you can hide stuff." I unzippered a little, then zippered her back up. "I keep stuff there," I said, and then I turned to look in his face. If he asked what I was hiding, would I really tell him? Yes. Maybe.

But all he said was, "Ah, right. I thought she was look-ing a little paunchy."

I sat Leopolda on my stomach. For a second I thought I was going to cry. Leopolda smiled at me, with a mouth that was happy but eyes that, without the eyeballs, were very, very sad. And this is another reason I loved her. Because she reminded me of Dad.

When people go to war, they change. I know this from my experience. From the accident Dad got a scar he called his "war wound" on his cheek, but that is not what I'm talking about.

Sometimes he would stare at the wall for an hour like it was a TV set. Sometimes I'd tell him I had a spelling test at school, and that night he'd forget to ask how I did. We used to play chess every night, he was teaching me how, but after he came back I would walk into the room with the set under my arm, and I would stand there and I'd stand there waiting, but after a while I'd walk away. And how I felt was a scream inside me, in my stomach. When you are not important to your dad, you are not important.

After Grandpa left, I unzipped Leopolda's dress and pulled out Dad's letter, not reading, just to hold it. This wasn't his letter from heaven, but another one, a one from earth that only me and Toby knew about.

Mom had wrote the fake letters when I had the only real one, and how would she feel if she knew? I should've gave the letter to her, I knew that. Like say Dad hid money somewhere, Mom should know. I thought maybe somewhere on the pages it said how he loved me especially, that he'd wrote a part meant just for me. "Lady Anna," he used to call me, or sometimes, "Madame Lady Anna." *Madame Lady Anna,* the letter maybe said, *It will be your job to take care of this family, because I love you more than anybody in the world.* And I wanted to be the one who read that first.

So the day after I took the envelope from Toby, I opened it. It was late at night, Mom and Toby were asleep, and I went downstairs and turned on the light. I sat in the chair that was Dad's, where he used to read and watch TV, the brown soft one with the beat-up arms and a bar that lifts up your legs. I put my hand on the chair arm where Dad's hand used to set, and I read the letter.

Here is the beginning part of it:

> I know I've told you I don't believe in heaven, but now I need to believe there's something more, and I know that I'll get back the parts of myself I've lost.

So. This was not the bad part. The bad part I read next and it made me start to shake, and I hear it all the time inside me now like hands that are strangling.

> I also need to believe there's something on the other side, so we can be together again. I'll be waiting until that day, because I also know I won't be truly whole without you.

That is where I stopped. I made a loud noise and Mom woke up and I heard her coming to the stairs, so I stuffed the letter fast under my pajamas.

Mom stood there, watching me sitting in Dad's chair. I was shaking and crying and she walked fast over to me and gathered me up and held me. And there we were, me and Mom, her arms pressing my back, her whispering and crying and me shaking and crying. "It's okay, it's okay," she kept saying, but between us was Dad's letter saying what he wanted.

Sometimes I think of Dad alone in heaven, lonely and sad and waiting for something I won't let happen. I have a picture in my head of him, sitting in a white chair with his hands between his knees, checking a watch, leaning forward, looking at everyone who walks through the gates.

There's more of the letter, a whole page and a half I stopped myself from seeing because I think it might say about how come he died. I have a feeling it talks about how I killed him, something I don't ever let myself think about.

Someday soon I know I'll have to read it, because until I know it will be kicking me and kicking. But now I feel like I can't. It is too much.

I tucked the letter back inside Leopolda. And this is what I told myself. That this weekend, I would look at it again.

21

Natalie

I threw my keys down on the entryway table, pulled off my coat, and climbed the stairs. It was barely ten o'clock but the house was dark and quiet, which was such a relief since I knew my face probably wasn't suitable for public viewing. I peeked into the children's bedroom and had a silent debate over whether to kiss them good night, the challenge being how to do it while preserving their unconscious state. Instead, I closed the door softly.

I sat on my bed, twisting my wedding band back and forth, back and forth on my finger, a new nervous tick. I pulled, felt the skin bunch up, squeezed my eyes shut and pulled again. The ring wedged against the knuckle, wouldn't come off, and I stared at it, then pushed it back down, stood, and reached for the phone.

"Nick," I said when he answered. "I'm sorry to call so late. This is Natalie."

"Natalie." He hesitated, then said, "Your move go okay? Are you settling in?"

"Yeah, I guess we're okay, pretty much. We're completely unpacked already, which probably has more to do with how little stuff we own than any kind of resourcefulness."

"Well, moving gets easier when you've done it a hundred times. You get a system." Then, uncomfortable silence.

I sat on the stool by my vanity. There were little sayings penned on the surface that I'd written in fat-looped childish handwriting (*Fail to plan, plan to fail; A candle loses nothing by lighting another candle*), back when I'd thought such things were profound. "So I'm calling now because I recently looked through the PDA Josh was keeping. He was writing down every little single thing, detailed entries on what he did every day and I realized—" I pulled in a shaky breath. "Nick, did you know how bad he was?"

"He was writing down everything?"

"Including what he ate for breakfast every morning. You must've seen him use it."

There was a beat of silence, and then Nick said, "Yeah, sure, I knew it was helping him cope. Having to remind himself about breakfast—I didn't know about that, but I guess I'm not surprised."

"How come I didn't know?"

He hesitated, then said, "You didn't know he had to write things down?"

"I knew he had problems, but he said it was getting better. He said it *was* better."

"I think it was, actually. He stopped getting lost in conversations, and he was finding all these ways to cope with things. He wanted to be able to show everybody that he could get by without help."

"That he could get *by*?"

"It's why I didn't say anything to our commanding officers. He didn't want to be discharged, even though he could've got benefits, disability. He wanted everyone to see he was doing okay, so I helped cover for him, helped him remember things, who he'd talked to, where he was supposed to go. I'd tell him and he'd repeat them over to himself, and I think it helped."

The heart of a fool is in his mouth, my desk said, *but the mouth of the wise man is in his heart.* "How much did he tell you?"

"It wasn't really something we talked about." Nick's voice was tight, almost pleading. "I mean, I know it was always there, under everything. He was struggling with it, but after the first couple months he didn't want to talk about it. He wanted to pretend everything was okay, so I guess I let him."

"Why didn't you tell me what was going on?"

"It wasn't really my place, Natalie. And I thought—it never occurred to me that you didn't know."

A smooth sea never made a skilled sailor; A good rest is half the work. I twisted my stool away to face the bed. "Do you think he was trying to protect me?"

"Maybe," Nick said. "Sure, that was probably part of it. I know he hated you having to deal with all he was going through. We talked about that after it happened, when we were still in Iraq, about your mother and how hard that was for you, and he hated himself for putting you through something that was so similar."

I stood and felt a sudden wave of dizziness. I leaned back against my bed and slid slowly down it, onto the floor.

"But back then he never seemed to doubt that it was going to get better. And he handled it so much better than I ever could've. Eventually he stopped talking about it, but I think that was because he wanted to believe it actually *was* better. He was probably planning to admit eventually how bad it had been, but not until he could prove to himself, to everybody, that he was okay."

"But he killed himself instead. Goddammit, Nick, what if I could've changed something?"

"You couldn't have done anything, Natalie. Nobody could. There was more going on than that."

"What do you mean?"

"Just…things were hard for him, okay? In a way nobody could make better. Things happened in the war and after we got back, and I guess he was having a harder time with them than we realized."

"What do you mean things happened after you got back? You mean things I did? Or didn't do?"

"No, that's not it. I don't know what I was trying to say, except…I guess I just meant he was struggling with memories. But none of it had anything to do with you."

"I know he had a hard time with things, but so did everybody who was there. *You* dealt with it, Nick, and people with injuries deal with them because they get the support they need from their families. Josh was pretty much the strongest person I know, and he would've got through it too if I'd just been there for him—if I'd seen it!"

And Nick said, "You *were* there," which maybe was what I'd been fishing for, that reassurance, why I'd called him. But it didn't help because I knew it wasn't true. My body had been there, but my attention had been with the kids, with my own thoughts. And with my longing for the Josh I used to know.

After hanging up with Nick, I pulled Josh's cloth heart out from my drawer and squeezed it in my fist. For the past year Josh had only pretended to be alive, and the pretense was as unforgivable a betrayal as the suicide. I'd done the exact same thing with my letters, had made Josh write through me, had actually thought I'd felt him writing. But I'd have to make sure they understood Josh was fully gone.

"Dear," I wrote, then stared at the word, put down my pen. Then picked it up again.

When I was done, I held the heart to my mouth, and whispered against it, "Good-bye." And then I went outside to the backyard and knelt next to a towering pine, a tree that must have been there longer than any of us had been alive. I dug into the earth with my fingers, deeper, my nails tearing, then laid the heart into the hole. I kissed my dirty fingers and touched them to the heart. And then, I buried it in the earth.

Last spring I'd woken to find Josh sitting at the edge of the bed and crying. He'd been having nightmares once or twice a week where I'd open my eyes to the sound of his scream and find him sitting straight up in bed, breath heavy. I'd pictured him dreaming of fire and fear and mangled bodies, and I'd tried to convince him that telling me would help. But he'd said the only thing keeping him sane was knowing that I didn't know, that there was a clear split between there and here, no crossing of boundaries.

Soldiers shouldn't have to face their conscience when they followed orders; it should be trained out of them so they could do the things they had to do. But Josh had never been able to stop second-guessing, worrying what was right and what was wrong. He'd killed people and it had killed a part of him, that's the phantom I'd believed was haunting him.

Now I rolled over and buried my head in the pillows,

but the thoughts wouldn't stop, Josh's nightmares playing in my mind and taking gruesome Hollywood war-movie shape: guns firing, heads without their bodies. Was that what Nick had meant when he said there was more going on than I knew? Or was there something else? Why did I have the feeling he was trying to protect me from something?

I went to my desk and searched on the computer for the section of the Code of Federal Regulations I'd read weeks ago, and reread the paragraphs that talked about suicide. My head felt so much clearer now, so maybe I'd be able to understand the legalese, and find a way to get out of the heap of crap for good.

(i) Affirmative evidence is necessary to justify reversal of service department findings of mental unsoundness where criteria do not otherwise warrant contrary findings.
(ii) In all instances any reasonable doubt should be resolved favorably to support a finding of service connection.

What the hell did that mean? Did it mean they *would* consider the suicide service-related, or that they wouldn't? Why wasn't this written in English? Because they hoped grieving families would be too desolate and overwhelmed to even attempt to understand it? That they'd do what I'd done and just trust the DoD to do the right thing?

They were still holding up our death gratuity while they reviewed Josh's medical evidence. I'd thought they'd been calling doctors to determine whether his depression had been triggered by the war—as I'd claimed—or had been an illness he'd suffered even before. Maybe they'd actually been looking into the extent of his brain injury, but wouldn't that make us more deserving? It made no sense, unless there was something more.

I addressed an envelope to the Department of Defense, then typed up a letter. Maybe they'd just forgotten about us. Maybe they just needed to be reminded.

I heard footsteps at the end of the hall, Mom's shuffling step on the stairs, one of her nighttime rambles. I walked down to watch her, make sure she didn't try and go outside, and followed her into the kitchen where she opened the refrigerator.

After seeing her slow sink into oblivion, how had I not realized what Josh had been going through? Or maybe the similarity was part of the reason I hadn't let myself look at it. Because I'd realized the two together would bounce off and amplify each other, be too much.

More than anything I wanted to believe my mother still existed somewhere other than her calcified brain cells, so impossible was it to understand how her life, her being could have been sucked out so thoroughly. I wanted to imagine that she was gradually leaving this world and joining the next, and so hadn't actually disappeared forever. It would be thrilling, and at the same time soothing, to believe that all this time she'd actually been in some other dimension, that there could be a way to talk to the self that had left her. Tell her all the things I wanted her to know.

"Can I get you something?" I said.

She hardly reacted to the sound of my voice, didn't seem surprised to see me. "So many things!" she said, gazing at the shelves. The dim refrigerator light erased the lines in her face; she could've been thirty.

"Well, I don't know about you, but I'm in the mood for empty calories." I pulled out a roll of cookie dough and sliced it onto a plate. "Remember when we used to do this? People worry about raw eggs now, but I don't think we ever got sick from it. Stomachs of steel."

Mom took a raw cookie and sat at the table, chewing on it contemplatively.

"Beer?" I said, then rose for a beer and a soda, twisted off the tops and handed the soda to her. "Cheers," I said, clinking the neck of my bottle against hers. "Now drinking beer with you is something I never used to do."

Mom took a gulp of soda and coughed.

"But I think we should start. Midnight cookie dough; we might get fat but we'll be happy."

So we sat there well into the night, not talking, just eating and being. Odd to think, in the morass of this new life, that this, sitting with the shell my mother had become, would bring me the first comfort I'd felt in days.

"Hey, Ma," I said softly. "This is nice, huh?"

Our eyes met and she smiled and set her hand on my wrist. "Natalie," she said, the first time since we'd come that she'd said my name.

22
Anna

When the bus dropped me off from school, Mom was waiting by the car with Toby. She gave me a hug and said, "How *are* you?"

I said, "Okay," but when we got in the car and started home she asked it again. "How *are* you?" So I knew something either had happened or was about to.

"Mom, can I go over to somebody's house Saturday?"

"Well, sure. Is it Annabelle?"

"No, it's somebody called Cameron."

I don't know why I didn't say Cam was a boy. I guess I knew she'd think there was something weird about it, and I'd have to explain what we had in common, which might take away some of her happiness for me. So when she said, "*Ah,* pretty name. Like Cameron Diaz," I said, "Uh-huh," and that was all.

We pulled into the driveway. "Where's Grandpa's car?" I said.

"He took Grammy for groceries. I asked him to pick up a few things."

Mom had just gone shopping yesterday. I looked over at the duct tape covering the window crack Toby made and said, "What things?"

"Toothpaste, batteries, just things. C'mon, let's go inside."

"You want to play basketball?"

She got out from the car and helped Toby off his booster seat. "Maybe later," she said. "But let's get a snack first, okay?"

We all went to the kitchen and Mom started a pot of water for cocoa, after which she sat at the table and smiled at us, a too happy smile that didn't show her teeth, like the kind you see on stuffed animals. And then she pulled an envelope out from her pocket, and gave it to me. "I found this today. In the bathroom cabinet, so let's read it, okay?"

"Okay!" Toby said, getting up on his knees.

I felt a kind of clumping in my throat. Was there something bad in the letter? On the envelope, instead of just one heart where the return address should be, there were hearts everywhere, front and back, like a rash. I suddenly wanted to hide it in my pocket and pretend like it disappeared.

"Cameron's really nice," I said. "I mean super nice." I dug around in my knapsack and pulled out the address Cam had wrote for me. "I'm going to bring my bike and we'll ride around downtown together." I looked up at her and said, "I can't wait!"

But Mom didn't even seem to hear me. She also didn't seem to hear the water which was boiling over and sizzling on the burner. "*Mom,*" I said. "The *cocoa.*"

She jumped up and turned off the stove, and then poured the water into cups along with packets of Swiss Miss. She brought them to the table and sat back down. I looked at the brown powder swimming on top of the water, then got up and brought back three spoons. "I really want to play basketball, okay?" I said.

"Sure," she said, but she didn't move. Me and Toby watched her.

"Mommy?" Toby said.

Mom nodded at the letter. "So, Anna, let's see what your dad has to say."

"Here." I put the envelope on the table and stirred at my cocoa. "He drew a lot of hearts."

"He did, didn't he? It shows he loves us very much." She opened the envelope and pulled out the letter, looked at Toby and then read slowly.

"Dear Anna and Toby and Natalie. I'm so glad you're settling in so well in your new home and your new school."

I glanced at Mom. My stomach hurt. It was a kind of hurt I've had before like a stick is twisting and twisting into your belly, fastening it together.

"I myself have met lots of incredibly nice people here, which makes me feel a little less lonely for all of you."

I didn't want to let this bother me, but in a little way it did. I mean I knew it wasn't real, I knew it, but I didn't want to hear our dad missed us less. When things are told to you, you feel them in your body even when your mind knows they are a lie.

"I remember leaving for Iraq, standing with you and I saw you all crying and I felt like my insides were dying. But then, Toby and Anna, you looked up at me and you both saluted, just the way I'd taught you. That showed me I was doing the right thing. That leaving was my duty and a way of hopefully making things better for you in the end."

I remembered that day. It was two weeks after the

birthday when I turned nine and I was holding the stuffed elephant he'd got me, which Mom had told me to bring. Dad was crying too, and when he kneeled down to hug us I could feel the wetness of his cheek on my cheek, and he was shaking which made me want to scream. They tried not to let us see what happened in the war, but I knew.

"There are times we need to do things that are difficult, but we do them because they're for the best. And now that I know how well you're all doing in your new home, I think it's time for us to say goodbye. Because you belong in the world, and I don't belong there anymore."

When Dad got into his bus, I touched my cheek and looked at my finger, wondering what part of the tears was mine and what was his. I put my finger in my mouth and kept it there, watching the bus disappear. How could anyone have thought that would be best for us?

Mom looked up, turned from Toby to me, and then went back to the letter. "I promise your mom will always, always be there for you, and in a different way I'll still always be with you too, watching down to make sure you're doing okay. Whenever you need me I'll be there in your hearts. I'm there for you now, can you feel me? A warmth in your heart to keep you strong. And I love you all forever and ever. Love, Dad."

She put the letter down. Then picked it up again and folded it and stuck it back in the envelope, her eyes on us the whole time. She wanted us to say something, but I wasn't sure what.

"It's okay." I watched her face. "We don't really need him anymore."

"Let's talk about it, okay? It's time we started talking

to one another about how we feel. So how I'm feeling now is I'm sad, I guess, but mostly I'm happy we have one another. And I also know what he says is true, that I'm going to be here whenever you need me."

Toby's eyes were wide as tangerines. His mouth opened too, a line of spit webbing between top and bottom.

"Toby…" She reached over to him, but he swung his arm at his cocoa and ran out of the room. The cup fell over and hot water splattered across the table. A sludgy puddle of cocoa powder dripped slowly onto the floor.

Mom made a noise and then stood. She glanced at me and said, "I'm going up to Toby, okay? Stay here and finish your cocoa, and we'll talk." But then she just stood there, staring out the door.

"Mom?" My voice was shaky. *Stop,* I wanted to say. *Stop it!*

"I'm sorry," she said. "Everything's fine, Anna, okay?" Her hair was mussed up, tufty like she'd been squeezing it, and I wanted to smooth it back down. The stick in my stomach twisting, twisting and I got up and tore off some paper towels and dabbed up the spilled cocoa, then stirred Mom's cup and stood in front of her, holding it.

Her face looked like a little kid. It was just the same way she looked at the funeral when Grandpa set a hand on her shoulder. She'd had on this exact same face, like she was asking him to make it all better, which got me scared. Because she was supposed to be the strong one.

"Here, Mom," I said. "You drink your cocoa." I wished there was something better I could say to her, but here's what I know. That sometimes there is no right thing to say. You could be the smartest person in the world, and still you would not be able to find anything that could help.

She looked down at the cocoa and then she smiled at me, the kind of smile you wear when somebody's taking a picture. "Thanks, Anna. I'm going to Toby." And then she left the room.

When she'd gone I walked slow to the stairs, and stood there listening to Mom's voice go up and down, like she was talking to a baby. And here is the word for how I felt: DROWNING. When I thought about our life, this is what I saw, all of us shaky and weak like balls of dandelion fluff, where if a wind came it would blow us into pieces. And if Mom got so sad that she wanted to die, she wouldn't have any friends to help make her better. It would all be up to me.

When I heard her come out into the hall, I went fast into the downstairs bathroom. I sat on the closed toilet and I tried not to cry, but my eyes had other ideas. It was not the kind of crying that makes noise, just gook flowing out my eyes and nose, like my guts were leaking.

There was a slow knock on the door. "Anna?"

I shook my head.

"Let's talk, okay?"

I shook my head again, and said, "I'll talk later."

She was quiet a minute, but then she said, "Okay. Okay, sweetie. I'll be in the kitchen, so just come sit with me when you're ready." She stood there a minute, waiting, and then finally she said, "I love you so much." And then she walked away.

I came out of the bathroom, quiet, and then went up to the bedroom. Toby was lying on his bed with his head pushed in the pillow, so I lay there next to him and put my arm around his back. We laid there while it got dark around us and I waited for sounds in the house, for Grandpa to come home, for Mom to maybe make dinner or turn on the TV. But there weren't any sounds. I wondered if she was still there at the table. I wondered if she'd drunk her Swiss Miss, or if both our cups were still sitting there, cold and waiting.

And then I heard a car in the driveway and I got out of bed and stood by the stairs, trying to hear.

There was the rustle sound of a grocery bag and then Grandpa said, "Well you'll have to apologize to Toby. I went to three stores and I still couldn't find the toothpaste with Barney on the tube. Big Bird I found, so he might have to settle for that." And then, "You okay?"

"Yeah," Mom said. She sounded not okay. "I'm good except my stomach's been bothering me. Would you mind doing dinner tonight?"

"It's that deli meat you been serving for lunch. I tell you, it's not real meat; Lord knows what they put inside it. Entrails, probably."

"Right." A chair scraped on the kitchen floor. "I won't buy it anymore."

I walked fast to Toby's bed and slipped back next to him, and laid my ear down on his belly like I used to do back when he wasn't talking. I listened to the thumps and gurgles his insides made, their conversation. They showed how he was still alive.

"Anna?" There was a knock on the door and I sat up, and Toby made a noise and rolled against me. "I made some dinner for the two of you," Grandpa said.

"I'm sorry." I put my hands on my belly and tears came out of my eyes without me even having to try. "We don't feel very good."

"You have the same stomach bug as your mom?" Grandpa came to lay his hand on my forehead. I closed my eyes and wished he'd keep his hand there forever.

When you are hurting in your body or your brain, a hand on your forehead, for as long as it is there, feels like a cure.

I don't know what time it was when I finally heard Mom come to say good night. I pretended I was asleep so that I could peek through my eyelashes.

She was standing there in the doorway and her face looked all puffy, like somebody had blown into her eyelids and her cheeks, inflated them. "Anna?" she whispered.

But I didn't answer, made my breath heavy and slow. She stood there a long time watching us, and then she turned away.

I listened to her get ready for bed, but then instead of going back to her room, she walked downstairs. I heard the front door open, and then close.

I slipped out of bed and went to look through the window, and there she was in her white nightgown, sitting Indian style on the gravel next to the front steps. I couldn't see her face, just her nightgown and her hair curling down her back. It was cold out and she started shivering but other than the shivering she didn't move, just sat there looking at nothing, the moon floating up through the trees and disappearing over the roof.

And then finally she got up and came back inside, but still I stayed there, looking out the window at the dark tree branches leaning to the windows and then back out like they were peering in and whispering to one another what they saw.

What would they be saying? This is what: Stupid people, no roots to hold them down. We'll be here forever but they'll just blow away and leave behind their sage burning and their shells glued on walls, like that could make any kind of difference.

I leaned my forehead against the window. And standing there I tried to believe that I could be still and steady, watching over Mom and Toby. But I knew the truth was in the trees, all shaking their heads and whispering. Waiting for us all to blow away.

23
Natalie

It was six A.M., almost time to wake the children. I'd slept fitfully, unable to stop thinking about the way Anna had hidden last night so she wouldn't have to talk to me, and Toby's unresponsiveness when I'd tried to comfort him. He'd cried in the same way as at Josh's funeral, not the way a five-year-old is supposed to cry, the full-force bawling of tantrums or scraped knees, but a trembling, closed-mouth, high-pitched wail, like the pain inside him was too big to let out, a molten-hot thing he trapped in his belly because releasing it would set him on fire.

What was wrong with me that I could only figure out the right way to handle things after I'd already screwed up my children? And my husband, because wasn't it also what I'd done with Josh, letting him drown in his depression rather than forcing him to tell me the reasons behind it?

Now I wanted to wallow. I wanted to crawl not just under the covers but inside the mattress, between foam and box springs, disappear. But I made myself go into the children's bedroom, leaned over the top bunk and touched Anna's hair. "Sweetie?" I said. "Anna, honey, can we talk a minute before school?"

Her eyes drifted open and she stared foggily into the

dim morning light before turning to me. Her face showed nothing.

"Come with me, okay? To my bedroom. I don't want to wake Toby up."

She sat up without speaking and climbed to the ground, and I took her hand gently and walked with her to my bedroom.

"Anna?" I sat cross-legged on the bed, facing her, still holding her hand. "We need to talk about your dad's letters."

Her face twitched, but she said nothing.

"Because I think...I think you know already why the letters had to stop. That they weren't real."

Anna's whole body stiffened, and she pulled her hand away.

"You knew that, didn't you? That it was really just us writing to one another? Which was important, it was good to tell me in your letter how you were feeling, but now we have to start doing things different. We have to actually talk about it."

She shook her head slightly, her eyes still on my face. Then she inhaled, a raspy gasp, and said, "How come? How come you did it?"

"Baby, I'm so sorry. You're so right." I felt my eyes start to sting and clutched the edge of my mattress, fighting the tears back. "And it wasn't okay of me to lie. We've all just been trying to make things better; I was trying to help Toby, and I guess find a way to help you tell what you were feeling, but that wasn't the right way."

Her eyes darted toward the door, and she stepped backward. "Are you going to tell Toby? Don't tell Toby, okay? Not yet, not yet because it helped him."

I thought of Toby's wild panic last night. Maybe she

was right. Not that I could keep lying to Toby, but that this wasn't the time to tell him the truth. "Okay," I said. "He's going through so much right now, so I won't say anything yet." I touched her cheek, as if I was brushing away tears, then said, "I know you don't understand why I did this, and I know you're probably mad."

She watched my face. "I'm not mad," she said slowly. "I know why you did them."

"Thank you, baby. I'm mad at myself, though. But it's over now, and we need to all start talking to one another, okay? We'll talk about things when they get hard, about what we can do to make them better. And I want to make sure you know it was true what Dad said…what *I* said in the letters, that I'll always be here for you. I'm not going anywhere."

At this, Anna's face flushed. She walked toward me, hesitated and then sat on my lap, her arms around my shoulders. She didn't fit; our heads bumped awkwardly and her weight cut off the circulation in my legs, but we held each other as best we could, my feet tingling to numbness.

I remembered holding her on a rocking chair when she was small enough to rest her head on my breasts, and then I remembered being pulled onto my own mother's lap, Mom's scent of coffee and shampoo. The loss of children, the loss of parents, how could anyone stand it? Little by little, life emptied you.

Anna started to shake, and then I heard her wet intake of breath and a keening sound of tears held back. And I realized suddenly that this was how you stood it, how my dad must handle caring for my mother, and how I'd cared for the kids when I thought my life was over. Because letting other people lean on you forced you to stand straighter, stronger. They leaned on you and somehow you braced against their pain, like it was an extra leg.

It would take time, I knew that, healing enough to talk to one another about the things that seemed impossible to even think about. But maybe finally we were finding a way to start.

24
Natalie

Make sure you reciprocate, okay?" I said as we drove to Anna's new friend's house Saturday morning. The map I'd printed directed me to a street of tired-looking homes, all in need of paint, fading flamingos and slow-turning pinwheels on the lawns. I suddenly pictured her friend in a spangled tube top, her belly bared, a cigarette dangling from glossed lips, and considered turning around and taking Anna back home. But then I realized these were the thoughts of the kind of woman I didn't want to be, so I made myself act chipper. "You could invite Cameron over next weekend maybe."

There was an uncomfortable pause, and then Anna said, "Maybe."

"You should have a sleepover! Toby can sleep with me and she could take his bed."

Another pause, and then, "Mom?"

"Yeah?"

No answer. I glanced in the rearview but could only see Toby, staring expressionlessly out the window. He hadn't said a word since I'd read Josh's letter, and I prayed to God he wouldn't go back to that dark place he'd been, his haunted silence. It was obvious he was listening when

I spoke to him and he did respond, nonverbally, to questions, so I had the feeling his words were right beneath the surface. I could only hope the silence was coming from anger rather than grief, a glowering silent-treatment kind of thing.

"You don't sound so excited to be here, kiddo. We could call and say you're sick."

"No, Mom. Just forget it."

"What's going on?"

Again no answer. I checked the address and then turned into the driveway of a small house, painted baby blue, its missing shutters making it seem lopsided. I pulled behind a gray pickup. "What?" I said. "Tell me."

"I said forget it." Anna unbuckled her seat belt and opened the door. "Could you pop the trunk?"

I got out of the car, opened Toby's door, and unbuckled him.

"What're you *doing*?" Anna said.

"I'm going to meet Cameron, tell her thanks for inviting you."

"But—" she started, and then she said, "Fine."

I pulled Anna's bike from the trunk, reattached her wheel, and then carried it up the crumbling concrete steps, the kids behind me.

A man with long sideburns answered the door. I held out my hand. "I'm Anna's mom," I said. "Natalie Graham."

He shook my hand and smiled. "Cameron's dad, Dan Carson." He turned to Anna. "Cam got a late start this morning. Still getting dressed, I think. Hey, Cam!" He backed away from the door. "Come in, all. Can I get you something to drink, Natalie? Anna? Anna's brother?"

"This is Toby," I said. "And sure, thanks, I'd love something." This would be my opportunity to make sure he didn't believe in recreational pot use. I took Toby's hand and walked inside.

The living room was much nicer than I would've expected—sage green walls, a large red Oriental rug, a white sectional that was only mildly stained. "Sit!" he said pointing at the sofa. "I have a semifresh pot of coffee if you're interested. And for you guys I have juice or Coke or milk, your choice."

"Coffee would be great for me," I said. "And Toby, Anna, what do you want? Juice?"

Both Toby and Anna shrugged.

"Two juices and a coffee," Dan said.

After he left we settled onto the sofa, and then a boy appeared at the door, wearing long shorts and an oversized, bile-colored shirt. "Hi," he said.

"Hi," Anna said.

"Want to come in my room?" the boy said.

Anna shrugged. "Okay."

I looked from the boy to Anna and back, and said tentatively, "Cameron?"

He smiled and said, "You're Anna's mom," with a firm authority, like he was telling me something I didn't know.

"Yes, I am," I said, feeling vaguely alarmed. Why hadn't Anna told me Cameron was a boy? Maybe because she knew this would be my reaction, that I'd worry she'd chosen a boy as her first new friend because she was looking for a replacement male, and so I'd reach the obvious conclusion, that she was destined to become pregnant at the age of thirteen.

Dan entered with a cup and two juice boxes, and Anna stood to take one. "Thanks, we're going to Cam's room now."

"That's rude, Anna," I said. "Drink your juice and then you can go."

Dan smiled as he handed me the coffee. "Guess we both better get used to being snubbed, because we have another decade of this ahead of us. She's Cam's first girlfriend, and obviously we're no competition."

Anna hunched back on the sofa. "I'm not his girlfriend."

I smiled at her and tried to give a knowing chuckle but it came out dry, my storytelling wicked-stepmother cackle. I cleared my throat to suggest the sound might be associated with chest congestion, then nudged Toby. "Say thank you for the juice," I whispered, knowing that of course he wouldn't. I shrugged apologetically. "He's not much of a talker these days."

"Cam was that way too, back in the day. Strangers would try and talk to him and he'd hide between my wife's legs and cover his eyes."

"The ostrich thing," I said. It was good at least to know there was a mother in the picture here, although I should've guessed it from the candles on the glass-topped coffee table and the faux sunflowers on top of the TV. "So your wife's not home?"

"Oh…" He sat in a faded leather armchair and propped his feet on the table. "She's not with us anymore."

I felt my face flush. Shoot, I should know better than to ask about a spouse before I knew the situation; it was like asking a heavy woman when she was due. Was it divorce? A recovery program? Incarceration? "I'm sorry," I said.

"Three years ago. Leukemia. It was tough, but you get used to things."

I shook my head. So this must be why Anna chose

Cam as a friend. The realization made me feel worse. "I'm sorry," I said again.

"Cam told me about your husband. Must be especially rough, it being so sudden and all."

I stared down into my coffee. There was something floating in it, a small white speck. I fished it out with my index finger. "Sure, yeah, it was," I said, and then, uncomfortable, I set down my cup. "Anyway, we should be going."

"Oh, I wish you'd stay. We don't get much company anymore." He gave an embarrassed smile. "People seem so awkward, or at least they did in the beginning, not knowing what to say. And then they got used to not coming over. I guess in the end they were her friends more than mine."

I tucked my hands under my seat. What was with this guy? I'd known him for five minutes and he was treating me like his shrink. I looked toward the door.

"But I'm sure you know what it's like," he said.

"Yeah, I guess the same thing happened to me." I smiled quickly. "People treated me like the death of a spouse was a contagious disease."

"Yes, exactly! How come they don't realize what it's like losing not just your spouse but your entire way of living? I miss Hillary so much, losing her was like losing my soul. But I also miss being invited to parties, and being able to take Cam out to dinner without people assuming it's one of my custody nights. Why can't they at least invite me to dinner?" He leaned back in his seat and looked into my eyes. "Tell me about your husband. What was he like?"

"I'm sorry, we really do have to go," I said. Didn't he understand how it would feel to discuss a dead spouse with strangers? "I'm doing a reading for kids at the local library this afternoon that I have to set up for."

But he went on like he hadn't heard. "We don't hear enough about war heroes, and you're just as heroic as your husband in a way. All military spouses are. You get married knowing what might happen, what kind of sacrifices you'll have to make. That's a more authentic kind of love than most people ever share. And here you are now, suffering the consequences."

I watched Anna and Toby, both looking up at me expressionlessly and waiting to absorb whatever I might say. I felt the coffee sloshing in my stomach, and I wanted to leave more than anything, just grab both of them and march with them out the door. But feeling their eyes on me, like knuckles nudging into my skin, I all at once saw the weight of the responsibility I carried, how in time their only vivid memories of their father would come from me. I steeled my shoulders. "He was worth it. Being married to him made it worth it."

"I'm sure it did," Dan said.

"He was more than just a hero, he was a good person too. A great person. Like he used to buy things at the PX in Iraq to give away, spent a fortune—and it's hard to spend a fortune there, they keep things so cheap. He'd spend all this money on clothes and food and knickknacks and then give it all to people on the street. Here he is, in the middle of all this hell and thinking he could really make a difference with colorful T-shirts."

"That's the simple kind of everyday heroism we never hear about," Dan said.

"But there was more than that, more than everyday stuff. Like..." I glanced at the kids. "Like last fall he got injured rescuing another man, and he never even told me how bad he was hurt. That's the kind of person he was. One of the Humvees in his convoy got struck by a roadside bomb, and he had to dodge sniper fire to drag the men out of the tank while somebody else called a medevac helicopter." I watched the children's faces as I went on, trying to see how much they understood. Anna was bent forward, looking down at the floor, and Toby's eyes were steady on my face. I laid my hand on Anna's back. "So just as it was about to land, he saw one of the snipers setting off an IED to destroy it, and he curled himself around the man he was carrying. He helped save the man's life."

"That's incredible," Dan said, sitting forward.

"He was an incredible man," I said. "He got a Commendation Medal for it."

"That's the most amazing story I've ever heard," Dan said. "I can't believe I haven't heard about your husband before. They don't tell his story but then they make up stories like they did with Jessica Lynch. They only tell stories with happy endings."

They didn't tell stories of suicides. If Josh had died in combat, would his story have been publicized? "Heroes die and people somehow forget everything they did. Now it's like Josh never existed."

"He died in the war, right?"

I picked up my coffee cup and took two lukewarm gulps. Of course Anna must have told Cameron that her father died in the war, because that was the story she'd told herself, and Toby, back when it first happened.

I glanced at her. She was watching my face, unblinking. "Yes," I said. "Because of injuries from the war." Which was, in a sense, true.

"Was he in Baghdad?"

Toby nestled against me, his face buried under my

arm. I tried to keep the panic off my face. "Fallujah," I said, pulling the name out of the headlines.

Anna stood suddenly, her face tight and pale. "Me and Cam are going to his room," she said, and then walked to the stairs. Silently, Cameron followed.

I watched after her, feeling a sudden pang of fear. Why had I let Dan talk about Josh's death in front of the kids?

Dan sat forward in his seat, and smiled an overly friendly, Santa Claus smile. "So listen, I'd like to ask you something."

Oh, Christ. He was going to ask me on a date. He saw this as an opportunity, two grieving souls taking comfort in each other, broken halves becoming a whole and blah-blah-blah. I'd have to make up fake-sounding excuses and find a way to avoid running into him at the grocery store.

He steepled his fingers. "Feel free to say no," he said. "But see, in my free time I write freelance for the *Herald*."

I watched him blankly. "Do you?"

"And they have a weekly segment on local heroes. Everyday heroes, we call it; cancer survivors and environmentalists, that kind of thing. Last month we wrote about an injured vet, and we've done a story on a war widow raising infant twins. And I hope this doesn't sound intrusive, but that was my first thought when I heard about your husband."

"Oh." Not a date. I didn't know whether to feel relieved or disgusted. "You want to write about Josh."

"Okay, it is intrusive, I know that. But they did my story too last year, about how I was raising Cam on my own, and I have to say, it actually helped to talk it out. First because these women from all over town started leaving baked goods on our doorstep." He smiled. "But mostly because it made me separate from it a little bit.

And them playing me up how they did, it actually did make me act a little heroically, be a better dad because the article portrayed me as the person I wished I really was."

Suddenly it occurred to me that his speech sounded scripted—that most of what he'd said in the past few minutes had. "I'm sorry," I said, "but no. Really generous of you to offer." I gave a smile I hoped he could read as sarcastic. "But it's really not my thing, being written up in the paper. It's a little boastful, and it's also embarrassing."

"I could take whatever angle you're comfortable with—the ultimate sacrifice angle? Or I could focus more on you and your kids."

He was an asshole, a salesman using me for his commission. "My life isn't your business, and it definitely isn't the business of the readers of the *Herald*," I said, standing. Toby scrambled up, buried his face against my hip, and I was suddenly furious with myself for even allowing Dan to bring up the topic in front of him. "Thanks for the coffee, and for watching after Anna. I'll pick her up around five."

"Right, okay, one sec." Dan rooted in his pocket, pulled out his wallet, and extracted a business card, which he handed to me. "Here's my number, so you can call if you change your mind. Just consider it, okay? People should hear this story." He overemphasized the words, the type of tone that should have a string music background. And then, to drive it home he said, "Josh *deserves* to have his story heard."

"Are you even listening to me?" I imagined the story making it into the *Herald*, being read by people who knew the truth of how Josh died, their scorn, the recrimination. I smoothed my hand over Toby's hair, and shuffled him toward the door. "Five o'clock," I said, then slammed the door behind us.

25
Anna

Want to see something?" Cam said.

Cam's bedroom was painted darkish green, with posters of lions and tigers and jaguars tacked all over his walls, clothes and junk all over the floor, and cut-out newspaper words taped on the front of a computer monitor. Not the kind of words you'd imagine seeing in a paper and thinking yes, these are worth keeping. They were words connected to nothing, words like *Triumph* and *Retribution* and *Contrive.*

He opened a drawer and pulled out a wooden jewelry box with an angel painted on the top, and then he sat on the floor next to me and held it in his lap. When he opened the box, it played "Silent Night." I listened to the music, trying not to think about what Mom said downstairs. It was too much to think about, so instead I tried to think what Cam's room reminded me of. This is the word I would use to describe it: *Jungle.*

He scooped out a handful of chains and beads, pretty things the color of sourballs. And then he slid out the red velvet bottom. Underneath it was a picture with smudged edges and bent corners, and a piece of blue paper with writing on it. Under the paper was a metal wheel, turning, plucking notes, slow, and then it stopped. Sudden silence.

Cam lifted the picture up by its corners. I reached for it, but he pulled it away and he held it flat in his palm.

The woman in the picture was skinny and not very pretty. She looked too old to be the mother of a kid. Her arms were just hanging there at her sides, and her mouth was in a flat line. Next to her was Cam, with rounder cheeks and shorter hair, holding on to her arm.

"She looks nice," I said because I didn't know what to say.

Cam touched his finger to the side of the woman's face. "She had leukemia inside her then but she didn't even know it," he said. "She felt sick all the time and tired, but nobody realized that was the reason." He ran his finger over her face and then down her body, slow like a little kid trying to read. And then he dropped the photo back in the box. "If I knew it and I'd told her, she'd still be alive."

I watched his face. He didn't seem sad, exactly, mostly just worn out. I wanted to show I understood, so I said something I'd heard another Marine's kid say once on the news. "If the Democrats had been in office, my dad would still be alive," I said.

But he didn't seem to hear me. He looked at the picture a long while and then set it back in the box. He handed me the piece of blue paper.

I opened it and started to read. As I read, Cam closed his eyes and whispered the words at the same time, so quiet I could tell he was saying them to himself and not to me. It was weird hearing his whisper over the inside voice reading in my head. Kind of like how I mouth words when people sing "Happy Birthday," because I'm too embarrassed to do it loud.

My Sweet Cameron,

    I wish I could've said good-bye to you in person, but I hope you understand why I decided this is best.

    I know I promised I'd be there for your seventh birthday, and I tried, sweetheart, with all my strength, but I'm not the one in charge. I have a gift your father will give you from me, a special gift that I got from my mother, who also got it from her mother. It's been handed down for over a century, a wooden box for you to store all the special things you will collect in your lifetime.

    There are a lifetime's worth of things I wish I could tell you, but since we don't have a lifetime I have to trust that the things I've already given you will last, and that you will know where to go to find the rest. You're a masterpiece I started that will be even more masterful because you'll finish it on your own.

    Please remember that even when it might not've felt that way, when I was too caught up in my own mind and then my own sickness and fear, I have adored you.

                               Mommy

Cam was crying when he whispered the last sentence. I could tell. So I wouldn't embarrass him I pretended I was reading much slower than I actually was, to give him a chance to get over it.

It was a weird letter, I thought, for a mom to give her kid when she was about to die. But on the other hand, it was better than what my dad had done to say godbye to us, which was nothing. The last time I saw him, I didn't know it would be the last. I should've paid more attention.

When I'd already read the letter three times over, I folded it and tucked it back into the jewelry box without looking at his face. "I have a letter my dad wrote too," I said, "right before he died. I didn't read all of it yet but today, or maybe tomorrow, I'm going to read more."

Cam didn't say anything. I looked up. He wasn't crying anymore, but his cheeks were wet and there was a bubble of snot in his nose. I tried to figure out if it would be worse to get up to find him a tissue or to have to keep looking at the snot. I decided not to get up, and tried to concentrate on not staring at it.

Finally he slid back the bottom of the jewelry box and closed the lid. "I dream about my mom sometimes." He put his hand on top of the painted angel and spread his fingers. "A lot of the time. And she doesn't know she's dead, or even that she was ever sick. She just acts the same how she always did. Sometimes when I'm talking to her I know she's not really there, but there's sometimes that I don't even know it. It just feels like everything's normal."

"Yeah," I whispered, then, "That happens to me too." I'd never told anybody this before. Partly because I didn't want them to send me back to a shrink, but mostly because it hurt too much to say. Every morning after I dreamed of him I'd get a stomach feeling. And it is not a feeling to bring back, if you can help it.

Cam shrugged and then shrugged again and got up to tuck his jewelry box back in the drawer. And watching him, this is what I thought. That even though I really should be glad somebody else had the same kind of dreams, even though it might mean that it was normal and not truly crazy, instead how I felt was worse. Cam's mom died three years ago, which meant my dreams, and the awfulness of waking up after, might go on forever for the rest of my life. And also because, looking around Cam's room, I couldn't be completely one hundred percent sure that he wasn't crazy too.

We rode bikes downtown. Cam's bike looked like it was about a thousand years old, half yellow and half rust, all the shine worn down. It also had a girl's pink basket on the handlebars, which was weird.

His dad gave us money for lunch, so that was the first thing we did: Palazzo Pizza. Cam ate four whole slices plus a large Coke, which was surprising. He was so skinny I didn't know where he fit it.

When I was done I just watched him keep on eating. He looked at his two plates, not at me, and he hardly seemed to chew. He didn't say anything, which made me not be able to think of anything to say, and I thought if this was how the rest of the afternoon was going to go, I had to go home.

When he was done he wiped the back of his hand across his mouth and then said, "Do you believe in always telling the truth?"

What kind of a question was that? "I don't know," I said. "I mean everybody tells a lie some of the time."

"Okay, but on a scale of one to ten, where one would be a little lie, like if you didn't tell your mom you ate cookies before dinner, and ten would be a way big lie like...you murdered somebody. On a scale of one to ten, how much of a lie would you be willing to tell?"

I poked my straw up and down in the ice from my

Coke. "Probably a three," I said, then glanced at him. "Like say if my mom ever told me I could write to my dad and wanted me to think he'd actually get the letter, I probably would decide to act like I believed it."

He made a face like I was a dweeb, so I knew I had to come up with something better.

"One time I stole one of my mom's necklaces? And I wore it to school and it broke, and I threw it away without saying anything." Remembering it made my insides feel squashed. The necklace was a gift to Mom from Grammy, and when she found it in the trash she knew it was me who broke it, so first she yelled at me but then, she cried.

"Okay," he said. "Okay, what if we didn't have money for pizza, but when we picked it up I told them we already paid when we ordered? Would you tell them that was a lie?"

I folded my plate in half, then in quarters, and I tried to remember if he actually had paid for the pizza. But yes, he must have. That is the rule of pizza: you pay first. "No," I said. "I wouldn't tell."

He nodded like I had passed the test, and then he plucked my plate out of my hand, got up and threw our plates and cups away and then walked out the door without saying a thing. I looked over at the people behind the counter and then I followed him outside.

We unlocked our bikes and started wheeling them down the sidewalk. When we got to a drugstore, he stopped and leaned his bike against the door. "So listen," he said. "There's these invisibility pens in there? And they're really cool. You write with them and the ink comes out clear so you can't see it. So what you do is there's another pen you use to color over the writing, and presto, it appears."

"Cool," I said. "We could write notes to each other in

class, and Mr. Benning would think they were just blank paper."

"Yeah." He kicked his foot against the wall. "But the problem is, I spent all the money I had on pizza."

I felt a cramp like someone had just dug a finger into my stomach. On the one hand, it was good he actually had paid for our pizza. But on the other hand, which made the goodness totally beside the point, I knew exactly what he wanted to do. I backed away from the door.

"You can make invisible ink out of lemon juice," I said. "I used to do it with my dad. And besides, they could catch us."

He smiled and kept smiling a long time before he said, "They won't catch us. I did it before. On weekends there's this girl works here, and she's always on the phone. You could stick the whole cash register under your shirt and she wouldn't even notice."

I imagined him sticking a cash register up his shirt and the way it would look, because he was so skinny, like a cash register under a shirt. He seemed all excited, and the excitedness scared me. But also, also there was something underneath it. I could feel it in me like a song playing under my skin and trying to come out. Maybe we didn't ex-actly *need* the pens, but… "I could get something for my brother too. And my mom."

"So you're okay with it?"

"I am," I said, then checked myself. Yes. I was.

He smiled. "So here's what we do, okay? You start looking at stuff near the counter, and if the girl gets up at all, ask her a question about how much something costs. Ask it loud. And when I get the pens I'll come back to the counter and you can pick up whatever else you want."

I nodded and hugged myself tighter.

"Okay, so you ready?"

I looked inside. There were smudges on the window, one from a hand and, next to it, a circle that was maybe from somebody's nose. "Yeah," I whispered, and we went into the store.

I saw right away what I wanted for Toby. It was up front in an aisle with toys. A Carbot: a car that could unfold its arms and legs to become a robot, and then fold back down when it needed to get going. I wouldn't have minded having it for myself.

Me and Cam looked at each other and then he nodded and ducked into an aisle. I walked up to the counter.

The girl sitting by the cash register was not on the phone, she was doing her toenails. Her foot was just out there in the open on a stool, cotton between her toes, nails turning hot pink. This made me homesick for Madison. I stuffed my hands in my pockets, looking at the rolls of candy, then picked up a bag of peanut M&M's and studied the nutritional information: 130 calories, 20 carbohydrates, 18 sugars. Madison used to read these numbers when she went with me to the commissary, to tell if a food was good or bad. She said a girl should never eat anything that had more than five grams of fat. She said that even if, like us, you had a tendency to be skinny, it would eventually appear on your butt.

Cam appeared and I set the bag down and without even looking at him I wandered up and down the aisles until I got to the makeup section. For my mom, I'd maybe get a lipstick. She hardly ever wore lipstick, but when she did it made her pretty.

I stared at the racks. Who knew there were so many colors? How did people ever decide which one was right?

I looked quickly at them, and chose the one that seemed to be the prettiest, light and shimmery. Silver City Pink.

How fast could a person's heart beat before they had a heart attack and died? I looked left and then right, took a deep breath, and then slipped the tube in my pocket. I thought what I did must be in my face, loud as a scar. Look at me and you think: Guilty.

I walked over to the toy aisle and picked up the Carbot. *Mighty robot with a magic transformational skill! Watch him change before your very eyes!* I stretched out the bottom of my sweatshirt and tucked it inside.

And then I didn't know what to do. If I went up to the counter the girl would be able to see my sweatshirt was lumpy, but if I just left, Cam might not realize I was gone. I folded my arms over my chest and walked behind the next aisle, and pretended like I was studying details on maxipads and grown-up diapers. I wondered if I should steal some diapers for Grammy.

But then Cam said, "Excuse me, how much does this cost?" and I froze, all of me except my heart. Apparently, a heart can beat very fast without you dying.

"Cam, I'm bored!" I said. "I'm leaving!" My voice sounded like I'd sucked on a helium balloon. My arms still over my chest, I walked fast to the door and out. The bell tied to the door jangled, and the girl must've heard it and now she'd be after me, and she'd take one look at my face and read the guilty. I imagined her running, how the pink on her toes would flash like a siren down the street.

I jumped on my bike, and Cam came out right behind me. He threw a pack of pens into his basket and we both raced down the sidewalk. As I pedaled my knees bumped up against the Carbot, crackling the plastic casing, the edge tickling my belly, and I imagined the girl charging up the street, saw her not just arresting us but also tackling us, yelling and punching. And part of me wanted that, to be punched and to punch back, because I knew it might help make my insides stop screaming. The inside-twisting in me was so bad that I almost had to steer away, off the road, to be sick. Which now I wish I had. I should've been sick in the bushes and stopped the day. Because, something worse was coming next.

26
Natalie

There were many foods Mark Mason loved," I read, "minestrone, milkshakes, macaroni and cheese. But every night Mark asked his mother, 'May I have some meatballs please?'"

The faces in front of me held the same mix of reactions as at every one of my readings, from restless to captivated to catatonic, based largely on whether they were due for a nap. Toby was sitting in the front row, hugging his knees, and bless him, he was one of the captivated. Or maybe one of the catatonic, it was hard to tell; he was a little too old for my book, and he'd certainly heard it enough times. But maybe it was because he knew it so well that he was so transfixed. It was comforting. A story from before.

The library was almost entirely unchanged from when I'd been a child. There was a chance I'd actually sat in the same spot, on the same round throw rug where these children were sitting now. It had the same meager, but brightly decorated, children's section, the same sour musty smell of old books. I thought I even recognized the children's librarian, her short blond hair turned to short gray hair. I waited to see if she'd recognize me, always the

first child to finish the twenty-book summer reading program and win the hot fudge sundae from Lickety Split.
But when she didn't recognize me, I was too shy to remind
her.

"Mark rubbed at his eyes," I read, "and reached for his
lamp, and he found something strange, soft and squishy
and damp."

The boy next to Toby, olive-skinned with a mop of
curly black hair, had been on his knees the whole time I
read, like he was still trying to decide if he wanted to stay.
Now, without warning and too adorable to bear, he bent
to kiss Toby's head. Toby blinked quickly with shy surprise, and I smiled at them, at this Kodak moment, until
the boy leaned all his weight on Toby and they fell backward, Toby's head conking on the tile floor. "Hey!" I said.

Toby squirmed to get out from under the boy and
then rose onto his knees, opened his mouth, and bit the
boy's cheek.

"Toby!" I jumped up, dropping the book, as the children stared at me dazedly, maybe unsure of whether this
was part of the story. Toby pulled back, looking almost
startled, at himself, at what he'd done, and then he started
to cry.

After a moment of shocked silence the boy started
screaming, and I knelt to him, staring horrified at the lines
of red teeth-marks startlingly close to his left eye. A
mother appeared, too young, in my opinion, to be a real
mother, wailing at the gathered crowd to dial 911, then
yelling at Toby. "Where's your parents!" she said.

I hesitated, then hated myself for hesitating. "I'm his
mother," I said, and reached for Toby, held him against
my shoulder. "I'm so sorry."

"You're *sorry?* Holy Christ, he almost bit out my son's eye! Is *he* sorry?" She was positively shrieking now.

Internally I was gnashing my teeth, but I forced my voice to stay in check. "Look at him. He is sorry; he's just been going through a tough time recently."

Around us children were being collected, soothing whispers, the librarian (who I now did not want to recognize me) scurrying toward us solicitously. "Is everything okay?"

"Okay? Look at my baby!"

Toby started knocking his forehead against my shoulder, and I pressed his head tight against me. "I'm sorry," I said again, and then carried him out the door.

In the car I got Toby into his booster seat. How could you love a child with your whole being, consider him as much a part of you as your own heart and mind and soul, and still screw up as badly as I was screwing up? How could you not understand what was broken inside him or have any idea of how to fix him?

I knelt on the pavement looking into his face, remembering the boy who'd been so quick to laugh, to share stories, to run to hug me and tell me in excruciating, barely intelligible detail, the minutiae of his day. (*And then…and then…and then…* he'd say.) This was my fault, I knew that; the biting was an expression of his pent-up confusion over the letters, over hearing Dan talk about his father's death. Press so much pain and fear into a boy too young to have any sense of how to process them, and no wonder it all came out through his teeth.

Suddenly, Toby's body stiffened against me. "I'm sorry about biting," he whispered, the first words he'd spoken since Thursday afternoon.

Hearing him speak startled me so much that I fell

back on my butt, staring at him. Slowly, I raised myself back onto my knees and reached to tuck a strand of hair behind his ear. "It's okay," I said hoarsely. "Oh, baby, I know and it's okay."

Back home, the first thing I did was dig out the number Seth had given me for the mortgage company. Then tried on my one and only business suit to make sure it would still fit.

After changing back to jeans I headed downstairs and sat on the couch, my legs folded under me, watching as Toby, unprompted, crawled up next to my mother and reached for the water glass in front of her, put it in her hand.

"Why, thank you!" she said, then gave it right back to him.

Ever since we'd gotten here, Toby had shown a sort of pride in having someone in the house less competent than he, making sure I cut the crusts off her sandwiches, trying to reteach her the alphabet. That's what kind of boy he was, the kind who'd check to make sure his grandmother was fully hydrated. Not the kind who'd bite another boy. I'd have to make sure his therapist understood that.

Therapy. A hundred fifty bucks an hour of which my cheapo insurance would pay, at most, half.

I turned to Dad. "Wanted to tell you I'm going to try to get an interview at this mortgage company Seth told me about. A receptionist job."

He peered at me over his glasses. "You know I'd pay you to watch your mom. It does get to be a bit much for me."

I watched Mom pick pills off her sweater with a shaking hand, and drop them onto the floor. Did he want me watching her so he could spend more time with Marlie? "I wouldn't let you pay me to take care of her, that's ridiculous. I'll watch her when I get home at night, but right now I need more than you can pay me. I'm looking to buy a house in the next few months. We can't stay here forever."

Dad's gaze shifted to the window and he gave a short nod. "Course you can't."

"But what I wanted to ask, when I'm working I'll need somebody to watch the kids after school. I'd pay you for it."

"Natalie," Dad said, then sat straighter and looked me in the eye. "Being with my grandchildren is my one pleasure in life. Me and your mother should be paying you."

I smiled at him, rose and hugged his head. "Thanks, Dad," I said.

How good it would feel to finally get *moving*, fulfill Goal 1 on my list of goals. And I'd work toward something else on the side, take classes toward teacher certification or nursing. I could be like the nice paramedic who'd held me against her chest, let me hide my face in her bosom while they carried Josh's body away. I could do it, why not? I was capable of doing good things.

I imagined myself in a white dress and stockings, holding a woman's hand while I told her that my quick thinking had saved her son, and I imagined her words: "You are a miracle, Natalie, and I'll remember you forever."

Here I was, on my way to creating a new life.

27
Anna

"This is Ms. Pinckney's house," Cam said when we stopped our bikes in front of an old white house next door to his. There were newspapers piled on the front porch, along with a broken chair and a mattress with a gray stain.

The shutters on the windows were different colors: Black, yellow, a different yellow, white. Like a disease. "It's gross," I said.

He gave a little nod and said, "She's evil."

"What do you mean?"

"She just is. One time the fire alarm went off? And my dad came here to make sure she was okay. But she didn't answer the door, so he went inside to check on her and guess what? She called the cops and they took him to the police station."

"He got arrested?"

Cam picked at loose plastic on his handlebars. "Also, I think she killed my neighbor's cat Chelsea."

We both stood there looking. I imagined an old woman standing behind her window shades, in rooms full of newspapers and magazines and empty soup cans, and possibly dead animals.

Suddenly Cam glanced at me and then he opened her mailbox. He pulled out a flyer and two envelopes, looked at the envelopes and then at me again, and then he threw one into his bike basket.

I widened my eyes at him, but he didn't even pay attention, just put the rest of her mail back in the box and rode away.

I watched after him, feeling shivery, in the same way nightmares do, where everything seems normal but you know it actually isn't. But even though part of me was scared of him, I also knew he was the most interesting person I ever met. Madison was still my best friend, but also she was like a stuffed animal. Always there, always happy to be with me, but the fact that we were friends didn't say anything about me. It didn't mean I was special and chosen as a friend because of my qualities, things she wanted to get to know. Whereas with Cam it seemed like he must see something in me that I didn't even know was there.

Inside his home, Mr. Carson was watching a hockey game and eating Goldfish crackers. "You guys have fun?" he said.

"We got pizza," Cam said.

"Ooh, bad choice." Cam's dad kept his eyes on the TV. "Hope you're not sick of it, 'cause I'm ordering pizza for dinner. Goldfish?" He held the bag to us.

"No, thank you, we're going up to my room."

"Just a minute." Mr. Carson looked into his bag of Goldfish and shuffled it like he was looking for a prize. "Tell me something, Anna. How does your mom feel about surprises?"

I watched him. "I don't know," I said.

"I mean if they're good surprises. Things she wouldn't

have expected, and maybe wouldn't have asked for, but that'll turn out good in the end."

There was something weird about Mr. Carson. When he looked at me, it made my skin hurt. "I don't know," I said again.

"Hmmm." He leaned back on the sofa and looked at the TV screen.

Me and Cam watched him a minute, and then Cam whispered, *"C'mon."* He grabbed my arm and we both went up the stairs.

When we got to his room, Cam pulled the pens and the letter out from his shirt and dropped them on the bed. Next to the bed was a little table with a drawer that was so full of stuff it wouldn't close, including comic books, a scarf with big red flowers, a license plate that said ♥Cameron♥, and something that looked like a bone. He reached into the drawer and pulled out a manila folder. I stared at the bone.

"Let's go," he said, and then he picked up Ms. Pinckney's letter, grabbed my arm again, and pulled me into the hall. He took me to the bathroom and closed the door behind us, and then he turned on the faucet.

"What're you doing?" I said. When he didn't answer, I said, "What do you think your dad meant about a surprise?"

Cam shrugged, watching the water, not answering.

I wanted to ask him if he liked his dad, or if he was a little scared of him. But Cam probably would not take that the right way. "He wouldn't do anything bad, would he?" I said.

Cam twisted his lips into a smile. "He wouldn't care if he knew what we did today."

"He wouldn't care you stole stuff?"

"Not really. He doesn't really think about things after he does them."

I frowned, thinking about this, how it might be like to grow up alone in this house with someone like Cam's dad. It would never be comfortable.

The water started to steam, and Cam held the letter next to the faucet. It was addressed to Susan Pinckney and it was from Citibank, in Detroit, MI. "One time?" he said. "Mr. Carroll, who's not his friend anymore, told him how he sometimes hated Mrs. Carroll? And Dad wrote about it in a newspaper article. He used different names, but it was obvious who he meant. And Mrs. Carroll read it and they got a divorce. That was the worst thing he ever did, but usually he doesn't mean for bad stuff to happen. Sometimes it just does."

"Your dad got somebody a divorce?"

"What he wrote did." Cam said this like it was no big deal, but I knew kids from Pendleton who had a divorce, and it was one of the worst things you could go through. I wondered if Mrs. Carroll had any kids.

Cam turned off the tap, then slid his finger carefully under the envelope seal. "What're you going to do?" I said.

He pulled out a paper with writing and a small envelope and said, "I did this before. I've done it with a couple other people too, but with her it always works."

I looked down at the writing:

Carson Liquor $49.99
Rent-a-Center $129.00
Petco.com Online $69.80

I wondered if she bought food at Petco to lure the cats.

Cam reached into his folder and pulled out a sheet of stickers. All of them said:

Accounts Payable
111 Star Street
French Creek, CA 90728

He peeled one off and stuck it on top of the address on the little envelope. "It's her fault for not even looking where she's sending her money to," he said.

I stared at him. "That's your address?"

"Nah, I don't even know if it's a real place. But this really screws her up, because she gets charges on her bill for not paying."

I watched him put the little envelope back into Ms. Pinckney's letter and press hard on the seal, and I got the feeling again of wanting to run away.

"You're not going to tell, right?"

I swallowed, shook my head.

"It's because she's evil. It's not like I'm killing her or anything, just making her poor."

It seemed to me that she was probably pretty poor already, but when I thought about what he said, what I really felt was angry. She called the cops when Cam's dad was just trying to help, which was just like the people who set a bomb on my own dad when he was trying to help them.

Mom told me not to be mad at those people because really it was the war that hurt him. She said the war didn't know what was right and what was wrong. But even though I pretended like I understood, deep down I knew that didn't make any sense. It was people who had hurt my dad, who had made him forget sometimes that we were important to him, who made me hurt him because he forgot we were important and made him die because I hurt him. And I hated them.

Driving home, Mom seemed to have things on her mind, so she hardly talked, just asked how my day had been. I told her fine and that Cam was a very nice boy, which I thought was what she'd want to hear. But then when we got onto our street she said, "I guess this is the first time you've made friends with a boy."

This was not true. When I was four I had a friend named Noah. We played house and pretended we were married, and he gave me baseball cards when he had doubles, and one time we kissed on the lips, just to see. But there was no sense in reminding her of that.

"Aren't there girls in your class you want to be friends with too?" she said.

"Well, yeah." I pressed my fingers against the hard plastic under my shirt. If Mom had asked why my shirt was lumpy I would have said Cam gave me the Carbot as a present. But she didn't ask. Sometimes Mom was so busy worrying about everything that she forgot to look at me. "I'm friends with girls too," I said, "just Cam was more interesting. He has a different way of living."

I waited for her to ask questions, but this seemed to be a good enough answer for her, because she said, "Hmmm…" and pulled into our driveway.

Sometimes I wondered if she really listened to me. Or she listened, which was easy, but I was pretty sure she never really heard.

After dinner while everybody watched TV, I went to my room and tried to figure out how I could give Mom and Toby my presents without them realizing how I'd got them. I could say Cam gave them to me, but what if she called his dad to say thanks?

I thought about this for a while, and then the idea came to me.

It felt like something I must've had in me all along but never let myself realize. Like when Madison pointed out that the mole on my cheek is shaped like a tear and I thought yes, all my life I knew I had a mole but this is the first time I have ever seen it that way.

I could fix Toby. And if I fixed Toby that might also fix my mom. A spark inside the new me was stronger than everything that was broken. Like superglue.

28
Natalie

I was dressing in my PJ's when I heard my dad's voice from his bedroom. I padded in my bare feet to my door, and slowly cracked it open to listen.

"...just funny," Dad said, "having to tell people where I'm going, and when I'll be home. I'm so used to nobody giving a damn."

He paused, then said, "Okay, I know, I'm just being cranky. Having them here is great, but it's making me feel my age is all. I'm used to having nobody to talk to besides you. And Meg too, I guess, but there's a huge difference between talking *to* and talking *at*."

I leaned my head against the doorframe and closed my eyes.

"When I talk to them, all I can say is, 'I used to do this,' and 'I used to do that,' and it makes me feel like everything's in the past, like there's no more 'doing' left."

Another pause and then he sniffed and said, "Well, thanks, hon. Me too. But no salsa dancing, never mind what you think it'll do for my flexibility."

I closed the door softly, walked to the bed, and lay down. Squeezed my eyes shut, then opened them again and stared at the ceiling. Hon. He'd called her "hon." He'd never called Mom anything but Meg.

Dad was on the phone for almost ten minutes, and when I finally heard him walk into the bathroom, I picked up my phone and dialed Seth.

"Hey," he said. "I've been thinking about you. You okay?"

"Yeah, I guess. You get used to things." Which wasn't exactly true, but I'd at least gotten to the point where thoughts of Josh's injury weren't invading every empty moment of my life.

I'd tried reading the PDA at least ten times since I'd last turned it on. And each time I paged through the entries, my hands started shaking uncontrollably, and it was all I could do to get my finger centered on the *Off* button.

Now I pulled out the PDA and turned it on, and started paging distractedly through the entries. I *should* be getting used to things. The awfulness of what Josh had kept from me should have percolated, permeated in the way shocking things do, should be sitting now inside me and becoming whatever sorrow or anger or guilt it would turn out to be. But all I felt now was confused.

Cut on hand chopping tomato, the screen said. I lay back on the bed. "Change of subject. My dad's having an affair."

"What?"

Took kids for Santa photos. I stared at the entry, then squeezed my eyes shut and flipped quickly to the next page. "What?" I said, then, "Oh. Yeah, I guess I'm just being ridiculously selfish. I mean, I want him to be happy, and it's not actually an affair when my mom's already basically dead, right?"

"She's not dead," Seth said, then, "Wait, so he's actually seeing someone?"

"Looks like it. It's this woman, Marlie, who used to be friends with both him and Mom. And I want to find something to hate about her, but so far everything she's shown me is pretty un-hateable. I don't know."

"Wow. I know how hard that has to be for you, and I feel like I should have something helpful to say but I'm coming up blank. Or actually, the only word in my head is *crap*. I know how it has to feel."

"It's okay, just needed to vent a little. I called because I was lonely, and this is helping."

I slipped my legs under the covers and read the next PDA entry. *Missing a black sock, and totally pissed off. What's it help to always be so pissed off?*

I ran my finger across this entry. I'd noticed anger last year, never at me or the kids but at traffic, or things he saw on the news. Had he thought the anger was a result of the injury rather than just anger at what had happened to him? Had he been scared that he'd turned into a different person? *Had* he turned into a different person? To distract myself I said, "I just got this total feeling of déjà vu; lying on my bed and talking on this very same phlegm-colored phone with you late at night. We used to sometimes fall asleep on the phone, it was so late. What did we possibly have to talk about that was so interesting and important it couldn't wait?"

"Apparently not much, if you actually fell asleep on me." He paused, then said, "I actually remember your voice drifting off, and then lying there listening to you breathing. It was kind of nice."

"Now I'm embarrassed."

"No, don't be. It's one of my happiest memories of childhood."

I raised my eyebrows. "Listening to me breathe was one of your happiest memories?"

He didn't respond.

Jamie expecting? Ask N. "You must've had a miserable childhood," I said, trying to put a smile into my voice.

"Maybe." His tone was suddenly stiffer, almost curt. "Anyway, I'm glad you're doing better."

"Well, you helped a lot the other night, so thanks."

"You're welcome. So, I have an early morning tomorrow."

"Oh! Okay, sorry. I was just calling to see if you're coming for Thanksgiving on Thursday. Marlie's going to be here too, so we can make her the token single person. And Anna's been asking me when you'll be able to show her that origami you promised her." This was a lie, but I thought he might see it as a compliment.

He hesitated, then said, "Oh, well, actually…Actually, I've been invited to dinner already. At a friend's house. A friend's party, but could I take a rain check?"

"Sure! Of course!" I ran my fingers across the phone's buttons. Outside the window, something fell from the sky, a leaf, a pinecone, bird crap. "Definitely a rain check," I said. Then hung up.

I wondered if it was rude of me to just hang up.

I wondered if I should've suggested a rain check date.

I wondered if after I'd fallen apart in his house, he'd been hoping to never have to speak to me again. And could I blame him? No. I probably wouldn't want to speak to me either.

I pulled the phone off my night table and hugged it against my chest, like it was a stuffed animal. A man.

I hadn't wanted to be alone watching Dad flirting with Marlie, making me think of what I'd lost. Seth was the only friend I had left, but he'd rather spend Thanksgiving alone.

I put the phone back on the table and looked again at the PDA. Everything hurt in me. It hurt so much and all the time, something I felt in me always. I knew I couldn't expect grief to have an edge I could step off from, but it should at least taper. I should at least be able to look into the future and see the possibility of tapering.

I remembered all the nights I'd lain here imagining Seth beside me, sure then that it would be my future. When Josh was alive, I'd thought back on those days as a teenage thing, a lesser kind of love. But what it had really been was an innocent love, without complications, without this kind of pain.

I missed that. And I hated myself for missing it.

But now I was on my own, and what choice did I have? To carry this question around the way some people carried tumors unchecked, because they were too afraid to learn how bad they were? I'd read through the whole thing because living with whatever I learned couldn't be worse than this question. This was the theme of my new life, bricks thrown at my head, coma, waking to find I'd somehow swallowed them. And maybe, in time, I'd learn how to absorb them.

Headache again, ask Dr., can't think. Took notes for class but no idea what they say. Ask for help? Who can help? I went down to the kitchen, poured myself a glass of wine, then came back upstairs and continued to read.

I spent most of the night reliving the minutiae of our lives, the straightforward facts without the emotions behind them. I wanted to read through every day, looking for clues. All these things he'd written in the way Mom had written her "memoirs," everything in her life set down so assiduously like she wanted to prove to herself that she'd lived it. I continued through the spring and summer, events I remembered and events I didn't, the turmoil Josh must've faced only evident in the frenzied tedium of his postings. Until I got to August 26, the last day.

I sat a long while with my eyes closed, squeezing the PDA so hard that my fingers went numb, trying to swallow down my nausea. Had someone cracked open my chest, I knew they'd find my heart slowly tearing into hundreds of shreds, unfixable heart confetti.

My eyes still closed, I turned the PDA off and without thinking, I threw it into my nightstand drawer. And then I sat at my vanity, gazing into my mirror, trying to center myself. *I look the same,* Josh had told me soon after returning last year, when his memory was worst. *I look in the mirror and I want to yell, What the hell's wrong with you?*

And that's how it was for me too; there were bricks inside me and I felt like my wrists had been cut, my blood drained. But yes, I looked the same.

In the middle of the night I heard a thump from the children's bedroom. I reached for the glasses I kept by my bed and started to rise, then saw Anna slip down the hall and heard the creak of the front door. I was about to jump up to see what she was doing when I heard the door close again, and her footsteps returning.

When she reached the hall, I called, "Anna?"

The footsteps stopped. A full minute later Anna appeared at the door, barefoot, ghostly in her white nightgown.

"What're you doing up?"

She shrugged, thought a minute and said, "I had to pee."

"Outside?"

"Yes. I didn't want to wake anybody up."

I raised my eyebrows at her and she said, "Actually, actually I thought I heard somebody outside, so I went to look and sure enough, there was a man."

"What?"

"Yeah, there was a man. And he put something in our mailbox."

Was she telling the truth? She looked pale, her eyes wide and shadowed, scared. I sat up, gripping my sheets. *Anthrax,* I thought. *Unabomber.*

Should I wake my dad up? I pictured him in the undershirt he slept in, skinny arms flailing wildly at a muscled man in a black ski mask. This was stupid; I had to get ahold of myself. Probably it had been a Jehovah's Witness or a small-time entrepreneur with a business card, offering us a reliable cleaning service. "Okay," I said. "You wait here, okay? Don't move."

Anna nodded.

"Everything's fine. I'll be back in just a minute."

Anna nodded again and I got up and slipped on my sneakers. On the way from the bedroom I kissed the top of her head. Just in case.

I opened the door and peered out. It was so dark out here, no streetlights, no neighbors; I couldn't see more than a foot in front of me.

I went to the kitchen for my Sandoku knife, then back up to my bedroom for a flashlight. Anna was sitting on the very edge of the bed, not looking at me. "Don't worry, sweetie," I said. "I'll be fine!"

Her forehead creased, and then she tucked her hands under her seat. "Uh-huh," she said.

I walked slowly down the driveway, the knife held at my chest, and then I slowly opened the mailbox and shone the flashlight inside.

It was a package, wrapped in spiral notebook paper. I read the neatly scripted words.

To: Natalie and Toby
From: Somebody who loves you

I exhaled, then smiled, then felt supremely embarrassed. I pulled the package out and walked back to the house.

Anna was standing in the entryway. She looked at the package and then stared down at the knife, and her cheeks flushed pink. I felt a sudden flash of anger. "You scared me, Anna! Why'd you say there was a man out here?"

Anna's face tightened. "Because there was."

"Look, it's okay, I'm not mad at you, but you should've realized telling me someone was here so late at night would scare me."

She watched me silently, then backed away from the door. I walked inside and sat on the living room sofa, patted the seat beside me. "It was nice of you to give me and Toby a present, though. We'll wait for tomorrow morning so Toby can open it, okay?"

She eyed the package, then hugged her waist. "That's not from me."

"Sweetheart, please," I said, and then suddenly, watching her, I understood what she must be doing. My letters from heaven had stopped, she'd seen how Toby was reacting, and now she was trying to convince us that the correspondence hadn't actually stopped at all. I felt a bewildering pain. How could she try to take this on herself?

I gathered her in my arms. "Oh, sweetie, it's okay, I know it's from you. And I think you're the most amazing kid in the world."

She stiffened, started to pull away, but I rubbed circles on her back and slowly, slowly she relaxed against me. I could feel her spine through her thin nightgown, so fragile, the knobbed shape and thickness of a Twizzler. "Actually, let's open it now," I said. "I can't wait to see what it is. I'll open it careful so we can rewrap it for Toby, and tomorrow I'll pretend to him it's the first time I'm seeing it, okay?"

Anna didn't move, her weight heavy against me, and then I felt her head nod against my chest. I pulled away and carefully peeled back the tape.

Inside was a black plastic action figure, with a square head and hinged joints, red lightning bolts on its legs. I bit back a smile. "Toby'll love it!" I said, then, "I love it too."

"No," Anna said curtly, then reached between the sofa cushions for something that had rolled from the wrapping. "That's just for Toby, but this is for you." She handed me a tube of lipstick.

"Really? Thank you!" I pulled off the top. It was the color of Pepto-Bismol. I smoothed it on my lips anyway. "How's it look?"

"Pretty," she said softly.

I kissed her cheek, leaving a shimmery Pepto-Bismol smudge. I wiped the smudge off with my thumb. "What a thoughtful gift," I said softly. "But how'd you pay for these?" I wondered if my dad had given her money. Last week he'd given me a hundred-dollar check, which I'd told him I wouldn't cash, pretending to be insulted but really more ashamed than anything else.

Anna took the lipstick from me, recapped it, and started wrapping it, along with the action figure, back inside the paper. "Cam's dad gave me the money."

I raised my eyebrows. "Well, that's really nice of him, but we'll have to pay him back. I'll give you money to give to Cam on Monday."

Anna paused a second, and then she said, "Okay."

I walked with her up to her bedroom, kissed her good night, and then rested my cheek on her forehead. And this was why I had to stop thinking about Josh. This was what was important, here in this house. I needed all my focus on the only two people who really mattered.

I set the package on the chair by their bed so Toby would see it when he woke up, then went into the bathroom and looked in the mirror. My lips looked like two sticks of spit-shined bubble gum. But I was going to wear that stuff every single day, until it was gone.

29

Anna

Toby woke me up by climbing up to my bed. He was not supposed to do this, because he might fall. But sometimes he needed to, and I never told.

It was light out, and first I couldn't figure out why I was so tired, the air like water, hard to move through, my eyelids gluey.

But then I remembered. And suddenly all of me sparked awake. I pulled the covers over my head and tried to open the door back to my dream, but it was no use. The thoughts started. I sat up.

I should've realized Mom would know the presents were from me. If I'd used wrapping paper, then maybe. But what real grownup would use notebook paper to wrap a gift?

Mom had put my package on the chair. I looked down at it, and then at Toby, and realized I had a decision to make.

Two years ago I had cut my baby doll Sadie's hair, and it came out bad so I cut it again, and then again so she turned out looking like a Koosh ball. I did it all without the right amount of consideration, but once it was done there was no going back. Before doing something big, you must think about it and then think again, see how the choices feel in your head. Usually one choice will make you feel scared and the other will make you feel sadly disappointed. When you know which of the feelings has the most weight, then you are ready to choose between them. It is not something to be done when you are tired. I lay back down.

Toby curled up against me. I slipped my finger into his hand, and I remembered how when he was little he'd make a fist around my finger and hold on tight, a little hug. I squeezed his fingers around mine, but when I let go his hand flopped back open. Sometimes it was like he wasn't alive. Or like the important parts of him had been sucked out, and replaced by oatmeal.

I sat up again, and just like that the decision made itself. "Look, Toby, you got a present," I said. "I wonder who it's from?" He stared up at me without talking so I pointed. "Look!"

He looked at it, but he didn't move, so I went down to get the package and brought it back up to my bed. I sat next to him and pretended to read my label. "Oh!" I said.

His face didn't change. I put my finger under the words. "It says, To Natalie and Toby, Love Dad." I clapped my hands softly and said, "It's from Dad!"

I guess part of me thought that might be enough to fix him, just like Dad's letters did before. I thought he'd tear at the paper and then find his words again, say, "It's exactly what I always wanted!" and, "Play it with me, Anna, okay?" And we'd play and when Mom got up she'd see us laughing and see Toby talking and have a surprise.

But no. His mouth twitched and then he smiled, but he still didn't talk.

I scooted closer and rested my cheek on top of his

head. At least I made him smile. I had put back the smiling part of him, and now I'd have to find ways to bring back the rest piece by piece: the playing part, the talking part, the laughing part. Toby was empty inside but my lies were filling him back up, returning everything Dad took away.

Toby was crawling around the floor with the Carbot when Mom came into the room. She was wearing old pajamas and her hair looked like someone had gone after it with a leaf blower.

I held out the lipstick. "Look," I said carefully, "a present for you."

She took it and opened the top, *ooh*ed like it was the first time she'd seen it. "Anna, look at this! It's beautiful!"

This was exactly the right thing for her to say. No mention of Cam or his dad, no thanking me. To stop her from saying anything more, I said, "I want breakfast."

Downstairs, Grandpa was sitting at the table, feeding Grammy eggs. Grammy had egg yolk on her chin, which made me not hungry. "Cheerios?" Mom said.

Toby unfolded the Carbot's legs and sat it on his lap while he ate. Watching him, I tried to pretend to myself it really did come from Dad. That him and God loved Toby enough to make that magic happen. I didn't let myself think about the stealing, or what we did to Ms. Pinckney. Sure it was there inside me, but it was in the back. Like the beginning of a stomachache where there's a chance you will later have to throw up, but at the moment even though you aren't happy and know something isn't right, you can focus on other things.

I looked down at my Cheerios, dunked them with my

spoon, and watched them float back up. Cheerios are the kind of food you can eat without tasting, and I usually have no opinion about them. But that morning I could feel them floating through the milk in my belly, swelling and getting soggy. I pushed the bowl away.

There was a hiss from outside, tires on gravel. "Somebody's here," I said.

Mom glanced at Grandpa. "Marlie?" she said.

Grandpa smoothed down his hair. "Could be."

"I should get dressed," Mom said. "Could you get the door, Anna? I'll get my clothes on fast."

So I went to the door. And who it was is my mom's friend Mr. Burns, who wanted me to call him Seth. "Oh, hi," I said.

"Hey, there." He wasn't smiling and I could suddenly feel the Cheerios in my belly. They felt like they were being stirred slow with a big spoon, and I wondered if I was going to be sick. "How are you, Anna?" he said.

"I'm okay," I said. "Pretty good."

"I brought you a little present." He reached into his jacket pocket. What he pulled out was a wrapped-up square. "Open it and take a look!" he said.

Inside the wrapping was paper, all different colors, shiny and unshiny, polka dots and stripes. "Mom told me how you've been wanting to learn origami. I'm pretty much a master now. One time me and my wife, my ex-wife, made about two trillion red, white, and blue origami balls to hang from the ceiling for Fourth of July, and I can put together an origami ball in about five seconds flat."

"Oh," I said, "that's interesting," even though there wasn't anything that I wanted to do less than make an origami ball.

Grandpa came out from the kitchen with Grammy, holding her arm. He smiled when he saw Mr. Burns. "Seth!" he said. "Good to see you."

"Mr. Hanson," Seth said, and they shook hands. "How you doing, Mrs. Hanson?" Seth said.

Grammy smiled at Seth and tilted her head. "I'm afraid I need the little girl's room," she said.

Grandpa rolled his eyes at Seth and smiled. " 'Scuse me," he said. "It's time for Meg's bath."

Toby came crawling out of the kitchen with his Carbot. We both watched him as he wheeled around me in a circle. "So I guess you're here to see my mom," I said.

He looked surprised at this. Also embarrassed. Why? "Is she around?" he said.

If I said no, would he go away? I watched him carefully. "She takes a long time getting dressed," I said. "Maybe an hour, or it could be more. I don't think you want to wait, but I could tell her you were here."

It maybe would've worked except just then, Mom walked into the hall. When she saw Seth, her face went the exact pink of the lipstick I gave her, which I knew was a sign. "Seth!" she said.

I only saw Mom turn pink one time before, and it was when Dad gave her diamond earrings for Christmas. She said, "Josh, you shouldn't be buying me things like this!" But you could tell she was glad that he had.

I looked from Mom to Seth and back to Mom. "Mom?" I said. "I have a stomachache."

It was the truth. But nobody was paying attention. "Hey," Seth said. "Can we talk a minute?"

"Sure, sure! You want to come in the kitchen? I'll put on some coffee." They both walked away.

I followed them, and stood outside the door to the

kitchen. They both looked at me. "Sweetie," Mom said, "could you watch your brother? See he doesn't get into any trouble?" So. I was dismissed. I walked back into the living room, sat on the couch.

When Dad gave Mom the earrings, she wore them every day. When she turned her head they sparkled little beads of light onto the wall. Until there came a day when one of the earrings fell off. We hunted everywhere for it, all of us crawling around and looking under sofas and beds and even inside the dirt in the vacuum cleaner bag. But it was gone.

She still kept the other earring, but it was pointless on its own so it just sat there in a drawer. Until Dad died and I started taking it out on sunny days, watching it make its magic again. I took it outside and watched it change colors, and I thought how this was what love would look like if you could hold it in your hand.

But then, one day, I did a weird thing. I don't really know why. I was just looking at the colors and remembering when there were two, and then suddenly the earring was in my mouth. I ran my tongue against it, bumpy, and then I swallowed and first it stuck, but then it finally went down. Into my stomach.

I'm pretty sure that it's still there now. Sometimes, when I close my eyes, I can still feel it.

30
Natalie

Seth didn't talk as I brewed coffee, so I tried to decide where in my brain to slot the fact that he was here. I poured us cups before the coffee had finished brewing, half cups at double strength. The stop drip on the coffeemaker no longer worked, so the coffee spilled and sizzled on the burner while I poured, hissed when I replaced the pot. "Cream?" I said.

"No, thanks. I've never understood cream in coffee."

"Good, because we don't have any. Don't know why I offered, just instinctual, erroneous politeness." I brought our cups to the table and sat.

He lifted his cup, blew on it, then set it back down and stared into it. "So," he said. "So I should explain why I kind of blew you off last night. Or actually I probably shouldn't, but I feel like I have to."

"Okay," I said, thinking *No, please don't.*

"It's just—you come back and I get this feeling like we can just pick up where we left off. I mean not in that way…" He pressed his palms on the table, not looking at me. "Not even craving the romance or the sex, because I think we had something more than that. You were my best friend, and now I'm trying to reevaluate things and I could use that friendship."

I felt heat rise to my face. "Sure." I tried to smile. "I can definitely give you friendship."

"Just things've been going on in my life, and I'm trying to work them out." He glanced at me, then away. "My work, the end of my marriage, all of it. Having you show up when you did, it just confused me."

I reached for my cup, and the reaching felt awkward; I couldn't move without thinking about every single part of my body. Do my fingers reach before my arms? Simultaneously? Does my thumb fit around the handle or just stick out separately? "Confused you how?" I said.

He slumped back in his seat, looking toward the window. "Oh, crap, I'm sorry. I just wanted to explain why I acted like an asshole over the phone. I really didn't come here to explode all over you."

"I exploded all over you the other night, didn't I?"

"Maybe, but you have a lot more right to explode."

I stretched a slim smile. "Honestly, I'd do anything to hear somebody else's problems. I could use something other than myself to worry about."

"It's not even problems, actually, but I decided to quit my job. Not today, maybe; first I have to figure out what I want to do with the rest of my life. But I got the job because of Stacey's father, and I don't want to ever feel indebted to her." He ran a finger back and forth along the rim of his cup. "So there I was this morning, living in a place that smells like pickles, and circling ads in the newspaper."

"Should I say I'm sorry, or congratulations?"

He smiled. "I guess what I realized is that I felt unaccountably okay about it all. I realized you can make decisions when you're young that can change your life. And then you either waste the rest of your life regretting them, or you find a way to accept that they were just mistakes and let them go."

I listened to the coffeemaker sputtering its last drops into the pot. "That's kind of what I've been struggling with, getting past things I regret."

"Yeah, but you never made decisions for the wrong reasons. You seem like you've chosen things because you know they'll make you happy—and not in a selfish way, in a wise way. You married your soul mate, you do work you like instead of getting caught up in corporate bullshit, you don't worry about money or prestige and all that."

I felt vaguely insulted. "And look how wonderfully it all turned out," I said. Then bit my tongue. Seth watched my face, unspeaking.

"Anyway," I said, "It's great you're reevaluating your life. When everything's flipped upside down, you either reevaluate or you get paralyzed and watch it all collapse around you." I smiled at him, then said, "Which is what I've been doing too, so congrats to us both."

He raised his mug, clinked it against mine. "To us," he said, then, "So what's your reevaluation?"

"Well, I'm going to call tomorrow for an interview with the mortgage company. And I don't know, I might suck."

"You won't suck. I remember you being good at everything."

"You remember me when I was twenty-one," I said. "I really haven't gained any skills since then."

"I sincerely doubt that."

"No, it's actually pretty much true. My crowning achievement was learning how to shave my armpits." I tilted my cup, looked into it. "I've just been so caught up in coping and helping the kids cope that I haven't had room for anything else, but who knows? Maybe all this is going to finally help me find my calling." I gave a self-mocking smile, but I had actually started to believe what I said. For the sake of my kids as much as for myself, I was going to find the life we were meant to be living.

"See? Most people would be just immobilized by what you're going through. But it was one of the things I loved about you, how you had this instinctive sense of what to do. You chose your friends because you liked who they were. You chose *me* because you liked who I was."

I glanced at him, considered saying I'd chosen him because he was so cute, then un-considered it, knowing he might take it as flirtation. Subconsciously, it might even have been flirtation. I remembered the winter we were ten or eleven, both of us singing carols around the town tree. We were friends, at least as much as girls and boys can be in fifth grade, and when he saw me shivering he took off his jacket and put it over my shoulders. Right then, that was the first time I'd ever wanted to kiss a boy.

"I'm real glad we're back in touch," I said, "because I kind of missed you." I hadn't meant to say this, but as I said it I realized it was true. Even when Josh was alive part of me had missed Seth, his friendship, his sense of humor, his periodic kookiness.

"Me too. You were my best friend." He set his hand on mine, then seemed to think better of it and pulled away. But I could feel the echo of it, and the loss of it; it was the same feeling I got when my mother smiled the same smile as always, then went suddenly blank to prove the familiarity was all an illusion.

"And if you don't hate me too much to reinvite me to

Thanksgiving, I'd love to come. I could even bring the frozen turkey that's now staring sadly up at me every time I open my fridge. I have to find some way to get rid of it, because there's no room for anything else."

"Donate it to a food pantry, or feed it to your cat. I ordered fresh, organic, free-range—probably caviar-fed for what I'm paying. You can bring the wine."

"Deal," he said. "Binky will love you."

"I doubt she'll make the association. Last time I saw her she acted like she thought I'd go out of my way to step on her tail."

"She's just jealous. She likes to think she's the only woman in my life, so you'll have to woo her slowly. But if she has any taste, she'll fall in love with you."

I felt the blood rush to my face, and I stood to dump my coffee in the sink so he wouldn't see. I didn't know why I'd be blushing. I guess it was because he'd implied that I'd have time to woo his cat slowly and had, kind of, implied I was now in his life.

Which was completely stupid, but I couldn't stop the sudden fluttering in my chest, flapping wings. And all I could think of were his last words, playing again and again in my head. Words which, albeit, were about his cat. Falling in love with me.

31
Anna

When Seth and Mom went to talk in the kitchen, I came upstairs, grabbed Leopolda, and sat with her. Because, I was getting an idea.

Here is the thing, something I only just realized lying in bed the other night, imagining me, Dad, and Toby playing ball in the same park where he first taught me how to bat. I could see his yellow hair, his favorite blue shirt and jeans. I could see his tallness but I couldn't see his face. And if you could forget a person's face, the most important thing of who they were, it would have to be even easier to forget how much you loved him. So what I understood, seeing how happy Mom was when Seth came to see her, was that she was already forgetting.

In Dad's real letter were his words, the last words he ever would tell us. And I knew I couldn't give Mom the letter. It said how Dad was waiting for us all to be together, and I knew what the words would do to her. But she needed to remember, and this was how I could bring him back, talking to her, the only words he had left to say. If I wanted I could tell her the words one at a time. I could make it last for years. If I wanted I could bring him back, just a few seconds a day, for the rest of my life.

I unfolded the letter, and how I felt was like I might break open, like if I looked down I really might see inside my ribs. I put my hands like I was about to pray, opened them a tiny crack, and then I held my breath and put my hands in front of one eye. This is what I saw:

man
back
pocket
newborn

I sat back and I thought about this, tried to figure out what it meant, what the sentence could be that used the words. Like:

The woMAN reached BACK into her POCKETbook which was big enough to carry a NEWBORN.

Or, *MAN, I wish I had BACK that POCKET Palm Pilot I had when Anna was a NEWBORN.*

But all I could come up with sounded stupid. I had to try again.

So here is what I decided I would do. I'd read one line. If it didn't say something I could tell to Mom, then I'd read one more. And so on.

I put my hands over the top of the note, covering the sentences I already read, then slowly opened them up until I could see the next sentence.

All year I've been remembering when you were pregnant, you keeping the children safe inside you while me, I was on the outside.

The words spoke in my head, in exactly Dad's voice. And hearing them something squeezed inside me so I couldn't breathe. I leaned over the carpet and listened to the sounds, the house creaking, Toby talking to Grandpa and the squeaking of Grammy's sneeze, until the squeezing let go. This was important, I knew. This was the most important thing in the world, so I let him go on.

> And that's how I know you'll all be okay without me. I never would've left if I didn't feel sure that you'll do better once I'm gone.

I threw the letter down, and flopped onto my stomach so I wouldn't have to look at it. I shouldn't have read it. It didn't bring Dad back, it was like him dying all over again. *Without me,* he said, *without me, without me,* and I rubbed my face against the scratchy carpet to make his voice go away.

I knew why Dad thought we'd be better off without him.

And here it is, something I never said to anybody. Something he might have wrote in his letter that I couldn't let anybody else see.

It was three weeks before Dad died, and I heard his door open. It was the first time I heard him leave his room in two days. I waited till the toilet flushed, and then I went out to the hall, and when he opened the door, I smiled.

He looked at me a long while, standing there, and then his lips twitched into something that was not a smile but was trying to be one.

"Hi," I said.

He put his hand on my head. I could feel it there, the

weight of it like a dead bird, and then he walked back in his room and closed the door.

I knocked. "Dad, guess what?"

He didn't answer.

"My molar's loose," I said, "and guess what else?"

Nothing. So I said, "What else is I learned a magic trick with my chemistry set, wanna see? It has to do with invisible writing."

He still didn't answer. I wiggled my tooth with my tongue, and then I walked into the bathroom and kneeled in front of the cabinet. I wanted to check if when Dad was in there peeing, he had remembered to put the heart. But, no.

So I'm trying to explain why, but I know there is no good explanation. I was angry when I shouldn't have been angry. I was angry and I was crying, and what I did is I went to my bedroom and wrote a letter and slipped it under his door. Which made Dad think I'd be happier without him, which made him die. Probably it did. Because this is what I wrote:

Dear Dad,

Sometimes all you care about is your own self. I don't care if you're sad because everybody gets sad! But they totally don't stop listening when their kids have to tell them something important. If there is something important, they want to know.

Like, what if I got hit by a car? You'd just be in your bedroom doing whatever and I could be dead! You'd come out someday and say where's Anna and Mom would say nowhere.

How come you don't play with us when you're

sad? I know you'd feel better if you did. Just try, okay?
And we can see if it works.

Love,
Anna

That is what I wrote to him. And then. It was three
weeks.

I can't think about it anymore.

32
Natalie

"Anna?" I called up the stairs. "What're you doing up there? Seth's carving the turkey!"

No answer. Anna had been hiding in her room all day, and I thought I had some idea why. Last Thanksgiving we'd been here at this same table. I'd made sure to change the seating arrangement: Mom next to Dad rather than at the foot of the table—necessary anyway with her new penchant for dumping full serving bowls of food onto her plate—and Seth across from the seat Josh usually took.

But regardless, holidays were hardest, just like everyone always said; they brought back memories, of course, but they also marked the time: first Thanksgiving, first Christmas, first Valentine's Day without Josh. I'd debated last month whether to even celebrate them. We could go to a movie, play board games, pretend this was just a day. But that would mean admitting our lives would always be less without him. We all needed to see that we could still forge new memories.

I started up the stairs. "Anna Michelle Graham, get down here!"

"I'm coming!" she said, and then a few seconds later she appeared from her room, glared at me, and then brushed past me down the stairs. I followed her into the dining room.

"This all looks amazing," Seth said, reaching for a bottle of wine and a corkscrew.

"Doesn't it?" Marlie said. "I always love how Thanksgiving's such a multicolored meal."

"It means we're eating lots of vitamin A," Dad said, and then he poured himself a glass of wine and lifted it. "Now in Meg's honor, we'll do the little round-the-table thing sappy families like us do on Thanksgiving, and I'll start for Meg, who's incredibly grateful to have you all. And me, right now I'm thankful to have a big stomach." He smiled, then said, "Natalie?"

Anna tilted her water glass, staring dully into it. I reached for her hand, and squeezed it. "My children," I said, "obviously, and also…" I smiled. "First Bank Mortgage for taking a chance on somebody who can't remember the times table without a calculator."

"You got the job?" Seth said.

"You believe it? I guess I impressed them during my interview with my button-pushing skills, and they hired me on the spot. I'm starting on Monday already, which I guess means I have to cancel my weekday storytelling gigs." I shrugged, trying to look more dismissive about it than I actually felt. "Which I'll miss, but this pays approximately a gazillion times more. Hopefully they'll trust me enough after a few weeks to actually give me a mortgage." I turned to Toby. "So okay, Toby, your turn. What're you happy about this year?"

Toby took the Carbot off his lap, and put it on the table. I smiled. "Okay, Toby's thankful for his new favorite toy. How 'bout you, Anna?"

She tilted her glass further.

"Anna? How about, are you grateful for your new friends at school?"

She tilted the glass even further, and suddenly it slipped from her hand, spilling across the table and onto Seth's lap. He jumped up and grabbed for a napkin, wearing a look of comical surprise. "Well now I'm awake," he said.

"Sorry!" Anna said, but I thought I saw a flicker of a smile.

I knew what must be going on. It must seem to her that Seth was trying to take her dad's place. So I didn't chastise her. I just righted her glass, chirped, "No use crying over spilled water!" and then quickly rose to bring a dish towel from the kitchen.

As I handed it to Seth, he raised his eyebrows at me, then said, "Wait, Anna, what's that?" He reached to Anna's ear and procured a quarter, then flipped it over in his palm, one of the inordinately stupid but surefire ways he'd used to cheer me up when we were young. "Cool, how'd you do that? You been noticing any hearing problems lately?"

Anna said nothing, but her whole body stiffened. Toby grinned, then ducked his head against my shoulder, watching as Seth draped the dish towel over his fist, tucked it in the crook between his thumb and index finger, then slipped the coin inside, gulped and made it disappear. "Deee-licious," he said. "Sorry, Anna, finder's keepers."

Toby crawled off my lap to look under the towel. "Do *my* ear. *My* ear!" he said.

I smiled as Seth reached for Toby's ear, then noticed Anna watching me, her fists pressed between her knees. I quickly dropped the smile and reached for the potatoes, and began heaping them on my plate so I wouldn't have to interpret the look on her face.

"Your mom's still got it," Dad said to me. We were playing, of all things, poker. Mom did not, in fact, still have it; the fact she'd ended up with two kings was undoubtedly pure luck. But it was bizarre to me that she could still remember rules for poker at all, when she couldn't even remember the names of the people she was playing with.

"One, two, one, one!" Mom said, stacking the chips. "Who knew I was this good at this game!"

Toby squeezed onto the sofa next to me, and began driving his action figure down my leg to the floor, and then back up again. I wondered again about his obsession with the toy. Maybe there were related toys I could buy him, truck-bots and SUV-bots.

"I'm broke," Marlie said. "Will, can you lend me fifty cents?"

"I'll lend you a fake dollar," Dad said, sliding four chips into her pile.

Toby started folding and unfolding his action figure rhythmically, *click-click, click-click,* then let out a little sob, and held up a broken limb. He looked down at both pieces, holding them in his fists, then suddenly, startlingly, started to cry.

"Oops, we have an injury," Seth said. He reached for the figure. "Luckily, I am a board-certified toy doctor."

Toby snatched the toy away. *"Toby,"* I whispered.

"He doesn't trust me yet, that's okay. Why don't you keep him on bed rest, Toby, and next time I'm here I'll see what I can do."

Toby looked up at me, with pained, watery eyes, and I said, "Well, it's patently obvious that it's past this one's bedtime. Anna might even be asleep already." I lifted him in my arms. "Say good night," I whispered, and he buried his head in my neck.

I climbed the stairs with him tucked against me, inhaling the salt smell of his tears, then set him down by the bathroom. "You get ready and I'll sit with you awhile," I said. He looked up at me mournfully, then entered and closed the door behind him.

I cracked open the children's bedroom door and saw Anna on her top bunk, holding one of her stuffed animals on her chest, the hippo Josh had bought from the hospital gift shop the day she was born. "Baby?" I whispered. She didn't turn to face me.

I stayed watching her silently until Toby emerged from the bathroom. He raised his arms to me and I carried him to the bed, set him down, and helped him change to his pajamas. After tucking him in, I stood. "You want to talk?" I whispered to Anna. Her eyes shifted to me then back to her stuffed animal, and she shook her head. I brushed the hair out of her eyes, kissed her, and then sat on Toby's bed, and stayed there rubbing slow circles on his back until he fell asleep.

Standing, I saw Anna was asleep as well, hunched in the fetal position like she was trying to take up as little room as possible. I pulled the covers over her shoulders, and went out to the hallway.

For a minute I stood listening to the sounds from the living room, the soft cadence of conversation, and then I went to my bedroom to pull Josh's PDA from my nightstand, slipped it into my skirt pocket, and walked down to the living room.

Seth was now standing by the bookshelf, stretching his back and studying the knickknacks Mom had set out years ago, seashells and Bakelite bowls, my school photos.

He lifted a framed photo from the TV and held it toward me. "Who's the pregnant woman with Josh?"

"That's not Josh, it's his dad. And his mom's pregnant with him." I'd put it there first because Josh was in this picture, hidden but there, and because Ken Graham looked so much like Josh, and yet was not him. The only actual photo of Josh that I'd unpacked was on the children's nightstand, so I could avoid it unless I really wanted to look. "His dad died in the Gulf War when he was a teenager."

Josh's mother hardly looked like him at all, so thin and almost sickly-looking. Only her deep-set eyes were Josh's, although looking into them you could tell there was something missing. "And his mom took it hard," I said. "Josh never went into detail, but I think she had clinical depression. And then when Josh told her he was joining the Marines she freaked out, basically told him to get out of her house and not come back. Which he didn't; I think they only talked once a year or so, maybe not even that. I guess she couldn't handle the thought of losing him the way she lost her husband, but I don't know. Who would decide they'd rather never see their son?"

"And then she didn't even come to the funeral," Dad said. "That's when I added her to my list of least favorite people, when she couldn't even be there for the kids."

"Well, seeing as she didn't even care enough to try to meet the kids when Josh was alive, why would she care now?" And then I turned to Seth, raised my chin. "Anyway, Seth? I'm hoping you could help me with the dishes."

They all looked at me quizzically, so I added, "Have you seen how many dishes there are? I'm getting dishpan hands just thinking about it."

"Sure," Seth said, looking toward the kitchen almost

reluctantly. He'd been enjoying himself, I realized. He liked spending time with my parents. Which was both really nice, and somewhat weird.

"I should be going anyway," Marlie said, then looked down at her one remaining poker chip. "Will, I owe you approximately five hundred bucks."

"I'll write up a deferred payment plan." Dad began stacking chips into the carrying case. "Me and Mom better get off to bed. I'd help with the dishes, but..." He shrugged and then winked. "I hate doing dishes."

"I know, it's okay." I kissed Dad, and accepted Marlie's hug. "Have a good night."

We walked into the kitchen, and I turned on the faucet and swirled in a spiral of dish soap, as Seth began bringing glasses to the counter. I stood a moment, letting the steam rise around me, and then I said, "So I didn't actually need your help with the dishes."

"Yeah, I figured that." He picked up a dish towel. "You seemed distracted all through dinner."

I shrugged, thought a minute, then said, "Hey, how'd you like to come somewhere with me and the kids this weekend? I've been thinking we should try and do more 'fun stuff' together."

His face brightened. "Really? Sure, I'd love to. Where were you thinking?"

"Maybe we could drive up to Shasta? Or no, they probably don't let you up this time of year, but maybe we could all drive out to the beach; I've been meaning to take the kids there. It'll be cold, but it should be warmer than here and I always loved the beach in the winter."

"That sounds great. Stacey wasn't an outdoor person—I don't know if she even owned shoes without heels—so I've missed that kind of thing."

"I don't think I even own a pair of shoes *with* heels," I said, then slowly started rolling up my sleeves. "I don't know, Seth. I have to do something to show them we can get past all this crap. Because everything seems so fragile now, the way Anna was, not talking to anybody tonight. And Toby, he hardly cried the first few weeks after Josh died. But now it's almost every day, and I usually have completely no idea why; it's like he's reverted back to his colicky days. We're all in this state of suspension like we're waiting for the next bad thing."

"I guess it's inevitable after you go through hell—you try and steel yourself against whatever's coming next, like that'll protect you."

"I'm not stupid; I realize going to the beach isn't going to fix it. What I need to do is find out what the worst is." I looked up at him, and then I reached into my skirt pocket and pulled out the PDA. "I've read all of it, except Josh's last day. And now I pull this damned thing out every few hours, and I turn it on and then I get completely paralyzed."

"Is that why you asked me to help with dishes? You want me to read the last day?"

"I want to do it myself, but I've tried, I keep trying and it's killing me. So I was just hoping you could maybe be here with me while I look at it. Just having an outside presence to ground me's going to help, I think."

He put his hand on my shoulder, but I shook it off. "Fine, I'm fine," I said. "It's one of those things I have to not think about, just push buttons without letting my brain process what my fingers are doing."

"I'll finish the dishes, okay? And you can sit with the PDA however long until you're ready."

"Thanks, Seth," I said, then brought the PDA to the

table. I sat with it, and kept my eyes on Seth's back as I turned it on and paged through, watching the screen through my peripheral vision. Lists and reminders, car repairs and doctor visits, highlights and lowlights of conversations, Josh's life blurring past in fast motion. Until I got to the last day.

Sunday, August 26: Josh had dressed in the green cotton shirt I'd gotten for his birthday. When he came down for breakfast it was not just on inside out but backward, the tag in front, and I'd teased him and then hooked my finger through it and kissed him on the lips.

I'd made French toast and he'd eaten five pieces, and we'd talked about yesterday's Padres game, an away game against the Phillies. He said he was buying tickets for the December 24 Chargers game as a Christmas present for us all, which of course, turned out to be a lie.

I told him I wasn't feeling well, the beginnings of a head cold that would end up plaguing me through the funeral preparations and then the actual funeral, surrounding me in a mucousy fog that in a way made the whole thing seem unreal and so a little more bearable.

Josh had put away the dishes with Anna's help, and then sat beside me to massage my sinuses. The feel of his callused fingers, both rough and soft, a discussion of whether it was warm enough to take the kids to the park; I'd repeated a dumb joke Toby had told me the night before—something to do with a cow—and he'd laughed. And somehow, slotted in with all of this, must have been his sadness. Because, fourteen hours later, he was dead.

"I can't do this," I said hoarsely.

Seth turned, reaching for a dish towel. "You want me to talk to you while you read it? I was listening to Bruce Springsteen when I signed my divorce papers which I wouldn't exactly recommend for this, but it helps to be distracted."

"I wouldn't be distracted if Bruce Springsteen was actually dancing on my lap. Just, here." I shoved the PDA at Seth. "Could you just tell me if it says anything I should know?" I crossed my arms over my chest, gripping my shoulders.

Seth took the PDA, looking into my eyes, then said softly, "Yeah, okay," and sat across from me at the table. He squared his shoulders, and then looked down at the screen. A minute later he looked up. "There's nothing really here, Nat, nothing bad. I think you could read this."

He handed me the PDA, and my hand shook as I took it. I forced myself to look down at the screen.

- !!!T wrote name!!!
- Nwsp dlvery paid
- Pick up milk—Nothing else
- Park, lunch, played tag
- Nklce ready—Littman's
- Refill Vicodin!
- N—9:30PM

I stared blankly at the list. I'd heard the message from Littman's the week after Josh's death, when I was deleting sympathy calls from the answering machine. I'd gone there on September 8, and been given a gold heart on a chain engraved *JG+NG Forever*, in the tradition of teenage graffiti. My anniversary present, and I'd held it in my palm with the chain dangling, feeling completely numb, then had given it back to them. "Thank you," I'd said, and left.

Now I leaned back in the chair, feeling suddenly

bleary with exhaustion. "I don't remember anything about nine-thirty. Was it something he was planning to do with me?"

"Where were you?"

"I went to sleep early. I felt crappy, so I went to bed right after I put the kids down." I glanced at Seth. "The medical examiner said Josh died around midnight. Look at all these entries—paying the newspaper, reminding himself to get milk—it's like he expected he'd have to know them later. Like he didn't expect there to be no later. It doesn't make sense!"

But it had to make sense, and this is what was running through my mind. That he'd needed something from me that night, had planned on asking me for help, and because I hadn't been there for him he'd suddenly given up. *She cares more about her cold than about me*, he'd thought.

Or what if he'd been planning to warn me at nine-thirty about what he was about to do? What if he'd wanted to say good-bye, maybe even offer explanations? If I'd been awake I could've stayed with him; I could've called the police, tied down his hands, hidden bullets, hacked the gun to pieces; I could've kept him here! Without thinking I threw the PDA across the room, and the battery cover broke open against the wall.

"Dammit!" I said, and then I turned to Seth. "Why? That's all I want to know is why? He could've at least said something to me, he could've left some kind of hint what was going on. I don't get it. I don't get it!"

"Did he seem upset or sadder that day? Or that week?"

"No, not at all! He'd been depressed off and on—I mean deeply depressed to where he could hardly get out of bed. But the last time was more than three weeks before he died."

"Which just goes to show how it's not fair to keep blaming yourself for whatever invisible pain he was going through. It's like blaming yourself when somebody dies of a sudden heart attack. How could you know?"

"Choosing to kill yourself isn't the same as a heart attack. Something must've happened that night that I'm not remembering, Seth. What was I supposed to do at nine-thirty?"

"Maybe he was just writing down the time you fell asleep. I don't know. But it's not going to help you to keep asking yourself the questions if there aren't going to be any answers."

"There *are* answers. There have to be, so how can I stop looking?" I slipped off my chair, crawled to the broken PDA, knelt to it and raised it to my chest. "I hate him, and how screwed up is that of me to hate my dead husband? But he left me here without giving a crap what the questions would do to us, and that's why I have to find the answers. Because I want to stop hating him."

Seth knelt beside me, and seeing him there I suddenly wanted to hit him. Because he was alive, because he wasn't hurting, because he thought he could help me when nothing could help. My hands shaking, I tried to slot the batteries back into the PDA, but they fell through my fingers into my lap, and I threw them across the room. "Damn this!"

Seth took hold of my hands, sandwiched them between his own, and raised them to his lips. "It's okay," he whispered against them, "it's okay, it's okay…" I wrenched my hands away and swiped at his chest, and then I fell against him, let him hold me. Sinking into his shushing sounds until there was nothing else.

33
Natalie

I woke up early the morning after Thanksgiving, and lay there playing over and over again the events of Josh's last day. I'd even written them down last night, the gist of every conversation, trying to remember the expressions on his face. But it had given me nothing. This felt like trying to piece together a crossword with no grid, and only a handful of obscure clues.

I lay in bed with my eyes closed, and tried to remember the little Josh had been willing to tell me about his life. The constant stream of adrenaline; how every time he got behind the wheel he'd find himself searching the Pendleton streets for IEDs; how he'd hear thunder and automatically duck; how when he saw kids sunning on the lawn he'd have to stop himself from checking for a pulse, looking to see if he could save them or should just pull a sheet over their heads and find their families.

It had been hard, I knew that, but there must be something else I was missing. It wasn't just the struggles with his injury, not just his memories from the war, because he'd been in war before. His first tour was during the shock-and-awe days, when he'd seen more bloodshed, more devastation, and had certainly felt more fear. And yes, it had haunted him after returning home. He'd been both repelled by and obsessed with war coverage, in the stunned, frantic way one is with serious illnesses suffered by friends. But after the first weeks he'd settled back into his body, a different person, but a stronger person.

So why had this tour affected him so much more? Those were the answers I'd hoped to find in his PDA, but now that I knew the answers weren't there, how could I come to peace with knowing I'd heard everything Josh had to say?

I was getting ready to make lunch when the doorbell rang.

It was Dan Carson at the door, clutching Cameron's shoulder. He smiled awkwardly at me, and for the first time I noticed a shyness about him, a down-home-on-the-farm sort of attractiveness. Or maybe it was just the way he held his son that appealed to me. I knew the burden he'd taken on. "Hey, there," he said.

"This is a surprise." I stepped away from the door. "Come on in," I said, then called over my shoulder, "Anna, guess who's here!"

"You have a good Thanksgiving?"

How to answer that question? "Sure," I said. "It was fine."

Anna straggled into the upstairs hallway. "Oh!" she said, and she and Cameron stood silently facing each other, glancing at each other and then away again.

"I think…" Anna said, "I think I have something you could help me with."

"Okay," Cameron said, then followed Anna up the stairs.

We watched them until they disappeared around the corner, and then Dan said, "I hope it's not imposing to stop by like this, but I have to tell you something."

I felt a sudden, prickling uneasiness. "What do you mean?"

"Let's sit." He glanced into the living room, then gestured to it. But when he saw I wasn't going anywhere, he ran a hand through his hair nervously, then reached into the inside pocket of his jacket and pulled out a rolled-up newspaper. He held the paper forward and I stared at it, a clammy sweat flushing my face. It was the *Herald*. "No," I said. "What did you do?"

"Just read it. I think you'll be really happy with how the story came out."

I snatched the paper from him, the Lifestyles section. And there it was, the headline: *A Family in Mourning*. I stared at it, stunned, and then I flung it onto the floor. "Are you *kidding*? What gave you the right? I told you no!"

"Just read it, Natalie." He picked it up off the floor, held it to me. "I know how sensitive this all is, it's the same way I felt with my Hillary; you want to make sure everyone understands how special he was, and that's exactly what I kept in mind when I was writing this. Please just take a look."

I tried to remember how much I'd told him. Maybe he hadn't written about Josh's death specifically. Or no, of course he must've, it was the climax to the story, but what if he'd just put it simply, a simple, irrefutable statement: *Josh Graham died on August 26, of a gunshot wound*. Period. And everyone could just assume what they assumed. I brought the paper to the living room, sat with it on the sofa, and started to read.

We see the numbers. Sometimes we hear their names or see their faces. But not often enough do we hear their stories. This is one man's story.

I almost rolled my eyes. It was schlock. Too schlocky for anything other than a tabloid, part war commentary, part tearjerker. Romance and reflection. The truth glossed over into something ridiculously idealistic, a perfect man and his perfect family, destroyed by war. It was our life, yes, but all of it, our sadness, our struggles, had been flattened onto paper so the world could read and think they understood. Anna's and Toby's names in print, the words trying to define who they were, trying to show what they'd been through while not really showing a fraction of their pain.

Natalie said Josh would never have thought of himself as a hero. But you can see the type of man he was by the look in Natalie's eyes when she talks about him, and by the bereavement on his children's faces when they listen to her speak of him.

It was cliché after cliché, and so I started hoping for an accordingly vague and cliché ending, until I read the final paragraph.

Josh was wounded in Fallujah this August trying to save an injured comrade, and tragically lost his life as a result. When asked to give details, Natalie could only shake her head and say, "He was a hero." Indeed, he was.

"No," I said. "What did you do?"
"What's wrong?"
"The ending, you put in how he died!"
"Well, yes. I mean, I had to."
"How could they print this without letting me know? Jesus, what kind of paper are they?"

"I guess...they thought you did know. Can't you see how it's a good thing? Like, a way to honor his memory."

I threw the paper at him. "I can't believe you!" What would happen if someone saw it who knew the truth? What if they called the paper? I'd have to disappear, go with the children to some far-off place, Montana or the Yukon or the Mojave Desert.

I started to pace up and down the living room. "You son of a bitch, I told you not to print this. I told you!"

I strode frenetically from the window to the door and back. "Get them to stop delivering the paper," I said, ridiculously. I didn't recognize my voice, a mix of fear and anger and pleading, so high-pitched it sounded like I was trying to sing. "Call the editor in chief, call whoever, get them to take it out!"

Dan watched me with his mouth open and then, shockingly, his eyes started to fill. "God, I'm sorry, I didn't think...I didn't realize you felt this strongly about it."

I punched the wall. "I told you!"

He shook his head. "I don't know, I guess I thought it might help you; you'll get an outpouring of support from everybody who reads it, and it didn't make sense to me why you wouldn't want people to hear your story. I thought once you saw it you'd realize how it's something to be proud of." His voice actually broke when he said this, like a kid who's been yelled at and can't comprehend the reason why.

"Don't they have fact-checkers at the *Herald*? Why didn't they call me to verify it?" I wanted to throw things at him, maybe to hit him, but I suddenly felt depleted by my terror. My knees buckled and I slid down the wall, onto the floor. "Dan, listen. It wasn't true, what you wrote. That's not how he died."

He blinked quickly. "What?"

"Josh didn't die in the war," I said hoarsely. "He didn't die in Iraq. He killed himself in our garage."

"Oh, hell." Dan knelt on the floor next to me, reached his hand toward my shoulder, and then dropped it. "Oh no, he—what?"

"He had a head injury that affected his memory, and post-traumatic stress; he was suffering from depression and he killed himself."

"A head injury in Iraq?" There was a subtle shift in Dan's expression. "But why didn't you tell me?"

"Because the kids were there! It wasn't exactly something I wanted to discuss with them at that moment. Dammit!" I slammed my fist on the floor. "What's going to happen if the truth comes out? What's going to happen to the kids?"

Dan knelt there, hunched slightly forward like he'd been punched. "Nobody's going to do research on exactly how he died. And most people won't even see the article. On weekdays, probably at least half of them only read sports and the front page."

"Damn you!" I stood, paced again to the window. "Get the hell out of my house."

"Natalie—"

I spun to face him. "Get out!"

He hesitated, then stood and walked toward the door. "I'm sorry, Natalie, honestly. Whatever you want me to do to make it right, I'll do it. Just call me if—"

I slammed the door in his face.

It was when I heard the sound of his truck that I realized he'd left Cameron behind. I opened the door and he looked up at me. Amazingly, he looked almost hopeful. "You forgot your son," I said, my voice lilting, mocking, to prevent myself from exploding—or bursting into tears. "Cameron! Your dad's leaving now."

Dan slapped his hand over his mouth in a parody of shock. Cameron and Anna appeared at the head of the stairs and Cam trotted down and out the door, not looking surprised that his father was already in his truck.

Anna started downstairs. "Want to see what I found?" she said.

"Not just now," I said. "I'll play with you later, okay?" I strode to the living room, grabbed the paper off the floor, and stuffed it into the trash bin.

I sat on the sofa, then stood, then sat again and folded my hands between my knees. Anna stood in the doorway, watching me. "How come you were yelling?" she said.

"No reason. I really shouldn't have yelled." I tried to smile at her. "Everything's fine, but I'm not really in the mood to play now. Why don't you play Clue with your brother?"

"He stinks at it."

"Anna, please. Play Sorry with him then, or Candy Land."

Anna started to say something, but then seemed to think better of it. She stood watching me a minute, then walked silently upstairs.

I sat staring at the fireplace, unseeing. I could hear my heartbeat, a dull thud in my ears. He'd put our story on paper. Or not our story but a fairy tale, written down in the way fairy tales are. Something to read to children at bedtime, something that would become, briefly while being read, more real than the room around us. Once upon a time there was a noble prince who died a noble death and left his family in ashes. A story without a happily-ever-after, without even a true ending. But then again, made-up endings were always more redemptive than truth.

I stood and retrieved the paper from the trash, stared blankly at the pages, and then, without thinking what I was doing, I pulled a pen from my pocket and crossed out everything Dan had written about Josh. I listened to the sounds from upstairs—Dad, the kids, the sound of blocks falling. And as I listened, in the spaces above each line, I wrote the story as I'd known it before the world had turned upside down. Starting with the father whose death had cursed Josh by steering him to join the Marines, the mother who'd sunk into a world shaped by depression and Valium, no room for anything else. I wrote about how despite all Josh had been through, he'd seemed incapable of bitterness or anger, and the way, despite his fear of loss, he'd been able to catapult himself into love.

I opened the paper to a full-page ad, and in the gray spaces wrote about our life, how we'd met, the astonishing frenzied thrill of our first days together. I wrote about the nights we'd stayed up talking until dawn, the almost pained joy in his face the first time he'd held our children, the reunion after his tour in Kuwait, after his tour in Afghanistan, and his first tour in Iraq. I wrote about his depression after returning last year, how he'd struggled to fight the illness with everything he had, and I wrote about how he'd used the cloth heart to show the children he loved them. And then I started to write about his brain injury and the truth of how he'd died, but then stopped. I scribbled out my last paragraph, and put down the pen. Josh hadn't wanted people to know the extent of his injury. So I sure as hell wasn't going to write it down.

I reread the pages. The truth of Josh was in here, and even without the lies about his death it was the story of a hero. I brought the paper up to my bedroom and pulled Josh's US Marines T-shirt out from under my pillow and slipped it on.

This must be one of the stages of grief, one right before, but an infinite number of miles away from, acceptance. I was finding myself wanting to dissect, in a way he'd never allowed me, every facet of his personality and every one of his secrets. And this was the irony and cruelty of this next-to-last stage of grieving, that in a way I loved him more now, more passionately and deeply and thoroughly, than I ever had when he was alive.

34
Anna

Before Cam came, I'd been lying next to Toby and looking up at my bunk, tracing my finger on the diamond shapes of the springs. Toby was napping and holding his Carbot, the broken leg fixed on with duct tape, and lying there I was thinking about how happy it made him, how he took it everywhere, how he smiled more, and listened to me when I talked. Which meant I had done the first step in fixing him, but giving it was like the duct tape on the Carbot's leg. Him and Mom both were held together, but take the tape off and you could see they weren't really fixed.

Last night I was sitting on the top step to hear what Mom might be saying to Seth. And I heard her, I heard her asking the same exact questions I had in me from the beginning. *I don't get it, I don't get it!* she said.

When Mom was writing letters from Dad, I think she felt like he was here, the same way like it felt when he was writing from Iraq, that sad-happy feeling we got when the letters came in the mail. But now the letters were gone, and Dad was gone, and her sadness was back because the question was back. And I was the one who maybe could give her an answer.

So this was my idea, that I would write a note from Dad that said the good parts of what was in the letter hidden in Leopolda. It would give her the answer she needed and also make her remember how much she loved him. I was pretty sure Dad's words could get rid of Seth forever.

But the problem was that A) I didn't remember exactly what Dad's letter said. B) Whenever I tried to write what I remembered it sounded stupid. C) Whenever I thought about reading it again to check, I felt sick. And D) My handwriting looked like my handwriting.

But every day Seth was kicking deeper and deeper into Mom, and I didn't know what else to do. So what I decided was that I'd try again, this time on the computer. It would at least take care of problem D and also help with B, because everything sounds better when it's typed.

Which is why, when Cam came, I pulled Leopolda off my bed. I went with him to Mom's bedroom, where I showed him Leopolda. "Look."

He raised his eyebrows, an *Are you mental?* look. "A cow?"

"She's a hippo," I said, and then I felt my face go hot, a tightness in my throat. "This is important, okay?" I unzipped Leopolda's dress, and took out the letter.

He reached forward, but I snatched it away. "What is it?" he said.

"It's…something my dad wrote, right before he died. And it's the only part of him I have left."

"He wrote it in Iraq?"

I didn't look at him. "Yes, in Iraq. He was holding it when he died, and it maybe has a secret."

"It touched a dead person?"

"Yes, okay? It's not gonna hurt you. It's not like you can catch being shot."

Cam stared at the letter. He looked a little sick, and part of me wanted to hit him. "What's it say?"

"I didn't read most of it. Because there might be stuff he didn't want me to know."

"Like what?"

"Like...why he died."

Cam stuck out his lips, thinking, then said, "I thought he died in the war."

"Okay, okay—look. D'you think I should tell my mom about it?"

"She doesn't know? You mean she never saw it?"

I watched him, shook my head. Cam let out a breath through his teeth. "How come you didn't show it to her?"

"Because. I don't know. Because it says Dad wants her in heaven with him."

"It says he wants her to die?"

"Not exactly those words," I said, "but if my mom read it she'd probably think that's what he wanted. And I don't know what she'd do."

"So what? It's not like your dad could kill her by just saying he wants her in heaven."

I stuffed the letter back in Leopolda. "You don't understand anything."

"I think you should show her," Cam said. "I showed my dad the letter my mom gave me."

"Your letter's completely different. Just forget it, okay? Forget I told you anything."

He thought a minute, and then he said, "You thought if she read it, she'd want to make herself die."

I felt suddenly on fire, like all my skin was scraped over gravel and bleeding. "Just look," I said. "I have an idea, okay? I want you to help me write something, and I want it to sound like it came from my dad. Whenever I try and write it, it sounds stupid, but I think you're a better writer than me."

"Who're you writing it for?" he said, and then he looked at me. "Your mom?"

"And my brother." I turned on Mom's computer, and sat at her desk. "There's stuff in my dad's letter that I think would help them, and I have to find a way to let them know. And plus, listen, you know that guy Seth I told you about? I think he's in love with my mom."

"Seriously?"

"And he *can't* love her, because she's still married."

Cam watched me but he didn't say anything, probably thinking marriage to a dead person didn't count.

"And I hate him; he's all trying to be my friend, but it's not because he likes me, that's obvious. He'd be nice to me even if he hated me."

"So what, you're going to give your mom a letter from your dead dad, to say he'll haunt her or something if she goes out with him?"

"No! She just has to stop being angry at my dad and remember how much they loved each other."

Cam squeezed in next to me, on the chair. "What's she going to think, that he just dropped out of the sky to bring it to her?"

"I'm not going to say he wrote it after he was dead. I'll make it something he wrote before, that we just didn't find until now." I typed Dad's last line into the computer, the words I'd been hearing in my head ever since I read them: *I never would've left if I didn't feel sure that you'll do better once I'm gone.* And then I turned to look at Cam. "Here's what my dad wrote that I want to tell her, and I just need something to say after it."

"How 'bout, 'If you really think this is from me, you are dumb.'"

I hit him with my elbow, and he said, "Hey!" But then he leaned on the desk, his chin in his hands and said, "Write this. Write, 'I wish I could've said good-bye to you in person, but I hope you understand why I decided this is best.'"

I looked sideways at him. "That's from the letter your mom wrote."

"I know. But it's a good sentence."

I typed it in, and then I thought a minute. "What was the last thing in her letter? About her adoring you?"

"It doesn't work. Because it talks about her being sick."

"My dad was sick," I said.

"What do you mean?"

"Just tell me. I'll type it and then I can see how it looks."

He looked at the computer, then shoved his fists under his arms and looked down at his lap. And then he told me the line and I typed it in: *Please remember that even when it might not've felt that way, when I was too caught up in my own mind and then my own sickness and fear, I have adored you.*

I blinked quickly, then smiled and typed, *I'm sorry I can't tell you why I died, because there really is no reason. I just couldn't live anymore, but please don't hate me for that. I need you to keep loving me. Love, Josh.*

We both read over the note. "It's pretty good," I said. And it was. It was pretty much perfect. "Now I just have to decide where to put it."

Cam tilted his head. "Does she have a secret place?"

I looked at him funny. "What do you mean?"

"Everybody has one. Like I have the bottom of my

mom's jewelry box, and my mom had under her bed where she kept tampons, and my dad has this little bench in his bathroom where you lift the seat and it has magazines of women's boobs."

I widened my eyes, imagining Cam's dad looking at pictures of boobs. It must be a long time since he saw real boobs. The pictures must remind him of his wife. "I don't know if she has one," I said.

"Want to look? It's probably in her bedroom."

But then I heard Mom. "Cameron! Your dad's leaving now."

Cam shrugged. "Next time," he said.

It totally made sense. Mom put letters in our secret place, so that we'd think they came from Dad. And I could do the same thing.

Before Cam came, I thought I was going to just give the note to Mom, maybe tell her I found it in one of the boxes we hadn't unpacked. She'd think Dad must've put it somewhere before he died, that we must've packed it without realizing. But this could work ten million times better. I could make it into a real letter from heaven.

Did Mom really believe in heaven? If she did then how could she start liking Seth, knowing Dad could see? So maybe she didn't really believe, but I could change that. This could be the first note I left, but if it didn't make Seth go away, I could figure out another one and another one until it did. It would prove there really was a heaven, that Dad really was watching down, and that he saw her with Seth. That he was probably crying.

I folded the letter careful so it would fit inside Leopolda, and gave Cam a little smile. "Next time," I said.

35
Natalie

The day of our beach trip, Seth showed up at the door wearing a cotton shirt with rolled-up sleeves, and faded jeans with a ruggedly appealing tear in the thigh. I looked at the skin behind the tear. Part of me wanted to touch it.

Instead, I gestured up at the gray sky and made a face. "Figures."

"It's supposed to clear up and get into the low sixties. This is what you call good driving weather." He tilted his head, studying my face. "You look good, Natalie."

The last time he'd seen me, I'd been huddled on the floor yelling at the universe. So what he actually meant was that I looked better than crap, not that I looked good. "I'm okay," I said. "The kids're upstairs, presumably packing up beach toys. But from how much time it's taking, I'm guessing they're packing half their closet. Is it drizzling out there? Come on in."

"Thanks." He scraped his feet on the mat, then touched the duct tape covering the crack in the window. "You want help with this? It looks like a standard size, so I could pick up a pane and install it next time I'm here."

"You know how to fix windows?"

"I'm a handy guy," he said, then set his forearm against the pane and touched his finger at the spot the window ended. "First knuckle," he said.

"Um," I said, "should I really trust someone to fix the window if they use body parts to measure it?"

Seth smiled. "That's called ingenuity. I can also use gum to actually fix the window in place, and the gum wrappers to repair your electrical wiring."

"Very MacGyver-ish of you." He followed me into the living room. "Hey," I said, trying to sound nonchalant, "you don't read the *Herald*, do you?"

"Oh." He gave me a crooked smile, then said, "Yeah, I saw it."

"Right. Probably everybody in the world saw it." I walked toward the window and then turned to him. "I didn't know about the article. The guy who wrote it didn't even tell me he was going to publish it, can you believe that? Apparently you don't need permission to screw with someone's life."

Seth raised his eyebrows. "It was a nice story, no? I mean, it sounded like it was written by an adolescent on quaaludes, but it didn't say anything too inappropriate."

"That's not the point. I already got three calls from people in town I haven't seen since I was a kid, and what if somebody gets curious and tries to find out more about how Josh died? It's not something I especially want strangers to know."

"Yeah, I noticed it didn't exactly say what happened."

"It told a complete lie about what happened. Because I didn't tell this guy anything, and he was apparently too lazy to look it up himself. I really don't want somebody asking my kids about it."

"I doubt people are going to be that insensitive."

"Maybe not." But I'd have to find a way to talk to the kids, I knew that, even if they still weren't ready to talk about it. I'd filled out an intake form for the therapist Toby would be seeing in two weeks, telling her as much as I could bear to about the situation. Maybe she'd be able to help us work through this where our family counselor at Pendleton had failed. Maybe she'd have some magical ability to make okay this thing that was so unequivocally not okay.

"I'm going up to check on the kids," I said. "They could've woven their own beach mats in the amount of time it's taken them."

It was drizzling as we started our drive, but by the time we got through the mountains the rain had cleared, the sky tufted with latherlike clouds. Both kids had fallen asleep, so Seth and I spent the rest of the drive talking about old times. And for the first time ever I found myself wondering what might've happened if I'd never met Josh. Insane to even let my mind go there, I knew that. For sure Seth and I would've broken up anyway—or if not, we'd probably be in one of those marriages where we pecked each other hello and good-bye, talked only about our children, and made love every other Sunday. Probably.

The kids had insisted on bringing their bathing suits, despite my warnings about the toe-freezing properties of Northern California ocean water, and in the parking lot they changed in the car while Seth and I looked out over the dunes, hunched against the brisk wind. He and I had been to Little River State Beach before. It was the month before we were leaving for college; we'd come out in the late afternoon and lit a bonfire and watched the sun set, then had stayed up all night, sometimes talking, sometimes kissing, sometimes just sitting with our arms around our knees and listening to the ocean. "I wish..." he'd said at one point, but he didn't finish. And I didn't need him to. We hadn't spoken about it, but we'd both known that would probably be our last summer together.

Now we followed the kids down onto the beach. The sand was littered with seaweed and limbs of driftwood, deserted except for an old man walking a dog that looked more like a powder puff with ears.

"Anna, look," Seth said. "Playground equipment." And then he handed me a Frisbee and towels, and jogged down the beach. He bent to a pile of driftwood and started pulling a large log sideways. "Could I have some help here?" he called.

I smiled at the kids, took Toby's hand, and walked toward him. Seth nodded at a rock. "Could you flip that so the crook's facing up?"

"What're you doing?" Anna said. But as soon as the words left her mouth her face seemed to all at once shut down, like she was disgusted at herself for admitting any interest.

"You ever play on a seesaw?" Seth said.

Her eyes dropped and she shrugged. "I don't think so."

"That's mainly because of eight-year-old boys who got a kick out of using it to knock the wind out of other eight-year-old boys."

"A whole generation is missing out," I said, digging my fingers in the sand to flip the rock on its side. Anna and Toby watched, both with their hands tucked up into their sleeves, Toby wearing a tentative smile. I bent to help Seth drag the driftwood over to the rock, then whispered,

"Wait," and turned to Anna and Toby. "I think we need some help," I said. "This thing's huge."

Anna and Toby dutifully traipsed over to us. I counted three, and we lifted the log to nestle in the shallow crook, then pushed it until it was evenly balanced.

"What's it do?" Anna said.

Seth gave the high end of the driftwood a test push, then smiled at it approvingly. "It's like one of those two-person swings, except better. Try pushing on the other end."

Anna reached for the opposite end, and she and Seth tottered the board back and forth a minute, before Anna said, "I get it, and it's kind of stupid."

"Nice try," I said. "You're just chicken."

"We kind of need you, Anna," Seth said, "or this thing's not moving anywhere. I think if you take your mom on your end, and I take Toby, we'll be more or less balanced."

I straddled the driftwood and reached for Anna's hand. "You coming?"

She did a little eye roll, but then climbed onto the board.

Seth swung a leg over the high end and then lifted Toby to sit in front of him. "Okay, we're set!"

I tried to push off, but the board went nowhere. I pushed harder—still nothing.

Seth laughed and tried bouncing in his seat, and the driftwood creaked but didn't move.

"Wow, this is fun," Anna said, getting off.

Still, my end stayed on the ground. Seth met my eye, grinning. "You're too fat."

"I'd slam you if my son wasn't on there with you." I stepped off and eased them down.

"You think I would've teased you if I didn't know Toby was protecting me?"

"Gosh, I'm so glad we're friends."

"Anyway, Toby thinks whoever came up with this seesaw idea is an idiot, and he wants to play Frisbee instead." Seth reached for the Frisbee I'd dropped by the pile of driftwood, then jogged down the beach. "Anna, catch!" he called, throwing it toward her, and I felt a sudden pang at his attempts to woo a girl who so obviously wasn't going to let herself be wooed.

The Frisbee landed at Anna's feet, and she picked it up, looked at it, then said, "I'm not really in the mood." She handed it to me, then walked out to the shoreline and I watched her, her big white sneakers and the bulky sweater she wore over her bathing suit making her look so impossibly thin.

I gave Seth an apologetic look and he said, "It's okay. Isn't she going to hate any man who's not her dad? After a while she'll realize I'm not a bad guy." He dug a line in the sand and then another line perpendicular. "I hope."

I wanted to tell Seth about the haunted look I saw sometimes in Anna's face and the sense I'd gotten that she blamed herself for his death, but instead I said, "I'm scared she doesn't like herself much either."

Seth nodded slowly. "That's the age you're sure nobody else in the world is as bad as you."

"Are you saying you've grown out of that?"

"You saying you still feel like you're the worst person in the world?"

I smiled. "Sometimes. Half the time I don't know what I'm doing."

"Of course you don't. Nobody knows what they're doing half the time, under the best circumstances. All's you can do is muddle through until you come to the few things you can fix."

"I don't think there's anything I can fix," I said. "I'm not old enough for this, Seth. I used to think I was an adult, but now I'm pretty sure I'm not."

Suddenly Anna yelped as a wave licked around her knees, and Seth said, "Whoa!" and grabbed my hand to pull me higher up the shoreline.

I tried to pull away, but Seth held my hand tighter, wrapping his other hand around it. I stared down at our joined hands, then quickly twisted away. "So let's play Frisbee."

Seth glanced at me, and then strode toward Anna. He stood a minute talking to her, and I found myself unsuccessfully straining to hear what they said. After a minute she shrugged and shook her head, and he touched her shoulder tentatively, then walked back higher on the dunes.

I arched my eyebrows at him, but he just raised his hands to me. So I threw him the Frisbee; the wind carried it yards away, but he took a running jump and caught it, hooting triumphantly. And there was something about his easy athleticism and childish elation that got to me, about the happiness in his face as we tossed the Frisbee back and forth, Toby running between us and trying to intercept it, while Anna stood alone looking out at the ocean. Because I worried that no matter what strides I made to piece our family back together, no matter how whole we looked, we would still always be broken.

36
Anna

Here is what happens in a new school. You walk in the classroom and you feel alone, everyone else in groups. You are surrounded by a bubble of empty space, miles all around, and people look in and whisper about you but you're too far away to hear. But then, suddenly, for no reason that you can understand, there is a hole. You walk through and listen to them talk and try to understand their language. And slowly your insides settle down. You find your place. This is how it usually works.

But at Bidwell, no. Maybe in the first week there was a hole, but Cam walked in and then it closed behind him. The two of us stood there in the bubble, together but not really together, watching out. Some days I was glad to have someone in with me, but then he would say something or do something weird, and I'd realize it would be better to be alone.

But then came the day Cam was out away and I was alone. And I realized I was wrong and that I wanted him to come back. He had flew the night before with his dad to San Clemente, which was funny because that was the town right next to Pendleton where I used to live. I'd thought about asking him to go back to my home to see who lived in my room, or to go back to my school to ask if they still remembered who I was. But what I told him instead was to get an ice cream at Custard King on California Ave., to sit at the table in the corner by the window and look on the table for an X carved in the wood.

Dad had took me and Toby there right before he left for Iraq. He carved on the table with his army knife, and he told us he'd always be around, like the X, even when we couldn't see him. Which had helped a little, and now I needed to know if it was still there.

I told about this all to Cam, and he promised me he'd look. So this is what I thought about the whole morning he was away. It was thinking about it that kept me okay without him, wondering if he was seeing the X *now*, or *now*. If he was touching it while Gary laughed at me for not being able to climb the rope at gym, if he was sitting in my dad's Custard King chair while I was eating lunch alone.

That morning was the worst time I ever had, being at school and knowing Cam was in the last place I had ever been happy. Seeing the X Dad carved to show us he'd always be around, when he'd never actually be around again. And knowing Mom had already forgot he even existed.

Because I saw them holding hands. I saw them holding hands at the beach, and all through the ride back home I tried to figure out what to do. More than anything I wanted to give Mom the letter that me and Cam had wrote, and I didn't know if I could wait till Cam came back and we found a place to hide it. It could be a mistake to give the letter in person. Since she'd pretended to write letters from Dad, she might know right away I was doing the same thing.

But they were holding hands. I was running out of time.

37
Natalie

In the mail was a letter from the Department of Defense. A letter that said nothing.

Ms. Graham,

This is in response to your letter of November 17, regarding Marine Staff Sergeant Joshua Phillip Graham. Unfortunately, because the case is still under investigation, we will not be able to provide details. We do, however, hope to reach a final decision on your eligibility within the month.

We, at the Department of Defense, extend our deepest sympathies for your loss.

Sincerely,
John Harrington
Benefits Officer
Division of Commissioned Personnel

I crushed the envelope in my fist. What did they mean the case was under investigation? It had been three months! They'd reviewed his records, they knew how badly he'd been hurt, so how could there still be outstanding questions?

Should I hire a lawyer? I couldn't afford one! I needed to talk to someone who'd know what might be going on, who might understand the convoluted policy on benefits following suicide. So up in my bedroom I dialed Nick's number. And got their machine.

"Nick, it's Natalie, and I really need to talk to you because I don't know who else to call. It's just I still haven't gotten our benefits money, and the little bit of information I found on what's supposed to happen is impossible to decipher."

I looked down at the letter, then threw it across my desk. "So I just want to talk to you, find out if there could be something going on with the benefits that I don't know about. The DoD mentioned an investigation, but what the hell could they still have to investigate when they know everything Josh went through? Please, if there's things you're not telling me, for the kids' sake I need to know what they are." And then, in a fit of irrelevant politeness, I said, "I miss you and I hope you guys're doing well." Then, hung up.

I stood a minute with my hand on the receiver, then turned on the computer and began to search for information on veteran suicides. A hundred-twenty vets a week killed themselves, over seventeen a day. I started jotting down names of survivors, contacts who might've fought the same battle and won, and could maybe tell me how long this was supposed to take. But as I searched through the articles, I found myself starting to read the soldiers' stories.

I'd done research when Josh had first returned from Iraq, on TBIs and post-traumatic stress, but always from a textbook stance, looking for direction on how I could best help him. But now sitting at the computer I read all the things Josh had conspicuously left out of his letters, the things he hadn't told me when he returned home.

I read blogs and message boards and wrote it all down, the conversations Josh and I should've had. As I wrote I felt the heaviness draining out of me and onto the paper, and by the time I finally turned off the computer, I realized that this was the next book I wanted to write. The book I had to write.

By mid-morning Sunday I had a partial outline. By lunchtime I had a title: *The Other War*. And after lunch I wrote an e-mail to Victoria, my literary agent, and I hit the send button feeling a sense of something close to panic.

Maybe I was fooling myself and this was crap, but it didn't feel like crap. I knew it wouldn't fully give me the answers I needed, but it would at least bring me closer to the truth. And I know this seems crazy, but I actually thought I could feel Josh as I read over the words I'd written. I sensed him smiling, and thinking, *Yes.*

"Here's the list of extensions," Rosalyn said. "Press pound to transfer and then the number, announce the caller and press pound again. It gets busy around lunchtime, so you'll have to keep on your toes."

Rosalyn was one of those people you'd have to say was of "indeterminate age." She had brown hair with gray roots and wore makeup in the wrong shades, like a face in a coloring book crayoned by a young child: burnt umberish cheeks and eggplant-ish lips and cornflower blue-ish eye shadow. She smiled at me and handed me a folder of things to copy, then squeezed my shoulder. "It's okay if you need to bring your kids here after school," she said.

"Long as they don't get in the way. People do it all the time when they can't get a sitter."

I stared at her. And, suddenly, I understood. Rosalyn read the *Herald*.

Since Friday I'd been waiting for the phone or doorbell to ring. For some busybody crone who'd read the article and had nothing better to do, to tell me she'd looked up Josh's records, found out about the suicide, and was planning to tell local news stations or write about it in an editorial. But no one had come forward, and I was beginning to believe we might have magically escaped inevitability.

"Thanks," I told her. "My parents are going to watch my daughter when she gets home at four, and I was going to have them pick my son up earlier too. But he gets awfully homesick." Toby's face, after I'd told him I wouldn't be there when he got home, had been almost enough to make me pick up the phone and cancel the job, screw the fifteen dollars an hour. "And it might be nice for him to get a picture of where I'm working," I said.

"Absolutely!" Rosalyn said, and she smiled at me with her eggplant-ish mouth. "Jackie brought cookies today, so we'll be sure to save some. Snickerdoodles, and according to her they're"—she made quote marks with her fingers—"the bomb."

Bless Rosalyn. I wanted to hug her. Working, I thought, was not so bad after all.

My only business suit was something I'd picked up at a used clothing store the year I'd graduated college, black skirt and jacket, both too big and not me at all. But almost everyone else in this office was wearing jeans, so after an hour of high-heeled discomfort, I took off my shoes and jacket and traipsed barefoot from phone to copier and back. The work was mindlessly difficult; each page was, ridiculously, the length of two and a half letter-size pages, and so had to be copied on three sheets and then stapled. Each was topped by photos of homes whose prospective owners had probably never had to make their own copies, but I liked that, the feeling I was helping them move into their perfect lives. The work distracted me from thinking about everything I couldn't stand to think about, and I was good at it; after an hour's worth of panic at dropped calls and paper jams, I got the hang of it all and the movements started feeling almost like a choreographed dance.

At noon, Rosalyn took over phone duties so I could pick Toby up from school. He'd been expecting my dad, and when he saw my car the happiness in him wasn't just in his face but in his entire body. He ran to me and wrapped me in a hug, like he hadn't seen me for days.

I spent the afternoon stuffing envelopes, speaking to Toby in low tones, letting him unpeel and stick address labels and stamps in crooked but approximately correct spots. We had a constant parade of visitors, rubbing Toby's head, commenting on his diligence, cracking jokes about child labor laws. "He really is a sweetheart," Rosalyn said.

A sweetheart. *Yes,* I thought, watching him press the moistened envelopes closed, feeling huge with pride. *My boy is a sweetheart.*

The fulfillment of their adoration lasted me through the drive home, Toby in the backseat silently playing with the multicolored paperclips someone had given him, stringing them into a chain and holding them up periodically for me to admire. It lasted through a stop at the Quik Mart for a pint of celebratory Chunky Monkey, lasted until I parked the car in the driveway, and waved hello to

Anna and my parents. But then I opened the mailbox and the fulfillment was sucked out of me, a balloon filled with nothing but air.

Because the mailbox was full, almost to the top, with letters.

38
Anna

When Mom walked up the driveway she was wearing her, what Dad used to call, pre-spontaneous-combustion face. What he meant was, she was mad. She went into the kitchen, like always, and we followed her for our cocoa. But she turned to us still looking like pre-spontaneous combustion, and told us to go play in our room.

Well. This made me a little mad too. But Mom was not in a mood to accept the word no, so me and Toby went to the bedroom. Toby sat on his bed with his Carbot, and I sat next to him and flopped backward.

Could I give Mom the letter now? Would her angriness make her angry at Dad?

I could hear her voice from her bedroom, yelling. I glanced at Toby, and then I went into the hall to listen.

"Did the *Herald* tell them our address? I mean for fucksake, Dan! I have children! What if somebody reads about Anna, realizes how vulnerable she has to be and decides she'd been dropped from heaven for their own personal enjoyment? Don't you ever watch TV? Don't you read newspapers? You tell them that if they tell one more person our address I'm going to have you arrested."

She'd said the f-word, and Mom never said the f-word. I couldn't show her the letter now. The way she sounded, she'd just tear it into pieces. Why did she feel bad having our story in the paper? Cam had told me his dad was writing about us. It seemed weird to me; I didn't get why anybody'd want to find out about us like we were the president, but Cam said he'd been written about too. Which shows that people will read about anything. I wondered how many people now knew who I was. It made me feel kind of proud.

She crashed the phone down, and then everything was quiet. I played with the top of the stair carpet which was flapping loose, kicked it up and back, up and back, and then I knocked soft on Mom's bedroom door, then opened it. Mom was on her bed, just lying there. She had her hands over her face. And she wasn't completely crying, but I could tell she wasn't completely not crying either. I watched her a minute and then I said, "Mom?"

She glanced fast up at me. "Anna," she said, then sat straighter on her bed.

"You okay?"

"Sure! I'm okay, just tired." She held out her hand to me, and I went to sit next to her. I looked up in her face, and then I hugged her with my cheek against her shoulder. She turned and I put my head against her boobs so I could hear her heart.

"Maybe we could do something good this weekend," I said. "Something fun like...go back to San Clemente."

"You're homesick, huh?" She smoothed her hand down my hair. "You know, Seth's coming this weekend to fix that window Toby broke, so maybe he'll show you what to do with that origami paper he gave you. That'd be fun."

Seth. I made a face into her boobs, then pulled away. "Could I call Madison?" I said. All day, thinking about Cam in San Clemente, I'd been missing her.

"You haven't heard from her in a while, huh?"

I shook my head a little, suddenly feeling like I might cry. Mom patted my back. "Go on," she said.

Madison had not kept up her promise to write me every day. In fact, she wrote every day for a week, but then nothing. I still wrote to her, but this is the thing that happens with writing every day: you run out of information. In the beginning the pages could hardly fit in the envelope, there were so many things. But then, the letters started getting shorter. And then shorter. My last letter:

Dear Madison,

Today we had a math test. We're doing fractions and I still hate math, so I almost definitely failed. But we also had a spelling test and I got everything right except "neighbor." So, I am doing medium.

How are you doing in school? Do you still hate math too? Do you understand fractions? Write back to let me know.

Love,
Anna

In the kitchen I dialed, and even pressing the buttons made me homesick. I had dialed that same number so many times.

"Anna!" It was Madison's mom. "You know I was just thinking about you? At the store this morning I bought a bag of tortilla chips out of habit, because I keep forgetting you're not here. Maybe I'll ship them to you."

I felt a sharp ache of missing Mrs. Hollis. She used to make fresh salsa just for me and my tortilla chips. "So how're you doing out there?" she said. "How is everybody?"

How could I answer that? "We're good," I said. "Is Madison there?"

"She sure is. Just a sec."

I sat at the table. I felt like somebody was wringing out my stomach. I wondered if Mrs. Hollis really would send the tortilla chips, since she and Madison didn't like them. I imagined how it would be to get them in the mail, how I'd hold the bag knowing it used to be in their kitchen, knowing somewhere on the bag were Mrs. Hollis's invisible fingerprints. I'd never eat them.

"Hi," Madison said.

I smiled wide. "Hi." She still sounded exactly the same. It's funny how there's trillions of people in the world and all of them have a one-of-a-kind sound, and all it takes is one word for you to recognize the people that are yours. I tried to think what else to say. But nothing came. "How are you?" I said.

"Okay, how're you?"

"I'm okay." Still nothing. I closed my eyes and imagined where she was sitting, in her blue bedroom, on her blue flowered bedspread, talking into her yellow cordless phone. "So, did you get my letter from Friday?"

"Yeah, did you get mine?"

What letter? Did she mean the one from weeks ago? Or did something maybe get lost in the mail? "You mean the one you sent where you were talking about your sunburn?"

"Yeah."

"Oh. Yeah, I got it." I hesitated. "So how's your sunburn?"

"It's better now."

"Okay. Well, that's good."

"Could you hold on a sec? Call waiting."

There was a click. "Okay," I said to nobody.

A minute later, she came back. "Anna? Sorry, it's Julie. Could I call you back?"

Julie Hunt. Julie was funny and nice and pretty, and always knew the right thing to say. It was impossible to hate Julie, but I did hate her. I thought about all my people, still there, going on the same without me like I never existed. I pictured them all in class, and in art and music and gym and recess, and having sleepovers and laughing with new secrets, and I hated them all.

After hanging up I sat on the floor in the kitchen and waited, in case Madison was planning to call back as soon as she was done with Julie. I sat there. And I sat there. And then I got up and went to my bedroom.

This is how much I liked Madison on a scale of one to ten: minus infinity. I was never going to write to her or call her again. If she called back, then fine, maybe I'd talk to her, but not because I needed to. Just because it would be rude to tell her how I had better things to do. From now on, me and Madison were officially divorced.

It wasn't fair that some kids' lives were perfect, like Madison's and Julie's, and some, like Toby's and Cam's and mine and cancer babies and African babies were crazy bad. I thought if I still believed in God, up there deciding and pointing and saying you and you and you, I wouldn't be able to take it.

I reached for Leopolda, unzipped her and took out the letter me and Cam had wrote from Dad. Every morning and every night I read it, and now it almost felt like it was really his, like his words were talking just to me. I sat with it and read it once and then again. And then I kissed the letter, put it back in Leopolda, and lay back down with Dad's voice still in my head.

39
Natalie

Money. It leads directly to reckless greed. This is how it starts; you are broke and your child needs a good therapist you can't afford, and whatever morals you once had go out the window.

I felt like a prostitute. The article was prostituting me, and lines Dan had included about our lack of income and the necessary move back to my parents' home were my garter belt and breast implants. By the end of the week we'd gotten thirty-two letters, and more than half had come with offerings: a gift certificate to Toys "R" Us, a subscription to Fruit-of-the-Month club, an offer from a financial planner for a free consultation.

And there was money. Of course there was. A person reads something that tears them apart, and sending money is the only way they can think to stitch themselves back together. A card with a five-dollar bill from "Ashley age 7," with a note that said, cryptically, "This is for shoes." A thousand-dollar check from "The estate of Harry Rees," with a Bible quote:

Not only so, but we also rejoice in our sufferings, because we
know that suffering produces perseverance; perseverance,
character, and character, Hope.

I'd gotten a sympathy card with a hundred-dollar bill
tucked inside and a letter blessing me and my family,
signed by C.M., who said she'd lost her husband and two
children a year back. The letter had no return address and
I thought about this all night, the goodness of a woman
who, in the midst of her grief, would anonymously send a
hundred dollars to a stranger.

That goodness made me resolve to send it all back and
donate the hundred dollars, which I didn't know how to
send back, to a third-world country. I even went so far as
to reseal the envelopes and mark them *Return to Sender.*
But then I sat in the kitchen with the envelopes on the
table, and I stared at them. Then opened them. The bills I
put in my wallet, but the checks I decided I would not
cash, because to bring them to the bank, to look a teller in
the eye and ask her to put them in my savings account,
would make me too much of an active participant in my
own corruption. This was where I arbitrarily set the limits
of my morality.

Until the next day. When I got my credit card bill.
Along with the Harry Rees check for a thousand dollars,
and I actually put the two side by side and looked at them
all afternoon: the bill, the check, the bill, the check. And
then I went to the bank.

How can you spend your whole life thinking you're
one sort of person and then find out you're another sort
altogether? I used to like myself. I used to think if I met
myself on the street I'd want to be friends, but it's easy to
be good when you have everything. A long time ago I'd

pulled a skin over the selfishness, to make myself look presentable to the outside world. So long ago that I'd even started to believe it myself, but now the skin had scraped loose and here it was, the core of me, my true self. When you lose your husband, your money, your home, your sanity, that's when you learn who you really are.

And so when Dan called me back with effusive apologies for giving the *Herald* our address, I-wasn't-thinking's and I-only-meant-to's, I told him it was okay, he was forgiven. And I asked if it might be possible for the *Herald* to tell any additional callers that letters and gifts should be sent to them, and then forwarded to me. I could hear the smirk in his voice when he said, "Of course." And there it was. I was accepting money through my pimp.

And then, a week after the article came out, I got a letter from Nick. I brought it into my bedroom and sat with it a long while before breaking the seal.

Dear Natalie,

We just want to make sure you know that we understand. Nobody here blames you for not talking about the suicide. And everyone loved Josh, so they won't do anything to dishonor his name.

I also wanted to tell you that I got your phone message, and I'm working with Captain Meyers to figure out what the hell is going on with your benefits. You're right that there's no way they should be holding things up so long, and I promise I'll do whatever I have to, to make sure you're all taken care of. They owe Josh, and you, the world.

All our love,
Nick and Rachel

I closed my eyes, gripping the letter, feeling the edges dampen against my skin. People had loved Josh enough to keep his secrets, and what would Josh have thought if he could see this? Would he feel proud or ashamed?

And they cared enough to help his family, figure out why our money was being held up. I'd gotten a reply yesterday from the wife of a Marine I'd e-mailed with a list of questions, and she'd told me her husband's therapist had showed the officials that his depression was service-related. Within two weeks their first check had come in the mail. There was no way Dr. Moore's notes wouldn't make that obvious too, regardless of how sketchy they were. So I'd wait another week, then call Captain Meyers to see what he'd found out. It had to be just a matter of time now.

40
Anna

I woke up early and went down to lie in Toby's bunk, burying my face against his hair. Today, Seth was coming, and I have to say it was not something I was looking forward to. Sometimes, I wish time was like a VCR, press one button and pause till you have had enough. And then, at certain times, press fast forward.

I wondered what Dad would think if he saw us now. It was like the four of us had been something fragile and Dad had held us all together. Like a cracker, you try and break off one corner and you hope the rest will hold, but no. There we were, three broken pieces with separate sadnesses and no way to come back together. We knocked on the door of one another's sadness, but nobody let anybody in.

I think in a perfect world, families would always sleep in one bed together. You have a nightmare and a hand reaches out to rub you back to sleep. In the morning you wake up and hear everyone's breathing, and you feel the warm cloud of closeness around you. Parents would buy beds the way they buy houses, the size based on the number of kids. Go to a mattress store and you'd find them in all sizes, from zero to ten.

Could I pick up Toby and bring him into Mom's bed without waking him up? I'd lie with him on one side and Mom on the other, and maybe I would fall asleep. When Mom woke up she'd see us here and the first thing on her face would be a smile.

I slipped out of bed and pulled back Toby's covers, slipped my arms under him and tried to lift. He made a little crying sound and then he stared at me with wide golfball eyes. Toby was the most broken one of all.

"It's okay," I whispered. "It's just me." I laid my head on his chest and closed my eyes and listened to his heart, and I thought about the blood running through him into every part. If you looked at his heart with the most powerful microscope, maybe you could see the sadness, a little black patch. What if that part of his heart was in charge of sending blood to one important piece of his body? Suddenly his little finger would fall off, or his toe, or even his nose. We'd look down at it, and we'd know that was his sadness.

I opened my eyes, and the Carbot under his arm looked back at me. Up close I could see scratches from its being loved too much. I remembered the look on Toby's face when he first got it, the wide open happy look. It was the look he used to have before Dad died, the look of the real Toby, and I wanted to bring it back. I thought about it, and then I stood up. "Guess what?" I said. "Look what I found."

I went to my desk, reached inside the drawer and pulled out one of the letters Dad had written us from Iraq. I brought it to Toby's bed and said, "He left it when you were asleep."

For a long time Toby didn't move, but then one side of

his face twitched. He looked up at me with questions in his eyes.

"I'll read it to you," I said, and I sat on the bed next to him. And then I saw my name in the middle of the letter. It was where Dad was talking about teaching me bike riding. *You remember, Anna, the summer you were learning how to ride a bike?* "Dear Toby," I said. "How are you?"

I was running alongside you, holding the seat and you kept yelling at me, "Let go! Let go!" You weren't anywhere near ready yet, but you wanted so much to be free. So you'd ride a little and then fall down, then ride a little more and then fall down.

"I am good," I said. "I was just thinking about you and how much I love you, and I wanted you to know I was thinking those things."

Remembering this made me realize that's how growing up is, in a way. There is no way to go on to new things without sometimes failing, but you keep on trying, get back up on the bike, and soon it will feel so natural you'll forget how hard it used to be. Remember that, both of you. It is important.

"Also," I said, "I am writing to remind you that I can still come down to see you whenever I want and I always will, so you should not miss me so much."

If I had the chance again, I'd pretend I was the slowest bike learner ever. But back then, I was so stupid. I didn't realize it was my last chance to be riding with someone running next to me. That chance only lasted for a week, and now I'd be riding alone for the whole rest of my life.

I started again. "Dear Toby. I'm glad you like the Carbot! Let me tell you why it is even more special than you think. Because, because…up here in heaven, one of my favorite things to do is ride cars. Up here, the cars have arms and legs and also, they speak English."

I watched Toby's face to see if this was too much, but

he was looking at the letter wearing no expression. It was impossible to tell what he was thinking.

"So anyway I used to ride my most favorite car all the time. But then I thought, seeing as you like cars and robots, wouldn't the Carbot be a great thing for you to have? Because I can do magic here, I brought it down for you to play with and think of me. I totally love you. Love, Dad."

Toby had no reaction, still didn't talk, didn't look at me. I touched his shoulder. "Wow," I said. "That was a nice letter."

Toby blinked quickly and then he frowned at the Carbot, like he was trying to decide what to believe. He touched its broken leg, and then its folded down head, and then his eyes got glisteny.

This is the thing. In a way the letters from Dad had knocked on the door to Toby's sadness, and he had let them in. I thought about all the parts of Toby that broke on that day, and how maybe the letters and my present were like little nails starting to fix him. And I wondered if I gave him enough presents, if that would work to put him all back together.

But no. I knew presents wouldn't be enough because I think he saw too much. What I really think is that he saw everything. That it broke him into so many pieces that if you tried to fix him you wouldn't even know where to start. Toby's pieces are as small as atoms.

I thought about this, and about Mom's face last night, and made up my mind. No matter what, I was going to show her the note today. And then, we'd see.

41
Natalie

"This enough?" Anna said, pushing her bowl across the table to me.

"Perfect," I said. "Now you guys can start spooning them out on the cookie sheet." This felt so wonderfully domestic. Sure the dough had come from a mix, but it had required stirring. We'd had to melt some butter. This was exactly the image I'd held of my life, in the midst of the hormone-induced sentimentality of my first pregnancy: me and baby Anna together in the kitchen, baking cookies for friends. Of course in that image Josh had come up behind me, wrapped arms around my waist and nuzzled at my neck. But still. Anyone watching us from the outside would smile and want this for themselves.

Anna and Toby propped up on their knees and started dropping spoonfuls of dough onto the tray. I stepped back to watch them, both of them looking so purposeful and proud, spoons in and out of the bowl and back and forth from the tray. Even if they weren't quite coordinated enough yet to be graceful, it still looked like a dance.

I was in a good mood this morning, partly because I'd gotten an e-mail back from Victoria, my literary agent. Of course it was filled with words like, "powerful," and phrases like, "wonderful to hear you're writing again!" which I read as pandering, the types of things she never would've said if she hadn't known about Josh. But she'd been at least moderately encouraging, telling me she'd be interested in seeing what I came up with. And it had made me feel almost like life was slowly sliding back on track.

"When that cookie rises, it's going to be the size of a baseball field," I said, splitting one of Toby's mounds in two.

The doorbell rang and I started out to the hallway, but my Dad got to the door first.

"Seth," he said, holding out his hand. They shook and then, in an unexpected move, my dad reached to squeeze his shoulder. "Good to see you, son."

Son? Had Dad ever called anyone "son" before?

"You too. Meant to thank you for telling me about that buffet table in your old shop. As of tomorrow, it'll be in my dining room."

"That's good! Knew you'd like it."

I stared at them. Dad had talked to Seth without me there? Recommended furniture? Dad's relationship with other men my age always seemed a little strained; with Josh I'd had the impression he was constantly thinking: *This man is sleeping with my daughter.* But with Seth he seemed pointedly jovial, almost like he was trying to impress him.

"Hey," I said, walking up behind Dad. "Come on in."

He gave a wide smile, then held up his hand in greeting as Anna appeared from the kitchen, dragging Toby behind her. "Hey, there." She stared up at Seth expressionlessly, then without saying a word she pulled Toby up the stairs.

I glanced at my father and Seth, then shook my head.

"Don't know what's got into her. I wish she'd at least said hi to you."

"We'll get there." Seth shrugged, but he looked slightly hurt. "So I'm going to get the windowpane from my trunk. You have any caulk?"

I frowned. "I don't even know for sure what that is."

"It's okay, I came prepared." He nodded at Dad, squeezed my shoulder, and went out to his car.

I went back into the kitchen, put the cookies in the oven, and started cleaning up. So much for my perfect domestic dream scene.

A few minutes later, Anna came into the kitchen. She was walking slowly, tentatively, like she was carrying something heavy, Toby trailing a few feet behind her, his Carbot cradled in his arms. "Mom, I have to show you something upstairs," she said. "Right now. This is really, really important."

My initial thought, God help me, was that Anna had gotten her first period. This was the way I'd imagined her telling me, this same momentous solemnity in her face, a ceremonial walk upstairs to see her stained underwear, tearful hugs, then a trip downtown for maxipads and a celebratory becoming-a-woman cake. I didn't know why she'd think it was appropriate to bring Toby to participate in this event, but it was in this spirit of excitement tinged with melancholy that I agreed to follow her upstairs.

She pointed to my bedroom. "In there," she said.

I raised my eyebrows, but she just strode into her own room and grabbed something (underwear?) from under her pillow. When Toby started to follow us to my bedroom, Anna said, "I just got an idea, Toby. You want to start building a fort with the blankets? I'll be there in a sec and we can hang out in it and read, okay?" And then she grabbed my hand and we stepped inside and she closed the door, looked up at me, and then her face flushed pink and she put a folded piece of paper into my hand. "From Dad," she said.

"What're you talking about?"

"I found it. I just woke up this morning, and there it was."

"It was where?" I unfolded the page. It was a short, typed note. "What is it?"

"It was on my bed. I found it there, but I don't really know where it came from. It just showed up."

I scanned the first sentence and my throat tightened. "Anna?" I whispered.

"Read it out loud," she said.

I stared at her, said, "Where did you find this?"

"Just read it! It doesn't say anything bad."

I sank onto my bed. "It says, remind them—" My voice broke and I swallowed dryly. "Remind them of who I used to be, and tell them how you all were the only thing that kept me alive this long. I wish I could've said good-bye to you in person…" I glanced up at Anna, my eyes glazed and my whole body slack. Had she written this herself? Copied it from a book? Or the Internet? "Anna, tell me the truth. Where did you find this?"

"There's more. Read the rest."

I shook my head slightly, then read, first slow but then fast. "I wish I could've said good-bye to you in person, but I hope you understand why I decided this is best. Please remember that even when it might not've felt that way, when I was too caught up in my own mind and then my own sickness and fear, I have adored you." My voice was weak, coming from high up in my throat as I continued. "I'm sorry I can't tell you why I died, because there really is no reason. I just couldn't live anymore, but please don't hate me for that. I need you to keep loving me. Love, Josh." The note dropped from my hands. "Anna?" I said.

It couldn't be real. All this time, I'd wondered how Josh could've killed himself without leaving a note. Was it possible Anna had been holding on to it all this time?

Anna picked up the note, her eyes wide and pleading. "I think…" she said, "I think he must've left it from heaven."

"Did you find it back at Pendleton?" I said. "Why didn't you show me before? How could you not show me?"

"I just got it this morning!"

I paced to the window, stood there with my breath heavy, leaning on the sill, watching blankly as Seth and Dad lifted the pane from the front door.

The words swam in my mind as I pictured Josh with a gun in one hand and typing with the other, his hand shaking so much he'd had to use a keyboard rather than a pen. He'd said he needed me to keep loving him, so there must've been a realization that there'd be an *after*. He'd wanted to know that even in that after, he wouldn't be alone.

How had it felt for Anna, finding this? Deep down she must know what this was, must know Josh had written it before killing himself. How had it felt for her, reading the letters from heaven I'd written when all this time she'd had Josh's real letter. What had it done to her, holding this inside her all these weeks?

I didn't know how to talk to her about this, didn't have the remotest idea what to do other than hold her. I turned from the window to find her watching me, her eyes unreadable. "Anna, come here, sweetie," I said.

She didn't answer, just stared at me. I walked over to

her, hugged her against me. "I know how you feel, how scary and sad and awful this is, and I wish so much you hadn't kept it inside you. Why didn't you show me before? Did you find this back at Pendleton? Was it with your dad's stuff?"

She pulled away from me. "I told you. I told you! Just forget it!" She threw the letter at me and ran into her bedroom, slamming the door.

42
Anna

I lay on the pile of blankets Toby had pulled off our beds, listening to the thumps of Seth and Grandpa working on the window. Maybe the window would fall and cut Seth into pieces. It was probably the only way left to make him go away.

I saw what the note did to Mom, made her look like she was going to break apart, and more than anything I wished I could take it back. She believed it, I could see that. Not that Dad had brought the note from heaven but that Dad had wrote it and that I'd found it after he died. Was it enough to make her get rid of Seth? I didn't know, I didn't know, but probably not. She didn't say the note made her remember how much she loved Dad, what she said was that it was scary and awful, which was the opposite of what I'd wanted. And now I had no other ideas left.

Toby pulled at the sheet under me. "Go 'way, Toby," I said.

He stared at me blankly, then tugged again, and I tugged back. "I know you want a fort, but not now, okay? I'm not in the mood."

He dropped the sheet and watched me, his arms hanging at his sides, and then he pulled a pillow off his bed, threw it next to me and then fell backward on the pile of sheets, with his arms out. Both of us stared up at the ceiling.

But in the quietness, my mind kept wanting to worry. I tried to concentrate it all away, wrapped a blanket over my head and looked up through it at the window. I blinked my right eye and then my left and tried to keep my head involved with blinking and the fuzzy light moving side to side, but it was no use.

"Okay, you want to build a fort?" I said, pulling the blanket off my face. But when I stood and looked down at the pile, I suddenly got a different idea. "I'm going to try something better," I said. "You should get up."

And that is when it happened. Something happened to Toby. It was something bad. Something real bad, and it was all my fault.

When Toby found Dad, he didn't scream. I don't know how long he was in the garage before Mom found him. What made him go to the garage at all? It is one of the mysteries of the universe. All I know is I woke up normal time, and I just knew that something wasn't right. Not in an ESP way, but because everything was too quiet. Usually there was Mom starting coffee and Dad starting his shower, but on that day all there was was nothing.

First I looked in Mom and Dad's room, but nobody. Then I looked in Toby's room, and then I knew for sure something was wrong. But of course I didn't know how really wrong it was.

I looked everywhere until I got to the kitchen, which is when I heard the sounds from the garage. I opened the door and they were there on the ground by the car, Mom holding Toby, and my first thought was that he was the one who was hurt. "Mommy?" I said, and then I started to cry.

She turned around and her face was white and she yelled at me, "Go inside!"

I jumped back and the door slammed shut in my face, and my legs felt like spaghetti and my brain was thinking, *please, please, please.* I went to the den and sat on the sofa, and buried my face in my hands.

And then Mom came in, carrying Toby. I ran over and tried to see what I could do to fix him, but he looked fine, no blood and no bumps and not crying even though his face was red.

Mom carried him to the sofa but as soon as she sat, Toby got off her lap and ran upstairs. Later, we found him under his bed.

Mom reached for one of my hands, and her face was doing weird twitchy things, like pieces of it were arguing over which way to go. "Anna," she said. Her voice sounded underwater. "Anna, something bad happened. To your dad. Last night." Then her face squinched together and she held my hand tighter.

In my brain I could hear her words, *to your dad, to your dad.* I wanted to say something, but those were the only words I had. And then Mom bent over me and hugged my head. She was wearing her green robe and her purple pajamas. She smelled salty.

"Anna, your dad got hurt last night."

My head started squirming. I stopped hearing the words and counted her heartbeats, *clump-clump* like something with rubber shoes walking in her chest. She didn't talk until I got to twenty, but then she squashed my head tighter and she said, "He got hurt bad, Anna. While we were asleep."

Her hand was pulling my hair. Later that day I put my hand back there and found it all tangled up, in a clump.

"He got shot," Mom said, her voice shaky. "Oh, baby, what're we going to do?"

My head was against Mom's boobs and it was dark. I wanted to bury all of me there, between her boobs, so I fell into the dark and the scrunching and letting go of her hand on my hair, scrunch and let go, hurt and not-hurt. I was there inside it, but also part of me was not. Part of me was up at the ceiling, over us all and looking down. And screaming.

This is the idea I had when I saw the pile of sheets. I decided to throw all our pillows onto it, and try jumping off my top bunk. First it was scary, but then I landed and it was fun and it only hurt a little, so I did it again, and then again, and then Toby climbed up next to me to watch. And it was seeing him up there that I got the idea of going all out and making him feel like Superman. I taped on a big red construction paper S, and tied a sheet through the label in the back of his shirt. I'd had to hunch over to fit under the ceiling, but he stood up straight with his arms out, and then he flew.

The problem was the sheet. It got caught on the top of the bunk bed ladder. Which I thought was funny, him dangling there, until he started to scream.

"I'll get you loose!" I said. He was hanging there, upside down, the bottom of his cape stuck on the ladder, like he was laundry hanging out to dry. And then his cape came loose out from his collar and he fell straight onto his head, after which he all at once stopped yelling, like he was surprised at what things had come to.

"Toby!" I ran over to him and held onto his head. "Toby!" I started crying, and Toby made a couple of choking noises and then he puked onto my lap. Mom ran into the room, her face pale and crazy. "What happened? What happened!"

"He fell!" I was crying so hard I couldn't even understand what I was saying. "He fell ohh-ve-e-er!"

Mom dropped onto her knees and pushed me away. "Don't move him! Toby? Talk to me. Where does it hurt?"

Things were running inside me, little rats with little claws scraping at my stomach and my lungs and the underside of my skin. Toby wasn't making any sound, and his eyes were different, not looking scared, not looking anything. Stuffed-animal eyes and he was dead. I had killed him and the rats were scratching bloody trails, the scream of them trying to get out but caught inside my throat.

Around me, somehow, time went on.

Mom: "Toby, look at me. Say something!"

Grandpa: "I'll call nine-one-one!"

Seth: "Okay, it'll be okay."

Mom felt Toby's wrist and then the side of his head, a lump, the size of an English muffin. Seth came to me and brushed the hair off my forehead. "C'mon, sweetheart, we're going to have to go to the hospital, so let's get your pants changed. Okay?"

I didn't really hear him and I had no thoughts until later, when I realized I was somehow wearing different pants and a different shirt, and everybody must've seen my underwear. But it didn't matter. All I saw was my mom there on the floor, and all I heard was her voice saying, "Toby? Toby?" and my own head saying, *Daddy!* and Toby's lump and his eyes and his ambulance, and it was all happening again, because of me.

43
Anna

People in white shirts took Toby out in a stretcher, and Seth drove us to the hospital. And then we were in a waiting room that had green walls and orange seats with wood arms and a smell of coldness, men yelling in Spanish and putting up a fake Christmas tree with no ornaments, and me watching it all from somewhere else, a movie through a blurry window.

This felt like a place where people had died. You'd die here and then your ghost would echo around, off the hard floor and hard walls and metal edges. There were a hundred trillion ghosts stuck here, bouncing around and not knowing how to get out, me with them and all of us screaming without sound. I wanted to hide under something, find a shadow, but everywhere was too shiny and spiky and cold.

"You eaten anything since breakfast, Anna?" Seth said. "Should I go down and check out what kind of processed food they're scrambling up in the cafeteria?"

I could hear the ghosts around me crying for the people they used to love, the voices of all the people who had sat here and had prayed here: *Daddy, Mommy, Husband, Wife and Sister, Brother, please God please,* all words that in the end went nowhere, listened to by nobody but me. I pulled my feet up on my chair and buried my face in my knees.

"I'll go down with you," Grandpa said. "See if I can find something Meg might eat. Anna, you stay with Grammy, okay?"

"Okay," I said to my knees, but nothing was ever okay. The okay-ness was just a rest before the next bad thing and then the next, and you could try to relax, but deep down you were always waiting.

Around me: a kid crying, a lady talking on her phone, a man holding his arm up to the lady behind the desk. "I can't bend it," he said. "Look at me, look—I must've broke it, see?" I got up and walked out of the room.

I walked down the hallway looking up so that I wouldn't see the sick people, at signs with long words I didn't understand. Until I saw a sign with not just words but also a picture of a teddy bear, the one friendly thing in the world of ghosts. I followed the sign and went in.

The shop was all balloons and baskets of flowers and cards and chocolates. I stood there with my head spinning, stuffed animals and snow globes, puzzles and colored pencils and a fuzzy green dinosaur hand puppet with cloth teeth. Back when everything was normal, Toby knew the name of every dinosaur that ever existed on the earth, and my hand put itself into the puppet and the puppet's mouth opened and closed.

Back when Toby was little-little, Dad taught him how to say *Tyrannosaurus rex*. He'd say it in front of company, and everybody would laugh. My hand shoved itself into my pocket, and the puppet slipped itself off inside.

"I saw that, young lady." It was the woman behind the counter who said it. She had a large bosom inside a fuzzy sweater that made it look like she had one boob instead of two. "Were you going to pay for that?" she said.

"Yes," I said, and then I started to cry.

She came over and put her hand on my shoulder, and I wanted to bury my face inside her fuzzy sweater bosom and just stay there. "My brother got hurt!" I said. "Maybe even dead, and I need it for him!"

The lady made a choking kind of sound and then reached for me. She squashed me, and her sweater wasn't soft and fluffy like it looked, but scratchy like a beard. I looked down at the floor. The tiles looked like square pieces of bologna.

"Here," she said, and she pulled away. She picked up a stuffed bunny wearing a bow tie and a bag of chocolate-covered peanuts, and she put them into a big bag. Then she took a shiny balloon, printed with *Get Well Soon*, and she tied it to the bag's handle. "For your brother," she said.

I stared at her. I wondered if I was supposed to pay.

She reached for a girl doll in a ballerina dress. "And this is for you."

I took the doll. Its eyes and lashes were painted on, staring painted plastic.

"You go on now," the lady said. "Stay with your parents. I'll say a prayer for your brother."

So I turned and left the store. I walked back down the hall to the waiting room. I felt like I wasn't inside my body, like my head was bobbing over me just like the balloon on its string.

Grammy was in the waiting room and I sat next to her. *Ow.* I stood up again and pulled the puppet out of my pocket. He looked squashed and sad, so I sat down and straightened his teeth, then smoothed him over my leg.

And then Seth and Grandpa came in with trays of food. Grandpa handed one to me: a sandwich wrapped in plastic, barbecue potato chips, an apple, chocolate pudding with whipped cream. I stared at it, and Seth unwrapped the sandwich and handed it to me, and I started to eat it but it wasn't me eating. I was bobbing over myself on a string, watching the sandwich go down, hearing the squish of it being chewed, until Seth opened the potato chips and I could smell them. I pushed the tray off my lap and it fell onto the floor. The apple rolled under my chair. The slop of pudding on the bologna-colored floor looked like blood.

"It's okay, it's okay," Seth said, and he bent to pick up my food. I watched him rub thin beige napkins over the pudding and then I bent my legs up on my chair again, to press my eyeballs against my knees.

And then.

"We're back!" It was my mom. I jumped up and started to run to her, then saw Toby. There was a bandage on his head, and under it a bag of ice, and his eyes were open and he was alive, he was alive! But he was in a wheelchair and I suddenly knew that he would never walk again. "Mommy?" I said.

She held her arms to me. "You been crying? Oh, sweet baby, it's okay, he's okay."

I ran to her and she held me, squeezing me against her, while she talked to the grown-ups. "He should be fine," she said. "Has a scary-looking lump, but his skull's not fractured and there's no sign of internal swelling."

He was alive.

"I just need to watch him all night to make sure he doesn't show any signs of distress, strained breathing or disorientation. But he's okay."

He was alive. He was alive, he was alive, and I suddenly dropped back into my body. I twisted away and bent to hug Toby's head.

And then, Seth came over.

He held out his arms so that Mom could walk into them and I saw her arms go around his back. I saw her hands grab on to his shirt and saw her and Seth rock back and forth before Seth whispered in her ear, "Thank God."

I stood up to watch them, saw Seth smooth back Mom's hair, saw Mom's face go pink when she smiled at him. And without even really thinking what I was going to do, I felt myself falling in between them.

"Anna!" Mom caught me and bent to look in my face. "Sweetie? What happened?"

"Sorry…" I put my hand on my forehead, closed my eyes. "I got all spinny," I said.

She pulled me against her and rubbed at my back. "Guess it's been a long afternoon," she said, then, "I think it's time to go home."

So, imagine this. Imagine I got some kind of sickness where every time I saw Seth, I fell over. This is what I'd be saying to Mom: *Make a choice.*

We brought Toby home and tucked him into bed, and Mom sat in the bedside chair. She made me go up to my bunk, but when I kept hanging my head over the edge, she let me come down and lie with him. So, I stayed there all the rest of the night. Watching Toby breathe.

44
Natalie

I woke up with my whole body feeling like a knuckle that needed to be cracked, stiff and wound into knots. I straightened my legs and slowly stood from the chair, testing my spine carefully, all of yesterday coming back gradually in spurts of shock, horror, sheer panic, and then relief. The bracing of Toby's neck, his whimpers as they lifted him onto the stretcher while I yelled at them not to hurt him. The paramedics questioning Toby and my fumbled explanations of his muteness, wanting to make sure they understood he wasn't mentally deficient in some way, didn't think him less deserving of their complete dedication. I looked over at Toby's bed and saw him lying there in his ridiculously large bandage, his hands resting on Anna's arm. Watching them I felt exactly like I had when the children were babies, standing over their cribs to watch them sleep, the conflicting emotions of pride at what I'd made and fear at how horribly vulnerable they were. The knowledge that I was inevitably going to screw them up somehow.

I knelt in front of them. They were both so beautiful. And, astonishingly, as a result of nothing I had done, they loved each other.

Here is what it will do to you, seeing your child unconscious, believing he might die; the immensity of that shows you that every other worry in your head is just background noise. Josh's suicide note was all just distant hisses and squeaks behind what really mattered. "Hey," I whispered, touching Toby's shoulder. "Can you wake up a minute? I need to make sure you're okay."

Slowly he opened his eyes, squinted, and then closed them again. I squeezed his shoulder. "Toby, wake up. Tell me how old you are, okay?"

He opened his eyes, looking quizzical, probably wondering why I didn't know, then held up five fingers.

"Good boy!" I said. I sounded like I was praising a dog, and he gave me the disparaging look of an embarrassed teenager. I sat on the bed and unwrapped his bandage, then touched the top of his head gently. "It still hurt?"

He nodded, then shrugged.

"They said you wouldn't need the ice pack today, so we can keep the bandage off unless the ice helps your headache feel better. I don't have another ice pack, but I guess we could use frozen peas."

He wrinkled his nose and I smiled. "Yeah, I agree."

Anna rose without speaking, and went to the closet. "Morning," I said, and she grumbled something unintelligible.

After Toby left for the bathroom and Anna emerged, I reached toward her. She hesitated, but then came to sit beside me and let me hold her. "I want to talk to you," I said, "about your dad's note and what happened yesterday."

I felt her stiffen, the breath heavy in and out through her nose. "I wasn't lying," she said, her voice trembling.

"Please, Anna. I'm not angry you kept the note. I guess

I understand why you did, and I'm glad you finally felt like you could share it with me. I know you have to feel guilty about it, but there's no reason to feel guilty and there's no reason to make up a story about him bringing it from heaven. But I really think we need to talk about the note and what it means, and what happened to Dad."

"I wasn't lying!" She pulled away.

"Natalie? How is everything?" Anna's gaze shifted to the doorway where Dad stood, squinting without his glasses.

I squared my shoulders. "Toby's okay," I said, hoping Dad was too nearsighted to see Anna's teary face. "He's walking around just fine, seems perfectly coherent. Probably more coherent than I am this morning."

"That's 'cause he's got brain power to spare. I guess all's well that ends well, and hopefully he's learned now that boys can't fly." He smiled at his own joke, then said, "I'm going to make some coffee."

"Be down in a few minutes," I said.

As he left, Toby came back from the bathroom. Dad bent to hug him and I listened to his muted words, tucking a stray hair behind Anna's ear.

"I'm going down to start breakfast. This feels like a French toast kind of day. What do you think?" I rose, kissed Anna's forehead, then Toby's, and went into my bedroom to change.

Josh's note was on my bed, where I'd thrown it when I'd heard Toby's scream. I picked it up, read it again. And holding it I felt a rush of adrenaline, like my body believed if it just ran fast enough, it could bring me back to the time when the note had been written, to fix things.

I didn't know what to do with it now. And how ridiculous to be faced with something so momentous and still have to deal with practicalities? What did people do with suicide notes once they'd read them? Throw them in the trash with their banana peels and used tissues? Have a ritual burning to commemorate the end to their loved one's sadness?

In the end I brought it outside and buried it with Josh's cloth heart. I'd expected that the heart would be somehow preserved, that in hundreds of years someone would excavate it and wonder. But instead it had been burrowed into by some subterranean creature, leaking its lavender insides. Already becoming one with the earth.

45
Anna

We were all in the kitchen when Seth came. I was the one who answered the door, and I stood there without letting him in. I had figured if I kept being mean, maybe eventually he'd decide this was a family he did not want to be involved with, but it obviously wasn't working. I was not the part of the family he cared about.

"Hey, Anna," he said. "I just came to see how your brother's doing."

Mom walked from the kitchen with Toby, smiling wide enough to show her teeth. "Seth! We were just finishing lunch. Come on in."

He looked over my head. "How're you doing today, Toby?"

Toby shrugged and smiled.

"You gave us a scare yesterday." He held up two bags. "So to celebrate your recovery, I got you a get-well-soon present."

Toby ran to him, and Seth handed one of the bags to him and the other to me. "And a being-a-good-big-sister present," he said.

The bag made me feel corroded, bad tingles up my arm. I dropped it and gave him an I-hate-you look.

"Toby!" Mom said, looking into his bag, big exclamation points in her voice. "A train set! It's beautiful, Seth."

It wasn't beautiful, it was just a train set, wooden, bright colors. "Say thank you, Toby," Mom said, but Toby was already gone, into the house with his train.

"He doesn't *talk*, Mom," I said. "Did you *forget*?" I knew I was being a brat supreme, but I didn't care. I hated everybody. How come they didn't understand? Mom was trying to put a new person in our family, but couldn't she see there wasn't any room? It would be like putting in a bacteria. Infection.

Mom gave me A LOOK. "Why don't you see what Seth got you?"

"I'm not interested," I said.

"Anna!" She reached for the bag, peeked inside. "Oh, wow, you'll love this." She held the bag to me.

Well, now I actually was interested. There is something about a present. The part of you excited about the mystery doesn't care about the rest of you. I took the bag and looked. Frowned. It was an American Girl doll. I raised my eyebrows at Seth. Did he think I was six? He didn't know me at all.

"My niece is crazy about hers," he said. "There's clothes you can buy for her too, and accessories and pets, and she comes with her own personal story."

Well, duh. That was the definition of an American Girl doll.

"I thought she looked a little like you," he said.

This made me start to feel a little sorry for Seth. He was trying so hard, and he couldn't help it that I hated him. So I pulled the doll out. The only thing we had in common was that she was a girl. "Thank you," I said, and I brought the doll up to my bedroom.

Toby ran up after me, and kneeled on the floor to open his train set. His Carbot was lying on its back by the chair, staring at the ceiling with its arms reached up, like a dying person. "How come you're not playing with the Carbot?" I said.

Toby smiled at me and held up a blue caboose. Why didn't anybody else understand what was happening? "That train's infected," I said.

Toby didn't even seem to hear me; he just started hooking the trains together. What was the best way to give him his new presents from Dad? If I gave them now, would he just keep playing with the trains? I couldn't deny the trains were a better gift.

I went to the closet, where I'd hidden the bag of hospital gift shop presents. Then I took the ballerina doll out from the bag, remembering the lady in the shop. If I was her I would've yelled at me, but instead she gave me a present, probably thinking I'd make it dance ballet, play with it, and for a few minutes forget about Toby. I robbed her and she wanted to help. It would've been better if she'd yelled at me instead. It would've felt better than this.

I stuffed the ballerina and the American Girl doll in the back of the closet and then snuck the other presents over to where the Carbot was lying. I made the Carbot sit on top of them, and then I sat on Toby's bed. "I have to tell you something."

Toby started running his train around the track, making honking noises and crashing noises, not even looking at me.

"This is important," I said, "so you have to listen. Because…" I checked myself. Was this what I wanted to do? "Because I've been talking to Dad," I said.

This got him. He started paying attention. He still held on to his train, but in a tight way. "He said he loves us very much, and that he was talking to me because he wanted us to know Seth was a very, very bad man." I heard Mom and Grandpa downstairs both talking to Seth, and it felt like a poking in my ribs. And then I remembered Seth at the hospital, acting like Toby was his to care about.

"Dad said that if you play with anything Seth gave you, he'll be very sad, but he got you some more presents to make up for it." I bent for the presents and brought them to Toby, then closed our bedroom door. "You can have these," I said. "They're secret presents, so you can't tell anybody you have them, and you can't play with them in front of Mom. It's just a secret between you and me and him."

The look on Toby's face made a little corkscrew turn in my heart. Maybe part of him knew it was a lie. But it might be that he made himself believe because he really, really wanted to.

I handed him the bunny, and he made a quick sighing noise, like somebody had just pushed on his lungs. He touched the top of the bunny's head, and then its left ear, and then its right ear, slow, like he was giving it a blessing.

"You like it?" I said. He just looked at me, not answering. I watched the bunny and it watched me back, smiling with its pink sewn-on mouth.

Next I gave him the dinosaur puppet, which I could tell he liked a lot. He put it on his hand, and then he used it to eat the bunny. "He wanted you to have it because he knows you love dinosaurs," I said.

"Where is he?" Toby said.

"Well, he's in heaven, right?" I said, and then I realized. "You talked!"

"But he came back to give me stuff."

"Yeah, I guess." I felt like I was walking careful, a spiderweb thread between him and me that would break if I said the wrong thing. "For just a little while, like for a minute."

"But he's coming back again?"

I bent down to hug Toby. I'd fixed him. I'd fixed him! I talked with my lips in his hair. "Definitely. Especially if you keep talking, then he'll definitely come."

"Could I see him?"

I pulled away. "No. I mean, he doesn't actually *come* here, just he drops the presents and his letters down, and his voice comes to me. I just hear him."

Toby looked inside the dinosaur's mouth, and then he put the open mouth over his own and talked into it. "Can you ask him stuff?"

"Sure, I guess." I sat back on the bed and hugged my waist. "What do you want to ask?"

He was quiet, the dinosaur still over his mouth, and then he said, "Ask if he can talk to me."

"I'm pretty sure he can't. I'll ask him, but I'm pretty sure."

"Why not?"

I traced my finger around the tread in the bottom of my sneaker. "Because. Because you're not old enough."

Toby looked up at me, the dinosaur still eating his mouth. I watched his eyes and the dinosaur eyes, both the same shape of round. "How come he got hurt?" he said.

I picked up one of Toby's pillows and examined it. Peanuts sheets, Lucy snatching up her football and Charlie Brown flying through the air. His face was partly embarrassed, but mostly scared. "I don't know," I said.

"Could you just ask him?"

I suddenly felt angry. A little bit at Toby, which I knew wasn't fair but I felt it anyway. A little at Toby, and a little at myself for starting this, but mostly at everything being up to me. "It's because of the war!" I said. "Okay? I told you that. The war!"

And then, when I said it, I realized who I was really angry at. More than anything, I was angry at him, at my dad, and I knew that was bad; it was worse than being angry at Toby. But I was, I was. It was because of him that everything had twisted inside out and wrong, and why didn't he think about that before he died? Did he think about us at all?

It was like last year when I fell off my bike, and I needed elbow stitches, and when I got back from the hospital I had to show him the bandage and the blood on my shirt and tell him how I had seen the under part of my skin, and how having a scar would change my life forever. I had to let him know, but he wouldn't open the door. He wouldn't even answer when I knocked because all he cared about was his own self, when I was the one who should've been important.

I threw Toby's pillow at the wall and then I picked it up and threw it again. Toby said something, but it was muffled by the dinosaur, so I picked up the pillow and threw, picked up and threw.

Toby spoke again, and something took over my arm and threw the pillow at his head, exactly on the lump. "I can't hear you!"

Toby stared up at me, and his face got red. He pulled the dinosaur away from his mouth and came up on the bed. I couldn't look at him, and so I lay down, and after a minute he lay down next to me. I let him curl up against me and pulled his shirt around my face. It smelled exactly like him, like salty milk, which sank the angriness back underground. I put my arm around him, and we lay there with my cheek against his hair.

Smelling Toby, there's no way you can be angry anymore.

46
Natalie

After Mom and Dad went up for their nap, I made some tea and sat with Seth on the sofa. "So how are you really?" he said. "Get any sleep last night?"

"I got a lot more than I should've, actually. I was planning to stay up all night to make sure Toby was okay, but I don't think I lasted past midnight."

"It was an exhausting day."

"Yeah." I stared down into my cup, the steam sweating my face. "You know what I realized? That Toby fell onto his head in almost exactly the same spot where Josh shot himself, just over his ear on the right side."

I saw Seth flinch, and I shook my head. "Sorry. It's just amazing, you know, that in a split second life can turn from okay into a nightmare. It feels like you have to be vigilant all the time, and I've been too caught up in myself and the kids' mental state and thinking what Josh might've kept from me to be vigilant about anything."

Seth rested his hand on my knee. "Stop," he said. "Regardless of what you seem to think, you're not superhuman."

I looked down at his hand, and a sudden fatigue swept over me, an ocean breaker of weariness that left me limp and sodden. Yesterday had been a nightmare, the blurry vagueness in Toby's eyes, the reek of vomit, then the sirens. Two policemen first, the same as with Josh's death, the questions, a checking of his pulse. The entire morning of Josh's death replaying, including my hatred of the paramedics for carrying my heart away inside their sterile white van, for still being alive when he was dead.

And then, before I could stop my self I said, "Anna gave me Josh's suicide note."

Seth widened his eyes. "What?"

"She had the note all this time; she just gave it to me yesterday. And the thing is? It said nothing. All this time I've been waiting for an answer, but the note was like five sentences long and it said, basically, that there was no reason for why he died."

Seth gave his head a little shake. "Are you sure it's real? That it actually came from him?"

"You mean did Anna write it herself? No; I mean, she's smart, but it wasn't a letter from a ten-year-old girl. He wrote to tell me there's no reason for him killing himself. How screwed up is that?"

"Maybe he was just trying to make you understand it wasn't your fault. Like, you weren't the reason because there was no reason."

"But this is worse. It's worse than thinking there's some answer I'll never know." I shook my head. "Who the hell writes a five-sentence suicide note?"

"Somebody in a lot of pain," Seth said. "Somebody who's so tired and confused all they can think of is one thing."

"And the worst thing is, how could Anna have dealt with this on her own for three months? I should've been there to help her understand it all!"

Seth rested his arm across the back of the couch. "Maybe she wanted to feel like her dad wrote it just for her? She'd just lost him, and she felt like she had this little piece of him she didn't want to let go of or share with anybody."

"Or maybe because she still doesn't want to face the truth about how he died." I crossed my arms and leaned forward over my knees. "You know we never talked about it? I haven't talked to either of them about how he died because I thought they were too young to understand the truth. And then I heard Anna telling Toby he'd died in the war, which back then I thought was the only reason she could think of for him to have gotten shot. I tried to broach the subject back in the first weeks, and again this morning, but every time she pushes me away."

"Well, you didn't do the wrong thing not telling them."

You didn't do the wrong thing. I watched him, waiting for more, then finally said, "What do you mean?"

"Suicide's hard enough for a grown-up to understand. I'm sure they'll process what actually happened when they're ready to, and at some point you'll have to discuss it with them. But for now you're just doing what you can to help them accept his death."

I heard myself make a strange, unbidden, high-pitched sound, then pressed my fist against my mouth and spoke from behind it. "I wrote letters. From Josh after he died, I wrote them letters."

Seth's face went suddenly still and watchful.

"I knew it was the wrong thing to do, I mean obviously, but Toby wasn't talking and I was desperate. So I left them letters saying Josh was okay, that he was happy in heaven, and he was still watching down to make sure they were doing okay without him. Which I know is so crazy."

"Not crazy." Seth paused, then said, "There's a difference between craziness and desperation."

"It gets worse." My voice shook. "It gets worse because I started letting them write letters back. I wanted to see how they were feeling, things they wouldn't tell me. I did it to get Toby talking again, and to try and get them both to open up, and now look! Anna's trying to convince me Josh's note just showed up on her bed yesterday, that he visited her, probably because she feels guilty for not showing it to me sooner."

"I used to think my grandmother was visiting me," Seth said softly. "For like a year after she died I'd see her sitting on the end of my bed, not talking really, just watching me."

"But at least your mother didn't try and convince you she was really there." I tried to laugh, but it sounded more like I was trying to cough up a hairball. "All I want, the only thing I want in the world is to make them better, but I don't have any idea how to fix this."

"Anna just misses her dad, so if she's actually pretending he's still around, it's probably a real comfort to her." Seth tucked me close against him. "You didn't do anything wrong," he said again.

I rested my head in the crook of his neck, let him wrap his arms around me. I'd told someone. Somebody knew how badly I'd screwed up my kids, but seemed to think they weren't screwed up irreparably. And finally, after all this time on my own, I had somebody to talk to, an adult to help me figure out how to get through this. Someone who knew what I'd done, and still was able to embrace me.

I was still on the couch with Seth when the doorbell rang. I wiped at my face, rose and went to the door to find Dan and Cameron behind it, dressed in identical brown T-shirts.

"I'm sorry for dropping by like this," Dan said. "But Cam was asking all morning if he could come over to see Anna today."

I looked down at Cameron. "No problem," I said although, of course, it was a problem. Because really all I wanted to do was crawl into bed with the kids, the three of us alone without a strange little boy in tow, insulated by the aloneness. "Anna'll be happy to see you."

"Where is she?" Cameron had the hyperalert look of a child with a secret, and I wondered again what exactly had drawn him and Anna together. Too exhausting to worry about, and so I ignored the uneasy twist in my gut and called for Anna. Cameron smiled at me, a knowing smile that probably should've been disconcerting, but there was too much inside of me fighting for attention.

"I'll have him call when he's ready to come home," I said.

Dan studied my face. "Are you okay?"

"I'm fine," I said, without stepping back from the door. "Just real busy today. I have this deadline for a book I've been writing."

Seth appeared in the doorway and raised his hand in greeting.

"Ah," Dan said. "So I see. Okay, I'll let you get on with your busyness." He smiled and started back toward his truck.

Anna appeared in the upstairs hallway and stood there

watching Cameron, then turned silently back to her bedroom. He followed.

"That," I said softly, "is a complex relationship."

Seth nodded at the stairs. "I'm sure he's harmless. Although no ten-year-old boys are completely harmless; he probably has a frog up his shirt, or is planning a science experiment involving fungus."

"That's fine; Anna's brought home her own science experiments. Long as it's not fungus growing on an amputated body part." I felt strange suddenly, almost weightless, like I'd just drunk too much wine in too few gulps. So when Seth laughed and slipped his arm around my waist, I hesitated but then rested my head against his shoulder.

I could feel his chest rising and falling against my ribs, like his breath was my own. This suddenly felt so completely natural, his hip notched against my waist, his scent so instantly familiar, a mix of wheat and wet earth.

I remembered the day before I'd left for college, the day after we'd convinced ourselves a long-distance relationship would be too hard. We'd stood together, looking down at my packed boxes, and he'd said, "We might still get married someday."

But I pretended I hadn't heard. I was too scared. That this was all my life would ever be; the predictability of it; maybe the fear that Seth might, in some way, turn into my father when I knew I didn't have the energy to become my mother, injecting life into something that would otherwise feel dead. I don't know. Probably it was just that I was too young. And when I didn't respond, Seth had pulled away and we'd never spoken of it again.

"I'm sorry," I said now.

Seth didn't speak for a long while, but then his grip tightened around my waist and he said, "For what?"

"I don't know. I guess for not appreciating what we had, the way things ended, all of it."

"Were you thinking our relationship shouldn't have been so complex?"

I squared my shoulders. Our relationship had seemed the opposite of complex, would never have been anywhere near as complicated as my marriage with Josh. Which, of course, was part of what I'd liked about Josh, the complexity, although now that I'd been through it, I could imagine how much easier this other life would've been. "No," I said. "I don't know what I was thinking."

"I guess I kind of was." Seth pulled away and stood a moment, head down, inspecting his shoes. "You told me about Josh, and over the years I kept thinking you'd change your mind, or he'd divorce you, and I'd be here." He smiled wryly. "I had this whole set of fantasies. Her husband will be boring! Selfish! Stupid! She'll realize what a mistake she made and come back, and we'll…I don't know, settle with her kids in Napa and open a vineyard—"

"You wanted to open a vineyard?" I said blankly.

He held my eyes, looking almost annoyed, then said, "I should've tried harder." And before I could even register what he'd just said, he turned and walked toward the kitchen. "Need more tea."

If I'd told him then that I wanted to get married someday, where would we be now? If I could've seen how things turned out, would I have given up the joy and pain of this life for the simplicity of that? Would I have felt like I was settling? I wouldn't have been unhappy, but of course there was more to happiness than the absence of unhappiness.

I listened to Seth pouring water, and imagined this was our life. I closed my eyes and imagined this was our home, a lazy Sunday where we'd made love in the morning, then jointly prepared the type of breakfast that required a griddle, had read each other stories from the paper and now would settle down to drink tea and watch football with the kids.

I walked slowly into the living room, and sank onto the couch. Pressed my fists between my knees, looking down at the orange juice stain on the arm of my blouse, courtesy of my mom who that morning had scooped French toast into her full glass.

How many people had lives that weren't complex? I remembered Josh telling me about his own mother, how absent she'd been while he was growing up, locked inside a depression even worse than his own. He'd told me how it was, wanting to share things with her but knowing she wouldn't listen, and I'd thought it was unimaginably awful. But now I was going through the same thing with my own mother, and the kids were going through it as well without Josh. Maybe that was an undercurrent of everyone's life, the needs that weren't met, this sense of betrayal.

And suddenly I felt something akin to anger, thinking of the mornings I woke up feeling completely blank, thinking *Josh, Josh, Josh,* like I was trying to reinforce the anguish. Where had this come from? This sudden rage surging through me painful as a broken rib, rage at everybody and nobody, at the universe. Like my confession to Seth had unleashed a flood of sludge that had been amassing in me, unlooked at all these weeks. Had it always been there?

Seth entered the room with two mugs of tea, set one on the coffee table and then sat in the armchair staring into the other. "I'm sorry," he said.

I stood and paced to the window, looking out, then spun to face him, my eyes suddenly stinging with a heat that felt more like sand than tears. "You know I'm pissed off at everybody? At my mom for having turned into a seventy-year-old toddler, at Josh for making me have to work a dead-end job and for what he's done to our kids, because they're never going to be the same again. They've lost something they'll never get back, and I'm mad at myself for not having any idea how to fix them, and at all the people who're going through normal lives, which is most of the rest of the world, which makes me mad at myself again for being mad at everybody. At Dad for managing to be so calm about all of it, and at you for having the choice of whether to keep your marriage, but ending it anyway."

"You're angry at me?" There was a broken, confused look on his face, which made me want to hit either my head or his head against the wall.

"Yes," I said. "Okay? I'm angry at you. Because here you are coming back into my life now. And because you're not Josh. And even if you don't realize it, you've been taking me away from him, and the fact I'm angry about it is so messed up I can't even stand myself." And with that, my knees all of a sudden gave way and I slumped onto the floor. "What the hell's wrong with me?"

"Natalie—"

"Just don't. You really think anything you say can fix things? They can't be fixed!"

He strode over to me and knelt beside me, and I saw his eyes, transparent to everything behind them. He tried to take me into his arms, and I punched at his chest to push him away. But still he held on and all at once something swelled in me. It was a longing that had teeth and fists that pushed me against him, burying my face in his neck and licking, biting at his skin.

He stiffened but I pressed my lips against his; he flinched away but then he made a small sound, pressed his hands at my ears, and kissed me back.

His arms, his smell, the muscles of his chest; my upper lip between his lips, his breath heavy and the sudden urgent swell of him against my leg. And in my mind, *Josh, Josh, Josh* even as I tried to push it away, as I pulled at Seth's shirt, my other hand cradling his erection.

Seth froze. "Wait," he said.

"Don't wait," I said, "don't talk. Don't say anything."

"Natalie." His voice was hoarse.

But I silenced him with my lips on his, focused on the feel of his lips and his tongue to silence the voice in my head. And I wanted to tell Seth I loved him, or I had loved him, or at least that I could love him someday, because I knew it was true; I'd known it the first time I saw him, and every time I saw him the knowing grew. But suddenly I could feel Josh in the room, not just the warning of his name but an actual physical presence encircling my throat.

I quickly pulled away and stood, then backed into the room with my hand against my mouth. "I'm sorry," I said from behind it.

"It's okay." Seth's face was flushed, his hair rumpled; he stood and briskly tucked in his shirt. "I should go," he said.

I nodded and he ran a hand through his hair, started to speak, but then closed his mouth again and gave a brisk nod. He reached for the jacket he'd thrown across a chair, and walked from the room without saying a word.

47
Anna

It was weird seeing Cam. I'd almost forgotten he even existed.

What I really wanted was just to be alone, in bed, looking over at Josephina Graham's smiling shell collection face so I could unload everything in my head, take it out and look at what it meant.

So when Cam came into the room, I said, "I'm sorry, but you better not come in. My brother can't have visitors." I glanced at Toby, who was lying on the floor. His dinosaur was eating one of his feet. "On account of he hurt his head yesterday, in an accident."

I did not mean this in a bad way, but it gave Cam a hurt feelings look, and I had this thought: that he had probably been in many circumstances where he wasn't wanted. So I said, "Never mind, I guess it's okay. I mean it's not like it'll make him die or anything."

"Cool." Cam's face changed back, the hurt wrinklings smoothing out. He sat on Toby's bed. "So you want to know how come I'm here?"

I looked up at him. "How come?"

"It's because my dad wanted me to ask you about your dad."

"What do you mean? Why?"

Cam shrugged. "Your dad's kind of famous now because of the article, so I guess he was just curious."

"People were sending my mom money," I said, then sat on the bed next to Cam. "What does he want to know?"

"Well, he wanted me to ask how bad your dad's memory was."

I narrowed my eyes, looking at him sideways. "What do you mean?"

"Like, if he couldn't remember things that happened to him. And he also wanted to ask if you know what made your dad sad."

Did Mr. Carson find out how Dad died? Did he tell Cam? "How did he know my dad was sad?"

"I guess your mom told him, after the article came out." He looked at my face, then looked quickly away. "I shouldn't've asked you. Never mind."

Cam did know. I could tell from his face. There was a sour, burning taste in my throat. I looked over at Toby who now was on his knees, wheeling around the Carbot with the dinosaur puppet over its head. "It was the war," I said. "He was sad because of the war, and he died because of the war."

"I know that. Forget I asked anything, okay?"

Why would Mom tell Mr. Carson? And why would he tell Cam to ask me? It was something private! Between me and Mom and Toby, our own private thing to hold inside us and know without saying the words. Not a thing for somebody I didn't know to look at and talk about behind our backs.

"My dad likes getting in people's business, which is why he's a reporter. He sucks sometimes, but we won't talk about it anymore." Cam put his hand on my shoulder, then pulled it away again.

I lay back on the bed. Did people at Pendleton still talk about how Dad died? Did the kids in my class? I was pretty sure they all knew. On my first day back after the funeral, a fifth grader called Craig Krafton saw me in the hall, smiled wide, put his finger up to his head, and pulled a fake trigger. Getting away from that had been the only good thing about leaving there and coming here.

"You want me to go home?" Cam said.

"No." I folded my arms over my eyes. "Just talk about something else. How was San Clemente? Did you see if the X was at Custard King?"

"No, sorry. I asked my dad but he said we didn't have time."

I kicked my feet up and looked at my sneakers. It was stupid, I knew that. It was just an X carved into wood. But I missed it.

"All we did all day was just hang out at this bagel place with outside tables."

"The Bagel Barn," I said.

"We didn't even order bagels, just drank Cokes, and whenever somebody wearing a uniform walked by, my dad got up and talked to them. We did that pretty much all morning."

"Why? What did he talk about?"

"I couldn't hear him, but he kept showing them this picture of some girl." Cam licked his thumb and rubbed at a smear on his jeans, then licked his thumb again. "It sucked we flew all the way down there just to drink Coke, and then eat at McDonalds. We stayed in this dumpy motel, and we woke up when it was still dark out to fly back home. The whole thing sucked."

"I loved it there," I said, and I wanted to be able to explain, but it wasn't the kind of thing that could be explained in words. I'd loved my house, my friends, but it was more than that. It was the last time I felt like I was myself.

There was a knock on the door and Mom came in, her face puffy and her eyes all red. Was she crying? "I just want to check on you, Toby," she said, her voice hoarse. What would make her cry? I rolled over to see if I could tell from her face and suddenly, too late, saw the dinosaur puppet. "Where'd you get this from?" she said, tickling one of its eyeballs.

I widened my eyes. "Cam!" I said. "Cam brought it."

Cam looked over at me, but I ignored him. "It used to be his, but he doesn't want it anymore."

"That's generous of you," Mom said. "Toby loves dinosaurs." She bent to touch Toby's bump, then said, "It feel okay?"

"I'm good," Toby said.

Mom stared at him, then actually fell back, onto her butt, and I realized this was the first time she'd heard Toby since he got his words back. It's funny how fast you get used to stuff. Already I'd forgot this was a new thing. "He just started talking again," I said. "For no reason."

Mom sat there with her mouth open. And then she pulled Toby onto her lap, and with her face in his hair she whispered, "I'm so glad, baby, I'm so glad."

I smiled at them, because it was working, exactly what I'd planned. And here is a rule that I have come to believe, that there are times when a lie should not count against you. Or even if it does count against you, you should not care.

Mom wouldn't let go of Toby, carried him downstairs so he'd be with her while she made dinner, and I lay back on the bed with Cam, holding my pillow.

I know it sounds a little mental, but I was actually starting to think of the presents as being from Dad. I was actually starting to believe he could've come down from heaven, maybe in the form of the gift shop lady. If there was actually a heaven, then those kinds of things would have to be possible. Dad was here and saying, "You'll know what to do." Maybe, he even brought me Cam.

Because what I needed was more ammunition. By "ammunition" I do not mean the kind that comes from guns, I mean the b) definition, enough things to prove a point. I needed things.

"How come you told your mom the dinosaur was from me?" Cam said.

I hugged my pillow. "I actually have to tell you something," I said. "I need your help."

Cam crossed his legs, and dirt from his shoe smudged on my sheet. The shape of a comma. "What?" he said.

"Okay," I said. "Okay, here's the thing. You're going to think this is weird, but just listen. Because I've been pretending to Toby and my mom that my dad came down from heaven."

Cam widened his eyes. "Awesome," he said.

"And that he brought Toby presents. First the Carbot I stole, and then that dinosaur puppet, and it made Toby start talking again. But then I told my mom the letter we wrote last week just showed up on my bed from heaven, which she didn't believe me."

"You thought she'd believe your dad wrote something after he was dead? No offense, but you're not a very good liar." He leaned all the way back on my bed, his legs hanging over the side. "Did she get mad?"

"No, not really but see, I need her to believe me because it's getting worse, with Seth. A lot worse." I tucked my hand in my pillowcase and felt inside, the coldness, remembering Mom's smile when she saw Seth at the door. "I think she's starting to love him back," I said.

"Oh…" Cam watched me a minute without speaking, and then he swung his legs, thinking. One of his laces was undone and it clopped against his other sneaker. "You have to tell her something only your dad would know, and pretend he came down from heaven to tell you about it."

"What kind of stuff?"

"Did you look for her secret place? Maybe she's hiding something there's no way you could know about, but your dad would be able to see it from where he is." He stood up. "C'mon, let's look."

I glanced sideways at him, then said, "In her bedroom?"

"It'll only take a couple minutes. She's making dinner, right? She won't catch us."

I felt all shivery and wrong, but I said, "Okay. Okay, let's."

So we snuck into the hall, walked into my mom's bedroom, and closed the door. "You check under the bed," Cam said, "and I'll look in the dresser." He went to open a drawer, and I wanted to stop him because Cam looking in her dresser just didn't seem right. But there was no way around it. This was something that had to be done, so I felt under Mom's mattress, and then under her pillow. And there, I found a secret.

I pulled out my dad's Marines T-shirt and held it up to my face, remembering how he used to smell after he came back from running. Mom always teased him, because he pretty much never washed the shirt and it used to smell like moldy potatoes. How when Mom teased him he'd open his arms wide and roar, and he'd try to hug her and she'd scream. I pulled the shirt on over my head. And then, I looked under the bed. And found another secret.

It was on a hanger, inside of see-through plastic. I sat on the floor and pulled it out. Cam looked at me, and then he came over to pat my shoulder. He didn't say anything, but you could tell he understood exactly.

I sat a long time with the uniform, and then I said, "It's okay." And, suddenly, it almost was. You can get used to things. You don't stop feeling them, but they turn familiar. They come back and you recognize them, like you recognize a headache—not fun, but not scary either. *Oh,* you think, *here it is again.*

Cam went back to the dresser and I pulled out my dad's jacket, touched the badges on the front pocket. I could imagine him in it, perfectly. I put my hands flat on the uniform and looked down at them, my nails dirty and too long. I remembered the time Dad wrote on them in magic marker, ANNABANANA. It stayed there a long time, but not long enough.

Cam opened my mom's underwear drawer, and then he just stood there without moving, looking all sunken. And I knew why. For him, looking at ladies' underwear was the same as me looking at my dad's uniform. It reminded him of what was gone.

Finally, he reached his hand inside and felt around. *"Bingo,"* he said, and then he pulled the drawer out all the way and scooped the underwear onto the floor. "Look."

There was a little nail on the bottom of the drawer, and when Cam pulled it the whole bottom came out.

Under the drawer bottom was: lots of papers, lots of photographs, cards in envelopes, a round plastic container,
and a tube of something called Spermicidal Jelly.

I picked up the tube and squeezed out a little jelly,
tasted it. Not good.

"Whoa," Cam said. "Look at this."

I knelt next to him and read the card he'd pulled out.

Natalie,

Surprise! I can't believe it's only been seven years
since I found you. You know I still have the first
message you ever left me saved on my cell phone?
You said something like, "Um, hi, um, this is, um,
Natalie Hanson..." You asked me yesterday why I
love you—well, that message is one reason. Another's
the way when I turn on a Cary Grant movie you say,
"Cool," unironically.

I hate that I have to leave again next week. You're
the only thing that keeps me sane out there.
Whenever I feel like hell I think of you, and it's like
taking a pill (Prozac? Ecstasy?) that makes the
hellishness go away.

I'm waiting for you now, in Bethesda Park. Take
the flowers with you, and I'll bring the champagne.
I've arranged for the babysitter to pick Anna up at
daycare, so don't worry about going home.

Love for an eternity,
Josh

Attached to the card was a blue Post-it note that said,
in my dad's handwriting, *Stop whatever you're doing right now
and smile, and give yourself a hug from me.* I unpeeled it and
touched the letters, and how I felt: weird. First, because I

never really thought about them having something together that had nothing to do with me and Toby. And second, because Dad had said he'd love Mom for eternity, but eternity hadn't lasted very long at all.

"There's stuff you could use from this. Like how they went on a picnic and drank champagne."

"Uh-huh," I said.

He started looking at the photographs, handing me each one after he'd seen it. My dad, sleeping. My dad in his uniform standing in front of a bus with other Marines people, looking almost about to cry. My mom in a puffy wedding veil, looking like a fairy godmother. And then, my dad laughing and holding a baby, maybe me or maybe Toby. I looked at this one a long time. Probably, it was me.

"Wait," Cam said. "Hey, look, this is her."

I looked over at the photo in Cam's hand, a girl wearing one of those hoodie things they wear in Iraq, with a big red mark on her face.

"The girl with the blob on her face," Cam said. "Who my dad was showing to people in San Clemente. Does your mom actually know her? Or your dad?"

"I never saw her before. How come your dad wanted to know about her? Who is she?"

"I'm pretty sure he's writing an article about her. I couldn't sleep in the motel, so I started looking at his notes. I wanted to know how come we had to go all the way down there and waste my whole day, just to show people her picture, and the notes were all about things that happened to her in Iraq."

"What things?"

"Well, it's not good things. It was all about her getting blood-gunned."

I felt a coldness in me, like I'd just swallowed an icicle. "Blood-gunned?"

"Blood-gunned with stones until she was dead, and other kids died too. Her dad was a translator. And he worked with Marines, I guess translating, and she got to be friends with them too."

"And she knew my dad."

"Well, I guess, yeah, since your mom has her picture. You should totally use that, say your dad told you about a girl he was friends with, who got blood-gunned with stones."

Dad knew a girl who got killed, and what did he think when he found out? Was that how come he was so sad? If I knew a girl who got killed, I probably wouldn't be able to come out of my room either. "Who blood-gunned her?"

"I don't know for sure, but my dad wrote questions about what happened after she died, whose fault it was."

I hugged my knees tight. "Whose fault was it?" My voice sounded weird, like an old lady's.

"He just was asking the question, he didn't write an answer. I think nobody in San Clemente wanted to talk to my dad, they all just gave him dirty looks."

"My dad didn't have anything to do with how come she died."

"I know that."

I stuck the picture on the bottom of the pile. "I don't want to do this anymore," I said.

Cam looked at me funny. "How come?"

"I just don't." I pulled off my dad's T-shirt, folded it, and stuck it back under Mom's pillow.

Here is what I wanted: I wanted to put all my memories of my dad into a box and make that box into something that was all mine. But now he was growing outside it, pieces of him that belonged to my mom in her veil and to the girl with the red mark on her face, and to the Marines on the bus to wherever he was going.

But even if I could find out all the pieces they knew, I still wouldn't learn even close to everything he should've been able to tell me. And that was probably what hurt most. It was all the things I might never get to know.

48
Natalie

I made pancakes for breakfast, more trouble than I usually went to on a school day, but I needed the distraction. And I knew this was just a postponement of the inevitable, that I hadn't let myself feel the questions that were trying to stab at me from behind it. After Seth left, I'd lain facedown in bed with my fists dug against my ribs, trying to keep my attention on the pain rather than the clawing panic. And now I'd make a good breakfast and go to work, focus only on moving my limbs in the right directions, until whatever was roiling inside me subsided enough that I could look at it, without falling apart.

Anna was tearing her pancakes into shreds, hadn't put a thing in her mouth besides her juice and chewable vitamins. I watched her pile the shreds in the center of her plate and then arrange them into circles. I tried prompting her into conversation, and then into actually putting some of these shreds into her mouth, but she gave one- or two-word answers to my questions, tore the shreds into smaller shreds, and rearranged them into rows.

"Your stomach okay?" I said.

She nodded and shrugged.

"I'll eat her pancakes," Toby said. I speared a pancake

off my own plate, and set it on his, still thrilled to hear his voice.

Dad stood for more coffee. "Anyone ever tell you about starving children in Ethiopia? Or is it Southeast Asia now? Know what we used to do when your mom was your age? She didn't eat something, we'd set it in front of her for the next meal, and then the meal after that. We'd give her the same bowl of oatmeal for two days straight, till she got hungry enough to finish it."

This wasn't strictly true. After Mom's first failed attempts, she'd inevitably dump the untouched meal in the trash and fix me something new. "She just scarfed it down!" she'd tell Dad, shaking her head in faux disbelief.

"I'm just not hungry, okay?" Anna pushed her plate away. "Mom, I have to talk to you. It's important."

I fingered a stray hair from her eyes. "We don't have a whole lot of time before the bus."

"'Course I'm not saying you should do that with your kids," Dad said. "'Specially not with food that now looks like it could line a hamster cage."

"Dad, you mind helping Toby brush his teeth and get his bag together?"

Dad raised his eyebrows at me. "One of these days, Anna's going to just evaporate." He snapped his fingers. *"Poof!"* he said, and then he stood and ruffled the top of Anna's head.

After they'd left, I pulled my chair up next to Anna's. "Okay, go on," I said.

She slipped her hands into her shirtsleeves, not looking at me. "It's about Dad. Something he told me that I didn't want to say, because it's not nice."

I suddenly felt dizzy, the drunk, nauseous kind of dizzy where your head doesn't feel quite connected to your body. "Tell me," I said. "It's okay if it's not nice, I won't get upset."

She glanced at me, then back at the floor. "You might get upset, though. Because it's about Seth. Dad doesn't want him coming over anymore."

Ah, yes. This should've been completely predictable. My head settled back where it belonged. "Anna, I know how it has to feel seeing me with a friend who's a man."

"He's not a friend and you don't know! Dad hates him!"

"Anna…"

"Dad came down from heaven and he talked to me, and I know you don't believe it but you should, because it's the truth! He told me other things, too, like about a time it was your anniversary and he got a babysitter for me and he brought champagne, and you went to a park to drink it."

Bethesda Park. It was the seventh anniversary of the day we'd met, and I'd brought the flowers he'd given me to the park and found him waiting there with champagne, a baguette, and Brie. That had been the night when we'd decided to have another child; could, in fact, have been the night Toby was conceived. "He told you about the picnic?"

"And he said I should tell you about it because he wanted you to remember how much you love each other."

Something was building inside me; a pressure under my ribs, part pain but part something else. I knew perfectly well not to trust the something else, but it had teeth. How easy would it be to let myself believe her, to float away on the possibility like I'd done writing Josh's letters?

"We do love each other," I said slowly. "I mean, we were very much in love. But he told you about the picnic when he was alive, Anna. And I know you feel confused right now—"

"No! Not when he was alive! I don't care if you don't believe me, but don't you care what he thinks? Doesn't it matter at all if he can see you?" She spun out of the room, and I heard her footsteps raining up the stairs, and then the slam of her bedroom door.

I watched after her, my mind strangely blank, maybe trying to avoid the pummeling thoughts in the only way it knew how. "But you haven't done anything!" I said the words out loud, but that didn't make them true.

Because it had been more than just a kiss. More than a physical or emotional reflex, more than a nostalgic longing for the simplicity of my past. It was an acknowledgment that I'd someday allow myself to stop grieving. It was a letting go of Josh.

49
Anna

All day it strangled me, thinking about Mom and Seth. It used to be where whenever Dad passed Mom in the hall, he'd reach for her and they'd stand there hugging without talking. And when we all watched TV, they'd sit together on the sofa with her head on his shoulder and him playing with her hair, sometimes pulling it over her face and to his mouth so he could kiss it. How could she forget about somebody who loved her so much? All day I went back and forth between wanting to cry and wanting to hit somebody, and all I knew was, I needed help.

I'll ask Cam, I kept thinking. *I'll ask Cam and he'll help.* But when recess came and we went to sit on the playground bench, he said, "So, did you tell your mom about the girl who got blood-gunned?" And it was like my skin closed up over the top of my words. Because I knew if I told him what I said to Mom that morning, the word he'd say back to me was, *cool.*

I curled my fingers under the bench seat and felt the piece of chewed gum I'd stuck there last week. It felt smooth but also wrinkled, like a scar. I could feel the imprint from my teeth. "No," I said. "I don't know if I'm going to."

"How come?"

"I just don't want to, okay?" I picked at the gum and it came off in my hand. I threw it across the grass.

"Fine, whatever." He looked over at the playground, then turned back and gave me a slow half smile, held it a long time and then said, "So by the way, my dad had your name on his notes too. On the back of the page where he talked about the girl."

"What do you mean? What did he say about me?"

"He didn't say anything, just your name underlined, and nothing else. Unless…maybe it wasn't you?" He was smiling all the way now, kicking his feet up to look down at his sneakers. "First I thought maybe he just got your name wrong."

I chopped his arm with the side of my hand. "Stop acting like this. What're you talking about?"

"Maybe nothing." He gave a slow shrug, still smiling. "But do you know somebody called Hannah Graham?"

"That's my dad's mom," I said slowly. "How did he know about her?"

"He's a reporter, duh. And maybe, maybe she called my house." He pulled his foot up on the bench and tightened the knot in his shoelace. "Maybe I know where she's living."

"My Grandma Graham called *you*?"

"Yep," he said, "she did. She called last night."

I chopped at his arm again. "Why didn't you tell me!"

"I *am* telling you. Jeez!" He rubbed at his arm. "She called last night, okay? She asked for my dad, but he wasn't home yet so she said he was supposed to tell her an address, and that he should call her at the Econo Lodge on Route 5. Which is a hotel. I didn't tell my dad yet, because I thought you'd want to know first."

I never met my other grandmother. All I knew about her was the picture we kept on the TV, where his dad looked almost exactly like my dad except skinnier, and his mom was also skinny except pregnant and didn't look like him at all. I tried to imagine her taking care of him, reading him books, playing ball, and I wondered how much she loved him. If she'd even loved him at all.

And it was thinking about it that I got an idea. I suddenly knew what I had to do. It would be the most grown-up thing I ever did in my life. But also...also the most important thing. "I'm sorry I chopped your arm," I said.

And Cam smiled. "Yeah, I knew you would be."

When me, Grammy, and Grandpa pulled into the driveway, Grandpa said, "May I get you a snack before your mom and Toby get home?"

"Sure," I said.

"How does an apple sound to you?" Grandpa always asked if I wanted an apple and I always said sure, the exact same thing every day. You would think he'd just go ahead and assume.

"Sure," I said again.

In the kitchen he reached for a golden delicious, my least favorite, and I sat across from him as he started to cut it. Grammy walked into the kitchen, and he turned to her. "Would you like some apple, Meg?"

"Oh, yes," Grammy said and reached for a slice.

He smiled at Grammy, and she smiled back and reached for another slice of my apple. She tucked it into her shirt pocket, and Grandpa pulled it out again. She started to laugh and he patted her hand. "It's okay," he said, then used his thumb to wipe away a lipstick smudge at the side of her mouth. This is how they were. He knew everything she needed. He took care of it without her even needing to say.

I watched his hands working on the apple, the hair on his knuckles, the bumpy veins, then stood up. "I'm not hungry anymore. Just give it all to Grammy, okay?"

He raised his eyebrows, looking a little hurt, so I reached to give him a hug. He made a kind of grunting sound and I didn't want him to let go. I wanted to stay there, with my cheek pressed on his shirt and my arms around him and breathing his wood smell until everything went away. "Well," he said, and patted my back. "Well, well." You could tell he did not get hugged very often.

I pulled away and said, "I'm going upstairs, okay?" I grabbed the phone book from off the counter by the phone and went up. Into Mom's room. Where I stood by her night table, looked up Econo Lodge and dialed, my skin going all prickly.

"Econo Lodge, can I help you?"

"Is this a hotel on Route 5?"

Quiet, and then, "It's the Econo Lodge."

"Which is on Route 5, right?" I dug my nails into my knee and said, "Is Hannah Graham staying in one of your rooms?"

"Graham? Just a minute."

There was a click. I bounced up and down a little on my toes. I knew she wasn't at all the same as my real grammy. She always felt fake to me, like all she was is a name and that one picture we had, like paintings of olden day people you see in museums. But here she was. She had a phone number, and soon she'd have a voice. And she knew things about Dad that nobody else could tell me.

And then even before I heard the phone ring again, Hannah answered. "Hello?" Her voice was scratchy and sharp, not what I expected.

I pressed my lips between my teeth. This was my grammy's voice, which had talked to Dad when he was just a baby. She knew him before anyone else. "Mr. Carson?" she said.

"Hello…is this Hannah?"

"Who is this?"

"Hannah Graham?" I gave a little cough, then made my voice deeper, more grown-up. "This is Anna Graham."

"Excuse me?"

"Anna Graham, who is your granddaughter."

She didn't make a sound. For a long time there was nothing, and I waited for her to get it. Then finally, "Oh my God."

"I just wanted to talk to you 'cause…well because you're my grandmother and I thought I should. And there's stuff I want to ask you about my dad. When he was a kid."

"Oh my God," she said again. There was a shuffling sound, and then she said, "Dan Carson told you I was here."

I looked down at my knees and said nothing.

"Anna, Anna…I have your baby picture. I keep it on my dresser."

"You do?" I tried to imagine this lady I didn't know putting my picture by her bed. Even though I never met her, it made me miss her a little.

"And your brother's too. Your dad sent them to me after you were born."

"I didn't even know he talked to you anymore."

She paused, then said, "Well, we didn't talk very often.

We didn't leave on very good terms, and he never forgave me for it, but he did call every year or so, and he sent me the pictures. I've been wanting to talk to you for such a long time."

"I was wanting to talk to you too," I said. And then, I felt shy; I couldn't think of anything to say.

"So how are you all? You and your mom and brother? It must be… Well, I can't even imagine how it must be."

This was just like at Dad's funeral, all these people I hardly knew asking how I was doing, if I was okay. And knowing they didn't want to hear the true answer. "No," I said, "you can't imagine."

"I'm so sorry. I'd give my life ten times over to bring him back to you."

I wanted to ask how come Dad didn't like her, but that didn't seem polite. Instead, I said, "Did you love my dad?"

She was quiet a long time, and then she said, "I loved him very much. After my husband, your grandfather, died, he was everything to me."

"Then how come you didn't come to his funeral?"

"Oh, Anna. I should've come, I know that, I just…" She made a little choking sound and then pulled in her breath and said, "I can't really explain it. It was like the one thing that scared me most in the world had come true, and part of me felt like I made it happen by being so scared of it, thinking about it all the time. So I just couldn't make myself face the fact that he was having a funeral."

It kind of made sense. Last year was when I started getting scared of something happening to Dad, when he'd go into his room and not come out. And one time I saw him sitting on the sofa and crying. I went and kneeled next to him and hugged his shoulders. I stayed with him for like an hour and he kept crying and he never hugged me back. All those times I got scared he'd go away forever, and then, it happened.

"Can you tell me something?" she said. "Did *you* love your dad?"

"Well, yeah, he was my dad."

"Was he a good dad? Could you tell me what he was like?"

"He was great," I said. "He was a totally great dad, and he was funny, and he liked to read big books and talk about them with my mom who also reads big books. And when we played games he always would lose on purpose, and one time he saved a bird that flew into our window."

That was my dad. All of those things together. I wrote them into my memory so that later I could add them to my list.

"You know, he wanted to be a teacher. If he hadn't joined the Marines that's probably what he would've done, study philosophy in college and get his certification to teach it. He loved learning about how the world and people work."

"Uh-huh," I said, even though I had no idea what she meant. I reached in Mom's nightstand for a pen, and I wrote down *teacher* and *filosofy* so I'd remember. How could Hannah know things I didn't? "What was he like when you knew him?"

"Well, he was wonderful, really. He was quiet, but not in a shy way; it was in a way that made you feel like he was always listening. And he cared about everything and everyone. Like there was this puppy we had when he was a kid, named Countess Chocula."

I smiled. "Countess Chocula?"

"And she was only about a year old when she got hit by

a kid on a motorcycle. Which she survived, but she had something called paralysis, which meant she couldn't walk. Josh's dad wanted to put the dog down, but Josh put her in diapers and wheeled her around on a cart. Oh, I probably shouldn't be telling you this. It's a sad story."

I could imagine it perfectly, Dad wheeling the dog everywhere he went. Even changing her diapers. "I never heard of a dog wearing diapers," I said.

"I'll tell you what he said to me, when Countess Chocula finally died. He said the dog was so sad about what she'd lost that he couldn't be sad about her death. He said there are worse things than dying, and I think that's what he'd say to you now. That you shouldn't be sad, because there are many things worse than dying."

I squeezed my fist around the pen, and drew a hard line across the paper. "Well, there aren't too many things worse than your dad dying," I said.

"No, I guess not." Hannah was quiet a long, long time, and then she said, "I was so scared to get in touch with you all. I wanted to more than anything after I found out what happened, but I thought you probably wouldn't want to talk to me. And then somebody called, a friend of yours."

"Mr. Carson."

"He wanted to talk about your dad, about what he went through after your grandfather died. He said he knew you all, that he lived in your town, so I came up. Because I thought maybe if I showed up at your door, your mom would be willing to let me meet you."

"He wanted to talk about Dad?" And suddenly, I understood. "Mr. Carson called you because he's writing another article?"

"An article honoring your dad, which is so nice, I think. You should be so proud." She was quiet a minute, and then she said slowly, "So now you've called, since we're talking…I'd really like to meet you in person, Anna. Would that be okay? And I'd like to talk to your mom too, and your brother. I'd really like to meet your brother."

Well, this wasn't good. I was getting ammunition about Dad, but if Mom met Hannah, she'd know where it came from. "Actually," I said, "you probably better not." I rubbed my hand fast back and forth over my leg. "Because Mom doesn't like you."

"Right," Hannah said, then, "Well, I guess I don't blame her, but she doesn't know the whole story. Although I guess even if she knew the whole story she'd probably still hate me."

I picked up my pen again. "What's the whole story?"

"Someday, maybe I'll explain it all to you. It has a lot to do with stubbornness and the bad habits of my relationship with Josh and right now, you probably wouldn't understand it. But I'd like to be able to convince your mom I'm not such a bad person."

She sounded sad when she said this, so sad that I started to feel bad for her. So I said, "I guess you could come see us."

"That'd be…amazing. Can you give me your address?"

I tried to balance the pen on its tip, watched it fall over. "Um, no," I said. "Actually, maybe you could come see me at my school first? Because I'm there all week, and Toby too, so that way maybe Mom could come and we could all go out for lunch, and maybe Mom could take you after, to our home."

"Okay," Hannah said slowly, "I guess that sounds okay. Just check with your mom first, and call me back or have her call if she doesn't want me to come."

"I'll check, but I'm sure she'll want to meet you. My

school's called Bidwell and it's on Jefferson Street, and you could wait for me, for us, outside the playground at recess."

So we arranged to meet tomorrow, and before hanging up Hannah said, "I'm so glad you called, Anna. It's like the most wonderful thing that's happened to me in years, getting to talk to you."

After I hung up I sat there in the chair, watching the sky go from the color of a bruise to the color of an older bruise. I sat there and I thought about how in my whole life I never really had a secret, but now I was so full up with them that I could feel them wanting to leak out whenever I opened my mouth. It was scary keeping so much in. It made me feel like I couldn't breathe.

But I had enough ammunitions to help convince Mom that I was talking to Dad, and if it wasn't enough, there was still more I could learn from Hannah, and maybe even from the real letter from Dad. I'd look at it if I had to. This was too important.

50
Anna

At Tuesday recess I stood with Cam looking around the playground.

A girl named Cheryl came over and smiled at me. "Want to play jump rope?" she said. Cheryl always wore the same thing, except in different colors. It was: a stretchy top that showed her shoulders, a necklace with beads, a watch that had switch-out wristbands, bobble bands on her braids. All of her always matched, all red or yellow or purple or turquoise, and just when you thought she must be running out of colors, there she'd be, all orange. Sometimes she even had matching eye shadow.

I looked over at the group of girls forming a line. I've thought of this before, that there could be a math formula to find out how useful it is to be someone's friend. You take the size of that someone's popularity and times it by your own, add on something based on how pretty you are. The amount the other girls liked me on a scale of one to ten was a zero, but Cheryl wasn't much higher so whatever extra she gave me wasn't worth the trouble. "You can go," I told her. "I don't really want to."

"Nah, that's okay," she said. "I feel bad for you, not having other friends."

Huh. This was what my life had come to.

"Actually," I said, "I'm supposed to meet somebody, a lady, and I want to find out if she's here. Want to walk around and help me look?"

"What lady?" Cheryl said.

"Just somebody who knew my dad. I never met her before."

So we all walked around the playground, slow and searching. How would we look from the outside, to someone who didn't know us? I thought of *The Wizard of Oz*, them traveling together, none of them matching, all of them weird in a different way.

We'd got halfway around the playground when Cam pointed. "That her?"

There was a woman standing by the edge of the playground. She had hair in a ponytail and old-person lines around her mouth, dark, sad eyes and a foldy neck. She was wearing all white, a sweatshirt and white pants. Even her skin and her hair were white, so she looked exactly like a ghost. She raised her hand up a little ways, by her shoulder.

"C'mon," I said. We walked up to her.

"Are you Hannah?" I asked.

She reached her hand out to me, then pulled it back. "Yes," she said. "Hi, Anna."

"These are my friends," I said, and then I thought about this. I should look up the definition of *friend* in my dictionary. It was more than just someone you spent time with; it was someone you'd spend time with even if you had other options.

"Hi, I'm Cheryl!" Cheryl stuck out her hand.

Hannah smiled and took her hand and they shook.

"Nice to meet you," she said, then, "So, Anna, is your mom here?"

I was scared a little. There wasn't any real reason to be, but scared is not something you can talk yourself out of. "Let's go there and I'll tell you," I said, pointing to a rock where kids sometimes played King of the Hill. And then I whispered in Cam's ear. "Keep watching us, okay? Don't look away."

When we got to the rock we both climbed up it and looked out over the playground, where Cheryl and Cam were just standing there watching us. "I like your friends," Hannah said.

"Yes," I said. "They're nice." Every single part of my body wished I was there with them, except my head, which was curious. I wanted her to tell me every day of Dad's life from the very beginning, all the words he said and the friends he had, and the toys he liked to play with. I'd ask her if he always knew he wanted kids, if he liked little girls back then or if he just learned to because of me.

Her mouth moved like she was shifting a candy from one cheek to the other, and then she smiled and said, "Can I tell you what I was wondering? I was wondering if you could do this." She bent her thumb backward in the shape of an upside-down L.

Huh. "Yes," I said, and bent my thumb back to show her.

"That's a genetic trait. Your dad could do it too." She was grinning like it was some talent I should be proud of. "How 'bout this. Can you curl your tongue?" She curled her tongue at me, and I curled my tongue back. Was this what we'd be doing until recess was over?

She uncurled her tongue and reached to touch my

cheek soft, then pulled away like I'd given her a shock. "So," she said, "is your mom coming?"

I felt my face get hot. "She couldn't. Or actually, she got mad when I told her how I talked to you. Like…mad enough to beat you up."

Hannah looked at me carefully, and her face said all kinds of things, skeptical, sad, angry, more sad. It was like the game me and Madison used to play where she'd make a face and I'd make mine into a mirror, and then I'd make a face and she'd make hers into a mirror: sad, surprised, angry, scared, crying, one after the other, and the first person who laughed is the one who lost. Hannah's face was like that, but all the feelings there at one time. None of them had anything to do with laughing.

"But she said it was okay if I saw you." I gave her a wide smile. "Because she knows there's stuff I have to ask you."

"What do you mean?" she said. "Like what?"

"Like…could you tell me something Dad wouldn't have said to me? Like a secret something you'd only tell a grown-up?"

She looked at me. "Why something he'd only tell a grown-up?"

I scratched my nails over the rock, felt the shiver of it up my arm. "Because," I said. "Because I don't know enough about him." And suddenly my whole body hurt, because it was so true. "I hardly know anything, and I just want to find the rest of it out."

She was quiet a minute, but then she said, "I don't know about a secret, but I could tell you more about his childhood." She frowned a little, then said, "He was quite an athlete, probably could've got an athletic scholarship if he'd wanted to go that route. He played football in high school, and all the girls were after him because of it."

"He played football?" You think you know everything important about a person and then you find out, no. I used to think I was the only one who had a trillion pieces but I was learning that everyone did, parts that nobody else can see from the outside.

"Up through junior year, and then he got a hernia." She made a disgusted face, like she'd just told me he had warts.

I wrote this into my memory. *Hurnia*. "What's a hernia?"

"It's a lump you get in your belly. He had a scar." She pointed to her belly. "From the surgery."

"I have a scar." I pulled up my sleeve and showed her my elbow. "I needed eight stitches."

She smiled. "That's quite impressive."

"You can touch it if you want. It doesn't hurt."

She touched it carefully, and then she said, "Your dad's was much smaller than that. But he had to give up football for the season, and I think that's when he decided to join the Marines. Become a real hero rather than just a sports hero."

"His dad was a Marine too. That's how he got the idea."

"You're right," Hannah said. "If your grandpa had been anything else, Josh probably would've had a very different life. He wanted his dad to look down on him from heaven, and be proud."

This was something I understood exactly. "Do you believe in heaven?" I said.

Hannah glanced at me. "When I was your age I believed, but I grew out of it. You should keep believing, though. Because even if it's all a load of hooey, when you believe it's serving its purpose."

Hooey. It was a good word. I tried it on my tongue. "Dad thought heaven was a load of hooey."

"Yeah, I guess he probably did." She looked so sad when she said this and I recognized her face. It was my mom's face, wanting to cry about everything that happened and everything that should have happened. Maybe my face too. To make her feel better, I said, "I have a picture of you."

"Of me?"

"You and Grandpa Graham. We keep it on the TV."

Hannah raised her eyebrows. "You do?"

Because she seemed suddenly happier, I tried to remember what my dad had said about growing up. "He told me his dad was a hero, and that he taught him how to bat, and also the names of the constellations. And he said . . . he said you were nice and you had a pretty name."

"He said I was nice?"

I slipped a finger inside my sneaker and scratched my foot. "And that you had a pretty name."

Hannah paused, and then she said, "He didn't tell you anything about me, did he."

"Actually, not really very much."

Hannah looked out over the playground frowning, then said, "Okay, it's okay. You know Hannah was my mother's name too? And my grandmother's. It means the grace of God."

"I didn't know names could mean something." If I had a baby, I thought I would name it my favorite word, which is *Twinkle*. "I don't think *Anna* means anything."

"Maybe not." She was quiet a minute, and then she said, "But it rhymes with Hannah." She said this seriously, her voice all deep, like she thought it was something important. I wondered if she was a little mental.

Suddenly I remembered something Dad actually did say. He knew how to make really good enchiladas, even better than Mom. And he learned enchiladas because Hannah didn't like to cook, and he found out everything in the kitchen tasted good with melted cheese and a tortilla. "He said when he was a teenager he made you dinner."

"He told you that?" Hannah's face went pink. "I used to make the fanciest meals with fresh garlic, spices I grew in pots. But your grandpa died when Josh was just fifteen, and I didn't have room in my head for cooking, or much of anything else really."

"It wasn't a bad thing," I said. "He wasn't mad about it, it just was cool he learned how to cook."

"Not that cool." Hannah looked down at her knees a long while.

"Your dad was a lot like you, you know. Smart, soft-spoken—but he liked asking questions. He was one of those kids you'd say was wise beyond his years."

I felt something in me like a hiccup, of happiness. Everybody said Toby was like Dad, because they looked the same. Nobody had ever said that about me.

She pulled a tissue out of her pocket and blew her nose, then talked with the tissue still on her face. "So I'm sure you have to have questions. It has to be…confusing."

"I'm not confused," I said. "I just want to know how come you weren't like a real mom. Or a real grammy."

"'Course you do. And I want to have an answer for you, but there isn't any good answer."

I looked down at Hannah's sneakers. They were the

color of dirt, and one was untied and had a hole in the toe. I could see her red sock.

"I just got angry at him for no good reason, and he got angry back." She started tearing her tissue into little scraps, letting them drop onto the rock. "Because I didn't want him joining up. I was trying to make him see how he was too much like Ken, your grandpa, that he didn't have the right personality for a war zone. Neither of them knew how to turn off their feelings, so I knew going to war would change your dad the same way."

This was too grown-up a conversation for me, and I didn't know how to help her. I had no idea. So I just watched the torn-up tissues fall, imagined they were paper tears. "I hate the war," I said.

"Yeah, me too."

I'd wanted to find out more about Dad, but how could I ask questions when she seemed so sad? "I was wondering," I said. "Could you come back tomorrow?"

She watched me a long while, and then she said, "I need to talk to your mom first. I really shouldn't have been talking to you without her here."

"But...she doesn't want to see you!"

"I know, but I at least want to have a chance to talk to her. Could you tell her I'll call? And if she wants me to leave after we talk then I'll leave, but I want to have a chance to at least try and explain."

I looked sideways at her. "Do you have our phone number?"

"Could you give it to me?"

Here was the thing. She wouldn't find us in the book. We were under Grammy and Grandpa's number, so she wouldn't know where to look. I smiled at her. "I'll tell Mom to call you."

She nodded, and then she touched my head, held her hand there a long while and then slid off the rock and brushed off her butt. "You can tell her I'm staying at the Econo Lodge. I really hope we'll see each other again soon." And then she smiled at me and walked away without turning back.

I watched her leave, replaying everything she'd said and everything I said. When I got home I'd write it down and look at it all in one place and try to understand.

I tried to imagine Dad playing football. When we used to watch a game, he'd give the air little punches during a tackle. When someone tried a field goal and the ball went short or too far right or left, he'd wave his arms in the right direction like it could help. It didn't matter what team it was, he wanted them to make it.

Cam and Cheryl got up from the bench and came over to where I sat. They stood there watching me, and then Cam said, "You okay?"

"She knew my dad," I said, and then I started to cry.

Cam and Cheryl looked at each other, and then they climbed up to sit next to me, one on each side. They sat with me, not talking. The way their shoulders touched my shoulders felt almost like a hug.

Here is my new definition of the word *friends:*

1) People who understand the messed-up, hurt parts of you without you having to explain.
2) People who will not let you be alone with hard things.
3) People who, when you start to cry in a big way that makes sounds, will sit in front of you so nobody else can see.

———

"Dad told me he used to play football," I said. All day Toby was asking me if Dad had come. And now I could tell him yes because, in a way, he had.

Toby stayed quiet, watching me, then said, "Who for?" We were on his bed with the lights out. Only moonlight, which made Toby's face look gray, like another moon.

I thought about this, then said, "The Chargers. He played tight end."

Toby's eyes went wide, and I smiled at him. "He was really, really good, but then he broke something in his stomach called a hernia that gave him a scar in his belly and he had to stop playing."

Toby huddled under the covers looking up at me. "What else?" he said.

"Okay, also he wanted to be a teacher, and teach philosophy."

"Fil..."

"Osophy." It wasn't in my dictionary so I had made up my own definition which, even though I knew it wasn't right, was something I could imagine him wanting to learn. "It means helping dying babies, but he decided to join the Marines instead. And also he said heaven is a really cool place, where everybody's nice and takes care of each other, and he plays football there too. On a team called the Angels."

I heard Mom in the bathroom, running water. Soon she'd come to check on us, like she always did. I pulled up Toby's covers so his new bunny was hidden. Mom had been acting a little weird today. Two times she'd gone to pick up the phone, stared at it, and then put it down without making a call. I wanted to tell her what I'd learned from Hannah, but I knew it would be better to wait until she was normal again.

"Did you ask if I could talk to him?" Toby said.

"You can't. He said he's sorry, but he's not allowed to."

"But why? Why not?"

"Shhh..." I looked toward the door. The toilet flushed. "Okay, I'll ask next time. We have to go to sleep, okay? When Mom comes, pretend you're asleep."

I climbed up to my bed and crawled under the covers, and watched through my lashes Josephina Graham smiling. Bits of her were already starting to fall off, mostly her hair but also parts of her face, including one of her eyes. We could fix her, but I'd always know those parts of her weren't from that day we'd first blessed the house. Peace, happiness, and ice cream, but other than the ice cream, it hadn't really worked.

When Mom went into her bedroom, I looked over the edge of my bunk to see Toby. He was lying there with the hidden lump of the bunny tucked under his chin. Sucking his thumb. Eyes open and staring. Wearing questions I didn't know how to answer.

And lying there, watching him, I let my brain go to the place I usually tried not to let it. I imagined the night Dad left for Iraq, how it could've been. I imagined where he could've been instead.

We are out in the park, Dad pitching and me batting. Sometimes other kids see us and join in, and usually Toby would be there playing too. He has a bat that's red plastic and almost the size of his whole body, and when he's at the plate he taps it and scuffs his foot like he's in the National League. But not tonight. Tonight it's only us.

Dad throws the ball, and as soon as I swing I can tell it's a good one, *SMACK!* And there the ball goes, up into the trees and then past the trees, up like a rocket into heaven. We watch it get smaller, a spot, a speck, a star, and then Dad is so happy for me that he runs and picks me up, holds me. "Anna, I love you!" he says and he kisses my cheek, swings me around. And then he starts to put me down, but I say "No!" so he just holds me. The call comes about the mission, and they want to take him away on their plane, but he's not home, and the Marines people wait awhile but then they give up. His plane leaves and my arms and legs are around him. He smells like when you take a walk in the woods. His whiskers on my cheek feel like electricity.

And then the sky gets light, and he puts me down and holds my hand. We swing arms and we walk. In the window we see Mom cooking breakfast. And then, we are home.

51
Natalie

Driving to work with Toby Tuesday afternoon, I felt like I was moving through a thick, wet cloud. Everything I did seemed to be riding on an undercurrent of fear. Toby was quiet in the backseat as we drove, kicking his feet up and down, then up again to study his new sneakers. And watching him, suddenly the idea of going back to the office seemed ludicrous. Pushing phone buttons, depleting rain forests to make replicas of columns of numbers, answering calls from strangers so they could speak to other strangers. I'd rather bang my head repeatedly against the wall.

"Tell you what," I said. "Instead of going to work, let's go see if Mr. Burns is home. I have a feeling there's another quarter stuck in your ear, and he's the only one I know who can take it out."

I pulled in front of the deli, one of those new storefronts remodeled to look like they hadn't been remodeled in a century, hand-distressed red paint and all. And there was his car, the kind of subcompact Dodge offered as the lowest-priced option at rental agencies. I wondered if I could read something in the way it had been parked, angled with its back tire up on the curb. Distraction; impatience; frustration.

I walked with Toby into the deli and ordered three sandwiches from the round-faced woman behind the counter, brought the sandwiches up the back steps to Seth's apartment, hesitated, and then knocked. Seth opened the door almost immediately, and from a distance I looked at the tiny thrill it gave me to see him, weighed it, and tried to understand what it meant. I held up the bag. "We brought lunch."

Seth watched me questioningly, then stepped back so we could enter. Toby smiled shyly up at him. "Could you do my ear?"

Seth glanced at me, then smiled back. "I can at least try," he said, peering into both Toby's ears while rooting in his pockets. "But I'm not sure I see anything in there. Although—wait? What's this?" He reached forward and plucked a coin from behind Toby's ear. "You're like an ATM. Except it's all earwaxy; you better take it." He handed the coin over.

Toby clapped a hand over his ear, grinning, and took the quarter with the other. And watching, I felt a mix of melancholy and joy, hard to decipher. Part of me wanted Seth here, and part of me wished he was Josh. I didn't know which part was bigger.

"I'm glad you came." He leaned back against the arm of his sofa, hands in his pockets. "I was actually going to call you about this cabin just went on sale. A really sweet place in the middle of the woods, fifteen acres of protected land. They're doing a rent-to-own, which means you could hold it for almost no money down, and it needs a little work, so the lease payments would be really reasonable."

I felt slightly discombobulated. "It sounds great," I said. I suddenly remembered a conversation we'd had our senior year about buying a cabin in the woods. "A place so far away from everything nobody can hear us fucking," I'd whispered, which in hindsight doesn't exactly sound romantic, but at the time the idea had made me feel almost faint. I wondered if he remembered.

"Well, *great* is maybe overstating it a little, but it has a lot of potential. I could take you next week, if you want."

"Okay, sure. Thanks." Awkward pause. I held my smile. Was that it? Should I hand over the sandwiches and leave now, and postpone any real conversation for another week? "So," I said, "sandwich? I got ham because it used to be your favorite, but there's also turkey."

"Do you mind if I have the turkey? I actually haven't touched ham since I saw *Babe* in the nineties, but if you don't like ham then it's fine."

"Oh! Oh, I shouldn't've just assumed."

"No, no, it's okay. I mean, I could have ham if you'd rather have the turkey."

My God, this was like junior high all over again. "No, my mistake. When in doubt as to preferences, always get a cheese sandwich, that's the rule," I said, then added, "Unless somebody's lactose intolerant." And then, I decided to shut up.

"I'll get plates," Seth said. "Toby, you want to see if there's any drinks you're interested in?"

Toby went to the refrigerator and looked inside, frowning. Seth's fridge was nearly empty, containing only Perrier bottles, a jar of olives, and various condiments. "Tell you what," I said. "I'll run down and get you some chocolate milk."

"Sorry," Seth said. "It's obviously time to go shopping."

"No, it's fine," I said, and dashed out the door and down the stairs.

When I got back from the deli, Toby was sitting with Seth at the table coloring in a notebook with Sharpie markers. "You've obviously never watched a five-year-old draw pictures," I said, "or you wouldn't be giving him permanent markers on an antique table."

"Toby's quite an artist," Seth said. "It might make the table worth something someday. Take a look at this; I asked Toby to draw me his favorite thing, and then his least favorite thing." He flipped back a page, and pointed to a large blue block with a head, next to three smaller, smiling heads attached directly to L-shaped legs. "That's a picture of you telling stories."

I smiled. I was Toby's favorite thing. "I need to lose some weight," I said, and kissed the top of Toby's head.

Seth flipped forward. "And this is his least favorite thing. What is this exactly, Toby?"

The picture was similar to the one he'd drawn weeks before of the night of Josh's death, two men beside a blue square. Anna's story about Josh dying in the war, confused with whatever he actually saw. Toby looked down at it, then began scribbling over it with black Sharpie slashes and swirls, like rage set onto paper. I quickly pulled the pen away from him and kissed his hand. "Let's have lunch," I said softly, "Okay?" I ripped the page from the notebook, folded it in half, and stuffed it into the deli bag.

We sat with our sandwiches, none of us saying much, Toby sneaking shy glances at Seth between bites. After a minute he looked up at Seth and said, "You know my daddy played football?"

"Did he?" Seth said.

"For the Chargers. He was a tight end and he was the star."

It was probably inevitable that he'd make his father into a sports hero or a movie star, or the president of the United States. I swiped my knuckle over a smear of mustard on his bottom lip. "You have a good imagination," I said.

"He had to stop because he had an operation in his stomach, called . . . I don't remember. Anna knows."

"Anna told you? About him having an operation?"

"And about the football; she told me last night. He plays in heaven for the Angels."

I'd have to talk to Anna again. This had to stop.

"And he got a scar on his belly, and then he went to college for helping babies."

Josh had a hairline hernia scar at his groin, right at the point where his pubic hair started. So delicate it had seemed, only visible close up, precious in the way the pulse at his neck was precious, or the inside of his elbow, a sign of his vulnerability. "Was it called a hernia operation?" I said.

"Hernia," Toby said. "Maybe. I don't remember."

Josh must've told Anna about the operation. And about the scar too, because there was no way she could've actually seen it.

"He's coming back tonight, I think," Toby said, scratching his nails back and forth over his chair seat. "I have to be asleep first and then he comes down."

The words hit me like saltwater over a wound. Daddy as Santa Claus. Toby was so little and so full of my lies and now Anna's lies, and his own truths that he could only express by drawing pictures and scribbling them out. All of it must be so jumbled in his brain that not even the hundred-fifty-dollar-an-hour therapist would be able to untangle them. How had I thought it'd be enough to just stop writing my letters, that it would absolve me of ever having to explain to Toby that they'd been a lie? Had I really thought they'd just go away?

"Oh, sweetie," I said, "I wish he could too."

Seth stretched a sad smile at me, then said, "Hey, Toby, why don't you check the big drawer by the fridge. I think there's a bag of Chips Ahoy, my personal favorite."

Toby slipped off his chair, and Seth turned to me and spoke softly. "You think it's because Anna gets comfort from imagining it? Or maybe because she's trying to help you and Toby like you were doing with your letters?"

"I didn't even think of that." It made perfect sense, of course. She'd understood what I'd been trying to do with Toby, and now was trying to take over where I'd left off. "You know what scares me most?" I said. "It's that she's not a liar, she almost never lies, so what if she really believes what she's saying? It's like you imagining your grandmother. What if Anna wants to talk to her dad so much that she's been having some kind of hallucination? Like taking stuff he told her last year and imagining he's saying it to her now."

"You want me to try talking to her? Maybe she'd be more comfortable confiding in somebody who isn't directly involved."

This was at once utterly sweet and completely delusional. "She told me Josh hates you," I said.

"What?"

"Not important. Don't talk to my dad about this, okay? I didn't tell him because at first I was embarrassed, and now I feel like he doesn't need our problems on top of his own."

Seth bowed his head. "Anna wishes I didn't exist, I realize that."

"That's not true. I mean…Maybe it's true." I shook my head. "But I think what I really have to do is get her back into therapy. I'm taking Toby to see somebody next week, and if she works out then maybe I'll set up something for Anna too."

Toby returned to the table with a bag of cookies and looked up at me questioningly. "You can have two," I said, more because Seth was there than to limit his intake of sugar and fat. For weeks Anna and Toby had eaten only the bare minimum necessary to stay alive, and now that Toby had started showing interest in food again, I would've been happy to let him eat the whole bag.

I watched him set two cookies on his plate, and envisioned us scurrying out the door when he was done, Seth and I having only danced around the real issue, pretending not to see it. If I left without discussing it, I'd have to avoid ever seeing Seth again. "Hey, Toby," I said. "How'd you like to bring those to the bedroom? Seth has a TV there, and I think *The Backyardigans* is on."

Toby started to balk, but Seth intercepted the balking by saying, "Piggyback?" then lifted Toby over his head and onto his shoulders, running around the table with him and depositing him at the bedroom door. "Bill for your transportation was exactly one quarter," he said, "including tip. But luckily, I see you're not tapped out." He reached again toward Toby's ear.

After Toby had gone into the bedroom, I closed the door and walked to the kitchen. Seth followed me, and I turned to him. "So, are we going to talk about what happened?"

"Yeah." He glanced at me. "I guess I wanted to let you come to me first. I'm trying to work this out in my own head, and I can't do that until I really understand what it is for you."

The underside of my skin felt suddenly sheathed with barbed wire. There it was, the question. What was it for me?

"Because I've been thinking you might be turning to me just because you need a shoulder. I mean I *want* to be a shoulder, I'm happy to be."

"It's more than that," I said.

Seth's face shifted into an expression that said, *Go on with that.* I dimly realized this hadn't quite been the right response, but it was all I had. "That's all I can figure out right now, Seth. It's not nothing."

"Well, how encouraging. Such enthusiasm." He sounded almost bitter, but then he shook his head. "I'm sorry. God, I'm sorry. I had the exact intention of not doing this. I was going to tell you I understand how you feel, and say how I'm going to go on like the other night never happened. That's what I meant to say, but I totally botched it."

"Don't apologize. I mean, I should be the one apologizing."

"Okay, awkward," Seth said. "Look, I'm just saying that I do realize some of what you must be going through, and I just want to be here for you all and do whatever I can to help. I'm not going to start looking for something that's not there."

"Thanks." I raised my hand toward him, then dropped it. "I don't know. It's just I think you don't even realize what you're getting into, being my friend. We're broken, Seth, all of us."

"But you're healing, can't you see that? Toby's laughing more, and Anna's tough but I think I can see her starting to open up. And you, I can see your face changing, your eyes. First time I ran into you on the street, I could see how hollow you were. But now it's like you're back inside your skin."

Back inside my skin? What did that even mean? I smiled crookedly. "Can I tell you the really messed-up thing? It's that I'm scared to stop hurting, because if I do it'll mean I'm letting go and accepting things, and that'll mean he's really gone."

Seth searched my face. "But it's okay for you to be happy."

"I know that." My voice sounded almost petulant, and I shook my head quickly.

I thought about last week when, coming home with Toby after work, I'd stopped by the front door at the sound of Dad's voice. I'd peered in the window and seen him there on the couch, rubbing lotion into Mom's spindly hands, singing "I'll Be Seeing You" in a soft, husky tenor. When he was done he'd pulled a stray lock of hair away from her eyes and said, "That better?" She'd tilted her head to look into his face and reached for his hand. "My pleasure," he'd said, and then they'd just sat there, hand in hand, heads bowed like they were praying.

At the time, I'd wondered where Marlie fit in this picture. When he and Mom held hands, did Dad feel her there? Was she between them? Around my mother like a sort of discoloring spectral aura? But now I realized Dad and Marlie were something altogether separate, not even touching what he still had with Mom. I'd wondered if he'd be relieved when Mom died, but of course he wouldn't be at all. His pain would be the same, but with Marlie he'd be able to go on.

"I mean I know it's okay to be happy," I said, "but I guess I don't *know* it. I swear, Seth, if I was you I'd drop myself like a live grenade, and run."

"I'm not going to drop you, I'm in love with you."

My eyes widened; they felt dry and separate from me like they'd been pasted on, and I felt a rush of joy followed closely by a coil of nausea. "Seth—"

"Oh," he said, stepping backward, his cheeks flushing pink. "I shouldn't have said that, I didn't mean to. It's just the words were in my head so long they somehow came out. I'm sorry."

"Don't be sorry." I hesitated, and then reached for his hand. "I like having you around. You make me forget things."

I knew I'd been avoiding this because it was so much easier to avoid it. When the real truth was, I'd already betrayed Josh. There was no way to move forward with anything without betraying him. I brought Seth's hand up to my face.

Our first kiss had been two decades ago, by the local theater, where we'd ditched our friends so we could see how it would feel to be alone. We'd stood there, not looking at each other, fourteen years old and terrified, and then he'd raised his chin and said, "You have the prettiest nose."

I'd wanted to laugh at this, the implication that the only thing he could find pretty about me was my nose. But then I saw the searching hunger in his expression, the earnest wrinkling of his forehead, and I'd tilted my face to his. "Yours too," I'd whispered, and he'd smiled and bent to kiss me.

Now I kept my eyes on him. "You have the prettiest nose," I said, and he smiled so I glanced toward the closed bedroom door, then leaned toward him.

"Natalie," he said, and then he tangled his free hand in my hair, his thumb tracing the outline of my lips. And he kissed me, just a brush of his lips before he touched his forehead to my forehead, then slid his cheek against mine.

I nestled my head in the crook of his neck, and without knowing it was going to happen, I started to cry. Seth stroked my hair and made a hushing noise, like this was the only reasonable reaction.

"These are happy tears," I said, then laughed.

He kissed the top of my head, then wiped at my cheek with his thumb. "I know." There was no pity in his expression; if there had been, I would've pulled away and tried to think of something funny and self-deprecating to say. But what his face showed was pain, and it was not just undeserved, it was unwarranted. I hurt for my children, for the mistakes I'd made and for what I hadn't been able to give them. But my own pain was more like a scar now than an open wound, something I could see if I happened to look for it, something that had left lasting damage, yes, but something I was able to forget when my attention wasn't drawn to it.

"It's like a roller coaster," I said softly. "But even if things never totally level out, at least we're starting to have moments where they do. That's all you need really, is periodic moments of happiness."

And actually, for a little while, I believed that might be true.

After dinner, the kids sat with my parents in the living room, kneeling by the coffee table, helping my mother with her endless job of mixed-nut sorting. "This is a tricky one," Mom said, holding up a broken cashew.

Anna squinted at it, then pointed at the bowl of cashews. "It goes here," she said. "See? It's the same except broken." She picked up one of the cashews and bit it, then held it next to the piece in Mom's hand.

Mom laughed at this, and said, "Maybe it goes here!" She held the piece to Anna's lips. Anna opened her mouth and Mom popped the nut inside.

Dad reached for an almond. "The relative concentration of peanuts in this batch seems to be growing. Keep eating and there won't be any point in sorting, Meg, you can just dump them all in one bowl." He looked up at me. "Why is it nobody likes to eat the peanuts? Even filberts disappear before the peanuts, and they're clearly inferior."

"Want a peanut, Grammy?" Anna said, handing one to her.

Mom took it and stuck it back in the peanut bowl. "This is difficult," she said.

"Anna," I said. "Can we talk? Upstairs, maybe."

Anna's face went suddenly still. She put her palmful of nuts back on the table. I held my hand to her, and she rose without taking it and walked ahead of me, up the stairs.

I sat on my bed, cross-legged, and she hesitated and then perched on the edge of the mattress, watching my face guardedly. "I wanted to talk to you," I said, "because I know you told Toby you talked to Dad. We discussed this already, Anna. I thought we both agreed it had to stop."

Anna clutched the bedspread in her fist. "We didn't

agree," she said which, strictly speaking, was true. I'd
agreed and she'd stormed out of the room.

"I know you want Toby to see what a hero Dad was,
but he doesn't need stories about pro football and helping
babies to make him heroic. He was a real hero. His true
story was heroic, and like I said before, pretending you're
talking to him doesn't make it true."

I could sense a sudden tension through Anna's body,
like a current. She bunched my comforter between her
fists. "I have to tell you, okay, Mom? I'll tell you everything, stuff I didn't say before." She held up one finger.
"Like how he had a dog named Countess Chocula who
got hurt by a motorcycle and then she died." She held up
another finger. "Also the dog had to wear diapers. Those
are just two of the things."

"Those are things he told you about before, Anna."

"Not before! He never told me those before, it was
yesterday! He told me about the dog, and then he told
about how Grandma Graham wasn't a good mom after his
dad died, and they got angry at each other, and she said
she never wanted to see him again."

"He told you that?" Why would he tell her that?

"He said it was only because she was scared when he
became a Marine, not because she was a bad person. And
then he said how sometimes there are worse things than
dying, which he told me because it was supposed to make
me feel better, and I know you don't believe me, but you
should."

He'd told Anna there were worse things than dying?
What else would Josh have told the children last year,
when his brain was probably too muddled to judge what
might be appropriate for their ears?

I closed my eyes, feeling suddenly dizzy. What else

had she been keeping from me? What if he'd told Anna what he was going through with his injury, and she'd kept it a secret all this time?

"When he told you that," I said slowly, "when he told you there were worse things than death, did he say what those things might be? This is important, Anna; what made him think there were things worse than dying?"

Anna watched me, her eyes glazed with sudden tears. "*Nothing's* worse than him dying," she said, and I suddenly heard what I'd just asked her. I'd just, in effect, asked a ten-year-old why her dad wanted to die.

"I'm sorry. I shouldn't have asked you that." I pulled her back into my arms. "Why didn't you tell me all this when you first heard it, Anna?"

Her face was red. "I did tell you. I heard it first yesterday!"

"Please don't do this, sweetie. I know you didn't hear it yesterday."

"I did!" Anna said. "He came because he wants you to know he still loves you. To make sure you can't marry anybody else."

I shook my head. "Who said I'm marrying anybody else?"

Anna hugged herself, her eyes suddenly fierce, and I smoothed my hand over the thin rails of her back. "Anna..."

"Also there was something else he said, about a girl."

"Okay, what girl?"

"She was somebody Dad knew, and she had this red scar thing on her face like she was burned, but then she died."

"Dad knew somebody who died when he was a teenager?"

"*Dad* wasn't the teenager, the girl was, and her dad did

translating for the Marines which is how they knew each other. She died, and other kids died too, but it wasn't Dad's fault at all. He didn't have anything to do with them dying. I don't know all of it yet, but I maybe could find out more."

"When did he tell you that?"

"I told you when, Mom. It was yesterday!" She flung out her arm, pushing me away. "How come you never believe anything I say?"

"Mom!" I heared the sound of Toby running down the hall, and seconds later he appeared in the doorway. "Don't yell at Anna!"

"I'm not yelling, Toby. But I need her to tell me the truth."

"Stop asking me; I told you! He comes down to talk to me, and he told me about her."

"She's telling you." Toby reached to hold on to the bottom of Anna's sweater. "Daddy comes down and he gives us stuff and he talks to her. We *saw* him."

"He told you that his friend died?"

"Because she was blood-gunned."

I raised my eyebrows. "Blood-gunned? You mean shot?"

"Blood-gunned with stones."

"You mean bludgeoned," I said. "She was bludgeoned with stones?" Would Josh have told her this? No, of course not. He was as adamant as me about making sure our children always believed the world was a safe place, where life was fair and good won out over evil. He never would have told her about a child being killed. "Who told you that, Anna?"

"Daddy told me."

"That's enough of this, okay? I know you haven't been talking to Dad; he can't talk to you now."

"But he can, Mom! You told me after he died that he could talk to me, and that's what he does. I can hear him in my heart, and that's what he told me."

"I meant you could feel him in your heart when you needed him, that he'd help you decide what to do. But he doesn't actually talk to you, Anna, not in words." Who the hell would've fed these things to her? Who did she talk to? And then I realized. "One of your friends from Pendleton said that to you."

"No!" Her face flushed pink. "They didn't!"

Christ, had people been gossiping about Josh, letting their kids overhear? "I know that's what must've happened, Anna. You don't have to cry, I'm not mad. Just tell me who it was." I'd call their parents and demand the truth from them. *You've told your child,* I'd say, *who's told my child, and so now you're going to tell me.*

"I told you! I didn't talk to my friends, they don't talk to me anymore. I swear to God and Jesus and the Bible they didn't tell me. It was Dad!"

There was a raw frustration in her face, no sign of wariness or deception. Why wouldn't she have broken down by now and told the truth? "Oh, sweetheart," I said, "I understand and I'm real sorry if I yelled. I'm not mad at you, okay? I know how much you want him back."

"You don't understand anything!" She swiped at me. "Just wait. Just wait. I'll prove it. I can prove it!" She strode out of the room, Toby following behind her, still gripping the bottom of her sweater.

I rose to go after her, but then the words she'd spoken began to sink in. A red scar on the girl's face. I went to my dresser, pulled out the false bottom, and rooted through the photos until I found the picture that had been in Josh's wallet, of the girl with the port-wine birthmark across her face. Could this possibly be the same girl?

I studied the picture, tracing my finger across the outline of her birthmark. Other than the birthmark, she looked a lot like Anna; I'd seen it before and even more now. They had the same pixie-like features, pointed chin, olive skin, wide searching eyes under a prominent brow. If Josh had known this girl, then maybe that likeness was why he'd been drawn to her.

Had she died? Been bludgeoned by stones? He might have kept the picture because his torture over not having saved this surrogate daughter was something he'd felt compelled to remind himself of. But he wouldn't have told Anna about it, that much I knew.

I set the picture down and went to the computer, searched on *Iraq, stone, 2006, Marine* and *translator.* And there it was. I clicked on the link.

There were two photographs, one showing the girl much younger, maybe ten or eleven with her hair in long dark braids, smiling as children do when told to smile. And the second, further down on the page, showed her on the ground. The large birthmark on her cheek was spattered with blood. I stared at this photo, my throat tightening.

Information has just been released in the brutal slaying of Leyla Memyan Chalabi, the 14-year-old daughter of Ramîn Chalabi, a Kurdish translator for the U.S. Marines. Miss Chalabi was stoned to death on October 22, 2006, in northern Iraq, as part of an "honor killing." Authorities indicated that she was attacked by her brother and cousins, after having been seen engaged in what they considered inappropriate contact with a Sunni Muslim man. It is not clear whether the two were intimately involved, but some Kurdish sects believe that mixing of any nature between faiths is an immoral act.

Most victims of honor killings are females, murdered by male relatives who feel her "immoral behavior" has shamed the family. An Amnesty International spokesman in Washington said that each year, dozens of honor killings are reported in Iraq, particularly in the predominantly Kurdish north. "The religious and social climate," she said, "is such that these brutal attacks can occur in daylight without intervention." Kurdish authorities have introduced reforms outlawing honor killings, but have failed to investigate them or prosecute suspects.

As soon as I finished reading, I closed the webpage so I wouldn't have to look at the girl's face. Anna said that Josh had known her, which was possible since he'd been stationed in northern Iraq last fall. Had she given him the photo before she died? Had Josh felt like he'd been given a chance to protect her, and had failed?

We'd had dinner the week before Josh and Nick had left for Iraq. Nick and Rachel had stayed until early morning, the four of us sprawled on our couches with goblets of red wine and quiet conversation, and later a ragged-looking joint Nick said was left from his tour in Kuwait ten years before. Josh had taken the joint, stared at its red tip. "This world is fucked up," he said. "Why is it our duty to leave our own families so we can destroy other people's families?"

Nick had propped his feet on the coffee table, watching Josh. "You shouldn't be fighting this war," he said. "I'm looking forward to it, actually. I want to shake sense into them, and if I have to do it with guns and grenades, then so be it."

Josh had handed the joint over without taking a drag. "I'm going to do this different," he said. "I'll talk to them, make friends with their kids, make them realize we don't hate them."

He'd started studying Arabic soon after 9/11, knowing a tour in the Middle East was probably inevitable. Had becoming friends with this Leyla girl been part of his grand scheme of how to change the world? I imagined him holding the photo and remembering what had happened, realizing he'd failed and what he'd lost in trying. That he'd sacrificed himself for nothing because it had been crazy of him to think he could make a difference.

The truth was, I had no idea what he'd really gone through in Iraq. Over the last few days I'd continued to research soldiers' stories for the book I wanted to write, the pain in their blogs such a striking contrast to the stoicism in their faces. I hated myself for not having forced Josh to admit to that pain, not having been able to talk him through it.

Why hadn't Nick told me about her when I'd shown him the photo back at Pendleton? If Josh had actually been friends with her, for sure Nick would've known about it. I'd seen a kind of stillness in Nick's face when I'd shown him the photo, like there was an image playing inside him that was taking his attention. Did he know what she'd meant to Josh? Would Nick have kept something from me in order not to hurt me?

Well, yes. Of course he would; it was what he'd done with Josh's injury.

I looked down at the photograph, and then I closed my eyes and prayed. For Leyla at ten, so much like Anna with her braids and strained little girl smile. Years later in her dark hijab, with eyes that looked like they had no smile left in them. And then at fourteen, on the dirt, hands flung up at her head to protect herself from her own brother, blood and birthmark splayed in a gruesome Rorschach pattern across her face. Her life beginning and ending, I prayed for her and then for Josh who had saved her picture for a reason I might never understand. To a God who must hear but never seemed to listen.

52
Natalie

I sat on my bed, staring across the room at the blank
computer screen. There was a weight on me, a fog surrounding my head, the images getting caught inside it. I
knew Josh couldn't have had anything to do with the girl's
death; there was no way. But if Nick knew something
about it, why wouldn't he have told me?

And then, something occurred to me. *N—9:30 PM,*
Josh had written the night of his suicide. What if the N
stood for Nick?

"Mom?"

Anna was standing in the doorway, watching me with
shadowed, shuttered eyes. Her cotton shirt had come half
untucked, her jeans were too short and yet so baggy in the
rear, and all I wanted to do was gather her up, swaddle her
in oversized blankets, and hold her. I shook my head
slightly, trying to clear it of the fog, and patted the bed beside me. "Come sit."

"I don't want to sit." All at once she flushed pink, her
face screwed up and she let out a thin, plaintive cry.

"Baby?" I stood and strode toward her and pulled her
against me, but she pushed me away.

"I have to talk about Dad." Her voice was pitched

high, so shaky I could hardly understand her words. "How come we never talk about stuff we did with him? How come you pretend like he's totally gone?"

"Oh, honey... You're so right, we should talk about him more. I guess I was worried it would make you sad, but that was stupid of me. We need to talk about him."

"Maybe you forgot about him, but even if you don't care, he's still my dad!"

I felt my eyes sting, and turned quickly away so she couldn't see my face. "You really think I don't care? Other than you and Toby, he's still the most important part of my life." I walked back to the bed and slowly sat. "You know what? You know what we should do? Next month's Dad's birthday. I think we should celebrate it, have a birthday dinner and then we can spend all night talking about the things we remember. We can celebrate him."

For a full minute she didn't answer, but then she said, "Would we buy him presents?"

I felt a tug in my chest. "Sure, why not. We'll buy presents and have a cake, and we'll get those windup car thingies he loved. Remember Toby's last birthday? How Dad kept winding them all up at once and sent them running across the table?"

"So he could steal our plate when we weren't looking." Anna smiled. "It got so annoying."

"I know. You guys were ready to kick him."

"But it was funny too."

I smiled. "Yeah, it was."

"If I could go back, I'd tell him he was funny."

"Oh, sweetie." I pressed my hands between my knees. "He knew how much we all loved him."

She thought about this a minute, and then she walked

to the window. "There's things I have to tell you. I just found stuff out. Something you don't know."

"Please, Anna," I said, "Come sit with me."

She rested her forehead against the dark pane. "He told me, he just told me that his memory didn't get better. He talked to me just a minute ago, and that's what he said."

All the breath in me expanded, pressed against my insides. "Turn around, Anna." Of course she'd known. Anna had been there watching, seeing what I should've realized all along. That her father had never really come home. "Look at me."

"He said he couldn't remember what work he did, or even how old Toby was."

Had Josh actually told her all this last year? Of course not, there was no way he would've burdened her with it, but where else could she have heard it? "Oh, Anna…" I said, thinking, *Oh, Josh.*

"And then, he talked about what happened in Iraq." Her words came in a rush, like something bottled and suddenly freed. "There were kids without legs, and a man who died carrying a photo of his baby."

I stared at her, stunned. *"What?"*

"And he looked at somebody he was about to shoot, and he was scared of going to jail—"

"Anna, stop!" I shook my head quickly. "Where did you hear those things? Nobody should've told you those things!" I stood to take both Anna's hands. "Tell me the truth now. You should never, ever have heard any of this. I need to know the truth."

"Dad told me! Today just now, and *then*"—she pulled her hands away and backed into the corner—"then this is what he did." She swiped at her eyes. "He told me how he really died."

There was a zigzag feeling inside me, all sharp edges poking under my skin. "What?"

"He did get shot, but it wasn't in the war because the real truth is he died in his car, because he wanted to."

Suddenly, before I realized what was happening, she slid down the wall, and hunched forward with her head buried in her knees. I stared down at her, frozen, part of me wanting to run out of the room, out from the house, to tear down the street, screaming.

I crouched next to her, rested a hand on her shoulder. "Anna?" My voice was shaking. She shoved my hand away, so I slipped my arm under her knees, the other around her back, lifted her, and held her against my chest. She smelled of salt and something long unwashed; if desolation had a smell, this would be the scent it would wear.

I carried her to my bed and, still holding her, I leaned back against the pillows. "I know, I know," I whispered, and suddenly, unexpectedly, I felt a cleansing sort of release. Like fevers that have to peak before a sickness can be burned away, I knew this pain of understanding had to be laid raw and looked at, made worse before we could heal it. I knew that. I'd known it all along.

She was shivering against me and I tried to still her, pressing her head under my chin. "How come, Mom?" she said. "Why would he want to?"

And there it was, the question, the only question that mattered and one we'd never be able to answer. "He was hurt," I said, "inside his head." Over and over I'd played with variations of this explanation, trying to find the right words, and each time the inadequacy of it had made me want to scream. "You can be hurt inside your brain, just like people can be hurt on their knees, or in their lungs or their hearts, and it made your dad's thoughts get all mixed up. He couldn't think clearly and he didn't know how else to stop the hurt he felt, so he just wanted to make that hurting go away."

She pulled away from me. "I hate him." Her eyes were suddenly fierce. "I don't care if he had a hurt in his brains, it's not the same thing as a real hurt, and I don't love him at all, I hate him!"

"I know." I worked to calm my breath, then said, "Of course you do, and sometimes I hate him too, but it's okay."

"It's not okay!" She flung herself at me almost violently, and I caught her in my arms. "It's not okay, it's not okay!" she said, and I rubbed at her back, hushing in her ear.

Anna tucked herself against me, and I tried to think of the right thing to say. "He never stopped loving you," I started. "What happened doesn't change that."

"I don't want to talk about it anymore."

"Okay, we won't talk about it now. Let's sleep, okay? You want to sleep here with me?"

She nodded and I kissed the top of her head, then lifted the covers around her. And I lay there with her, rubbing at her back, holding her until she fell asleep.

I dialed Nick and Rachel's number from the kitchen. Nick answered, and in the background, I could hear the sound of people talking and glasses clinking, and beneath that a jazz saxophone. I felt a wash of homesickness. "Nick? This is Natalie."

A beat of silence, then, "Natalie! How are you?"

"Nick. Nick, I have to ask you something. Somebody's been talking to Anna, telling her things about Josh, about his injury and also about his childhood. Was it you? Have you talked to her recently?"

"What? No, of course not!"

"Then I'm hoping you can give me some idea who the hell it could be. Who else at Pendleton would know about Josh's childhood?"

"No one that I know of. He didn't talk about his past much, even to me. I swear, I find out somebody's been screwing with Anna, I'll have their heads so fast they'll think they've been hit by a roadside bomb."

I rubbed my hand up and down my leg, then said, "Did you see him that night, Nick?"

Nick hesitated, then said, "What?"

I squeezed my eyes shut. And told a little, calculated lie. "He wrote it in his PDA for that night. That he talked to you. So did he?"

"He wrote he talked to me?" Nick said, then quickly, "Oh, wait, wait—okay, I think I know what that was, what it must've been. Because he'd been acting not great on Friday, and I told him to call me Sunday night, just to talk. So he said he'd call but then he never did, and the next thing I heard…Well, the next call came from you."

Silence, the words circling around us and tightening. Had Josh been planning to talk to Nick? Tell him what he intended to do? I'd been so horrified at the thought he'd wanted to ask me for help that night, but it was even more awful knowing he'd wanted to go to someone else instead.

I heard my dad switch off the TV, swiveled my head toward the door, then whispered, "Someone's also told Anna about this girl he knew in Iraq, who died as part of an honor killing. Her name was Leyla and I showed you her picture the night before we left Pendleton. And you said you didn't know anything about her or what she had to do with Josh, but were you lying?"

"Somebody told Anna about Leyla?" Nick paused, swore under his breath, then said, "Okay, hold on, okay? I'm walking into the family room."

I heard him talking to someone in a low murmur, and then the sounds of the party faded. "I'm back," Nick said. "And in the time it took me to walk across the hall, I realized I can't talk about this over the phone. You have to understand that, don't you? I'm going to come up there. I should've come a long time ago."

"Why? Talk about what?"

"I'll fly up tomorrow, call in a sick day. Can I meet you tomorrow morning? I'll call you from the airport as soon as I get in."

"Just tell me, Nick. Did he do something wrong?"

"I love you, Natalie, and I'll talk to you tomorrow." He hung up.

I sat there gripping the phone, holding it tight to my ear as I listened to the dial tone, like it might be hiding subliminal messages. And then hung up the phone and stood.

I walked upstairs, to the children's bedroom. Toby was asleep, and I pulled off his shoes and drew the covers around him. And then, quietly, I started to search.

I checked Anna's dresser, pulling out her shirts, pajamas, underwear. I checked the pockets of all her pants, then looked inside her desk drawers, pulling out old homework papers, drawings, *Jack and Jill* and *Girls' Life* magazines, then went to her bed to feel under her mattress, inside her pillow. I felt under her covers, shoving aside the pink hippo lying face-down on her quilt. And heard a crinkling.

I lifted the hippo. Felt the unnatural stiffness of its dress, and slowly I unzipped it. And there, tucked inside, was a crumpled wad of paper. Filled with Josh's handwriting.

My knees went weak. I sat down abruptly, almost missing the desk chair, and leaned forward to rest my forearms on my knees, staring at the wall. I stayed like this for nearly five minutes, then forced myself to look back at the page.

Natalie,

I know I've told you I don't believe in heaven, but now I need to believe there's something more, and that I'll get back the parts of myself I've lost. I also need to believe there's something on the other side, so we can be together again. I'll be waiting till that day, because I also know I won't be truly whole without you.

All year I've been remembering when you were pregnant, you keeping the children safe inside you while me, I was on the outside. And that's how I know you'll all be okay without me. I never would've left if I didn't feel sure that you'll do better once I'm gone.

I want to explain what I've been dealing with this whole year. I hid how bad things were, and even though at first the doctors told me it would get better, now they say it never will. If I close my eyes, after a minute I won't remember what room I'm in. I don't know what I did at work today, and there's days I don't even remember what work I do. I don't know how old my son is. I don't remember the first sentence in this paragraph. And I couldn't have lived with myself if I made you have to deal with what I've become. You would've handled it, you would've been strong enough, but you shouldn't have to be.

Nothing makes sense anymore. I can't think and I can't breathe and my head hurts and the pictures keep coming. People, piles of people dead in the street, children without legs and legs without children. Looking at the man I'm about to shoot, and seeing him look back, terrified. Reaching into a dead man's pocket for ID and pulling out the photo of a newborn. All I have inside me is death.

I'm under investigation for something horrible, but I'm not even sure exactly what that thing is. I'm scared of things I might've done that I can't remember, because all I remember is a girl's bloody face and my own screams and the things other people have told me that don't feel true.

I can't stand to think of how you're going to look at me when you realize the things I didn't tell you. I can't stand the thought of not being a Marine, because what else can I do with my life? There is nothing else, it's who I am. But worst of all is the knowledge that I have it in me to do wrong, that I have this virus spreading and infecting everything that used to be inside me. I'm scared if I stay that in time I'll hurt you too.

I love you and the children more than anything. I love you more than my life, and someday you'll see that's why I had to leave. Please, don't let them ever forget me. Remind them of who I used to be, and tell them how you all were the only thing that kept me alive this long.

                                                    Josh

I sat with the letter, reading it again and again, hearing it in his voice. This was what Josh had faced, those days he'd hidden behind our bedroom door. These were the fears he hadn't been able to tell me in life, but had realized he'd have to tell me in death.

What had he meant about an investigation? What would've made him afraid he'd face jail? Could this have something to do with the delay in getting benefits money, because he'd done something wrong in Iraq? What the hell could he have done?

I squeezed my eyes shut, trying to stop the thoughts from coalescing. Until I learned from Nick whatever there was to learn I'd focus on the one truth I knew: that Josh would never hurt anyone he didn't have to.

I recognized the line from the note Anna had given me the morning of Toby's accident. I didn't know how Anna had found Josh's real note; it was something she never should have seen. But I'd talk to her about it; I'd talk to her and do what I could to help her reach peace with it and from it.

This was the explanation I'd needed from Josh, why I'd been so distraught reading both Anna's version and the last entries in his PDA, and seeing it wasn't there. The more times I read this letter, Josh's words from beyond the grave, the more I saw what he'd been trying to help me understand. How there was nothing I could have done; there was probably nothing that could have saved him. Because Josh had died long before his heart had stopped beating.

I knew it would take me a long while to reconcile this in my mind, what war had done to him. It would take time, but the thing this letter showed, the thing I most wanted the children to realize, was that Josh had never stopped loving us. That he'd thought about us before he died. And that he'd not just wanted us to find peace again, but had known we could.

53
Anna

Mom was sleeping and I turned on my side so I could breathe her breath. What I have noticed is you can catch sleep from a sleeping person just like you catch yawns or colds. But this morning, no. My brain had too much to say.

I heard my dad say this about the war, which I didn't understand when he said it, but now I really do. That when you first start, you know what you're there for and you believe it is the right thing and you feel proud. But then, the badness goes on. You see how it might go on forever, always bad. You wake up every day and the first thing you are is scared. You start to wonder why you came.

From the time when Mom wrote that first letter from Dad to us, I could feel all the lies inside me, like bee stingers that hurt a little and then a lot, the poison of each lie spreading through me. And maybe this says something bad about me, but how it made me feel was mad. Not mad at myself for lying, which I should have been, but mad at her.

I pulled the pillow up around my face until I couldn't hardly breathe. I should suffocate. I wished I could. In kindergarten there was this girl Mary who got so sad when her mom left every morning that she used to hold her breath until she fell over. That's what I wanted. To just stop.

Oh I wished I hadn't read Dad's note. I wished I hadn't read it! Why would he think this would help us at all? Sadness was a disease like my grammy's disease; it hurt her, but it made other people hurt even more, so why didn't he get that he'd gave the darkness to us too? Like how those first days every time Mom saw me crying she also started crying, you couldn't tell about your own sadness without hurting the people who loved you. Dad was the only one of us who wasn't hurting anymore.

Now I lay here, watching Mom sleep, and I thought about how all over California girls were waking up from their moms saying *Good Morning,* how at Camp Pendleton girls were in bed listening to reveille, hearing their dads taking their showers or their parents waiting for them in bacon-smelling kitchens, talking sweet to each other in low voices. All over the world girls thought these things were just normal; they didn't even pay attention. They had no idea how it all was a miracle.

54
Natalie

Nick had called from the airport, so I'd been expecting him, but still when he showed up at my office it was a shock, two worlds colliding. I felt almost like I'd become a new person in the past few weeks; the woman I'd been at Pendleton would always mourn, but I'd begun to separate from her so that I could go on.

"I was thinking we could have an early dinner at the sandwich place next door," I said. "The sandwiches suck so it's usually pretty uncrowded." I'd asked my dad to watch Toby after school so we could talk alone. But now I almost wished he was here so Nick and I would have to censor our conversation, talk about anything other than the one thing we needed to.

There were only three couples in the Blue Moon Sandwich Shop, all in their seventies or eighties, the shop's typical demographic. We both ordered at the counter and then slid into a booth. We sat a moment, awkwardly, and then Nick said, "You look great, Natalie. Or maybe I shouldn't say that."

"It's never wrong to say a woman looks great. Generally it's universally appreciated."

He smiled. "I just don't want it to sound like one of

those stupid things people say a few months after someone dies, as a way of figuring out whether you're over it.
What I really mean is you do look good. You look...
lighter."

"I've gained seven pounds, mostly because of beer," I
said. "But thanks. I don't know if I'd say I'm great, but I'm
getting there. Things're falling into place." And it was
true, things actually were falling into place. Such an
eerily fitting expression; everything in our lives that for
weeks had fallen through seemingly bottomless space was
now clicking piece by piece into shape. Job, books. Seth. I
jammed my soda straw on the table to break through the
wrapper. "We have a long way to go, but at least we're
starting to talk about the things we have to talk about."

"The kids're adjusting okay?"

Adjusting. The word sounded so crude; he must mean
adjusting to life in French Creek rather than to life without Josh, but it was another weirdly applicable word for
all of it. Adjusting our minds and shifting our vision for
the future by a hundred eighty degrees. "Yeah, they're doing okay," I said. Which was not altogether true, of course,
but maybe not altogether untrue. "They're learning how
to adjust," I said.

Nick gave a sad smile. "They're strong kids."

"Yeah," I said. "They are."

"So I have some news for you, good news, although I
don't know details. But I heard from Captain Meyers that
you should be finding out about your benefits any day
now. He got someone to press the VA, and you get somebody with the right rank asking the right questions to the
right people, you can make things happen. It's inexcusable
what they did to you."

I looked into his face. "They said they were still

'reviewing his case.' Which I thought meant the suicide, but there's obviously more."

Nick rocked his Coke cup back and forth on the table. "I guess I can give you some idea what was going on, although I have no idea how Anna would've found out because there weren't too many other people who knew."

"Okay." I met his eye. "Tell me."

"How much do you know? About what happened before Josh left Iraq?"

"Nothing," I said. "Josh didn't tell me anything that happened."

Nick studied my face as a waiter set our plates on the table. "Maybe we should wait till after we eat."

"I've waited for months, Nick."

"I know." He pulled a napkin from the dispenser, and looked down at it. "Well—Josh didn't do anything wrong, okay? He was trying to save the girl."

"From the stoning? He was there?"

"We were both there. Josh had become her friend; she was the daughter of a translator, and she used to come talk to him almost every day, practicing her English. He'd buy her these little gifts from the PX, and she'd bring him drawings or little treats she baked. I think he saw her as a chance to show at least one person of the next generation not to be scared of us. But things were getting strained between us and the Kurds—they were starting to hate having us there, and some of them were still really old-school and thought it brought shame on the family for one of their girls to be spending time with an American man."

I stared at Nick, something slinking down my spine, an icy trickle of water. "The article I read. It said she was stoned for having inappropriate contact with a Sunni."

"Well, it wasn't a Sunni, it was Josh. Not inappropriate,

except that she was a Kurdish girl and he was an American soldier and—I don't know, maybe she had a little crush on him. After his injury she spent even more time with him, I think she gave him her picture to make sure he'd still remember her. But apparently her brother started seeing them together, and made some kind of demand that she stop. Which she told Josh, but I guess he forgot because after a few days he went to her house to find her. And the next day she was attacked."

All this time I'd been wondering what had happened and now I'd found the answer. Had he blamed himself for Leyla's death? Yes, of course he had. The last year of his life he'd been living with the guilt over what had happened to her. It must've consumed him, all those times he'd looked so distant. Every day he'd been bleeding, and how could he possibly have lived through it alone all those months?

"A friend of the girl's, of Leyla's came running to us for help, but by the time we got there, she was already in pretty bad shape. So we shot in the air to stop them, and the girl's brother started throwing the rocks at us, hitting us with the rocks while the rest of the group was still going after her. And then the boy pulled out a gun and waved it around, yelling, and Josh started shooting."

"To protect himself," I said.

"Basically, yes. And maybe he should've realized how young they were, or shouldn't have fired so many times, I don't know. But it was a crazy situation, there wasn't time to think, and you don't know how it is out there. The boys that age are so desensitized they'd just as soon shoot you as shake your hand, and it wears on you."

I looked down at my salad, shuffled the onions with

my fork, then said, "He was shooting at them, and you weren't."

"That doesn't mean anything; if he hadn't started firing then I might've done it myself. There just wasn't time to think."

"Okay. Okay, so then what was he being investigated for? Did you tell all that to the NCIS?"

"Of course I did. But I guess you could say there was a difference of opinion." He set the napkin by his plate and looked up at me. "Right after it happened we both had to report the details, but Josh couldn't remember any of it. This was back when his memory was worst, only about a month after he got hit by the IED, and he couldn't really tell them anything so they just had to go on my word."

"And they thought you were trying to protect him."

"At the time they talked to other people at the scene, civilians, and the things they said were all over the place, no kind of believable, definitive statements about what happened. But then, a few weeks before Josh died, a handful of them came forward."

Nick stared down at his plate, his eyes clouded with pain. "I don't know if it was revenge, or if they were trying to get something out of it, but they said Josh was shooting wildly even after it was obvious Leyla was already dead. So there was an investigation into it, into Josh's mental state. They pulled his medical records this summer and he was interrogated again. And he couldn't answer their questions."

I stared at Nick. "Why didn't I know any of this? Why the hell didn't anyone tell me?"

"We couldn't tell you. There were allegations he shouldn't have been let back into combat after his injury, which to tell you the truth, he probably shouldn't have.

But if any of that leaked, the media would've had a field day."

"Did you really think I'd leak anything to the media? I mean you personally, Nick. Did you think it wasn't safe to tell me?"

"First of all…first of all, Josh really didn't want you to know. If anyone was going to tell you, it should've been him. And I had my job to worry about, Natalie, and if they found out I said anything, I could've gotten into so much trouble."

"Well, I had my *husband* to worry about. I should've been there to help him through it!"

"But you couldn't have helped. Whatever you did, he still would've been broken. You're wondering about the delay in benefits? It was because right before Josh died they'd decided to discharge him, and with all that was going on they were making the decision on whether to make it a dishonorable discharge. The circumstances would've affected whether you were eligible, which meant everything got bogged down in bureaucracy."

Nick dragged a fry through a puddle of ketchup, then dropped it and pushed his plate away. "Regardless of whether it was honorable or not, he still would've been discharged. And the idea of not being able to serve, not even knowing if he'd be able to keep supporting his family that on top of the injury and his PTSD is what killed him. There's nothing you could've done to save him from that."

"Did they tell him?" I said. "Did they tell him they were considering a dishonorable discharge?"

Nick's face twitched, like he'd been slapped. "He knew."

I felt a hollow churning in my stomach, at the difference between the question I'd asked and the one he'd answered. "Did they tell him?" I said again.

"Natalie…"

The entry in the PDA the night he died. *N—9:30 PM.* "That night," I said. "You told him the night he killed himself."

"I'm so sorry." Nick's voice broke. "You don't know how it's been haunting me; I've been reliving it every single day since, thinking how I could've changed things. I called him that afternoon to say I needed to talk to him, and then I came by late. I guess you were asleep." He glanced at me, as if looking for confirmation, then said, "What I told him is that I agreed with them, that he shouldn't be fighting. The month in Iraq after his injury, half the time he didn't know where he should be going or what he should be doing. If I hadn't been there to help him, there's no way he could've coped."

I felt a dull pain behind my eyes. If Nick hadn't come over, if he'd offered to help Josh fight back, if I hadn't gone to sleep early, *if, if, if…*

"He said he was going to protest the decision, prove to them he could go back, but I knew he wasn't ever going to be fit to serve and he had to understand that. Which I hate myself for now, you have to realize that—I wish I'd done this completely differently, because he must've felt so ganged up on." He shook his head slowly. "Ever since the allegations came out he'd started questioning whether I was telling the truth about what happened, and I guess he started questioning what anger might make him capable of. I don't know, maybe he got scared of the things he didn't remember and the parts of himself he didn't recognize, and those were the parts he was trying to get rid of."

Josh, alone with this terror, not knowing the man living in his body. He'd written about anger in his PDA, how much it scared him, and had he felt like this was his only option? To kill, not himself, but what he saw as the new Josh he didn't understand? "Why didn't he tell me? If it was me, if I was scared of myself, I would've gone to him first."

"I guess one of the hardest things he was facing was that he didn't want you to change your impression of who he was. He kept telling me how you thought he was a hero, how he needed to be a hero, so maybe he thought if he died, whatever he'd done could be buried with him. If he stayed alive you'd have to find out."

I pressed my thumb and forefinger against my eyes and saw spots spinning, red blotches swirling through the dark. There was Josh, alone that night after months of pain, knowing his life was over. "You should've woken me up that night instead of leaving him there alone. You just left him there."

"I know. Of course I know that now, but I was upset myself that night, and I wasn't in any state to talk to you. Plus we must've woken Toby up—he was standing there at the head of the stairs—so I wanted to just leave and wait until Josh calmed down before I talked to him again. It never occurred to me he was that upset."

"Wait," I said. "Toby was there?"

"Just for a second; I guess he saw us fighting and then he went back to his room. But I knew we couldn't keep talking if he could hear us."

The picture Toby had drawn of the two men fighting, it wasn't of the war; it was of Nick and Josh. Toby's was the only bedroom facing the front of the house, and he'd heard their voices; that might be what had woken him. After Nick had left, he must've waited for the sound of Josh's footsteps up the stairs and then, not hearing them, had gone down to find him.

The things he'd drawn were the things he'd seen: Nick

and Josh fighting, and then Josh dead in his car. And maybe the fact he hadn't drawn his father holding a gun to his own head meant that he hadn't actually seen it. Probably he hadn't, because how long would Josh have hesitated with the gun in his hand? Not long. He was brave. He wouldn't have wanted to give himself time to second-guess what he was about to do.

"I'm so sorry," Nick said hoarsely. "I'll never forgive myself for leaving him there. And I know I should've told you all this when we talked before, but I had no idea how to talk about it. And I guess I convinced myself you didn't need to know."

It was all so screwed up—so many things that should've happened, could've happened, mistakes, lies, blindness—but could I blame Nick? Not any more than I blamed myself.

"He didn't tell you how much he was hurting because he wanted to keep as much as possible of what you had before the injury. He loved you so much, Natalie, and that's what he kept telling me that year, was how scared he was of jeopardizing everything."

He'd still loved us. I'd thought there was no way he could've stayed distant enough to lie about his injury, and care for us at the same time. But he'd kept his secrets *because* he loved us, because he wanted to protect our family. And maybe that was the answer to the only real question I'd had, the question behind all other questions. Whether he'd still felt the same.

"Thank you," I said. "For telling me now, for coming up here to tell me."

A slow flush rose from Nick's neck up to his face, and he brought his fist to his mouth. I reached for his hand,

and when he pulled it away I rose to slide into the booth beside him and gather him in my arms.

Sitting there, holding him, made me feel strangely wise and wistful. Older. I'd aged a hundred years in the past few months, and it was clear to me suddenly that the sadness would never fully go away. But I was learning how to absorb it, in the way one might absorb a chronic illness. Always there, coloring but not defining.

55
Anna

When I opened my eyes, the house was quiet, only the TV on downstairs, and I was still in Mom's bed. I sat up slowly and looked at the clock.

It was already afternoon. Mom had let me sleep through school.

And suddenly I got a fever, a burning-upness that took over all of me. My whole head and stomach and bones were screaming, they were full up with screams, and I bit my teeth together hard to keep them from coming out. And then, I don't know why, I dug my nails into the back of my wrist. It hurt, it hurt but I dug hard until the blood came, then wiped the blood across the front of my shirt.

I looked down at my shirt, a streak brighter red than I thought blood would be, and a sound came out of me, a little hiccup. I went into my bedroom, trying to rub the streak away, and I was about to climb up into my bunk when I saw Leopolda there. Unzipped, and empty.

I sucked in my breath and grabbed at her, felt under her dress, then threw her on the ground and pulled off my covers, *no, no no!* I searched the bed, throwing off my sheets and my pillow, then started throwing other things, clothes, all our toys. I threw them on the floor, at the wall, at Josephina Graham's face, and then I started tearing apart her face, my shell collection, her hair, her eyes, her smile. I threw it all into the trash and then I threw away everything else, the Carbot, the bunny, the dinosaur puppet, and then I heard a noise, a sucked-in breath. I looked up and saw Grandpa and Toby standing by the door, watching me. They both looked scared.

I went to Toby's bed and crawled under the covers, pulled them up over my head.

"Anna?" Grandpa asked. "Goodness, what happened in here?"

"Go away!" I said from under the covers.

He came to the bed and sat, and rested his hand on me. "Looks like you're having a bad day," he said.

I hit out at his hand, and he stood up. "Okay," he said. "Everybody's allowed a bad day sometimes. But we better get things straightened up in here before Mom comes home."

Toby came to lie on the bed next to me, and he put his hand on my back. "Anna?" he whispered.

I didn't answer, just squeezed my eyes shut. I could hear Grandpa start to put away my things, hang up my clothes, put toys back on my shelves. And the sound of it helped. He was taking care of things, putting them where they belonged. He didn't care if I was the worst, most evil person in the world. He wanted to help.

I peeked over the edge of my covers. He was at the closet, trying to bend with his hand on the bottom of his back. So I got out of bed and picked up the clothes to hand to him, let him slip them over hangers. And then Toby got up, and knelt to pick up Josephina's stones and shells, and we worked without talking, them next to me, putting away everything I ruined. Until it all was in its place, my shell collection in a pile on the floor, the toys I threw away sitting on the desk.

"Why don't we let Anna rest?" Grandpa said, holding his hand out to Toby. "She's feeling unhappy today." Toby looked up at me and then came to hug me, squeezing his arms around my back. And then he took Grandpa's hand and without saying anything, they left.

I made Toby's bed, feeling quiet inside me, empty, like I was watching me from far away. When I was done, I picked up Leopolda and slowly zipped up her dress, then kissed the top of her head and hugged her against my neck. If she was real she'd be glad to have got rid of my secrets, I knew that. She never would've asked for any of this, just like dad wouldn't have wanted it when he bought her on the day I was born. All she knew was how to be a stuffed animal, and be loved.

I petted the top of her head, and then brought her down to the living room, where Toby, Grandpa, and Grammy were on the couch, watching TV. "I'm sorry," I said.

"It's okay." Grandpa smiled and patted the seat next to him. "Want to watch with us?"

"Okay," I said and went to sit between Grandpa and Grammy on the couch. And when he put his arm around my back, I leaned against him and I listened to him breathe.

56
Natalie

I noticed a quietness as soon as I stepped in the door, despite the TV being on. They were asleep on the sofa, all four of them breathing through their mouths, Toby next to Mom and Anna between my parents with her head resting in the crook of my dad's arm. I watched a minute, feeling a rush of love for them. This family, this little everyday intimacy, all brought together by me. I switched off the TV which, ironically, served to wake them all simultaneously.

I smiled. "Boring show?"

Anna gazed drowsily at me until, all at once, her face sharpened. Her eyes were pink. Had she been crying? "Everything okay here?" I said.

Anna watched me, unblinking. My dad stood slowly. "Somehow, getting older, I sleep worse at night and better in the day. I think if I moved to Japan I'd be right on track."

"You okay, Anna?" I said.

She kept her eyes on me and gave a quick nod.

"I want to talk to you, okay? There's a couple things we have to discuss."

Still she watched me blankly, then stood and left the room without answering. I watched after her, then turned to Dad and tried to keep my voice light. "I was going to make burgers for dinner, if you're okay with that. And Tater Tots."

"They still make Tater Tots? I ate those growing up, and I blame them for my angina. Take a CAT scan and you'll see my arteries plugged with breaded potato cylinders." He smiled. "But they're still the best thing you can do with an Idaho."

I followed Anna upstairs, but stopped in the hallway at the sound of her voice from my parents' bedroom. "I just need to talk to you," she said. "Okay? Maybe tomorrow you could come to recess, or the next day but tomorrow would be better because this is *so* important, and I'll try calling again tomorrow morning, okay? Okay, bye." I heard the phone clunk down, and stayed in the hall as Anna emerged.

"Anna? Who were you calling?"

Her face blanched a shocking shade of white. "Nobody. Just Cam."

"You didn't ask Cam to come to recess tomorrow." I watched her face, so many disparate thoughts spinning so frantically inside me that all I saw was the blur of them. What if it was one of the Iraqis who'd seen Leyla die? Or a relative of one of the boys Josh had shot, who was now seeking some kind of twisted revenge by telling Josh's daughter their version of what had happened? "You've been talking to somebody. That's how you found out about Leyla. Who the hell's talking to you?"

"No!" All at once she started to shake, an awful, epileptic sort of shivering.

"Anna, look at me."

She kept her eyes on the far wall, so I cupped my hand under her chin and turned her to face me, made my voice sound far stronger, firmer, than I actually felt. "I need you to tell me how you heard about the Iraqi girl Dad knew. This is important, Anna. It's the most important thing I've ever asked from you. Because whoever told you about what happened did a very wrong thing, and I need to talk to them."

"It was no one, Mom!" Her eyes filled and she batted my hand away.

"Anna, tell me the truth! If you don't tell me, then I'm calling the police." I reached for her, and suddenly noticed a patch of angry, partially scabbed-over gouges on her arm. "Anna, what happened?"

"I got hurt." She made a sobbing sound. "Today I got hurt, and it hurts when I touch it and I think I better go to the hospital."

"Okay. Okay, let's go look at it in your room where the light's better, okay?"

The first thing I noticed in the kids' bedroom was Anna's shell collection in a pile on the floor; the shells, stones, and branches we'd decorated with when we first moved in had been ripped off, bits of glue still stuck to the wall in the shape of a ghost heart. "Anna, did you do this? Why?"

"I couldn't find it." Her voice shook.

"Find what?" And then I realized. "You mean the letter? You were looking for Dad's letter?" I led her over to Toby's bottom bunk, sat and turned on the lamp on the nightstand so I could see her arm. There were four small cuts, approximately fingernail sized, in a semi-circle. "Oh, baby," I whispered. "Did you do that to your own arm?"

She looked up at me, the answer in her brimming eyes, and I felt my stomach twist. Anna was my easy child, my strong child. She never asked for help, and somehow I'd managed to convince myself she didn't need it. Toby had forced me to look at his pain by not talking, but Anna had to hurt herself before I realized how much help she needed too. It was the same way I hadn't seen the pain Josh was in, because I'd lived in this fantasy world where everything was just as it appeared on the surface. I was the nurturer, the breastfeeder and the diaper changer and the boo-boo kisser, so how could I have been too caught up in my own suffering to notice hers?

"It's okay," I said softly. "I found Dad's letter, and I know you've held on to it all this time. And I know it's scary and awful, but we need to talk about it, what he said."

She stared down at the floor, and I could see her whole body shaking. "I didn't have it this whole time. Dad gave it to me yesterday."

"Anna, please stop this."

"He gave it yesterday! He said we all needed to know why he died, that it'd help us know how it wasn't our fault."

"Of course it wasn't our fault." I watched her face, her red eyes, then reached for both her hands. "Anna, you didn't ever think it was your fault, did you? How could you think that?"

"I wrote to him," she said, and then gave a single, convulsive sob. "I wrote something bad, I wrote to him and he thought I hated him and then, and then—!"

"Oh no..." I got on my knees and looked into her face. "Oh no, Anna no, don't you *ever* think that. It was the hurting in his head, that's what this note's about, how much the war made him hurt. It has *nothing* to do with you. You were the reason he stayed alive as long as he could."

Anna made a tight mewling sound and I reached for

her and hugged her against me, like she was an empty toothpaste tube I was trying to squeeze the truth and the pain out from. She flinched away but then fell against me, her arms wrapping tight around my back. And I knew it must be hurting her; the cuts on her wrist were still open and raw, but still, she held on.

After dinner that night, I slathered Neosporin on Anna's wrist, and then sat with the children reading bedtime story after bedtime story so I wouldn't have to think. If I let myself think, I knew I'd start hating myself.

I read until Toby fell asleep against me, then tucked him in and turned to Anna. "So you got rid of Josephina Graham, huh?"

Anna looked over at the blank wall. "She died."

I raised my eyebrows. "Guess she was starting to look a little ragged. Want to make something new out of the shells this weekend? We could make her brother... Jeremiah."

Anna's expression loosened, in her face a wistful look I didn't understand. "Making a face is stupid."

"Well! I'm sure Josephina would be highly insulted if she could hear that." I tucked a stray hair behind her ear. "You want to sleep in my bed tonight?"

She hesitated, then said, "You snore."

"I do?" I tried to smile. "Your dad used to say I snored, but I never believed him. That's embarrassing."

"You only snore a little." She smiled back. "Okay, I'll go to your bed."

She swung her legs over the side of the bed and I lifted her into my arms, the first time I'd tried to carry her in years, with her legs around my waist. I tucked her into my bed and rested my cheek against her forehead. "I love you, baby girl," I said.

I sat with her, holding her hand until she fell asleep, then rose to go into my parents' bedroom where I picked up the phone, and pressed *redial.*

"Econo Lodge, can I help you?" A woman's voice.

Econo Lodge? I felt my heart thump down to my stomach. Who the hell had she been calling? Somebody at the Econo Lodge had been talking to my daughter.

"Yes," I said, "I'm wondering...there's a girl who called your hotel this afternoon. A little girl, and I was wondering if you might remember the room she was calling."

"I'm sorry, ma'am—"

"She might've called multiple times, but the last time was tonight, around six."

"I'd need a room number, ma'am..."

I suddenly heard myself, the desperation in my voice. "I'm sorry," I said, and hung up. I hesitated and then walked to my bedroom, knelt by the bed and put my hand on Anna's shoulder. "Anna?" I whispered.

She twisted away from me.

"Anna," I said louder, "who were you calling at the Econo Lodge?"

She squinted at me, and then her face blanched. "I wasn't," she said.

"I know you were. Anna, sit up and look at me. Who're you talking to?"

She shook her head slightly, and then she said, "It's Cam."

I could feel something akin to panic rising in me. "It's not Cam, I know it's not. You've been calling the motel, and whoever you're talking to, you have to stop, you hear me?"

"I'm not!" Anna threw the blankets off. "It's Dad, okay? He comes down to talk to me and he gave me a number to call him, and he said you wouldn't believe me but it's the truth!"

"I don't know what to do anymore, Anna. I don't know why you'd lie to me, but I know there's somebody at the Econo Lodge you're talking to, and I need to find out who it is. He's a bad person, Anna."

"It's not a bad person!" She jumped up. "You never believe anything. It's like you *want* him to be dead and not see what you're doing, but he can!" She swiped at my jaw and then tore out of my room and into hers, slamming the door shut behind her.

"Anna—" I brought my hand to my chin, tears blurring my vision. This had to make sense somehow. Did she really believe she'd seen her father? That she'd been able to talk to him on the phone? Called him at a motel?

And the image came to me then, fully formed in all its horrendous glory in the way these things do: a pedophile who'd read about Anna in the paper, a little girl needing a surrogate father, ripe and ready to be seduced by any man who claimed to love her. Who'd looked up whatever information was available about Josh, maybe even talked to somebody at Pendleton, and used it as part of the seduction.

Shaking, I grabbed for the phone, dialed Seth's number, and even before he could say hello I said, "Seth, you have to meet me at the Econo Lodge downtown."

"Natalie? Wait, slow down, what's going on?"

"There's somebody there that's been talking to Anna! Somebody at the motel she was calling who's feeding her all kinds of information about Josh, and I have to find out who the hell it is."

"Okay, okay." The anxiety in his voice shot another spear of adrenaline through me. "Give me a few minutes and I'll come pick you up."

"I'm not waiting, I'm going down there now. Just… meet me there, okay?"

I hung up, grabbed my jacket, and ran downstairs to the living room where Dad was reading an old magazine, Mom's head lolling against his shoulder. "Dad, I'm going out."

He raised his eyebrows. "At nine-thirty?"

"I can't explain right now, just… I'll tell you later, okay? I'll tell you all of it."

I grabbed my purse, ran out to the car, and shot down the driveway, my hands tight on the steering wheel. The fog had come in, thick as milk, the curves of crossed tree branches in the moonlight like letters in a foreign alphabet, black on white. I felt floaty, the way you do after a long, not particularly restful sleep, the feeling of not completely inhabiting my body. Thoughts came, turned corners, and went again; none of them stuck.

Finally, after twenty minutes that seemed to last ten years, I turned into the motel's cement parking lot. The lot was nearly empty and I scanned it for Seth's car, then pulled into a space near reception.

And it was sitting there, looking out at the motel's worn blue doors and vertical blinded windows, that I suddenly knew.

Why hadn't I realized it before? Christ, how had I missed it? Josh had never talked about his past, even to me. This was how he'd been able to move on, by pretending the past never happened. He wouldn't have told his friends about it, no matter how intimate their wartime conversations were, and he sure as hell wouldn't have told

Anna. Who else would know what a crappy mother Hannah Graham had been, except Hannah herself?

I got out of the car and, my knees shaking, I strode to the reception desk. "Please," I said, "Can you tell me if… What room is Hannah Graham in?"

The gaunt-looking woman at the desk gave me a weary, put-upon gaze, and slowly entered something into her computer. "Thirty-four," she said.

"She's here?"

"Room thirty-four," the woman said again.

I let out a breath through my teeth. She was there, she was here. *Hannah*. Who'd been too selfish to drop whatever crucial prior commitments to go to her son's funeral, couldn't even talk to me when I'd called after his death but who, for whatever half-insane reason had come behind my back to talk to her granddaughter. "Thank you," I said, and rushed outside in time to see Seth pulling into the lot.

I ran to his car. "Seth, I know who it is." I pushed my hair back with both hands and scrubbed frantically at the top of my head. "It's Hannah, Josh's mother. Why the hell would she call Anna without talking to me? How dare she!"

Seth looked bewildered; his shirt was half untucked, his hair scruffy. "Josh's mother? Do you know which room?"

"Thirty-four," I said, and without waiting for him I strode down the lot, scanning the numbers nailed to the gray shingles. When I found the room, I banged on the door with my fist.

It took a full minute before the door swung open, barred by the security chain. The woman behind it was wearing a red plaid nightgown, a sleep mask pushed up on her forehead. She looked terrified, like a night animal dragged into the light, and her eyes, they were Josh's eyes. This woman was wearing Josh's eyes.

"Who are you?" she said, looking from me to Seth. "What's going on?"

She was older than I'd expected, her skin crepey, frown lines in her forehead. But her thin frame was the same, and her sharp pixie chin—it was Anna's chin. Josh's eyes and Anna's chin, and this was not one of those situations where crying was appropriate, but I just couldn't stop my eyes from brimming. "You know who I am," I said.

Silence. And then, "Natalie..."

I tried to figure out what to feel for this woman. Outrage? Disgust? Fear? None of these seemed quite right; they were the feelings you'd have for a cockroach in your kitchen, but I felt all of them. "How could you?" I said. "How dare you talk to Anna behind my back?"

"You didn't know?" She sounded almost in awe.

"Did you tell her not to tell me? You haven't been here for her or Josh all these years, but now you think you have the right to confuse her like this?" I slammed my fist on the doorframe. "You filled her head with things Josh never would've wanted her to know!"

"Natalie, listen. You have to realize I never would've talked to her without you knowing. She called me first, and she said she'd tell you! Just...hold on." She closed the door, then opened it again with the chain unlatched. "Come in," she said.

Seth and I stepped into the room, wood veneer furniture, faded orange carpeting, and an unmade bed covered with blocky tangerine-colored flowers. "She called you first?" I said.

"Don't be mad at her. Maybe part of me knew something wasn't right. But…I guess it was just so good to talk to somebody about Josh, to tell her some of the things I should've told him. Her and Toby are the only parts of him I have left."

Hannah pulled off her sleep mask and looked down at it, then scrunched it in her fist. "Listen, I know you're never going to forgive me for not being there for Josh. And if you want me to leave and never come back, then I'll leave. But I feel like I owe you an explanation first. I think maybe it'll help us all heal."

"What the hell do you know about what'll *help* us?" Seth put his hand on my arm, squeezed it, but I brushed him off. "You think you can change my opinion of you? Do you really think there's any explanation?"

"I know I should've come sooner, for Josh's funeral. I actually booked a flight, but I couldn't make myself get on the plane."

"What, you have flight-o-phobia? What could make someone miss their son's funeral?"

She raised her arms to me, then let out her breath and dropped them again. "I did the best I could at the time, really I did."

"You should've been here when Josh was alive," I said. "Do you have any idea what it did to him not having you there for him after his father died? Or when he was injured or when he was scared? Not celebrating when our kids were born, or when he was honored for service—don't you realize there was always something missing in him?"

"I know. Of course I know. There's no way you'll be able to understand it." Hannah walked to the window and stood there looking out. "Or maybe you can. Imagine Toby telling you he wants to join up. My husband was only dead three years before Josh joined the Marines, and Josh was so set on honoring Ken's name and doing him proud even if it killed him. And you know how he told me? He just sits next to me and slaps a dog tag on the coffee table, printed with his name, O-negative, and the word Episcopalian, and seeing that, it drove me over the edge."

She flung her sleep mask onto the bed. "Not even so much that he wanted to be a Marine, but that he needed his blood type and religion on some tag. So I told him not to come back because I thought it'd be easier not knowing, imagining him doing okay, not having to worry that someday I'd get the call. Which I knew I would. I knew he'd die, and how could I take that?"

Seth set his hand on my back, and I tried to absorb peace from it. I thought of Josh growing up with this woman as his mother, forced ever since his father's death to fend for himself. Which is what he'd done this whole last year. He was used to weak women, and so expected me to be weak.

"It was so awkward the few times he called me. He was so bitter, which of course he had every right to be, so to keep things at least halfway amicable, the whole conversation we'd hardly do more than talk about the weather. I wanted to absorb the sound of his voice and keep him on the phone as long as he could stand to talk to me, but then the conversation would just trickle out and he'd say goodbye, and I'd have to wait another year."

"I know he sent you photos of the kids. He was reaching out to you, Hannah."

"I think he was just trying to show me what I was missing. Or maybe he *was* reaching out, I don't know, but he sure wasn't willing to reach very far. I asked him after Anna was born if it might be okay for me to come out and see you all, and he said he didn't want to subject Anna to me. He was so stubborn, and after that I felt so... *dismissed*, that I became stubborn back, I guess to protect myself."

"But you were the parent."

"I know." She stood a moment staring out the window, then slowly turned to face me. "I was falling apart not being part of his life, but I also knew I'd literally die from worry if I knew he was out there fighting. Every day I'd expect to hear from him, and every day he didn't write I'd die inside. As it was, I was obsessed with war coverage. I lost my job because all I could do was watch CNN. And I know I should've told him that. More than anything I wish I'd told him how much I needed him."

For the first time I started really looking at Hannah, trying to remember what Josh had told me about her. The few times he'd talked about her had seemed to cause him so much pain that I'd learned not to ask questions. He'd told me that he'd had to take care of her after his father had been killed, shopped and made her sandwiches to keep her from starving, sat with her well past midnight every night, holding her hand as she stared blankly at the TV. Which showed he'd loved her. Of course he'd loved her. She was his mother.

Maybe she was right, and hearing whatever she had to say about his past would help us heal. One of the things that had been so hard after Josh's death was realizing I'd never learn another single thing about him, that I'd have to just replay the old things over, trying to find meanings that probably weren't there.

I hesitated, said, "Why don't you check out of this dump, and come stay with us?"

"What?"

I glanced at Seth who'd stayed silent throughout this

conversation, looking like he'd rather be anywhere else. But now he smiled and took my hand. I looked back at Hannah. "You'd have to sleep on a pull-out sofa, but at least it won't smell like dirty laundry." I stepped sideways, toward Seth. "I'm not going to lie and say I'm glad you're here, but I know it might be good for Toby to meet you. And I have photos I can show you, of the kids growing up, of Josh over the past few years. I have a photo of his medal ceremony; he'd want you to see it."

"Thank you," Hannah said, sounding almost incredulous, gripping the sides of her nightgown, the way shy kids do when waiting to be introduced. "I'd like that."

"Do you have a car?" Seth said. "I can drive you."

"Thank you," she said again. "I'm not much of a driver, so I've been taking cabs. I mean, I could take a cab."

"No, Seth'll drive you." I squeezed his hand in thanks, then said, "Just one more thing. The last time you talked, did he tell you anything about what happened in Iraq while he was there? About the girl he knew who was stoned to death?"

"We didn't talk about Iraq. I figured he must've gotten deployed there at some point, but I didn't want to ask and he didn't tell me."

Then how had Anna known about Leyla? It was like an algebraic equation, taking $x+y+z$ and trying to come up with the numbers. Hannah was x, his suicide note was y, so what was z? Had Anna overheard someone back at Pendleton talking about what had happened?

Now I'd found out about Hannah, Anna couldn't keep up the charade of having gotten the information from her father. I'd have to talk with her, find out how much she knew, and make sure she understood the true story, that Josh hadn't done anything wrong.

"Why don't you get changed," I said, "and we'll wait outside."

Seth and I walked out to the parking lot, and I leaned against the wall and closed my eyes. "Did I just invite her over? Was that stupid?"

"I actually think it was exactly the right thing to do. Not that you'll ever be friends, but forgiveness feels a lot better than blame."

"I haven't forgiven her," I said. "I'm doing this for the kids. Because like it or not, she's a part of them." I pressed the heels of my hands against my eyes. "And maybe Josh would've wanted me to forgive her, so I hope there really is a heaven. I want him to see what's going on, that we're trying to make things better."

I remembered the times I'd tried to convince him he should invite Hannah to stay with us: after Anna's birth, after Toby's, at his own medal ceremony. *What would I say to her, exactly?* Josh said with more bitterness than I'd ever heard from him before. *It's been awhile! Let me introduce you to the grandkids you've shown no interest in meeting! I know you think joining the Marines was the stupidest thing I've ever done, but why don't you come to a ceremony celebrating my stupidity!*

But I'd recognized even then what was behind that bitterness. It was fear that his mother would refuse to come. It was yearning.

And standing there, in the dark parking lot, realizing Hannah probably would've come if he'd called her, and that now he'd never get to see his mother fall in love with his children, I felt it completely, with every ounce of my being. That Josh was gone.

57
Anna

I lay in bed staring at the ceiling, and here is what I was thinking. How in first grade, when Mrs. Jakes told Mom I wrote a bad word on Karen Rolly's pencil box (which in fact I did not) what Mom said back to Mrs. Jakes was: "Not only would she never write a bad word, if she'd known the word was there she would've erased it before Karen could see." And then she said, "Anna is the kindest, most considerate child you will ever have the fortune to know."

That is who Mom thought I was. Now, today, she was finding out the truth. That I was exactly the opposite.

Think of the Commandments: I was a liar and a stealer, I didn't honor my mother, I bore false witness, I didn't love God with all my heart and my soul and my mind. I already broke all the Commandments except killing, and maybe adultery which I didn't even know what it meant. How long would it take for Mom to figure out all of it? I knew she'd never love me the same way again.

So I couldn't stay here. If I saw Mom's face, the change in how she looked at me, I would feel like I was cracking into pieces. Like I was dying. I knew Cam would help me if I asked. Maybe I could hide in his basement and he could bring me food. And I didn't want to stay there; Cam's house felt empty even when both him and his dad were home. But in the end it would be a good thing. I'd think about what kind of person I turned into and how I became her, and I'd figure out how to turn back. Just like there'd been a before-the-war Dad and an after-the-war Dad, there'd be an after-the-basement Anna.

What would Mom think when she found out I was gone? She'd be sad, I knew that. She'd wonder what she did to deserve me. And the answer was, she didn't deserve me. I'd have to make sure she realized that.

I got out of bed, quiet, and went to my desk to write a good-bye letter in the dark.

Dear Mom,

I know you are probably mad. Which I deserve since I told a lot of lies, and I am so so so so sorry. And I wish I didn't lie to you except it's too late to take it back.

But now I will tell the truth. Because here is the first thing, that Dad didn't come to talk to me, which I guess you already know that. I found out about Dad's hurnia and his dog from my other grammy Hannah, who's not a bad person, she's just kind of sad. I found out from Cam about the girl who was Dad's friend, because Cam's dad was talking to people from Pendleton and asking them about the girl, because he's writing another article about Dad. And the note Dad wrote before he died is something me and Toby found that day, not last week. That is the whole truth.

Now don't worry but I have gone away for a few days to stay with people who are pretty nice. I don't

blame you if you can't forgive me except I hope
you do.

Love,
Anna Graham

P.S. Please tell Toby

I stopped. Put down the pen. What could I tell Toby? I
could say I loved him, but he already knew that and it
wouldn't be enough. It would be like knowing Dad used
to love me. Yeah, but so what?

I put the note on top of my bed, and then I knelt in
front of Toby's bed and looked down at his face. His eyes
were moving back and forth under his eyelids, and I
hoped he was dreaming about us playing Wiffle ball, or
him on my lap watching *Bob the Builder* on TV, or about
Mom reading us stories. All of me wanted to hug him
good-bye, but I knew that would wake him up. So instead
I just looked a long while at his face and hugged him in
my heart.

I opened my closet, pulled down a sweater and jeans,
and changed as quiet as I could. I packed another sweater
in my knapsack, along with socks and underwear and my
Garfield PJ's. And then I took the photo of Dad off my
nightstand and stood there with it.

Was he watching me now? I couldn't think about it.
The only thing worse than knowing Mom was disappointed was knowing he would be too. I put the picture
down and walked away.

In the bathroom I packed my toothbrush, and then I
snuck down to the kitchen to call Cam. The house was all
dark and quiet, and even after I turned on the kitchen
light it felt like I was the only one awake in the entire

world. It didn't feel real to be alone downstairs so late at night. It was like a dream, one of those nightmares where nothing you can see or hear makes sense, and you can't remember why you are wherever you are, and all you want to do is be with your mom.

I looked up at the phone, practicing in my head what I'd say when Cam's dad answered. That something had happened to Toby and I was all alone and scared, and could he please come get me and take care of me until Mom came back next week. If he said he didn't want to, then I'd tell him how I could clean his house, that I knew how to cook eggs and macaroni and cheese, and if he wanted I could even tell him things for his article. But I knew he'd help me. He had to help me. I picked up the phone.

I was just starting to dial, when I saw a flash of light. There were tires crunching up the driveway, and I widened my eyes and dropped the phone to look out into the entryway. Where suddenly, the key turned in the lock.

I slapped my hand over my mouth to stop myself from screaming, and ran fast out the back door. And then I stood there on the back steps, breathing heavy, trying to think. I had to go, to get out of here. I could hide in the woods and eat berries and drink rain, and I could build a lean-to and sleep on leaves and maybe make a fire. I used to be in Girl Scouts, where we made frying pans out of coffee cans and learned what kind of plants were safe. You could stay warm by digging yourself a hole, and tell directions by looking at where moss grew, and if you got really hungry you could eat bugs. It would be gross, but I could totally do it if I had to.

I started sneaking around the side of the house, looking for a place to run to. This was a night of fog, clouds down to the earth, the moon washing everything into no color. The fog smelled like a refrigerator, so thick that it stuck to me when I walked, like I was rolling through snow.

I couldn't remember having started crying, but my mouth was making shaky choking noises and it suddenly felt like my whole body was full up with tears. I forgot my knapsack, I wasn't wearing shoes or a coat, and it was so cold and empty here, like I was swallowed up by the fog, like I was the only person left in the world. Or like there was no world, like I blasted off flying into white space with no way back. And I imagined living like this forever, able to see the house, people coming and going, with nobody seeing me. Maybe that was how it was like being dead.

I snuck around to the front corner of the house and saw Mom waiting by the door, blurry in the fog, like watercolor paintings where you use too much water. I held up my hand, to wave her good-bye. And then, I walked into the woods.

58
Natalie

Seth's car pulled into the driveway, and he and Hannah got out from the car and walked toward me. How had he introduced himself to her during the drive? Probably, hopefully, just as an old friend.

"So I'll be heading home," Seth said. "Call me if you need anything?"

"Thanks," I said. "For everything. Especially for driving out in the middle of the night to keep me from freaking out." I found myself wanting to hug him good-bye, which of course I couldn't do, not with Hannah here.

"Call you tomorrow," he said.

Hannah and I walked inside and I saw her scanning the entryway, maybe wondering how I could afford maple floors and the mahogany balustrade. "This is my parents' house," I said. "We're just staying here until we can get back on our feet. I'm actually going with Seth next week to look at a cabin to lease; he's...my real estate agent."

"Ah," she said. Nothing more, which made me suddenly shy. I gave a little cough, smiled, then said, "So here's the living room, where you can sleep. You want to pull out the couch, I'll go up for clean sheets and a pillow."

I started toward the stairs, but then she said, "You

said there's photos?" I turned back to her and she shifted her gaze to the middle distance, as if speaking to somebody over my shoulder. I had to stop myself from turning to make sure there was no one there. "I probably won't sleep much tonight. I mean, I have a hard time sleeping anyway, and this has been one of those nights that've made a mess of my body chemistry. So I was thinking, if it's okay, more than anything I'd like to spend time with Josh. I mean, with his pictures."

"I know what you mean." I watched her face, then raised my hand to her. "Come upstairs. I'll show you in person."

"But...it's so late."

"I know. But I haven't looked at the photos in a long time; I guess I was scared to. Which is stupid, because I don't want to stop thinking about the best parts of my life."

Hannah stretched a slow, almost shy smile, the type a child might give when praised by an adult. "Thanks, Natalie. I'd like that."

In my bedroom, I bent to slide my box of photographs from under the bed. Hannah dropped to her knees beside them, and began studying each framed photo I handed her, arranging them on the floor. And then she knelt above them looking down, her arms straight at her sides. Our wedding photo; Josh and I holding Anna's hands to swing her off the ground; Josh with Toby on his lap dressed in Spider-Man Underoos, reading about Mike Mulligan and his steam shovel. The life she'd missed out on. "Josh looks happy," she said finally, then lifted a photo of the four of us and sat back on her heels, holding it in her lap.

The photo had been taken last year, in the summer. It was the photo I'd used for the Christmas postcards I'd ordered in August but never sent. Josh had tickled my waist the way he always did for pictures to get me to smile, and I'd tickled him back in retribution. And he did look happy, caught mid-laugh, one arm around me and one hand on Toby's shoulder.

"The kids look so joyful in all the pictures," Josh had said when we looked through the prints, deciding which to enlarge. "Happiness should always be that uncomplicated and reflexive, like breathing."

That was what he'd taken from them, the simplicity of their happiness. So this was my job, a job I'd take on until the responsibility shifted to their spouses: to find the happiness I knew must still be intrinsic in them, unearth it from the muck life had thrown at them, and make it, if not ever uncomplicated, at least easier to find.

I thought about my father, who every day moved further away from the future with Mom he must've dreamed of, but still seemed to have found peace, even contentment with his new life. And Josh, who'd lost his father and then, in effect, had lost his mother; he'd figured out how to be a parent, to get over whatever fears of intimacy he must've had, and love us with every ounce of his being. It was part of life, moving on after your world collapsed. Every day life collapsed you but you picked yourself up again because you had no choice. It was that or, as Josh had eventually done, you gave in and let it destroy you. He'd survived the loss of his father and mother, but not the loss of himself.

Hannah traced a finger back and forth over the bottom of the photo, everything she was feeling stamped clearly on her face. I watched her hunched shoulders, and then reached to set a hand on her back.

I still resented Hannah, probably would always feel

bitter for what she'd done to Josh, for deserting him when he needed her most. But I could see how much she'd suffered, that she blamed herself too. And even though I couldn't make myself care whether she forgave herself, I still could empathize.

"Hannah," I said, "you're here now. You came to be with your grandchildren, which isn't nothing."

She looked up and met my eyes, frowning slightly like she was trying to work out a puzzle. I squeezed her shoulder in a way I hoped was reassuring. "You can't go back," I said. "But I can tell you about him, and you can tell me, and then we'll both tell the kids. We can show each other what we missed."

59
Anna

I watched from the trees, my eyes wide and something heavy pressing on my lungs. Hannah was here. She was here with Mom, and it was like one of those dreams you get after a day filled with too many things. Where they all jumble together, your teacher sitting on top of your dining table, playing Scrabble with you and Jimmy Neutron: Boy Genius, and you know it doesn't make sense, but there it is. Hannah was in my home.

And I was trying not to make noise, so I covered my mouth with both hands. But as soon as Mom and Hannah got inside the noise escaped, a sound like someone about to throw up. And Seth heard it.

"Who is that?" he said, peering into the woods. He walked closer, startled back. "Anna?"

I shook my head, my hands still over my mouth.

"Anna, what're you doing there? You okay?"

I dropped onto the ground, then started crawling into the woods, the sticks and rocks digging into my hands and knees. Bumping into a tree, a scrape on my cheek and I screamed and scrambled back.

"Anna!" Seth grabbed at me and I tried to push him away, knowing Dad could be watching and how would he feel? Angry and sad, loving me so much he hated me, just the way I would be seeing Dad hold another girl. "Go away!" I said.

But he was on his knees holding me, his arms around my back and rocking me side to side. I couldn't move and I couldn't breathe because the hug felt exactly like Daddy. An after-nightmares hug, a back-home-from-war hug, and I buried my head in his neck and breathed him in. "Go away, go away!" I said, but I let him pick me up, one arm under my butt and the other one around me. I closed my eyes and sank.

"It's okay," he whispered, rubbing at my back. "I'm not going to hurt you, nothing's going to hurt you." And I couldn't help it. I put my arms around his neck, and let him hold me.

Seth followed me upstairs, and when we reached the top, I whispered, "Don't tell Mom where I was."

He looked like he was going to ask a question, but then he just nodded and bent to whisper in my ear, "You all ready for bed? You need help with anything?"

"No, thank you," I said. "You can go."

He made an okay sign and stayed by the stairs as I walked down to my bedroom.

I could hear Mom's voice across the hall, and she didn't sound angry. She was talking low and slow and she sounded sad but it was a quiet kind of sad. I peeked into her bedroom and they were there, Mom and Hannah both on the floor and looking at pictures.

"This was our trip to Bear Mountain," Mom said. "It was the first time the kids saw snow; crazy, huh? And you should've seen how surprised they were, like we'd taken them to the moon or something."

I remembered that trip, from when I was six. One time me and Dad snuck up on Mom to shove snowballs under her sweater. The look on her face was the funniest thing ever. If time was like lunch food where you could give away all your just-okay stuff, carrot sticks and cheese crackers, for a half a Ring Ding or a Toll House cookie, this is what I would do: trade all the days in the future for that five minutes, Dad whispering in my ear, helping me pack a snowball, trying not to laugh while we snuck quiet through the snow.

"This was Anna's seventh birthday," Mom said. "About five minutes after Josh took this picture? I went to the kitchen for a cake server and Toby came at the cake like a linebacker. I mean, literally dove into it with both his hands and his face."

I smiled, remembering. We'd started cracking up, then all of us started grabbing at the cake with our fists and shoving it in our mouths, Mom laughing so hard she had to jump up and down to keep from peeing. Dad grabbed at Mom, both of them covered in icing, kissed her lips and then mine and then Toby's, his head looking like it had no face. And thinking about it I made a hiccupping sound, a mix of happiness and awfulness, and I clapped my hand over my mouth but it was too late. Mom turned.

"Anna?" She looked confused. She also looked like she'd been crying. She glanced at Hannah, and then she reached her hand to me.

"Mom…" I took a step closer, then back again, and she came to me and dropped on her knees and pulled me into a hug. "It's okay," she whispered. "I know, sweetie, and it's okay."

I could hear my heart, the thump of something trying to get out, until I turned into spaghetti, my legs and arms and shoulders folding and collapsing. She held me tighter.

There should be a word to describe this because I could put together a thousand words and not even come close to the mix of badness and goodness of it.

Think of: You are lost in a store; there are people everywhere, all tall and hurrying, no way to see around or over. You're trying to get away but they're pushing at you, stepping on your feet and yelling in some language you don't understand. And then, you hear from right behind you a voice that says, "Anna?"

You turn and there she is, your mom, and she's been stepped on even worse than you, scared and bruised and bleeding.

But she takes you home.

Epilogue

Natalie

I'd debated for days the best way to throw a party for a dead person. Did we leave a chair for him? Put his photo by his plate the way you did at funerals, to remind us of how he'd looked in his prime? It all felt obscene.

What we did was to bake a cake and, so I wouldn't have to consider the chair question, bring it to Santa Lucia Park. I laid a blanket on the grass, and set a drinking glass in the center, holding wildflowers the kids had picked, everything from yarrow to dandelions. I unstacked three *Blue's Clues* plates and cups, left from Toby's last birthday, then lifted the cake plate lid. The cake was somewhat the worse for wear, dented on one side from the car trip, and the letters on top were barely legible. "It looks stupid," Anna said, sounding almost in tears. That morning she'd slowly, earnestly, squeezed the words *We Love You Dad* in multicolored icing. Now, it looked like it had been sat on.

I set a hand on the small of her back. "I think it's perfect," I said. "Especially for Dad, because he wasn't the kind of person who liked perfection. It's like how he used to wear his favorite shirts until they fell apart, because he liked them all soft and raggedy. And how his favorite thing of all time was that photo of you, Anna, with your mouth and hands all purple from a Popsicle, and you're laughing so hard your nose is running. He brought that picture to Iraq and he kept it by his bed."

I watched her think about this, sure at first she was going to smile. Instead she said, "That is the most embarrassing thing I ever heard."

I grinned. "Here, let's light a candle." I opened a box of birthday candles, considered how many to add, then just pulled out one and stuck it in the center. I didn't know what we'd do with the candle. Sing "Happy Birthday"? Just blow it out?

But after I lit the candle, the children's reaction seemed almost instinctive; we joined hands, and watched in silence as the candle burned down. And even after it finally spluttered out in the icing, we kept our eyes on the cake without speaking, until Anna said, "I miss him."

"I know," I said.

Toby glanced at me. "He probably misses us."

"Yeah, I'm sure he does." I looked up at the sound of two boys who were dribbling a soccer ball. Followed them with my eyes as they darted back and forth, laughing as they tripped over each other's feet. This is what I wanted for my children, that unmitigated glee, the sense those boys must have that the world was made just for them, that their future was a blank page no one else would have the power to write on. "But you know what?" I said. "I bet it's getting so when he thinks of us, he can feel happy instead of sad." I squeezed Toby's hand. "What can you remember about Dad that makes you smile?"

Toby flipped his plate up on its edge, thinking, then

said, "When he was teaching me batting? And he did the voice. That makes me smile."

Toby in his T ball uniform with a fat plastic bat at his shoulder, swinging his little hips while Josh called plays in his Howard Cosell voice: *And here's the Lions' slugger Toby Graham up at the plate, and the crowd's on its feet. It's an oh-and-two swi-i-ing…And a miss! But amazingly, Graham's chosen to run the bases anyway. Folks, rarely has this reporter witnessed such determination…*

Anna thought a moment, then said, "Strawberry picking! Remember that time he ate so much he almost puked, and he had stains everywhere, on his hands and his face. And when you said people were going to think he just killed somebody? He pretended to eat my nose. That was funny."

"Those are great memories," I said softly, then saw Anna's eyes start to fill. She turned away from me to swipe the back of her hand across them, and I shifted closer to her and pulled her against me. I reached my other arm to Toby as he scooted toward me, and I held my children, stroking at Anna's hair. "Remember that night we stayed up late to watch shooting stars?"

The children were quiet a long while, and then Anna said, "We were making wishes. And I wished every night there'd be shooting stars."

It had been the week before he'd left for Iraq. We'd lain on our backs in the grass, Toby on Josh's chest and me and Anna by his side, and I'd wished with all my heart for the war to end, for him to be kept safe, to come home to us soon. I'm sure that's what we all were wishing, even though we only mentioned new bikes and Dodgers wins, and an end to the Santa Anas. The real wish not spoken, like that might bring bad luck. But spoken or unspoken, this wasn't a fairy tale. The universe made its own decisions.

"Dad wished an anonymous person would put a flat-screen TV outside our door," Anna said.

"And I told him his wish could come true if we bought the TV and paid for delivery," I said, smiling. I watched one of the boys dribbling the soccer ball on his knees, his face bright with excitement at his own talent, and I held my grieving children, listening to Anna laughing through her tears, thinking about the roller coaster of the aftermath of tragedy. "Remember when…" I started again, and *Remember when* and *Remember when*. On this, the anniversary of Josh's birth, we celebrated the best parts of his life, and we rode the memories wherever they chose to take us.

The morning after Hannah had arrived, I'd found Anna's note in her bedroom. She'd wanted to run away, maybe for some of the same reasons I used to wake every morning wanting to run. But she'd changed her mind, maybe for the same reasons I went on every day. Because I knew we would, in time, regain some of the hope we'd lost.

I'd talked to her that day, told her as much as I could about what had happened, to make sure she understood Josh hadn't done anything wrong. It was a story she should never have had to hear—but then again, all her life she'd been faced with daunting stories. She'd been through war, and worse. She was strong enough. I'd known there had already been too many secrets kept.

After hearing the story, she'd asked if we could send the toys she'd stolen to Leyla's family. I'd suggested we send them to an Iraqi orphanage instead, and both children had agreed. That Toby would have the selflessness to give away gifts he still wanted to believe had come from his father just stunned me. This, I thought, was the one good thing Josh's death had given them: empathy. Empathy, compassion, and kindness; heartbreaking but also heartening in a way, to know the goodness in them came not just from Josh's life, but from his death.

Along with the toys I'd sent a check, including a letter telling the orphanage who I was. My name had been splashed everywhere in the U.S., in every paper and on every news channel, so I knew it must have reached Iraq as well. I wanted to make sure they didn't think I was trying to make amends for what Josh had done, or assume that I thought their children's lives could be bought. When what I was really doing was making amends for myself.

I sent three thousand dollars, roughly the amount I'd gotten in the mail after Dan's first article had been published, plus the money I'd gotten from the *Herald* for my own article telling the truth about what had happened in Iraq, and how Josh had died.

I'd written the article to preempt Dan. He'd apparently learned there'd been a shooting where Josh's troop had been stationed and that Marines had been at least peripherally involved, although since the investigation was sealed I doubted he would've been able to uncover much more. But I'd known it was only a matter of time before he, or someone with more perseverance, found out what the civilians who'd turned on Josh were claiming. Since I knew the truth, I'd wanted to make sure this story was told right.

We'd finally received our benefits money, so once I got an advance on my book I'd try to send the orphanage more. Last night I'd finished a partial draft, printed it, and packed it in an envelope to send to my agent. And sitting there, with the package in my hands, I'd felt a hopefulness I hadn't felt in weeks. Writing the book, sending it into the world—I knew it would cleanse me somehow, in a way I didn't even quite understand.

It was a book about the lives of wounded soldiers in general and about Josh in particular, a book I hoped would say something big and true. I'd write the things I was learning about war, its impact on both the people fighting and the people trapped inside that fighting. I'd say what Josh had done and how he'd died and why, and I knew readers would understand it was the war that had killed him. And that he really was a hero.

I didn't know if I could bear to write about Leyla, her brother, and her cousins, immerse myself in the world of the boys my husband had shot. I was scared of what it would do to me. But maybe, in the end, it would help me truly absorb what had happened, and I'd learned from dealing with the pain of Josh's death that you needed to fully absorb things in order to get past them. The pseudo-psych term was *closure*. And no, I hadn't reached closure yet.

I was out front of the new house, playing basketball with Seth and the kids, when the mailman came to pick up both packages. I watched him drive away, then turned back to see both Seth and Toby bent over Seth's shoe. Seth looked up and smiled. "We're working on the art of shoe tying, bunny ear method."

I smiled. "Guess I can't keep him in Velcro sneakers forever."

Amazing to think Seth was teaching him something that would stay with him for the rest of his life. In thirty years he'd still be using the bunny ear method, something I myself had only learned from Seth in high school and had never gotten the hang of.

"So," I said, "I just sent a check and a letter to the orphanage."

"Oh…" He stood, studying my face. "How are you?"

How great, I thought, that he'd ask how I was, rather than what was in the letter. That for him, this would be the bigger question. "I just hope they don't blame me. Or think I'm looking for forgiveness."

"Honestly, I realize this shocks you, but I doubt they'll even think of blaming you. Nobody's near as hard on you as you are on yourself."

And of course, that was the thing, wasn't it. Josh, Anna, and me, we'd all lied in misguided attempts to help one another, and then hated ourselves for lying. I only wished Josh could've seen the support I'd gotten after the story came out. Not just the military pardon but also the outpourings of sadness over what he'd gone through, both in Iraq and after returning home. Maybe it would've helped him forgive himself, like I was learning how to forgive.

Last week, Anna asked if we could invite Hannah for her birthday. When I'd called to invite her, Hannah had started to cry, which of course made me start to cry too. Had Anna realized how much the invitation would mean to her? Well, yes, of course, she must have seen it. Hannah's guilt scars were deeper than any of ours, and like us she needed to feel forgiven, forgivable.

Now Anna took a jump shot, using the wrist-throw method Seth had been teaching, and the ball flopped onto her toes and rolled down the driveway. She looked mournfully after it. "I suck," she said.

I scooped the ball up, smiling, and bonked her softly on the head. "Blame the teacher," I said.

"Let's do me and Toby against you and Seth," she said, "except you guys have to keep one hand behind your back."

"We're gonna break another window," I said, as I put my left hand behind my back and tried to throw. Miraculously, I made the basket, nothing but net. "Apparently someone up there's on my side," I said. "You guys're in trouble. Two-zip, your ball."

And so we played, the most graceless basketball game ever in the history of mankind, all laughing as we charged at the ball, Seth and I trying, and usually failing, to catch it against our chests. And as we played I remembered sitting with Hannah and the children before she'd returned to Arizona, imagining Josh watching down and wishing he could join us. Thinking how strange he'd find it that now, months after his death, the family he'd created was sharing his stories with the family he'd been born to. Sitting there, all I'd felt was the loss of him, that essential missing piece, an orchestra without the percussion.

But now I realized that this was the percussion. *This.* The children and I together were the underlying beat, and all this time I'd been in mourning I'd neglected it, hadn't even let myself consider it might be enough. Maybe by bringing her father back, Anna had been trying to re-create the underlying rhythm of our family, and it must be my job to show her we didn't need that, that we could find a new rhythm.

We could find a way to be whole again without him.

Anna

Here is what my dictionary says about the word *family:*

1) a group of individuals living under one roof
2) a group of people who come from the same ancestor
3) a group of things that share characteristics, such as related plants or animals

Which I guess is all true, but here is what Mom said about the dictionary last year when I told her how much I liked it. She said she loved words, but not dictionaries. Because words are like plants, with parts you see which are the parts they can put in dictionaries, and also the underground parts that feed the words, make them be alive. I thought that was the most true thing anybody ever told to me.

So I'll give my roots-explanation of the word family. It was something Mom told me after Dad died which at first I didn't understand it, but now I really do.

Think of a puzzle with pieces. The picture it makes, of a puppy or the Empire State Building, that picture is the family. Sometimes the pieces break off and go to heaven, and that means you are less. But you still always know the picture's there, behind the missing pieces.

And then sometimes pieces come back together, like Hannah, maybe even like Seth did for Mom. And they smooth the edges of the broken pieces. You see more of the picture, you can imagine what the person taking the picture must've seen, the things behind him, the smells and sounds of it. And more than that you start to see where you belong inside it.

This is not the kind of thing you could ever put into a dictionary, but it is the real meaning of a family. When I grow up I'm going to be a writer, like Mom. And what I'll write is the true meaning of things.

There's robins whose home is in the juniper tree out front of our new house. This spring was the first time I ever saw birds building a nest, picking in the gravel for sticks and carrying them away. They were working so hard, so what I did to help was take the bits of the broken-apart bird's nest I had used for Josephina Graham's hair, and I spread them on the driveway. And you could tell they were appreciative; they flew right to them and then back to their tree. So when Josephina's hair was gone, just for fun I cut off a piece of my own hair, and they picked that up too, and brought it to their home.

I imagined them living there, nestled in my hair, and just like that, I knew exactly what to do. I asked Mom for her hair, and then Toby and Grammy and Grandpa, pretending it was a science experiment for school.

All spring, when I watched the babies grow, I felt the beginnings of being happy. Which maybe sounds stupid, but I don't care. It was the first time since Dad died that I remembered how happy could be. And when the babies flew away I had Mom take the nest down for my collection. I look at it pretty much every day. You can see the gray in it, the brown and the yellow with the bits of left-over eggshell, and you look at it and can see how it would be a comfortable home.

Next year, in the new nest, I'll add Hannah's hair. I invited her to my eleven-year-old birthday where I'll show her the nest and ask if it would be okay. I don't know if she's really part of our family; she doesn't really fit into the puzzle yet. But you can see the part of the picture that's on her, and where she might fit in someday. So next year's nest might be a different color. But I'm pretty sure that it'll still make a good home.

Acknowledgments

I'd first like to thank all the readers who wrote to tell me what *Pieces of My Sister's Life* meant to them, as well as everyone at the amazingly awesome book groups I spoke with. Hearing from you, your generous words, wise insights, and inspiring, sometimes heartbreaking stories, made this dream seem both real and worth doing. If you enjoy *Promise the Moon,* I hope you'll check out my website at www.ElizabethJoyArnold.com, where I'll post scenes deleted from the book, and will be conducting "story polls," the results of which I'll use in my next novel!

I want to thank Kim Lionetti for her feedback and the cheerleading, ego-boosting, and pick-me-up therapy sessions that kept me going throughout this entire process. Caitlin Alexander is an absolutely brilliant editor who could turn a block of wood into a Stradivarius. Deep thanks for her unwavering encouragement as well as her tireless efforts and impeccable intuition in shaping this particular wood block. Thanks also to Katie Rudkin, and the whole sales and marketing machine at Bantam, miracle workers whose enthusiasm and hard work helped get my first book into the hands of more readers than I ever expected in my wildest dreams. And thank you to all the amazing booksellers I've met over the past year, especially those who've graciously hand-sold my first book or put it on their staff pick shelves.

Much love to my mom, on whom the character of Natalie's mother was loosely based, and to my dad, who has ten times the dedication of Natalie's father and in general is one of the most incredible men I've ever met. Love also to Rebecca, and huge hugs and kisses to little Auria who, as I write this, is turning three days old. Also to the family I married into who, I think, have told half the population of New Jersey about my books. You all are amazing!

And of course most important, I want to thank Jerry, my secret weapon, for the countless hours you put into helping me craft this book, for your brilliant suggestions and deep understanding of what it was supposed to be. On top of your enthusiasm for and belief in this book, you gave me endless patience, love, and support (as well as countless backrubs) when I was too harried or obsessed or lost in this imaginary world to give back much of anything to the real world. At the risk of sounding like a Kay Jewelers commercial, I adore you.

About the Author

ELIZABETH JOY ARNOLD is also the author of *Pieces of My Sister's Life*. She was raised in New York, and has degrees from Vassar College and Princeton University. She now lives with her husband in Hopewell, New Jersey, where she is at work on her next novel.

Visit her website at www.elizabethjoyarnold.com.